THE STRAGORI DECEPTION

Also by the author

Sic Transit Terra
(Edge Science Fiction and Fantasy Publishing)
Book 1: *The Genius Asylum*
Book 2: *The Otherness Factor*
Book 3: *The Relativity Bomb*
Book 4: *The Genome Rally*
Book 5: *The Cockroach Crusade*
Book 6: *The Identity Shift*

Sic Transit Stragon
Book 1: *The Stragori Deception*

The Nash'terel
The Earthborn
The Bloodstone

Adventures in Godhood
Imaginary Friends
Weekends Can Be Murder
Remains to Be Seen (forthcoming)
The End (forthcoming)

THE STRAGORI DECEPTION

Sic Transit Stragon book 1

ARLENE F. MARKS

Milton, Ontario

First edition, January 2025
Published by Brain Lag
Milton, Ontario
https://www.brain-lag.com/

ISBN: 978-1-998795-20-8 (softcover)
ISBN: 978-1-998795-21-5 (ebook)

Cover design by Catherine Fitzsimmons

Library and Archives Canada Cataloguing in Publication

Title: The Stragori deception / Arlene F. Marks.
Names: Marks, Arlene F., 1947- author.
Description: Series statement: Sic transit Stragon ; book 1
Identifiers: Canadiana (print) 20240461371 | Canadiana (ebook) 20240473620 | ISBN 9781998795208
   (softcover) | ISBN 9781998795215 (EPUB)
Subjects: LCGFT: Science fiction. | LCGFT: Novels.
Classification: LCC PS8561.R2868 S77 2025 | DDC C813/.54—dc23

"The most effective way to destroy [a] people is to deny and obliterate their own understanding of their history."

—George Orwell

ONE
ON STRAGON

Isabela Bakshi quickly hauled up the rope ladder, first coiling it on the ground, then kneeling to conceal it from casual view. She'd done this many times before and had no need of even the feeble light of Stragon's distant moon. Practiced hands kneaded the pile of knotted fibre into a nondescript brown lump before shoving it to its accustomed spot in the tall grass at the rim of the bluff. Only by close inspection would anyone detect the metal spike to which the top of the rope was fastened and recognize the lump for what it was: an escape route down to the beach.

When done, Isabela got to her feet. She stood alone, staring blindly out at the vast murmuring sea as she waited for the pounding of her heart to subside.

They were gone. Extracted. Ten Earth Intelligence Service agents, whisked away to safety on Daisy Hub aboard a cloaked ship that had landed and lifted off at low tide in the darkness of night. Their mission on this world had been aborted, and hers along with it. Isabela was deactivated, free to get on with her life, such as it was.

At least her cover as a schoolteacher was still secure. She knew she ought to feel relieved about that. And yet, her mind was roiling with dread, because the danger was not over.

The Stragon those operatives had left behind was a powder keg waiting to explode. The population was dividing into moderate and radical factions, each with its own strident fringe groups. Their common target was the Directorate. The moderates, including many loyalists, believed it would be sufficient to rein in its power over their lives. The radicals wanted every Director dead and gone, and some of the more extreme groups apparently no longer shrank from blowing up public buildings and killing innocents in order to make their position clear.

There was no backing away once that line had been crossed. Security was doing its best to head off the violence (a number of bombing attempts had already been foiled), but their efforts were only delaying the inevitable—a long and bloody Stragori civil war.

The powerful Forrand family, among others, would no doubt be in the thick of it, tailoring the conflict to their own benefit. As they'd already demonstrated on Earth, they were experts at pulling profit from the misery and disaster that afflicted others. Why should things be different here on their own home world?

Isabela had just helped ten Terran agents to escape—the nine that "Gervais Forrand" intended to scapegoat and Olivia Townsend, the EIS's Chief Intelligence Officer. According to Olivia, this impostor's plan was to repair the fracture in Stragori society by giving the native population an "other" to hate.

Labelling the Terrans as terrorists would certainly accomplish that. It would also open the door to expelling the twenty-seven million refugees from Earth who now occupied the former gulag on "the island", as the land mass south of the mainland was called. But sending them all back to where they'd come from would be expensive and time-consuming. Who would rescue them if the war broke out first? Or if one of the more violent radical groups decided it would be simpler to blow up the island instead, with the Terrans on it?

The restless mutter of waves on the beach had been growing steadily louder. The tide was rushing in, bringing with it a spray-laden wind that reached right through Isabela's many layers of protective clothing and pressed clammy fingers against her skin. She shivered, only partly from the cold, and drew her outer cloak more tightly around her shoulders.

She could have been extracted as well. Olivia had begged her to climb down the ladder and join her inside the ship. But that would have meant abandoning other people Isabela cared about. Her students. Her young teaching assistant. And her brother, Carlos, and husband, Vikram. Isabela had earlier vowed not to leave this planet until she'd gotten to the bottom of both their deaths and procured justice for them.

At last, with reality accepted and her path firmly chosen, she turned her back on the water and set out for home.

Even in the dead of night, Isabela navigated unerringly through the Wilderness Zone. She had spent so much time out here that she needed no more than the glow-rod's pale whisper of illumination to guide her footsteps through the woods to the access gate. At the edge of the treed area, with the exit from the Zone in sight, she stopped to extinguish the handheld device and adjust her clothing.

The Zone formed a natural barrier between the inhabited part of the island and the sea. Like The Flats around New Chicago back on Earth, it was an uncurated swath of dense forest, occasionally opening into large, overgrown clearings. Isabela was a xeno-biochemist, and this was where she had come to gather the native plants she'd used to fill "special orders" from EIS operatives working undercover: knock-out drug, paralyzing serum, memory inhibitor... For five years, she had gone back and forth with her baskets, finding and picking the needed greens and wildflowers without difficulty and pretty much unnoticed—because the Zone proper was untouched by the close surveillance technology that seemed to pervade every aspect of life on Stragon.

The Zone was still observed from orbit, of course, like all the other parts of the planet. However, the island's soil was toxic—developed areas were all paved over or covered with artificial turf—and the wild flora that grew in the Zone so dangerous to Humans that the Stragori Directorate had apparently decided no further security measures were necessary there.

The tall chain link fence that separated the Zone from the various urban districts, though, and the access gates distributed along it...? Those were a different matter. The fence line fairly bristled with monitoring gear.

Isabela routinely took precautions not to be identified during her comings and goings, but tonight they were especially necessary. An explosion had taken out the below-ground level (and with it the main server) of the Directorate's Capital City offices on the mainland the previous day. An investigation was already underway. Fingers were pointing toward the Terrans, and the authorities would soon be hunting for whoever had helped the "terrorists" to escape off-world.

So, she pinned a veil in place to conceal her features. Then she slipped through the gate in the dark, staying tight to the post in order to pass unseen by the surveillance cam mounted atop it. She did the same thing at the gated entrance to the urban district where she lived.

The streets were empty at this hour. They were also well-lit, providing nowhere for "bad actors" like herself to hide. Hunching her shoulders to make herself look as bulky as possible, she took a circuitous route to the quadplex housing her apartment. The longer she spent outside, the riskier her situation became, but it couldn't be helped. The last thing she wanted to do was bring Planetary Security home with her.

At last, she was on the final approach to her building. It was time to make use of all that Earth Intelligence training.

She passed by the walkway to the entrance, looking straight ahead and not slowing her pace until she was nearly at the next cross-street. Then she activated the device in her pocket, temporarily jamming all the mics and vidcams on the block. In that instant, adrenaline-propelled, she spun and sprinted across three lawns, directly to the front door of the quadplex. A breathless race up the stairs, a thumb pressed to the lock... and several heartbeats later she was safely inside.

"How did she take it?"

Angeli's voice coming at her just as the apartment door slid closed behind her nearly launched Isabela out of her skin. Exclaiming in surprise, she whipped her head around and saw the other woman emerge from the second bedroom.

It took a moment for Isabela to recognize whom she was now looking at. This was no longer the Angeli she knew, and it certainly wasn't Angeli's cover identity, Anna Sturtevant. Scrubbed of all makeup and framed by a tangle of short, light brown hair, with pale blue eyes fixed in a steely expression... this was her real face, the face of a Forrand fully engaged in the shady side of the family business.

Isabela's anger flared. "How did she take it? How did you think she would take it? Olivia was devastated. She held everyone up, waiting for you to arrive at the rendezvous point, then was informed by someone with the tact and empathy of a sledgehammer that your dead body had been pulled from the rubble of a collapsed transportation tunnel. The timing could not have been worse. I wish I had never agreed to keep your secret!"

"I know. We were best friends for more than thirty Earth years, and believe me, if there had been any other option..." Angeli let out a sigh of resignation, then drew herself up, resetting her features. "If she'd thought I was alive and staying behind, she would never have left. This was the only way to get her safely off-world and untie all our hands, including yours."

"According to Dennis Forrand," Isabela supplied bitterly.

"You want justice for Carlos and Vikram? You're going to need Dennis's help."

"And you're certain he will keep his promise?"

"I'll make sure of it, Bela. I can do a lot more as a ghost than I could while maintaining a cover. Dennis has a plan. He assures me it's a good one."

"And of course it involves me. You realize I will very

shortly have a new apartment-mate...? Or has Dennis decided that I will have to die and be reborn as someone else as well?"

"No, that won't be necessary. Dennis has arranged for your next co-tenant to be someone who's in our camp. You already know him. It's Dr. Quinian."

Isabela's eyes widened. "He wants me to trust the person who betrayed Moe to the authorities?"

"Did he? You told me yourself that Quinian's behaviour felt 'off' when he questioned you about your little friend camped out in the Wilderness Zone. In any case, Dennis doesn't care whether or how far you trust Dr. Quinian—that's your decision to make. He just wants the two of you to work together on an assignment."

"Which will be...?"

"...given to you in due course. I've already packed everything I'm taking with me and gotten rid of anything of mine that could compromise your cover. Go back to being a teacher. Don't change anything that you were doing before, including how you interacted publicly with Quinian, and don't try to contact me or Dennis. We'll get in touch with you when the time is right."

Spring on Stragon was a temperamental time of year. Blustery one day, tender the next, it was definitely not Angeli's favourite season. Today, a chill westerly wind was sweeping across the strait, stealing the sun's warmth from the air. It made the exposed outer deck of the ferry to the mainland an uncomfortable place to be. So, naturally, that was where Dennis had chosen to have their meeting—on a boat plying its way between the shores, rocked by choppy waves.

The situation could have been worse, she realized. There could have been Waste Management barges moored upwind of them. And she could have been prone to seasickness.

Angeli placed her go-bag on the deck beside her feet. She layered the fronts of her black woollen coat one over the other and snugged her sash, then folded her arms across her chest to hold everything in place. Unfortunately, that left her no way to stop the wind from lashing her hair around.

Dennis didn't have that problem. Standing beside her at the railing near the port bow, he wore a grey knitted cap that covered his ears and came down his forehead all the way to his eyebrows.

Angeli and Dennis were the only two passengers on the open deck, so there was no need to worry about being overheard.

"I gather there's been a development," she said.

"There has. I've obtained a map showing the locations of all the objectors."

"And? Have you spoken to them? Are they coming onside?"

He paused. "No one has spoken to them yet. That will be your assignment, and before you start giving me your litany of reasons against," he added, raising his voice to pre-empt them, "just hear me out."

Reluctantly, she swallowed the arguments that had already leaped onto her tongue.

"When I first recruited you," he went on, "and you had to pick a new name for yourself, I told you it could be anything except Forrand. You weren't happy about that."

"Damn straight, I wasn't! All I wanted back then was to

be acknowledged by my biological father. You refused to do it. I was mad as hell for a while."

"And your anger made you reckless and impulsive."

"You did call me a 'loose cannon' once or twice," she allowed.

"Yes. I was beginning to wonder whether hiring you might have been a mistake. Then you teamed up with Olivia Townsend—"

"—your granddaughter, to whom you'd also denied the family name," she remarked dryly.

He shook his head. "Not true. Olivia rejected it. Calling herself Juno Vargas was entirely her own idea. She was making a statement."

"Mm-hmm. Probably because you weren't in *her* good books any more than you were in mine."

"Be that as it may," he said, impatience putting a sharp edge on each word, "as I was about to say, your long partnership with her was mutually beneficial. For you, it was calming. It gave you purpose, smoothed out most of your rough edges—"

"Only most of them?"

Dennis batted her question away. "It prepared you for the important role you would play in bringing about the Reformation on Earth, as I had always hoped it would. It also gave Juno the necessary confidence in you to step back, making you the face of that social movement. And because one of the 'ordinary folk' was its apparent leader, people were willing to sign onto it, and the Reformation was a success. That would not have happened if your last name had been Forrand."

She couldn't argue with him there. Angeli gazed expectantly into his eyes, not saying a word.

"The downtrodden have an ingrained distrust of those who wield power and privilege," he said, "and with good reason, would you not agree?"

"And the Forrands have more power and privilege than they know what to do with. I understand that," she replied, chilled nearly to the bone and wishing he would get to the point already. "We'll be consolidating and weaponizing popular unrest. On Earth, revolutions have always been *against* the upper classes, never begun *by* them. That explains why it's a bad idea to send a known member of the Forrand family to talk to them. Okay. Fine. I know the drill. But it still doesn't answer the question: Why is this *my* assignment, when I'm sure you have other associates you trust just as much?" *...or even more,* she added silently.

"Because the Terran Reformation was a rehearsal for what we're about to do here, and when you've got a winning team and a successful strategy, that's not the time to make changes. You're going to do for me what you did for Juno Vargas back on Earth—travel around, get disparate groups onside, and lay the foundation for an uprising that will confound and perhaps topple the highest levels of government on the planet. Meanwhile, I'll be working behind the scenes with a handful of dependable allies, just as Juno did. And when the time comes, the role I've played will fade into the background, and you will take your rightful place at centre stage."

For a moment, she was at a loss for words. Finally, she managed to ask, "You want a Terran to be the face of a Stragori Reformation?"

He chuckled. Combined with the hissing of the waves and the moaning of the wind, it was not a reassuring sound.

"You may have been born on Earth, my dear, but you are

half Stragori. And when this is all over, you will be more than a face. You will be a revolutionary hero."

Angeli bit back her first response. A revolution? The Reformation on Earth had been a bloodless coup—a con worked on the planetary High Council to force them to negotiate with representatives of the Ineligible population, to make concessions, and ultimately to *avoid* a revolution. But the Terran High Councillors had been flesh-and-blood Human beings, with memories, and emotions, and vulnerabilities that could be exploited. The Stragori Directorate, as she and Isabela and Olivia now knew, was little more than a collection of files on a Thryggian super-computer housed in a top-secret bunker underneath the island. (A computer that some clever radical had apparently already hacked into in order to impersonate Gervais Forrand, the Directorate's most recent inductee.) Each Director's memories had been translated into data and stored in a discrete organic matrix that drifted like one of more than a hundred jellyfish in a tank of hyperconductive fluid, also installed beneath the island by the Thryggians.

Could there even *be* negotiation and compromise when dealing with entities such as this? Or was a revolution with mass murder the only path to change?

As though sensing her reservations, Dennis continued: "According to the public records, the objectors have been nursing their grievances against the Directorate for a very long time. They're the survivors of a decision that only a computer would have made. Now they live like prisoners, confined to gulags all over the northern land mass."

"And we're going to liberate them?"

He smiled. "You're going to promise them justice. Justice for the eighteen million who reportedly died of toxic poisoning on that damned island while waiting to be transported to a world that was no longer ours to give them. Nothing less than a revolution could ever compensate them for that.

"The Directorate looked at the numbers and unilaterally handed over our entire space colonization program to the inhabitants of another planet. For a computer, it was an either-or. No compromise. No middle ground. That was when many on Stragon realized that we'd surrendered too much power over our lives to a bloodless machine."

"...and they formed the two factions."

"Not right away. But they protested strenuously against what was happening on the island. That's probably the only reason an antitoxin was developed, and now there are a couple million survivors for us to recruit to our cause."

"To incite to rebellion, you mean," she pointed out. "Tell me, Dennis, which faction am I part of now? I thought we were moderates, but this plan of yours sounds like something a radical would cook up."

"Since you're the one who planted the bomb that destroyed the server and then collapsed the adjacent transit tunnel to fake your own death—"

Angeli's nails were digging into her palms. "I died on your orders, don't forget!" she spat. "And I may have planted an explosive device in the computer room, but that wasn't what killed all those people. What I set was a standard EIS heat grenade, designed to fry the mainframe without harming anyone or anything else, and it was timed to go off in the middle of the night when no one would be around. A blast strong enough to bring down an office building at the height of business hours...? That wasn't my work, and you damn well know it. I was sick to my stomach when I saw the casualty numbers crawl across the bottom of my screen. Olivia's plan—"

"—included explosives, and that's why you agreed to it. Even as a child, you thought blowing things up was great fun." His shrug was an *Oh, well!* of acceptance. "Quite honestly, daughter, I don't think you're constitutionally capable of moderation. That's what makes you perfect for something like this."

They were coming up on the mainland shore.

Angeli had to swallow the taste of bile that had risen in her throat before asking, "The surviving objectors... How much do they know?"

"They don't hate Terrans, if that's what you're worried about. They know where your people are living right now and consider them to be kindred spirits, in more ways than one. Whatever animus the objectors possess is aimed squarely at the Directorate."

"How can you be sure of that?"

He pulled a data wafer out of his coat pocket. "I have people on the inside. They've proven to be reliable sources of information in the past. You'll be wearing a shell identity I planted among the objectors years ago. Your undercover name will be Eva Moss."

Of course. Forrands have spies everywhere, she thought bitterly, reaching for the wafer. He placed it deliberately on her palm and closed her fingers over it.

"This is old technology on the rest of Stragon, the only kind an objector will trust. Guard it with your life," he advised her. "It's Eva Moss's biowafer. It will identify you to my agents at each of the gulags."

"How many gulags are there?"

"Twenty-two. Enough to spread out two million

dissidents over an entire land mass and keep them from mounting any sort of unified challenge to the Directorate's authority. You'll be visiting each one separately, so figure on spending about a year on the road."

This assignment had a familiar ring to it. Angeli's decades-long relationship with Juno Vargas had begun with just such a field trip.

"And will I have a companion on my journey?" she wanted to know.

"No." He produced a second wafer and showed it to her. "You need to be able to make and execute quick decisions. A shadow would only complicate things. You've divested yourself of anything from the mainland, I trust? All traces of advanced technology are gone?"

Her EIS-issued encrypter had come with her from Earth, so as far as Angeli was concerned, it didn't count as advanced technology from the mainland. She elevated her chin and nodded.

"Good. I shouldn't need to tell you what will happen if you're found up there with so much as a signal-jamming device on your person. Keep this one concealed," he added, and finally gave her the wafer. "It contains a map and a list of the operatives you're to seek out on the northern continent, along with as much about my plan as you need to know for now, and instructions for contacting me without tripping any security alarms. Can I assume from the size of that tote bag you carry around that you're ready to travel at a moment's notice?"

She nodded again.

"Good, because the moment has come. I've arranged for someone to meet you on the dock when we land and spirit you away to another ship, where you'll find everything else you need for the completion of your mission. I'll expect a brief verbal report when you leave each location," he continued, "and a full one when you return."

With that, he spun on his heel and went below.

Angeli was still standing at the railing, her mind aswirl with ever-darkening reflections, as the ferry bumped up gently against the mainland dock.

Isabela stepped through the front door of the school and found Dr. Reston Quinian, the island's Supervisor of Education, pacing back and forth in the corridor. Short and slender, he was fairly emanating nervous energy. Quinian had never struck her as being particularly happy in his work—his customary expression was one of disapproval—but today his lean features were even more pinched than usual.

Instinctively, Isabela slowed her steps, envisioning another full day of inspection and criticism of her teaching practices. Or was there another reason for his visit?

He glanced up, frowning, at her approach. Isabela licked her lips and squared her shoulders before greeting him.

"Dr. Quinian, welcome. I was not expecting to see you back so soon."

"Is there somewhere private where we can talk?" he asked. His voice was deceptively deep. It conjured the image of someone twice his size. Right now it was also taut as a drawn bowstring.

Wordlessly, she led the way into her office and closed the door behind them. When she turned back to face him, a familiar-looking device was sitting on the corner of her desk.

Angeli's signal jammer.

Isabela's mouth went dry. "What is that?" she inquired softly.

"I think you know what it is," he replied, easing himself onto a guest chair. "I got that from a mutual acquaintance of ours before she left on a special assignment for another mutual acquaintance. She assured me that as long as the green light is flashing, we can speak without fear of being overheard. Truth?"

"Truth," she told him after a pause, and crossed to the chair behind the desk. "And what is it that you've come to say that must remain between the two of us?"

He leaned forward and lowered his voice. "I bring you a warning from Dennis Forrand. It's something that can't wait. How much do you know about the history of this island?"

More than you or Dennis would even suspect, she thought. Aloud, however, she replied, "A little, based on what I've seen. Evidently, it used to be a prison."

"It was a processing centre for objectors before they were sent off-world. It became a prison after that option for dealing with them expired."

His choice of words raised red flags at the back of her mind.

"Objectors? Are you talking about dissidents? Exiles?"

"Yes, all of the above," he confirmed. "According to the public records, there were more than twenty million of them on Stragon at one point. Throwbacks, some called them, because they clung to the old technology, refusing to upgrade when it became obsolete. They formed online communities, then built themselves a private communications network that the intellinet could not shut down or shut out.

"The Directorate saw this as subversion. It responded by enlarging and upgrading its network of spies, connecting undercover agents and civilian volunteers directly to the electronic surveillance grid. The tactic succeeded so well that the network was expanded again, this time to include as many Stragori as possible."

Isabela stiffened in her chair. "Are you referring to optimization?"

"Yes." His expression became positively grim. "The procedure had been originally developed for the military, then customized for other fields of work, including espionage. It wasn't difficult to sell the general public on the advantages of being linked directly to the net—having all that information available at the speed of thought, without any external devices to carry around. Now, roughly ninety percent of us carry the implants... and a fair number of the Terrans on Stragon are optimized as well, living and working on both the island and the mainland. What no one has seen fit to tell them is that they've been turned into monitoring gear on legs."

Isabela felt the colour drain from her face. She'd suspected this all along. The first time Joanne had mentioned that her parents were giving her the implants as a birthday gift, Isabela had wanted to say something to the girl, to warn her... but she'd held back, hoping she was wrong to worry. Now, if Quinian was to be believed, Isabela's worst fears were confirmed.

Unbidden, fragments of an earlier conversation with Joanne surfaced in her memory.

"...integrated right into my nervous system... The brochure says they'll last a lifetime... Just one downside, though—once in, they

can't be removed or I might die."

Isabela swallowed hard. Still, anger kept rising like a scalding tide in her throat. What kind of parents would inflict such a thing on their sixteen-year-old daughter?

"You spend your days among children who are too young for the procedure, so none of them should be a source of concern," Quinian continued evenly. "However, your teaching assistant..."

"You mean Joanne. She received her implants nearly a year ago."

"And that's what Dennis wanted me to warn you about. The procedure is on record. The gift card may have been signed by her parents, but the gift itself was subsidized by a government grant. Think back to when she was posted to your school. It's a small facility, with only twenty-four students. You ran it on your own for four years without any problems."

"Other than you, you mean."

A smile tugged at his lips. "Other than me," he allowed, then added, "Had you requested an assistant?"

"No. Getting her was a blessing, though. She's a born educator, quite good with the children, and she has added invaluably to their instruction... Wait a minute. Are you suggesting the Directorate suspected me of something?" she demanded indignantly. "That they put her here purposely to spy on me?"

"If you were the object of their suspicions, you would already be under arrest. What's more likely is that they were onto someone close to you." He paused, visibly choosing his words.

Isabela already knew what he was about to imply. She waited silently, unwilling to make this easier for him.

At last, he braced himself and said, "Your husband. You believe his death was not an accident."

"Correct. I have made no secret of that."

"Well, you're right. It wasn't. And Dennis believes—and I happen to agree with him—that the timing of Joanne's arrival at your school was no accident either. Be very careful around her, Mrs. Bakshi. Be mindful of your words and actions, and I'll do the same."

With that, he got to his feet, scooped up the jammer, and slipped it into his jacket pocket. Isabela stared him out the door, a terrible suspicion writhing at the back of her mind.

She'd been assigned her assistant shortly after Vikram had begun his analysis of the soil at various locations on the island. It was part of a feasibility study, laying the groundwork for a proposal to build hydroponic greenhouses. The concept was sound. Terrans growing their own food would have made the immigrant community more self-sufficient and less of a burden on the Stragori economy. In the course of his field work, however, Vikram had discovered the roof of the secret bunker, the one housing the Directorate... and then he had died, ostensibly while trying to break up a street fight.

Isabela had never believed that official explanation. She knew in her soul that he'd been murdered. But what if she bore part of the blame? Had something she told Joanne, some comment dropped in an unguarded moment, led to her husband's death? If that were true, however could she live with herself?

Drew Townsend had never enjoyed waiting, even in his mother's womb. He'd been born two weeks early, impatient to take his first breath. As a child, he'd bristled at being forced to spin his wheels while others did things for him that he was sure he could have done for himself.

Then, at the age of twelve, he'd been turfed out onto the streets of New Chicago, where the leader of the Warrior Kings gang called the shots. The next six years had been a crash course in self-control. For five years after that, patience had served him well in the confines of a detention cell. He'd also put it to good use after his release, working as a District Security field investigator.

By then, he'd come to see waiting as a necessary evil, one with a payoff at the end. He did it when he had to, but there remained a spark of resentment inside him. Drew had spent nearly his whole life hemmed in by rules he dared not break and orders he dared not disobey, and what was the payoff for all *that* waiting?

Apparently, it was here and now. Drew was the station manager of Daisy Hub, CEO of The Repository (formerly called the Earth Intelligence Service), and *Hak'kor* of House Daisy Hub (trusted ally of House Trokerk of Nandor). He was neck-deep in titles and authority, the big hat who made the rules and issued the orders. By rights, his waiting should have been over.

But it wasn't. Ironically, each of those titles brought with it a myriad of obligations that hung about his shoulders like a heavy woollen cloak, and he seemed to be waiting more than ever these days. Waiting for news. Waiting for a reply. Waiting for a report. Waiting for an arrival, for a departure... Right now, though, he was waiting to learn the outcome of the extraction mission to Stragon, and for the near-constant burning sensation in his stomach to give up and go away.

The spark had reignited a flame. At least, that was the way it felt, like a slow fire inside his rib cage. His gastric ulcer was back. Doctor Ktumba's diagnosis had been firm. Her instructions had been even firmer.

Just what he needed—more rules to follow. Peachy.

Unable to sit still at his desk any longer, Townsend crossed the Administration and Communications deck to Lydia's work station. He paused behind her chair and let out a sigh.

"It's acting up again, isn't it?" she said.

Lydia Garfield, the Hub's senior commtech specialist and third in command after Ruby McNeil, swivelled her seat and gazed up at him, her blue eyes brimming with sympathy. "I can order some yogourt for you from the caf," she offered.

He shook his head. "The antacid tablets in my desk drawer will do for now. Still no word?"

"If everything's gone according to plan, they're on their way back and will reach the Gate in roughly a standard day and a half. The *Night Cloud* is a cloaked ship, Drew. Gorse isn't going to risk transmitting a message to us from Stragori space."

"I know. It's just—"

"The waiting. It's hard. I understand. She'll be aboard it, Drew. Your sister will arrive here safe and sound, you'll see," Lydia assured him. "You'll have time to set things right between you."

He knew that too. Still, the heat inside his rib cage was intensifying.

"Maybe I'll go down to the caf after all," he said. "See what the daily specials are. And you'll notify me...?"

"The second they pop through the Gate, I promise."

TWO

ANGELI

The person who met Angeli as she stepped off the ferry was a rather slight woman with luminous grey eyes and a cap of curly white hair that at first glance might have been mistaken for a hat, it hugged her head so closely.

"I understand you need a ride," she said in a voice even warmer than her smile. "Come with me, please."

A hundred metres from the dock and concealed behind a row of trees, a small copter sat on a landing pad. Avcraft were noisy and impossible to ignore. This was Forrand's idea of being "spirited away"?

Or was it Forrand's idea at all?

Alarms sounding at the back of her brain, Angeli stopped walking and asked, "Who sent you, exactly?"

The woman stopped also and spun around, wearing an expression of childlike excitement. "Your father warned me not to mention his name until we were away from the dock and alone together. Never fear, *minona*. Your mission is important to his plan, so we are taking every precaution. I am an excellent pilot. Come!"

"And you are...?"

"Linda. It isn't safe here. We need to go."

Linda. Dennis's mother. Angeli's grandmother. And she'd called Angeli *minona*, which meant "sweetheart" in Stragori.

Olivia had told her about the volatile relationship between Dennis and his parents—about their opposition to what Gervais appeared to be doing and their mixed feelings toward what their son was doing. In particular, Olivia had emphasized how protective Linda was of her family. She could always be counted on to provide help if it was needed, regardless of the reason.

And she evidently knew that Angeli was her granddaughter and had called her by a term of endearment.

Stifling the impulse to give her new-found grandmother a hug, Angeli followed her the rest of the way to the landing pad and climbed aboard the copter.

It carried them past the mouth of the strait and along the cliff-bordered western coast of the land mass the Stragori referred to as "the mainland". Looking down, Angeli saw dense stands of trees, their tall trunks crowding the edge of the drop like an army waiting to repel a water-borne foe. There were also grassy areas atop the plateau, and more than one sandy beach at its bottom. Now she understood how this ride could be considered "spiriting her away". They were flying over a Wilderness Zone.

As though reading her mind, Linda said, "Do you remember, *minona*? On Earth, we used to call buffer areas like that 'The Flats'."

"On Earth they still do," she replied. "But where are you taking me now? To the next urban district?"

"No, a populated area would be too dangerous. The

radical movement has spread all over the continent, and any unfamiliar face could become a target for suspicion or worse. There's a transportation nexus at the narrow end of that firth just ahead."

Angeli looked where Linda was pointing, at an inlet that appeared to have been chopped out of the coastline with an axe. Buildings clustered around the bottom of the 'V', and three fair-sized vessels sat at anchor toward its middle. That was all there was to see.

Even on Stragon, a nexus was supposed to be an intersection, a point of transfer from one mode of travel or transmission to another. However, this "nexus" was apparently only reachable by water. There was not so much as a dirt road leading to it at the top of the bluff, and no steps or ladders in evidence going down to the beach.

"Not many people are aware of this place," Linda continued. "That's the way they like it."

"They?"

Linda banked the copter for its approach. "It's best if you don't know, *minona*."

"But they're all right with you dropping me off here?" Angeli persisted, her skin prickling a warning as the copter descended rapidly and finally came to rest on a patch of ground behind one of the buildings.

Linda set the controls to idle, then twisted in her seat to face her granddaughter and said solemnly, "Here are your instructions, word for word, as given to me by Dennis. Without attracting attention to yourself, find a ship named *The Parable Priest*. Its captain and crew have been well paid to delay their departure for the northern land mass until you have slipped quietly aboard, and to ignore your presence during the voyage. Should the *Priest* be stopped and searched while en route to its destination, they will swear up and down that you must have stowed away. Your contact on the northern land mass is named Bennin Krall. He'll be in uniform. Don't leave the ship to seek him out. He will find you. Any questions?"

"Just one. Dennis told me that everything I need to complete the mission will be aboard that ship. What should I be looking for, and where?"

"I have no idea," she replied cheerfully. "He said nothing to me about it. But your journey will take a couple of weeks. That should give you enough time to figure things out."

It had to be a test. Or a punishment.

As the afternoon shadows lengthened, Angeli crouched behind a shipping container, staring with disgust at *The Parable Priest*. The medium-sized freighter was streaked with grime and rust. It was also riding high in the water, a good fifty metres away from the dock. If it possessed any launches or shuttles, they were already put away in preparation for departure, and there were no small craft visible that she could steal, either beached ashore or tied up to the pier.

There was only one way for her to sneak onto that ship unnoticed. She would have to swim out to it under cover of darkness and climb up its side. And what were the odds that the boarding ladders had all been retracted and stowed away as well?

Angeli glanced around her once more, at the cluster of metal-walled storage sheds she'd seen from the air. All were in the same sorry condition as the freighter. She would have to break into them, one by one, in search of something she could use to pull herself up and onto the deck of the ship. At least she didn't have to worry about being caught while doing it—the crews of all three ships had boarded their vessels earlier in the day and there was no one else around.

The swim was going to be a different kind of challenge. Her woollen coat kept her warm as long as it remained dry. Saturated with water, it would only weigh her down. When the time came, she would have to either waterproof it or leave it behind.

The go-bag would also impede her. Its contents were what mattered, though, and Angeli always travelled light. The irreplaceable stuff could be transferred to her pockets and the bag itself abandoned. That was the third problem solved. As for the second...

Damn! And she *loved* this coat...!

Two hours later, the only light in the inlet was the tentative yellow glow that trickled off a lantern mounted on the bow of each ship. Concealed by her coat, and wearing a skein of the sturdiest rope she could find slung over one shoulder and across her chest, Angeli stole to the end of the dock and eased herself into the water. Once the shock of the cold had subsided, she pulled her arms out of the sleeves of the coat and let it sink away behind her. She checked to ensure that the grappling hook was securely fastened to her belt. Then she fixed her gaze on the inky silhouette of the *Priest* and kicked off from one of the pilings, launching herself into the breast stroke.

If everything she needed to complete the mission didn't include a jacket and a change of warm, dry clothing, she decided, she was going to be more than a little pissed.

Angeli had no idea what this rope was made of, but it clearly had not been waterproofed. Within moments, it felt as though she had an anchor wrapped around her body, bent on dragging her to the bottom of the bay. Every metre of forward motion was a battle won, and the effort required was taking its toll. By the time she was close enough to the ship to toss the grappling hook, she was shivering violently and aching all over.

She was also madder than hell. There was no ladder and the deck was deserted. Apparently, Dennis hadn't paid off the crew to help her stow away, just to wait and perhaps watch through a porthole while she fought to do it herself. They were probably hoping she would drown, so they could claim to have fulfilled their part of the bargain and waltz away with Forrand's bribe. Well, *that* wasn't going to happen!

Angeli dug deep inside herself. Determinedly treading water, she swung the hook around her head four times, letting the line play out a little longer with each circuit through the air. Then she let it fly. Miraculously, the grapnel caught and held onto the deck railing, and, summoning what felt like the last of her strength, she gritted her teeth and began to climb.

It was a painful process. Every muscle in her body was burning. If she hadn't thought earlier to knot the rope at intervals, she might not have made it to the top at all. However, she did finally manage to haul herself aboard and fall, gasping, onto the deck. She lay there in the dark for several long minutes, drawing and expelling huge lungfuls of air while the jelly in her legs turned back to bone. Then, as soon as she knew they would hold her weight, she made her way below and found a hiding place, just in case she'd been right about the crew wanting her dead.

Angeli's to-do list was short: steal a blanket, dry her clothes, and find the package Forrand had left for her. After that, all she had to do was wait out the rest of the voyage.

It was easier said than done. Stowaways didn't get assigned berths or eating privileges in the mess. Over the next fifteen days, as the ship made stop after interminable stop to take on freight and Angeli prowled every part of it in search of the promised parcel, she found herself scavenging scraps from the waste bins in the kitchen and curling up in dark and dirty corners to sleep. Once, in desperation, she hung an "out of order" sign on the door to the head, locked herself in, and stood under the lukewarm shower with a purloined bottle of soap, cursing Dennis Forrand under her breath in rich and heartfelt language while she washed first her body, then her clothes. Unfortunately, neither came quite clean again.

There was no parcel either, none that she could locate. The more she thought about it, the clearer it became to her that Dennis had already given her everything she needed to fulfill her mission, on those two data wafers pinned into the inside pocket of her trousers. So, he had lied to her, most likely to make sure she boarded this ship for the first leg of her mission.

Someone had once told her that running other people's lives was the Forrand family business. In this case, she thought sourly, *ruining* them would have been more accurate.

A commotion on deck pulled Angeli from the darkness of her reflections and sent her to peer out the nearest porthole. The *Priest* was docking at a transportation nexus. She had reached the northern continent, at last! Through the glass, Angeli could see cultivated fields sloping away into the distance, and grey paved roads winding between them down to the shore, and lines of large, boxy vehicles waiting to take on freight.

Stay aboard ship, Linda had advised her. Let Bennin Krall come to her. So, Angeli retreated to the auxiliary control room and stared out the window, watching a procession of packing containers on dollies roll past it as she waited for her contact to appear. Eventually, the cargo parade drew to an end. There was another flurry of activity overhead as lines were cast off and the *Priest* began edging away from the dock.

What now? Had something happened to Krall? Was the mission blown already?

All at once, the door opened and a large man wearing a light blue, long-sleeved shirt stepped over the threshold. He was tall and solidly built, with sepia-coloured skin and dark brown eyes that scanned the room, his piercing gaze coming to rest at last on its lone occupant.

Too angry and uncomfortable to be intimidated, Angeli met his look with a challenging stare of her own.

"Is that supposed to be a uniform?" she demanded.

He tugged at the top of one sleeve to bring a green, orange, and white shoulder patch into view. "It is where *I* come from," he replied, and gave her a lopsided grin. "Eva Moss, I presume?"

"And you are...?"

"Warder-in-Charge Bennin Krall." He looked her up and down again and let out a low whistle. "He told me you would fit the part. He also warned me you wouldn't be happy about it."

"Well, he was right. I'm not. Now, can you please get me

the hell off this rust-bucket?"

"We'll be disembarking when the *Priest* docks again. It should be within the hour," he told her, dropping onto a chair and pulling something out of his pocket. "He instructed me to give you this."

It looked vaguely familiar.

"Is that what I think it is?" she asked.

"It's a data card reader. He told me to give it to you while we were still on the ship. He was very specific about that. And to assure you that it's rogue technology, whatever that means."

"It's a Terran expression. It means the device is undetectable, because it isn't connected to any network. And by giving it to me here and now, you're keeping a promise he made me two weeks ago." *...that slippery, hair-splitting bastard...*

Krall leaned back in his chair and tilted his head. "You're from Earth? You speak Stragori like a native."

"I've had five years to learn how. And what part exactly am I supposed to be playing?" she reminded him.

"Not the one he originally envisioned for you, unfortunately. There's been a development, so I've had to improvise. You are now a fugitive that we've been hunting for a while. A thief who escaped to the Borean interior with some things of great personal value that did not belong to her. She's been living on the margins of society ever since, popping up, stealing, and then disappearing again."

"Like a stowaway on this excuse for a ship. Looking the part. Got it," she said tartly.

"You were always going to be a stowaway, but the new story is this: following up on a reported sighting, I tracked the thief to the port we just left and—tipped off by the captain—I boarded the ship and found her. Found *you*. When we get off, my partner will be waiting with a vehicle, to take you north to be tribunaled. So will the local authorities, with an arrest warrant issued by Mainland Security."

"*What?!*" Stunned, Angeli fell backward onto the other chair in the room. This couldn't be happening. She'd followed Dennis's instructions to the letter. She'd been so damn *careful*...!

"That's the unforeseen development. Apparently, they get anonymous tips on the southern continent too," he continued. "Someone fitting your description is wanted for questioning with regard to the recent terrorist activity down there. Fortunately, there's no love lost between local and Continental Security. It shouldn't be hard to convince the locals that there's been a mistake and you belong in my custody, not theirs. After they've torn up the warrant, we'll transport you to Westgrove, supposedly to face justice. Your role in this charade is simple: just act scared and don't say anything. I'll do all the talking."

Angeli swallowed hard. *Act* scared? That was impossible for her right now. When she was genuinely frightened, it always came out looking and sounding like something else—anger, impatience, sarcasm... at times all three at once. Olivia had known how to read her moods. Maybe sending her away hadn't been such a bright idea after all.

"I don't do scared very well," she informed Krall. "How do you feel about defiant?"

He frowned, his expression darkening. "How do *you* feel about being roughed up? Because if you give me attitude in front of those other officers, I'll have to show them I can put you in your place. You understand? They won't hand you over to me otherwise. So you need to keep a straight face and your mouth shut, or your mission is over before it begins."

Grudgingly, she promised him, "I'll do my best." Then she retreated into her thoughts.

Silence swelled like an inflating balloon, filling the space in the room. Hogging the air. Making the very act of breathing a chore.

Within the hour, as promised, the *Priest* dropped anchor a short distance up the coast, where someone had built a small-goods store and vehicle fuelling station. The dock that came with it was clearly designed with much smaller craft in mind, making it dangerous for the freighter to get too close. Angeli hoped the motor launch tied up to the pier would be her transportation ashore. She didn't relish the idea of another swim in that cold water.

Through the porthole, she could see three people in uniform waiting at the foot of the dock. The one in light blue had to be Krall's partner. The other two, a man and a woman wearing shades of grey, were most likely local Security, poised to take her into custody and ship her back to the mainland.

"Damn," muttered Krall over her shoulder. "That's Continental Security. All right, I can handle them. Just remember what I told you."

Angeli's first impulse was to snap out a retort. She stifled it.

Krall escorted her topside, where she had a clear view of the approaching launch and its stern-faced pilot... and of the freighter's captain, standing on deck with his hand outstretched, palm upward. Krall dropped a small pouch onto it. The captain peeked inside, uttered a grunt of satisfaction, then pocketed the payment, wished them good luck, and left.

"What was that?" Angeli demanded in a whisper. "An insurance bribe?"

"The balance owed. Captain Turner is a pirate at heart. Forrand knew better than to pay him everything in advance," he whispered back, then added in a louder voice, evidently for the benefit of the grey-jacketed man drawing his boat up alongside, "How do you think I knew which ship to search?"

Standing on the waterside porch of the small-goods shop, with the second warder firmly gripping one of her arms and the female Security officer hanging onto the other, Angeli willed the churning in her midsection to subside as she watched the animated discussion taking place on the dock. Krall and the male officer were apparently exchanging heated words. Facial expressions were stormy. Hand gestures were quick and sharp. How much of this was for show, she had no idea. All she knew was that her fate, her mission's fate, and quite possibly the fate of the entire Reformation depended on its outcome, and the suspense as it dragged on was becoming unbearable.

At last, the talking was over. The two men turned and strode together toward the porch. Neither one of them looked happy. Angeli couldn't help noticing that they hadn't shaken hands to indicate an agreement had been reached. Was it a compromise? Was she to be passed back and forth and interrogated after all? Her skin prickled icily at the thought.

Then Krall said to his partner, "She's ours, Andy," and

Angeli's knees went a little wobbly with relief.

As Continental Security got into their dark green land car and drove away southbound, Krall put her into the back seat of the second vehicle, this one dun-coloured and square-bodied.

"What did you have to give up?" Andy asked him as Krall settled himself behind the wheel.

"In the end, I was forced to use blackmail," he replied, the disgust in his voice reflected by the look on his face as he glanced over his shoulder and added, "I hope you're worth it, Eva Moss. I just burned a lot of capital to keep you north of the channel."

"Thank you," she said stiffly. "I'll do my best not to disappoint you."

He made no response, and any thoughts of relaxing that she might have been foolish enough to entertain promptly evaporated. By the time the car pulled up at the building on the border of the gulag, Angeli was wound tight and ready to explode.

The structure was rectangular, with a bright red door and small, barred windows, and dark brown walls that appeared to be made of the same two-way composite material as the ferry terminal on the island (opaque from the outside, transparent from the inside). Tucked into a clearing on the edge of a densely overgrown forest, the building sat at a point where paved road ended and dirt trail began.

This was where the vehicle carrying Eva Moss to Westgrove came to a stop, and Krall and his partner got out.

"I'll let Trim know we're relieving them," said Andy. "He and Rory can take her the rest of the way in."

"You do that." Krall opened the rear door and bent to look inside. "There's a wash-up room inside the warders' station. Want to stretch your legs?" he asked her. Without waiting for a reply, he reached in, grabbed her by the arm, and manhandled her out of the car.

It was the final straw. As soon as both her feet were on the ground, she flung off his hand and took a swing at him.

Bennin Krall was a big man, but surprisingly quick and agile. He easily avoided her roundhouse punch, then spun her, pinned her arms, lifted her bodily off the ground, and carried her, kicking and yelling, inside the station.

"No charges. She just needs to cool off for a day or so," he told the other warders. They stood aside, watching with amusement while he toted her into a two-by-three-metre cell and dumped her unceremoniously onto a piece of furniture.

It was a bed—an actual *bed*, raised off the ground and longer than she was tall. So what if the mattress was a little skimpy? Angeli extended her legs with a sigh of contentment. She watched Krall return to the other side of the bars. Then, as soon as the door clanged shut behind him, she closed her eyes and fell asleep.

The next twenty-five hours gave Angeli more than just time to calm down. They also came with three full meals (dinner, breakfast, and lunch), served to her on compartmented metal trays, and a set of borrowed clothing to wear while her own was being properly cleaned. Krall evidently understood more than she'd given him credit for—he let her keep her personal effects with her, and he saw to it that she was afforded privacy while she showered and exchanged her dirty and bedraggled garments for freshly-laundered underwear, blue bib overalls, and a pearl grey long-sleeved shirt.

They were even the right size. Such civility!

Angeli was in a much better frame of mind the next day. So was Krall, although his facial expression was still far from cheerful. At the end of his shift, he packed her into the back seat of a smaller vehicle than before and drove it along the narrow dirt road, through the forest and into Westgrove.

The gulag was not at all what she had expected. For one thing, as they emerged from the woods and it spread out before her, the setting sun glinting off windows and metal rooftops, she could clearly see that what they were approaching was a town—or what towns must have looked like on Earth before the Reorganization emptied them and left them derelict. It was definitely not a prison like the island, with its high fences and intrusive surveillance technology.

Westgrove had a barrier zone, to be sure, a wild and difficult terrain to cross on foot, but so did every urban district on both Earth and Stragon; and, like those urban districts, it also had its name on a sign at the side of the road:

Welcome to Westgrove

Population: 127,607

Angeli gaped out the window of the vehicle as Krall negotiated a series of turns, navigating a maze of above-ground streets that also had their names on signs: *Martinsen Avenue, Hellene Road...* There were houses here, not stucco barracks squatting like rows of orange and yellow toads but actual homes made of stone and wood and showing distinct, personalized faces to passersby. She saw windows with curtains of different lengths and in a rainbow of colours, and tidy, railing-lined porches flanked by arrangements of multihued blossoms and flowering shrubs; and planted in the middle of nearly every manicured front lawn was a hand-made sign identifying a product or service that was apparently available within:

Computer Repairs

Plumbing Supplies and Solutions

Toy Hospital

Krall pulled to a stop in front of a two-storey building with a dark blue door and matching trim around each window. No shrubbery here, just a gorgeous river of flowers that seemed to spring from the huge planter beside the entrance and flow along the front and side of the house. The number painted in white on the door was 11, and the sign halfway to the street said *Baked Goods*.

Angeli stared a question at him.

"This is Eva Moss's new home address," he replied. "Your landlady is waiting for you inside. Or not."

She looked where he was pointing and saw a tiny woman with rouged cheeks and fluttery hands burst through the front door and scurry down to the road to meet them.

"You've brought her with you! Splendid!" the woman gushed. She was bouncing in place beside the vehicle, obviously impatient for its passenger to step out of it.

Angeli paused, momentarily dismayed. She had expected to make a much stealthier entrance.

"If nobody has actually seen Eva Moss, how can they be sure...?"

"...that you're really her?" Krall supplied. "They can't. But memory is a funny thing. Think about something often enough and it will become a fact in your mind. Forrand is a master at planting false memories. Some of these people will swear up and down that they knew you for years before you disappeared. Just one thing: the northern-born don't call this 'the northern continent'. Southerners do. We call it by its name—Borea. You need to do the same, or you'll blow your cover.

"You'd better go inside now, before Lyla explodes with excitement. Her full name is Lyla Claire, by the way. You've been eating her cooking for the past twenty-five hours, and wearing clothing from her daughter's closet, and if Lyla offers to teach you how to make pies, let her do it. She's an even better baker than she is a cook, and you'll need something to barter with soon enough."

Angeli got out of the car and was immediately pulled into a welcoming embrace. This birdlike woman was much stronger than she looked. She gave an astonishingly powerful hug.

"Your timing is perfect," she declared. "Dinner is nearly ready. Ben, I've reserved your usual place at the table. Come and wash your hands."

"Yes, ma'am."

Her mind now swimming with questions, Angeli let herself be shepherded to the front door of the house. From there, the beckoning aroma of something spicy and delicious drew her the rest of the way inside.

THREE
ON DAISY HUB

Sixteen hours after it had entered Earth space, the *Night Cloud* was parked on the Hub's landing deck. Drew and Ruby went up from AdComm to greet the extracted Terran agents as they debarked. Thirteen had been embedded on Stragon: nine operatives, three support techs, and the mission coordinator. Olivia had made it fourteen. Of those, ten had made the flight. The mission coordinator had been killed by a terrorist bomb, and the surviving support tech, a biochemist named Isabela Bakshi, had elected to remain behind and be deactivated.

Lydia had been half-right about Olivia earlier. Drew's sister was aboard the vessel. However, she was the last to leave it, and she was definitely not safe and sound.

Something twisted in Drew's chest as he watched her. The one thing he'd never doubted about Olivia had been her strength. As Juno Vargas, this woman had single-handedly brought the Earth High Council to its knees. She had orchestrated a worldwide societal shift. She had been

Dennis Forrand's choice to take over running the clandestine Earth Intelligence Service and had managed it successfully for nearly fifteen Earth years. She'd been a powerhouse, practically invincible, ever since he could remember.

Now, Juno Vargas was dead, and Olivia was the shell she'd left behind. She moved as though things were broken inside her. Her expression was dazed. Gorse had to help her down to the landing deck. He placed her bag at her feet, then paused, evidently expecting her to collapse and himself to catch her.

Setting his jaw, Drew sent the other passengers on ahead. Ruby went with them to help them find their quarters and get settled. Meanwhile, Gorse and his mate, Ixbeth, climbed back inside the ship and closed the hatch, leaving the brother and sister standing alone, separated by two metres of silence.

When Olivia finally raised her eyes to meet his, Drew could see that she had been crying. There were tears in her voice when she spoke.

"Drew, I'm sorry. I know you don't want me here, but I have nowhere else to go."

In that instant, decades of pain and recrimination melted away. He went to her with open arms and she toppled into them and hung on tight, burying her face against his chest.

"Angeli's dead," she said, choking out each word. "She was my best friend, and she died on Stragon, and I had to leave her there."

He held her close, sifting his mind for the right words to say, while heaving sobs wracked her body. Drew knew precisely how she was hurting. It hadn't been so long ago that he'd lost his own and only best friend, Bruni Patel.

Bruni's murder had been a senseless crime, still unsolved, as far as he knew, and Drew had been shipped off-world to Daisy Hub the day after it happened. The investigation had been aborted, the file erased. It had taken time, but he had finally accepted that he might never have closure. Perhaps Olivia would find acceptance too.

He hated himself for even thinking this, but there might have been a silver lining to Angeli's death. It gave brother and sister a shared experience. A reason to bond. A way to forgive.

A way back to each other.

Drew lowered his head. "I'm sorry," he whispered into her ear, "for everything. Welcome home."

Olivia tightened her arms around him in response. "Me too," she replied in a muffled voice.

The nine agents from Stragon had arrived on Daisy Hub rumpled, ripe, and irritable—just as one might expect them to be after several days spent in tight quarters together. Drew decided to delay beginning their debriefings until they'd all had a shower, a couple of good meals, and a full night's rest in an actual, private bedroom.

Olivia he would leave for last, giving her time to gather herself.

She was grieving for Angeli. Drew understood that. Eventually, the full reality of losing her best friend of more than thirty years would sink in and she would need all the support Daisy Hub could give her. But for now, he just wanted her to hold things together long enough to deliver some semblance of a report.

Over the next few days, the other extractees painted a

grim picture of the situation on Stragon. They described a fractured society plagued by extremist bombings and street violence. A political climate fraught with lies and deception. Widespread public unrest. And the Terran population in ever-growing danger of being targeted as the cause of the problem.

It wasn't easy to listen to. The worst part was that it was entirely credible. The Stragori were Human, whether they liked it or not, and Human history had a nasty habit of repeating itself.

After five days, it was Olivia's turn to give Townsend her perspective. Her stay on-world had been brief. With luck, their discussion would be short as well.

Olivia stepped off the tube car on Deck C, crossed the deck to her brother's office, and took the guest seat he indicated on the other side of his desk.

Offices on Deck C, informally referred to as AdComm, were surrounded by transparent plastiplex walls, giving their occupants an unimpeded view of all the duty stations, and vice versa. Drew understood how unnerving it could be to find oneself in a goldfish bowl. He'd only recently gotten used to it himself. But Olivia had demanded that he not treat her any differently than he did the other operatives under his command, so here they both were.

"We don't have to do this today if you're not up for it," he told her.

Olivia shook her head decisively and replied in a voice thick with tears, "I want to. No, I *need* to. I need to get it out."

Drew leaned back in his chair and gave her an appraising look. Drawn expression, red-rimmed eyes... What she *needed* was to spend time in grief therapy with the Doc. But the old Olivia was re-emerging, and she was stubborn. The situation on Stragon was critical, she'd insisted. She had intel that no one else possessed and it was already an interval old. The EIS had to be informed, and since Drew Townsend was now its top-ranking administrator, that meant he had to debrief her without delay.

"All right, then," he said, and pressed the *Record* button on the keypad inside his desk drawer. "Tell me what you know."

"There are Thryggians on Stragon. They're scientists, observing the progress of their experiment."

"We already know that the word 'stragori' means 'control group' in Thryggian," he told her, not unkindly.

"We met them. The Thryggians. They're also the guardians of the Directorate. And they're not the villains everyone thinks they are."

Townsend's memory flashed back to a vidclip Captain Takamura had shown him. It was the deathbed confession of a Thryggian the *Marco Polo* had rescued from a crashed alien ship.

"Make diseases, they ordered us. Make them sick. Make them die. Keep their numbers small so they won't attack..."

Drew leaned forward again. "Okay, stop there for a moment. '*We* met them'? Who is 'we', exactly?"

"Isabela, Angeli, and me. The Thryggians have been living underground—well, so have a lot of the wealthier Stragori, but on the mainland, not the island, and not in a bunker concealed under a metre of toxic soil—"

"What about the Directorate?" he broke in, disrupting what threatened to become an avalanche of words. "You said they're its guardians?"

"They manage the server that houses the Directorate.

They supply the matrices that protect the integrity of the Directors' memories when their consciousnesses are uploaded into the computer. Drew, the technology that enables the Directorate to exist is Thryggian and always has been. The Stragori only *think* they've been doing this themselves. And the whole thing is a ploy to fool the Great Council into leaving the Stragori alone. The Stragori are more than just the control group of a Thryggian experiment. The Thryggians have been keeping the experiment going to make sure that whatever happens to Earth, whatever dastardly scheme the Great Council cooks up to wipe us all out—and make no mistake, that's what they're aiming for—the Human race will still survive."

For a moment, Drew was at a loss for words. When he found them and could speak once more, his voice was half an octave higher than normal. "You're telling me that the Thryggians—the ones who unleashed the Angel of Death plague on this arm of the galaxy, destroying half of our colonies and killing more than a million and a half Humans in the process—those Thryggians are actually our saviours."

"Yes."

That she could say this with a straight face was in itself astounding, he thought.

"And they control the Directorate from their base on Stragon?" he said.

"I don't know how much influence they have on Stragori policy-making, but they're as close to the seat of political power as it's possible to be without actually joining the Directors inside the server," she replied.

"And it's impossible for there to be any backup copies of the Directors anywhere else on the system or the planet or on any external device? Just in that Thryggian computer where their memories are?"

She nodded.

So, he'd been right earlier to shut down the AI that claimed to be Gervais Forrand. Good to know. However, something else had captured Townsend's imagination.

Raising a hand to pause the debriefing, he punched the intercomm button on his desktop array. "Ruby, would you call O'Malley up here, please? There's something he needs to hear."

"Sure thing, Chief."

As though conjured by the sound of his name, Robert "the ratkeeper" O'Malley, Daisy Hub's hacker extraordinaire, arrived on C Deck. The youngest-faced member of Townsend's crew, O'Malley would probably appear to be half his age for the rest of his life. It was easy to underestimate someone who looked as though he was playing hooky from high school. In fact, that was something he and Townsend had both been taking advantage of for some time.

After a rapid glance around AdComm, O'Malley came to stand in the entrance to Drew's office.

"What can I do for you, Boss?" he asked, flashing a toothy grin.

"Pull up a chair. You'll want to be sitting down for this. And nothing that you hear is to leave this room." To Olivia, he added, "Tell him what the Thryggians have been doing on Stragon."

O'Malley paused, wide-eyed, with his butt halfway to the seat. "There are Thryggians on Stragon?"

"Yes. They've been there from the beginning," she said, "monitoring their experiment."

"Huh!" He eased himself the rest of the way down. "I thought Earth was the experiment, and the Stragori were the control group."

"That's what the Thryggians have led the Great Council to believe," she confirmed.

"Their orders from the Council were to remove Humanity as a threat," Drew explained, "preferably by annihilating us. But the Thryggians apparently decided to disobey their masters by doing what scientists do best. They set us up as an experiment. Experiments have control groups, and control groups are observed and measured but not interfered with."

"You're thinking they did this deliberately to foil the Council's plans for us?" said O'Malley.

"I know they did," Olivia cut in. "We found their bunker and spoke with them."

"And by 'we', you mean...?"

"Angeli, Isabela, and me. They swore us to secrecy, but now that Angeli's dead and Isabela is deactivated... I just felt it was really important for someone else to know."

"But blowing their cover would not be a good idea because as soon as the control group realizes what's going on, it won't be a control group anymore. That will end the experiment, along with the protection Stragon currently enjoys against the Great Council's interference. Got it," O'Malley concluded soberly.

"What I find most impressive about this ruse," said Drew, "is how long it's been going on. If I understand correctly, the Stragori were removed from Earth thousands of years ago."

O'Malley's grin returned. "And the whole thing's a con that they're running on the Great Council. That's brilliant.

What would be even more brilliant would be piggybacking our own con onto it somehow."

"My thinking exactly," said Townsend.

"You're planning a con on the Great Council?" Olivia said. "From here?"

"We're planning on planning one," Townsend clarified. "There's still a lot of groundwork to lay down. It could take us years. But eventually, I want to expose the Great Council as the criminal enterprise that it is and make them accountable for the harm they've done, not only to Humanity but also to the other races in this arm of the galaxy."

"That's... a great and noble cause," she declared. "I've had enough of them for one lifetime, so I'll be sitting this one out, but I do wish you luck with it. And since I've nothing more to tell you, I believe this interview is over."

Frowning, O'Malley opened his mouth to say something. Drew silenced him with a look.

Then they watched wordlessly as Olivia got to her feet and made her way out of the office, across the deck, and into a waiting tube car.

"It's too soon," Townsend told him quietly. "She just lost someone she cared about very much, and it's left her a bundle of raw nerves. When the time comes, Olivia will be on board. She won't be able to help herself."

"I sure hope you're right about that, Boss," O'Malley replied. Then he left the office as well.

FOUR
ISABELA

Isabela Bakshi returned home to her apartment at the end of the school day and found a technician she recognized kneeling at her front door.

"What are you doing, Alfred?" she asked.

She'd uttered the question reflexively, already knowing the answer and sure that she wouldn't like it. The absence of Dr. Reston Quinian from her life during the past few days had felt like the unnatural calm before a storm. Now he was moving in with her, and there would be no escaping him, either at home or at school.

Madre!

Her question had startled the tech. As his gaze whipped toward her, she saw him flinch, as though to avoid a projectile. (Still? It had been a single small vase, just the one time. Would they *ever* let her live that down?)

"I'm reprogramming the lock to admit your new co-tenant," he told her, then shifted his weight and paused for several beats, evidently gauging her reaction, before returning his attention to the task at hand.

"It's too soon," she informed him. "When my husband died, the grace period I was given was four weeks, not one."

"That was before the rules changed. Now it's two weeks for the loss of a family member, one for the loss of a friend," he recited to her over his shoulder. "And living space on the island—"

"—is at a premium," she snapped. "I know."

A moment later, he got to his feet and stepped back from the door. "All done."

"When will the new tenant's personal belongings be arriving?" she said frostily.

Alfred gave her a careless shrug. "No idea. Far as I know, he'll be bringing them here himself."

On reflection, this made a lot of sense. Quinian had to know he was moving to an already-furnished apartment. And it wasn't as if they were a couple, merging their households in anticipation of a long and happy life together. Quite the opposite, in fact...

...which was why she saw no point in catering to any stereotyped expectations he might have. Isabela went inside and busied herself preparing dinner for one.

She ate alone that evening, and the next. By the third day, she was becoming annoyed. She contacted his office and was told that he'd taken some personal time and had instructed them to hold or handle his calls until he returned. No one knew when that would be. And no, they did not give out the private information of anyone on their staff for any reason short of a dire emergency.

By the fifth day, Isabela still hadn't heard a word from him and was growing concerned that something might have happened to him. It irritated her deep down to be worrying about him this way. He was a grown man, after all, and he'd been a thorn in her side for the past five years. Why should *she* care whether he was safe?

Instantly, the answer came to her: because carrying out Dennis Forrand's plan with Quinian as her partner was the price of justice for the death of her husband, and no partner could mean no mission, and ultimately no justice. And that simply wasn't an option.

The second bedroom was waiting for Quinian, exactly as Angeli had left it. Each day, Isabela came home from school anticipating that she would find something of his cluttering up the hall, or Quinian himself, fussing about the disorderly state of his new quarters. Each day, however, there was no sign of him, and the weight on her mind increased.

How *dare* he torment her like this!

By the time he walked through the door of the apartment, a full eight days after the lock had been reset, she was torn between giving him a relieved hug and ripping his head off. She did neither. Instead, she nestled more deeply into her blue and gold striped easy chair, crossed her arms over her chest, and glowered at him.

He'd brought two large containers fitted with antigrav units. Once he'd wrangled them inside, he dialed the units down, let the containers settle onto the floor, and took a look around. His gaze paused briefly when it came to the jamming device blinking silently on the coffee table. Then he noticed Isabela shooting dagger looks in his direction.

"What?" he demanded. "I just got here. What could I already have done to make you angry with me?"

"You are a week late," she replied, each word honed to razor sharpness.

Frowning with puzzlement, he stepped closer to her.

"Late for what?"

"You should have let me know you wouldn't be moving in right away."

"I waited the full two weeks. It's protocol after the death of a roommate."

Isabela swallowed a sigh. Of *course*, he'd followed protocol. Reston Quinian, Doctor of Curriculum and Supervisor of Education for every school on the island, was all *about* protocol. In this case, however, he'd erred.

"Two weeks if the deceased roommate was a family member," she corrected him tartly. "Only one if they were a friend. I've known Anna Sturtevant for many years, but we are not blood-related."

"I was aware of that," he said. "But there are two kinds of families—the ones we're born into, and the ones we build around us as we go through life—and a loss from either one hits us equally hard. Anna may not be dead, but she's still gone, for who knows how long. Given how many losses you've suffered in the past five years, I thought you might appreciate some extra time to yourself before the Forrand family circus came barrelling back into town."

Isabela's jaw dropped. Had she heard him right? Had this prim, excessively correct, *very* Stragori pedant just used a Terran metaphor comparing the Forrands to a *circus*? That he'd used it correctly was a marvel, since the closest thing to a circus on Stragon was the fun fair she had fought to have at the school two years earlier. Clearly, the man had been tainted by all the time he'd spent on the island, trying to get Terran content removed from the lessons of educators like herself.

"Got it!" Quinian had been rummaging for something inside one of his boxes. Grinning triumphantly, he came up with a shiny rectangular container.

"I never cook without these," he said, and removed the lid to show her a collection of small, labelled bottles. Their contents looked familiar.

Spices? And then, because it was the second unbelievable thing she had learned about him in the space of less than two minutes, she exclaimed aloud, "You cook?"

"What? Men don't prepare food on Terra?" he demanded.

"No, of course they do. It's just—"

"—you never saw me as the kitchen type," he supplied archly. "I'll bet you never even tried."

"I did once attempt to imagine you stirring a pot of something that was simmering on a cooking surface."

"And?"

She grimaced. "To be honest, the apron clashed so loudly with your business suit that it gave me a headache."

"Business is the whole point of wearing the suit," he said. "It projects a certain image that helps me to do my job."

His calmness was infuriating. She decided to ruffle it a little.

"Oh! So, you *want* teachers to see you as a stiff-necked doctrinaire."

This jibe hit its target. Quinian drew himself up and declared in the officially disapproving voice she'd grown so accustomed to hearing, "The education we give our children is what shapes our future, Mrs. Bakshi. It's a solemn responsibility, not a popularity contest. So, as long as the teachers I manage respect my professional authority, I don't much care what they think of me personally. And while we're being brutally honest, let me point out that if you followed the standard curriculum and focused on the safety and well-being of the students in your care instead of taking them on unsanctioned adventures to dangerous places, you would hardly need to see me at all."

"You never take it off, do you?" she remarked with calculated pleasantness. "The suit. Even when you are not physically wearing it, you're still inside it."

Silence.

His lips pressed tightly together, he expelled a long, thoughtful breath through his nose. Then he reclosed the container of spice bottles and placed it deliberately inside the shipping box.

"All right," he said in a soft, controlled voice. "Let's start over. I'll go out and come back in. And this time, we *both* leave the suit outside the door. Agreed?"

The look he gave her caused warmth to rise in her cheeks.

He was right. Isabela had always believed and taught that a woman's power came not from conquering obstacles but rather from making unpredictable choices fuelled by anger. However, if she and Quinian were to become working partners, picking an argument with him was not the most productive way to begin.

"Agreed," she said. "And since we are going to be sharing accommodations, shall we also agree to be informal with each other outside of school hours? You may call me Isabela."

He nodded assent. "My friends call me Quin."

He has friends? She stifled the uncharitable thought before it could reach her tongue. Besides being provocative, it was also a reminder of her and Angeli's earlier suspicions about his political leanings. If Quinian was an undeclared radical, his friends could very well be the sort of people

Forrand and company were trying to bring down.

As she watched, Quinian stepped out into the hallway. The apartment door slid shut behind him. When it reopened, he strode across the threshold and went directly to the shipping box.

"Hello, Isabela," he said with forced heartiness, turning a rictus-like smile on her as he retrieved his container of spices, along with a half-filled brown cloth sack. "I've had a rather full day of meetings. We can discuss them later. In the meanwhile, why don't we begin making dinner with these ingredients that I picked up on the mainland before coming here?" He thrust the sack toward her and gave it an enticing shake.

Meal preparation was normally a relaxing activity for Isabela. It would have made a good place for their partnership to begin. However, her mind hadn't kept up with Quinian's words. It had tripped over one word in particular and couldn't seem to move past it: *meetings*.

He'd had a full day of meetings during his personal time? One of them had to have been with Dennis Forrand, she was certain. Well, she knew things Quinian couldn't possibly be aware of, so if these two men thought she would accept a subordinate role in Forrand's mission, or quest, or whatever it turned out to be, they'd better think again.

Isabela got to her feet and followed Quinian into the kitchen.

She pulled the quantum knife out of its special compartment in the cutlery drawer. Stragori vegetables were uniformly tough-skinned, yielding only to a blade that vibrated at a molecular level. "You'll be needing this for any roots or stalks," she said, setting the knife on the cutting board.

"Actually, I won't," he told her. He upended the brown sack and spilled its contents onto the counter. "These were a little pricey, especially the meat, but I wanted to make a good first impression, so..."

She let out a snort of laughter. "*First* impression? A little late for that, is it not?"

His brows drew together as a shadow crossed his face. "It's our first dinner under the same roof," he pointed out, enunciating carefully. He was clearly holding onto his temper with both hands now. "And do you want to see what kind of chef I am or not?"

"Of course, I do," she replied. Then she noticed what was inside the paper-wrapped bundle he'd just finished opening. "That's the meat?" she asked faintly. "And it's blue?"

"Yes, because it's auroch, properly aged and shipped all the way from Galandra. It's only available from a handful of gourmet shops on the mainland."

Isabela could already feel the indigestion it was probably going to give her. However, he'd clearly gone to some trouble for this meal and she didn't want to launch another argument over it. So, she pinned a friendly expression on her face and lied. "I can't wait to taste it."

To her relief, the other foodstuffs were instantly recognizable and the right colour. She watched him peel and dice a few of the vegetables using an ordinary serrated knife. Then he poured some oil into a frypan, dialed the temperature up to high, and added a large cupful of thinly sliced dannoli—a tall green stalk with a fiery orange bulb at one end. As it browned, it filled the kitchen with a peppery, garlicky aroma that instantly made Isabela's taste buds perk up and take notice.

"Are the vegetables pre-boiled?" she wondered aloud.

He shook his head. "Imported, like the meat. I have a source who has a source, on the northern coast."

There was little for her to do but observe, as a dark, savoury-smelling sauce took shape in the frypan and was then poured into a small pot to thicken. By now, Isabela's mouth was watering in anticipation.

He sprinkled three different spices over the auroch steak and used a spatula to press them into the meat before turning it over, placing it in the frypan, and repeating the process.

"My mother created the recipe for this dish," he remarked offhandedly, raising his voice to be heard over the sizzle of meat being seared. "I make it whenever I can, but quality ingredients can be hard to find. And it never turns out well from a quick-oven. The old-tech way works best."

A fresh salad completed the meal. Quinian's mother had invented a recipe for the dressing as well, and it was delicious.

Well, Isabela thought later as she was arranging cookies on a small plate to go with the pot of tea she was brewing, it might not have been a first impression, but it was certainly a good one. Not only did Reston Quinian possess serious culinary skills—the steak had been fork-tender and quite tasty—but when he wasn't wearing his suit, he could also be a surprisingly sociable dinner companion.

Of course, that might have been because he was on his best behaviour, avoiding mention of Dennis Forrand until the meal was over and they were sitting in the living room, comfortably sipping a second cup of tea.

"You were going to tell me about your meetings," Isabela reminded him.

He cleared his throat, then deposited his cup and saucer on the coffee table. "Yes. Well. Dennis and I had breakfast together a few days ago. He gave me our assignment. After that, there were some people I needed to talk to before I moved in with you. That's what I was doing today—talking to them."

...which explained the gourmet dinner. Of course. He'd known from their earlier interactions how she would probably react to his being made the more important partner for this mission, so before breaking the news to her, he'd tried to soften her mood by plying her with this (admittedly outstanding) meal.

All by itself, Isabela's head began swivelling back and forth.

Speaking rapidly, he went on, "We have to turn the Terrans still living on the island against the Directorate somehow, preferably without letting the ones who are optimized find out what we're doing. You're the linchpin of this operation and have to maintain your cover. I've been on personal leave, with high-level contacts inside the Directorate's staff, so Dennis has given me the job of supporting you."

There was a lot wrong with that plan, but one thing in particular leaped out at her.

"I am the linchpin?" she repeated, unconvinced.

"That's what he told me."

"And you are to support me how, exactly?"

He shrugged. "However you need me to. But if you'd like me to be specific... As your trusted co-habiter, I can make this apartment a space in which you don't have to worry about blowing your cover. I'm also a fount of useful information—thanks to the contacts I've made over the years—and a not-too-shabby decoy when a diversion is required to distract attention from what you're doing behind the scenes."

"A decoy," she repeated, frowning uncertainly.

"What? You can't picture me playing that role?"

Actually, she could. The word "decoy" had conjured in her mind's eye the image of a carved wooden duck, with Quinian's face where the bird's bill would have been.

"Think about it," he urged her. "You're the dedicated Terran educator championing the best interests of your students. Not a partisan bone in your body. Meanwhile, I'm the government stooge from the mainland who may or may not be affiliated with one of the fringe groups. I know you and Anna suspected me earlier of being an undeclared radical, and you're not the only ones. All I have to do is make a bit of noise in the right company at the right moment and everyone's going to be paying attention to me—and none to you."

He looked so proud of himself. It was almost a shame to burst his bubble. Nonetheless...

"The public record shows by now that we are sharing this apartment. How does that not suggest we are collaborating?"

"So we're living together," he said. "That doesn't mean we're getting along. After all, since the moment we met, we've been at odds, you and I, never accepting each other as colleagues, let alone friends. Neither one of us has made any secret of that. I'm sure you've complained bitterly about me to others, just as I've done about you. And now that we've been forced into close quarters by a heartless bureaucracy, that can only exacerbate the situation. In fact, it's probably taking all of our self-control just to be civil to each other right now."

He had no idea how truthful that statement was.

"Then what would you have us do?" she demanded.

"In private, we work together on our assignment. In public, or whenever we know we're being monitored, we keep doing what we've always done. That becomes our cover. We butt heads over educational issues, and we complain about having to live together to anyone who'll listen, all the while making the best of a bad situation."

Let people see her barely tolerating a man who had been making her life difficult since the day she'd taken up her teaching responsibilities on the island? Certainly, Isabela thought grimly, she could do that...

FIVE
ANGELI

"You've just enough time to change and freshen up. Let me show you to your room."

The bedrooms were upstairs. Lyla led Angeli up a flight of runnered wooden steps to the second-floor landing and swung open a door, the middle one of three.

"This one is yours," she said, adding, "It was Kate's before she moved out on her own."

"Is Kate your daughter?"

"Yes. She made those clothes you're wearing, and the ones in the closet. You're the same size as she was before the baby came, so feel free to borrow. And welcome home, Eva. You were missed."

With that, Lyla went bustling back downstairs.

Angeli took a moment to survey her new surroundings, flushed with a sense of *déjà vu*. The soft, warm colours, the furniture arrangement, the large curtained window, the broad, comfortable bed amply supplied with plump cushions—it all looked so familiar. Then something clicked into place in her memory. Thirty-three years fell away in an instant, and she was on Earth, staying in Isabela Bakshi's house in Veggieville, responsible for the safety of Juno Vargas, a bold and stubborn teen in a dangerous place, and wondering how her life could possibly get any more complicated. How little she'd known back then...!

Shaking off the past, Angeli checked out the closet and found the clothes she'd travelled in—and swum in, slept in, and showered in—hanging up, all clean and neatly pressed. She also discovered a selection of tops and bottoms in a wide range of colours and a variety of woven materials, all in her size. In the dresser drawers were other garments: changes of underwear, a couple of nightgowns, and some knitted sweaters, with and without button fronts.

For a moment, she hesitated, feeling like an interloper. She was in a borrowed room, wearing borrowed clothes, using an assumed identity. Then she reminded herself: if this assignment was going to take a year, Eva Moss needed more than one outfit to wear. And hadn't Lyla invited her to help herself?

The lock on her bedroom door was little more than a token gesture, so whatever she chose would have to have a pocket large enough to hold the two data wafers. Angeli picked out a pair of emerald green trousers and a matching green and white striped blouse and proceeded to dress for dinner.

Lyla's kitchen was by far the largest room in the house. Angeli stole a glance through the door and saw a huge pot bubbling on what appeared to be a four-burner cooking surface, and a square central counter on which sat three iced layer cakes, along with half a dozen round pies cooling on a pair of metal racks. The air was so full of delicious aromas that just standing there and inhaling it might have added a few grams to her mass.

The dining room wasn't nearly as spacious as the kitchen, but it still held a long, sturdy-looking wooden table, set for ten. Seven of the chairs were already occupied by guests. This wasn't just dinner—it was a dinner party. Clearly, Eva Moss's homecoming was considered an event to be celebrated.

So much for entering unnoticed and keeping a low profile. Angeli paused on the threshold to assess this new situation.

A man in a dark red pullover sweater whose greying beard placed him in his middle years sat folding and refolding his napkin for the apparent amusement of the small boy beside him. They were watched fondly by a young, auburn-haired woman to the child's immediate left—his mother, Angeli guessed.

Meanwhile, another woman had taken the seat at the foot of the table. Plain-faced, with a thick fall of wavy blonde hair pulled back and caught in a metal clip at the nape of her neck, she glanced up, smiling, as Angeli appeared in the doorway. Krall sat to her immediate right, still in uniform.

So, the third bedroom is probably not his, otherwise he would have changed his clothes as well... and yet he has a customary seat at dinner? Interesting.

The blonde-haired woman gestured to Angeli to take the vacant chair to her left, across from Krall and one place setting away from a pair of young men who bore a strong family resemblance to each other. Both had neatly trimmed dark hair, long noses, and angular jawlines. Twins in taste if perhaps not in fact, they were identically dressed in blue denim trousers and long-sleeved grey and green striped tops. They had been quietly chatting until Angeli sat down. Now they turned their attention to the new arrival.

"So, this is the famous Eva Moss?" the nearer one said, his tone of voice indicating that he was less than impressed.

Reflexively, Angeli stiffened in her chair.

"Mind your manners, Adam," Lyla scolded him as she emerged from the kitchen, pushing a serving cart.

"Sorry," he said, making it sound more like a description than an apology.

On the cart were the large pot from the stove, a shiny metal soup ladle, and a cloth-wrapped bundle in a round woven basket... and memories of the past burst free and inundated Angeli's mind once again. She and Juno Vargas had served themselves from pots just like that, sitting at tables like this one, in community dining halls all over the Industrial Wilderness of Americas. The friendship they'd forged during that year of travel had lasted for decades. It should have lasted a lifetime, but it hadn't. And whose fault was *that*?

Krall was right—memory *was* a funny thing. Right now it was constricting her heart in her chest. Next it would make her cry.

She mustn't let it. As Forrand would no doubt delight in reminding her, she had made her choices. The face of a revolution needed to be a whole lot tougher than this.

A hand gently patting hers broke into Angeli's thoughts. She looked up and found herself gazing into a pair of sympathetic blue eyes.

"I can see you've had a rough time of it. Whenever you're

ready to share," the woman at the foot of the table assured her softly, "know that you're among friends."

Among friends? This lady had no idea who she was talking to.

Lyla wheeled the cart to the head of the table, reached down to a lower shelf, and brought up nine bowls, all different colours but the same size and made the same way. Then she dipped the ladle and began serving the soup. Or maybe it was a stew. It was certainly thick and hearty enough, with plenty of bread and dumplings to go around.

As the meal progressed, its warmth loosened the knot in Angeli's stomach, making her comfortable enough to speak.

"I'm at a bit of a disadvantage here," she said. "You all seem to know *me*, but—"

"Oh, dear!" Lyla interrupted her. "I was so thrilled to have you at my table that I forgot my manners. Please forgive me."

She was thrilled? Eva was famous? What had this shell identity been up to since Forrand had planted it here?

"Warder-in-Charge Krall you've already met," said Lyla with a lilt in her voice that was too suggestive to be unintentional.

Angeli threw Krall a questioning look and saw a mischievous—and confirming—tilt to his grin. So the landlady was a matchmaker as well? Wonderful.

"Adam and Michael Skinner are our twin bards," Lyla continued. "They broadcast our local news online and gather interesting items from other towns to report to us as well."

Hmm. If Westgrove was part of a comm network with other towns, that could prove useful later on.

Angeli exchanged pleasant nods with the brothers on her side of the table.

"Mariah Naughton is a mind-mender," Lyla continued, indicating the woman to Angeli's right. "She shares a medical office with four others, including a pharmist. Their clinic is just around the corner."

A psychotherapist, then, in Terran terms? That explained her earlier behaviour.

Angeli nodded toward her as well.

"Roger Walker is an electronics wizard who keeps our computers running and creates wonderful games and toys in his spare time, in addition to being our newly-appointed Oath Binder. Tannis Ludvigsen is his daughter—she's our top-rated kilnist—and Charlie is her son," Lyla concluded.

No more than five or six years old, the child was having trouble meeting Angeli's gaze. She lowered her face to his level and gave him a wave of her hand. He smiled shyly and waved back.

"Kate was supposed to be our tenth, but it turns out that she's feeding a group of her own tonight. You'll be meeting her soon, I'm hoping," Lyla explained. "She's a clothing maker, the best in the region."

That wasn't just a mother's pride talking. Angeli had admired how expertly fashioned the garments were in the closet upstairs.

"I'll look forward to it," she replied.

When the stew was gone, everyone passed their spoons and empty bowls to the head of the table to be stacked on the cart, and Lyla announced, "Dessert will be three-fruit pie, washed down with hot *klummeren* tea."

Lyla rolled everything back into the kitchen. They heard a muted clatter of dishes from the other room, and then the cart reappeared, freshly laden with a rectangular baking dish, a serving utensil, and nine plates, made the same way as the bowls and most likely fired in the same kiln.

The pie had a bottom that was more like a large soft cookie, and a smooth custardy sauce in place of a top crust. The fruit between these two layers was sweet and plentiful. As with the stew, not a bite or a crumb was left over. While the empty plates were being collected and the tea was being poured, Michael piped up, "So, when do we get to hear about some of your adventures, Eva Moss?"

"What makes you think I've had adventures?" Angeli replied, genuinely curious.

He stared at her as though she'd just sprouted horns on her head. "What makes us—?" he sputtered, then flung his arms wide for emphasis and exclaimed, "Because you've been *travelling*. You've seen things. You've done things. You've crossed to the southern continent and explored it, front to back and top to bottom. You've been to places we've only ever seen on a map and wondered what they would be like to visit. And now that you're back, you can *tell* us what it was like."

"We all want to know," Adam chimed in. "Not just Michael and me. Everyone in Westgrove. You're a celebrity now. You owe it to the rest of us to share your experiences."

Realization burst like fireworks in Angeli's brain. So *that* was what Eva had been doing! (In someone's imagination, at any rate.) Well, these twin bards were right about one thing: she did owe it to them to share what she knew. That was what her mission was all about. The problem was, she was beginning to question the veracity of what she knew— or rather, what she *thought* she knew. And something Michael had said was niggling at her.

"None of you have been off this land mass? But what

about when you travelled from here to the island and back?" she asked, directing her question to everyone at the table.

Baffled looks crisscrossed the room for several heartbeats.

Then, "Some of us did leave here once," Roger replied slowly, "to go off-world. A lot of us, actually, according to my grandfather. But that was a lifetime ago, two and a half centuries, give or take. Well before the time of anyone here present."

...and well before the Stragori made first contact with the Terrans on Mars in 2230 C.E., if Angeli remembered her history correctly. She performed some rapid mental calculations. A Stragori century was equal to 94.3 Earth years. Assuming Roger's estimate was correct, this mass emigration from Stragon would have begun around 2170 C.E. That was two years before the second pandemic wiped out half of South America and decimated the populations of every other continent on the planet. It was also a good ten Earth years before Adam Vargas and his team ended the dark age following the pandemic by instituting the Great Terran Reorganization; and it certainly predated the Directorate's cancellation of Stragon's space colonization program, a decision which (according to Dennis Forrand) infuriated the radicals and stranded millions of objectors on an island polluted with toxic waste.

This wasn't right. Roger had to be mistaken. The timing made no logical sense.

"Did anyone return to Borea?" she asked.

Frowning, Lyla tilted her head quizzically. "From off-world? No. But some who changed their minds about emigrating did come back home from the processing centre on the island."

"Did they tell anyone why they'd changed their minds?" Angeli persisted. "For example, was there sickness at the processing centre?"

"No, there wasn't," Roger replied. "Is that important?"

"You look upset, Eva," Mariah observed. "Is something wrong?"

Angeli opened her mouth to respond, then closed it again. Somebody—she wasn't sure who—was apparently rewriting Stragori history to suit their own purposes, and the local mass media were sitting two seats away. She needed to find out more. At the moment, however, it was more important that she choose her words carefully.

"That's... not what I was told," she said after a pause.

"By the technoslaves on the southern continent?" Lyla drawled. "What a surprise."

"I want to know the truth," Angeli told her. "It's vital to—" Catching herself up, she concluded, "to my well-being."

Roger cast a significant glance down the table at Mariah. "She needs to talk to Derwin."

"All right, I'll authorize it," the other woman said with evident reluctance, "but keep in mind that he's old and he's frail. You mustn't get him too excited."

"Who is Derwin?" Angeli inquired.

"My grandfather," Roger replied. "Derwin Mak. His parents were among those who changed their minds. He was in his teens at the time. I could tell you what he told me, but I have a feeling you'd rather hear it from someone who was actually there when it happened. Tomorrow midmorning, I'll come by and pick you up, and we can visit him together."

"Thank you. I would appreciate that."

Any questions Angeli may have had about the remaining pies and cakes in the kitchen were answered when the dinner party broke up. They were apparently parting gifts. Each of Lyla's guests was handed a sealed container on their way out the door, including little Charlie.

Roger and his family were the first to leave. Charlie had school the next day and it was already past his bedtime. Mariah thanked Lyla and departed a few minutes later, followed by Krall. Adam and Michael expressed their disappointment at Eva's reticence at dinner, but they cheered up considerably when she consented to give them an interview in a few days' time. Then Lyla shooed them out of the house.

"Alone at last!" she declared, quietly but firmly closing the door behind them. "Let's have another cup of that *klummeren* tea. It's quite delicious, isn't it?" she added, leading the way back into the kitchen. "One of Petra Blankoff's special blends. I trade her pastries for it."

Special, yes. It was a translucent lavender colour, and seemed to be naturally carbonated. It sparkled in the mouth. Angeli had never tasted anything like it. Intrigued, she said, "It has a unique flavour. Does she grow the tea herself?"

Lyla laughed. "Heavens, no! That would take up her whole yard. She gets the leaves from a plantation run by her family in one of the eastern districts, and barters for the spices and other ingredients with local residents."

Lyla poured out two cups of the still-steaming liquid from the urn beside the stove, handed one to Angeli, then led the way again, this time into the cozy parlour. It held seating for six, on a loveseat and four differently designed chairs, all upholstered in the same black-and-tan-striped material and all within arm's reach of the large, square wooden coffee table in the centre of the room.

"Out of curiosity," said Angeli as she and Lyla settled onto adjacent chairs to sip their tea, "who sleeps in the third room upstairs?"

"It used to be Kate's work space. Now it's a spare bedroom in case we have guests from out of district."

"So you are free to travel between districts, as long as you don't leave this land mass."

Lyla laughed again and said, "Well, of *course* we're free to travel, anywhere in the world we want, including to the southern continent. We simply choose not to go there. You've been away too long, Eva. We're not prisoners up here, no matter what those thick-headed southerners might have told you."

"Then why did Adam and Michael make such a fuss about where I've been?"

"Because you're a daredevil explorer, with a longing to visit distant and dangerous places." Leaning forward confidentially, she continued, "The fact is, you're our avatar, Eva, one of very few that Borea has produced. Some northerners would be content to live in a bubble of ignorance, pretending that the southern continent doesn't exist, but the vast majority of us are aware of the need to stay informed, especially in these troubled days. People like you perform a valuable public service. You make it possible for us to find out what the southerners are up to without the risk involved in linking our technology to theirs, or going among them ourselves. It truly is an honour to have you at my table."

Uh-huh. So Angeli was a double agent—a spy for the objectors as well as for whichever faction Forrand had conscripted her into.

"That's what makes you perfect for something like this," said Dennis's remembered voice in her head.

"You called the mainlanders 'technoslaves' earlier. Would you like to know what they call Boreans?"

"Probably something a computer would spit out—something accurate but dull and unimaginative."

"Objectors."

Lyla arched her eyebrows and flourished her free hand in a *ta-dah!* gesture. "See? Absolutely colourless. So tell me: do they at least understand what we're objecting *to*?"

"The ones I've spoken to think you have a stubborn resistance to new technology in general, and to the implants in particular."

Lyla uttered a disdainful syllable. "The implants are just a symptom of what's wrong down there. What we truly object to—and have always objected to—is the childish compulsion they have to find and embrace the next shiny new toy. Those fools have been leaping from one technology to another without stopping to analyze and evaluate the effects of any of them, on their bodies, their society, and their environment. They call that progress. We call it insanity. That's why we prefer to live up here, and no one with implants is allowed to set foot on our shores. That's by *our* choice, not theirs. We may not be able to block their orbiting surveillance satellites, but we can certainly keep their 'optimized' drones off our property."

"Really!" Angeli leaned forward now and lowered her voice. "You can detect the implants? How?"

Grinning conspiratorially, Lyla leaned in as well. "We 'throwbacks' aren't as unsophisticated as those southerners would like to believe. We developed a technology sensitive enough to detect the faint radioactive signature the implants give off. And we've kept it to ourselves all this time, leaving the Directorate and its minions guessing."

"That's quite an achievement," Angeli agreed. "But what happens when their implant technology evolves beyond the need for whatever is generating the signature?"

Lyla raised a reproving eyebrow. "You think our technology has been standing still, child? Trust me, whatever the Mainland throws at us, we'll be ready for it."

Angeli's thoughts were spinning so hard inside her head that it was a wonder she was able to keep her balance as she climbed the stairs to her bedroom that evening. Everything the Earth Intelligence operatives planted on Stragon had found out about the objectors had been wrong. What was much more important, however, and much harder for her to wrap her brain around, was that everything Dennis Forrand had told her at the beginning of this mission was wrong as well.

Either Forrand had lied to her or someone else had lied to Forrand, or both, if he'd known the truth all along. Wait—What was she thinking? Of *course* he'd known the truth. He just hadn't wanted *her* to know it. Not in advance, at any rate. Like the ordeal aboard the *Priest*, discovering what was true or false was probably just a part of her mission that he'd neglected to mention.

Behind the closed door of her bedroom, Angeli took out the card reader and the secret second data wafer. Forrand had warned her she might have to make quick decisions and act on them right away. One of them just might be triggered by the contents of this wafer.

Angeli pushed it into the slot in the side of the reading device, then released the breath she'd unconsciously been holding as rows of text—in Anglo, not Standard or Stragori—appeared on the screen:

If you're reading this, then you've made contact with Bennin Krall and arrived in Westgrove as Eva Moss, a prodigal daughter of the northern continent. Congratulations! You've achieved the first objective of your mission. Now you need to orient yourself. Spend some time getting to know the people who live there. Your next goal is to determine what will motivate them to take action that will weaken if not silence the radical movement on the mainland. The radical groups are your targets in this operation—not the Directorate, and not the individual who is impersonating Gervais Forrand. There are others assigned the task of dealing with them.

Once you know what button(s) to push, formulate a plan. Be unpredictable and think outside the box. Be the loose cannon that I know you can be. Recruit as many northerners in as many towns as possible to our cause, but don't rush the process. You've got roughly a year to get things right.

Bennin Krall is one of my most trusted agents. You can confide in him and enlist his assistance without fear of being betrayed. He is also your conduit for getting in touch with me as long as you are in Westgrove.

Press 'P' on the keypad to project an image of the map onto a flat, plaincoated surface. It will help you plan your itinerary. Report to me through Krall when you are ready to leave for the next town.

Eva Moss's backstory is contained in a separate file on this data wafer. So are the names of the operatives I've planted in each town and the recognition codes you're to use. Your birth name and your thumbprint are required to open it.

Good luck.

SIX

ISABELA

Isabela awoke with a start from a nightmare in which the apartment was being demolished around her and found herself in a place that may have looked dark and peaceful, but was even louder and more disturbing than her dream.

For a surreal moment, she thought the harsh, rasping noise that filled the air must be the death scream of a wall being ripped apart. Then she remembered that she was no longer alone, and she recognized the racket for what it was.

Reston Quinian was in the next bedroom, snoring loudly enough to rouse not only Isabela from a deep sleep, but most likely other residents of the building as well. How a sound that powerful could be generated by someone as compactly built as Quinian was, was a mystery. (Even more of a mystery was that a society as advanced as the Stragori claimed to be had not yet figured out how to cure or prevent this annoying problem.)

Now thoroughly awake, Isabela rolled onto her back and lay staring blindly at the ceiling. In truth, it wasn't only the commotion emanating from the next room that prevented her from getting back to sleep. It was also the eddying of her thoughts in reaction to learning what Forrand had in mind for her and her new co-tenant.

According to Quinian, Forrand wasn't expecting a miracle—they were only two people, after all, and the island was a large place. It was also infested with surveillance hardware. Granted, she and Quinian were able to jam any local monitoring signals, and they'd been given a year in which to complete the assignment... but still...

More than five hundred thousand Terrans had accepted optimization. They lived in every urban district on the island, and many of them commuted to jobs across the strait. Even if she and Quinian were somehow able to identify them and track their movements, doing anything subversive among the general population without the Directorate's knowledge was going to be a task of Herculean proportions.

As well, there was something else to consider. The Directorate had provided twenty-seven million Humans safe refuge from an interstellar war, had ensured that as many as possible could be transported here from Earth, had warned and inoculated them against the toxins in the soil on the island, had given them work and educational opportunities on the mainland and equal access to Stragon's advanced technology, had freely shared food and supplies with them... In short, the Directorate had shown the Terrans every generosity, every reason to be grateful—and that would surely translate to loyalty in the event of a planetary conflict.

True, the Directorate may also have turned half a million of them into unwitting spies... and the justice system hadn't exactly proven to be a level playing field so far... but those were minor hiccups in the grander scheme of things. The millions of Terrans now living in relative comfort on the island would never hate the Directorate as much as the Stragori did. Certainly not as much as Forrand wanted them to.

Dennis had to know this. He had eyes and ears everywhere. So, what was he *really* trying to accomplish?

At once, an answer came to her. She didn't like it, but it was the only one that made sense. Whatever his end game was, Isabela's last-minute decision to remain on-world instead of leaving with the EIS agents must have thrown a wrench into it. He needed to sideline her, to prevent her from nosing around in his business while he dragged Angeli into the middle of his latest plot. So, he'd made Isabela the "linchpin" of an impossible mission that would focus her attention on the island, and he'd foisted a live-in partner on her for good measure, someone he knew she disliked, who would keep her on edge and off-balance, as well as out of the loop.

Forrand had promised to get justice for Vikram, once his own purpose had been fulfilled. Of course. She should have known he was only telling her what she wanted to hear, to ensure that she would follow his orders. He'd talked Angeli into faking her death for much the same reason—to make Olivia leave Stragon because it was what *he* wanted. It untied their hands, Angeli had said earlier. She'd been wrong. The only hands Forrand was interested in freeing up were his own.

Sadly, this was not the person Isabela had known and respected back on Earth. That man had fought to procure a decent standard of living for agricultural workers by setting up Veggieville as a model community and putting Isabela and her brother in charge. *That* Dennis Forrand had found ways to funnel resources to them, and to expedite their building permit applications. He'd been a humanitarian. The man she was dealing with now had a moral compass pointing in quite a different direction... if, indeed, he had one at all.

The current Dennis Forrand enjoyed playing with people's lives. Was he playing with Angeli's as well, making her believe she was doing important work while sending her on some hopeless errand? Did Quinian realize he was simply another pawn in what Forrand saw as a game? Would it matter if he did?

She made a face at the ceiling. Then she remembered more clearly what Angeli had said, and Isabela gasped aloud. "...all our hands, *including yours.*"

Was this an invitation to take independent action—to be a "loose cannon", as Angeli had once put it?

Dennis had ordered them to destroy all the EIS technology in the apartment, but Angeli only followed orders that she agreed with, regardless of who had issued them, and neither she nor Isabela had thought this one made sense. So, Isabela's small, ornamental-looking signal jammer still sat beside the flower vase on the coffee table, and her commpad and EIS-issued encryption device—keyed to her DNA, useless to anyone else—remained tucked away at the back of a drawer at the bottom of her wardrobe.

Hmm. Perhaps it was time to contact Angeli's former handler at the Earth Intelligence Service and read Ops Control into this situation.

Isabela spent the rest of the night carefully drafting her

message. It was encrypted as a letter to "Uncle Henry"—the code name Barry Novak had used when communicating with Angeli on Stragon.

Communicating back to him was another matter, something that had been strictly controlled for security reasons. As the mission coordinator, Angeli had had special codes for that purpose programmed into her encrypter—which wouldn't work for Isabela even if the other woman had left it behind in the apartment. Olivia had once supplied Angeli with codes to send a message directly to Drew Townsend, the station manager on Daisy Hub, but that had been a one-time-only use, to request the emergency extraction—and again, the information was not accessible to lower-ranking members of the organization.

Getting an update to someone at the EIS had suddenly become much more challenging.

Then a name popped out of Isabela's memory: SecuriTech. It was the business Barry Novak ran as a cover for EIS Operations, in New Chicago on Earth. If being deactivated meant she was cut off from covert communication channels, then she was left with only one option: the more open and conventional method of transmitting messages would have to do.

With luck, her report would find him. If not, then at least she would have tried. In either case, Isabela had no way to know whether Novak would be the first to read "Uncle Henry's" letter, so the wording of both the encrypted and the unencrypted text was important.

By the time she was satisfied with both versions, rays of sunlight were slipping past her curtains to paint golden stripes on the ceiling of her bedroom, and she could hear Quinian moving around the apartment. Today was a school day—a work day for her. Quickly, she transferred her communication onto a blank data wafer, then thrust it into the inside pocket of her jacket and replaced her commpad and encrypter in their secure hiding place.

A plan firmed up in her mind while she was choosing a blouse to wear with her brown, tweed-patterned trousers. (They'd been pricey, as Quinian would say, but the "smart fabric" was programmable. It could imitate everything from linen to leather, in a range of colours, and a single pair was touted to last a lifetime.)

The school was running low on snack food for the students' breaks. This gave Isabela a perfect excuse to run an errand. The district's food distribution depot was less than a block away from the local commhub. She could place her order at the depot's front desk, leave the school's antigrav cooler there to be filled, go and take care of her business at the commhub, then return to the depot to pick up the cooler and bring it back to the school.

Joanne could manage the class for an hour or two. She'd done it before, during Quinian's annoyingly frequent inspections of Isabela's curriculum. If Quinian was right about Joanne's being purposely placed at the school to spy for the Directorate, they wouldn't be any the wiser. And if Isabela played things right, neither would Quinian.

When Isabela finally left her bedroom, she found her new apartment-mate sitting at the dining table, unshaven, wearing a dark blue robe and scowling at the bowl of cereal grains in front of him as though it had just confessed to throwing out the approved curriculum and cancelling all summative assessments of its students. His spoon was nowhere in sight.

This did not bode well for the rest of Quinian's day.

Meanwhile, Isabela was enjoying the irony of the situation: the man whose snoring had probably kept their whole building awake looked as though he himself hadn't slept a wink.

Smiling inwardly, she went to the kitchen and poured herself a bowl of cereal as well. Then she took two spoons from the drawer and the container of milk from the refrigeration cabinet and carried everything over to the table.

"Good morning," she said, firmly placing one of the spoons beside his bowl.

Silence.

She tried again. "What's the matter? Is it refusing to show you its lesson plans?"

This time he looked up at her, blinking in confusion. "What—What did you say?"

"I said, 'Eat your cereal. You'll feel better.' You know," she added between mouthfuls, "I heard somewhere that people who snore may sleep, but they don't really get any rest."

He stiffened in his chair. "I don't snore," he informed her.

"Really! Then that must have been a demolition crew I heard last night, tearing down the buildings to either side of us." Before he could utter any further denials, she changed the subject. "How much leave time do you have left?"

After a pause to add some milk to his bowl, he replied, "I put in for two weeks, so there's another few days to go. And I can extend my absence if necessary. Why?"

"Any more *meetings* to attend?" she inquired softly.

He swallowed hard, and apparently too soon. Judging by

the expression on his face, the partly chewed cereal hadn't gone down without a fight.

"No," he said in a strangled voice. Then he cleared his throat and tried again. "No. We've got everything we need for now. I'll set things up here while you're at school and give you a demonstration when you get back."

If he was going to be working in the apartment all day, then the risk of his dropping by the school while she was running her errands had just dropped to zero. Isabela barely managed to mask her relief. Then she washed her dishes, put on her jacket, threw a "See you later, then," over her shoulder, and walked out the door.

Everything went like clockwork. Even the unpredictable spring weather went along with her plan, the overcast sky threatening but not delivering its fall of rain until after Isabela had returned from the depot with a month's worth of snacks in the cooler—sweetroot, cheese chews, nutribars, and juice jugs—and a brand-new transmission log in her pocket.

Other than "Uncle Henry" and the imaginary relatives that figured in his encrypted messages, Isabela had no surviving friends or family that she knew of back on Earth. She had consequently never had occasion to send a message to anyone off-world until today, and had no idea how to go about it. Fortunately, the clerk at the commhub had been quite understanding.

A very earnest young woman with an abundance of facial jewellery, she had walked Isabela through the steps involved in opening a secure account, had shown her how to fill out a transmission requisition, and had even taken the time to locate the destination code for the only Barry Novak residing in New Chicago, Americas, Earth.

These services, the clerk explained patiently, were provided free of charge. However, the transmission itself came with a price tag: fifty credits for standard delivery (arriving in anywhere up to a month or more), or two hundred and fifty for an expedited message (guaranteed to arrive sooner than that).

"It's the energy you're paying for," she went on, warming to the topic. "A commburst is a commburst at our end. It uses the same amount of energy whether it's carrying one message or a thousand, so it's just a matter of mathematics, dividing up the total cost among the senders. Depending on the distance involved, it can be a lot. In the case of a transmission to Earth, you've got the initial push plus five signal boosts with redirection to the next space gate—that's where the real expense lies—ending up at the comm centre nearest the destination planet. To make standard delivery affordable for our Terran residents, we don't transmit fewer than a thousand messages at a time. It can take a while for them to accumulate here, and another while before they're all delivered to the individual recipients at the other end."

"And what about the ones marked 'expedited'?"

"The minimum number for transmission is much lower, taking less time to reach, and with fewer senders the cost per message is proportionately higher."

"But you're still waiting to fill a quota. If it takes longer than expected—"

"It won't, trust me," the clerk assured her. "We've got twenty-seven million Terrans, most of them staying in touch with family back home. I transmit an expedited commburst every couple of days."

"And if there's an emergency communication that has to be transmitted right away...?"

"Commhubs don't handle those. They're passed to the Directorate's offices, where they're screened, marked urgent, and sent via a special diplomatic frequency to the nearest Terran space station for immediate forwarding."

Hmm. The nearest Terran space station to Stragon was Daisy Hub, and its manager was part of the EIS. How fortuitous!

Projecting what she hoped would be taken as a reflection of the clerk's own wide-eyed earnestness, Isabela asked, "Could I redirect my message to Daisy Hub?"

The clerk's features contracted into a thoughtful expression. "As long as the recipient is posted to or resident on a space station," she recited, "they can receive personal communications there, of course. But the recipient of your message, Barry Novak, lives on Earth."

Isabela mentally crossed her fingers, then leaned in confidentially and said, "Actually, Barry is the 'in care of.' The actual recipient is his father, who travels a great deal. It's time-sensitive but not an emergency yet, and two hundred and fifty credits is more than I can afford to pay. Meanwhile, a close friend of the family recently moved to Daisy Hub. This person has forwarded my messages to them in the past. And since Daisy Hub is so much closer to Stragon than Earth is..."

Still looking doubtful, the clerk consulted the screen of her computer. "One space gate, minimal boost required... Says here that it's doable, but the message goes as a single transmission, and if you can't afford a share of a normal expedited burst..."

A pause.

The clerk narrowed her gaze and locked eyes with Isabela across the counter. "Out of curiosity, who would you be sending this missive in care of if not Barry Novak?"

"The station manager, Drew Townsend."

"Townsend," the clerk echoed. "Townsend. That name sounds familiar." She returned to her computer. A moment later she was reading from the screen in a hushed voice. "*Dio!* He's the grandson of—"

The clerk inhaled sharply, then raised huge eyes to Isabela's face. "You should have led with that, you know," she scolded. "It would have saved us both a lot of time. All right, then, no problem. I'll open the channel and send this myself."

"And the cost?"

"There is none. He's a Forrand. Anything going to or from a member of one of the founding families travels free of charge, by order of the Directorate. But I will need your name and your thumbprint to seal the transaction, just in case there's any problem with delivery."

"Done!" Isabela declared.

Together, they completed the first entry in Isabela's log book, and she left the commhub with a spring in her step. Being a loose cannon, she'd decided, was going to be fun.

The unbroken layer of clouds overhead had been steadily darkening all morning until it looked like dusk outside and felt more like midnight than noon. No more than five minutes after Isabela had accompanied the cooler through the front door of the school, there was a sharp *crack* of lightning and a drumroll of thunder and the skies split open, unleashing a wind-driven downpour of rain.

Students ate their lunch and worked at their various lessons to the sound of fat drops tattooing the roof and splatting against the windows. This was no gentle spring shower—it was a barrage. Under its relentless pummelling, the walls of the school seemed to draw closer together somehow. The air felt heavier. And the students became restless.

Isabela couldn't blame them. She was having some difficulty focusing on the task at hand as well.

The classroom was heated, but its radiant thermal units weren't strong enough to dispel the chill one imagined while watching trees bend in the storm raging just outside the window. Students went to the hygiene room and returned wearing sweaters, their cuffs unrolled all the way to the wrist. At snack time, Joanne made a pot of hot chocca. It was instantly every child's favourite beverage. When it was time to leave, twenty-four students and a teaching assistant bundled up before braving the weather.

Isabela stayed behind to record her assessments and prepare the following day's menu of assignments. It was nearly five o'clock when she headed out the door. By then the rain had stopped; however, the cloud covering persisted, dimming the sun like an age-yellowed lamp shade. Meanwhile, the wind continued to blow. It rippled the puddles and rattled the tree branches. Moaning like a spirit in torment, it raced along the rows of low- and medium-rise buildings that lined the five blocks between the school and the quadplex. It gusted at Isabela's back as though urging her to hasten her steps.

She walked briskly, feeling the chill penetrate her light jacket and wishing she'd picked a heavier one to wear that morning. As she entered the apartment, she was mentally sifting through the selection of tea blends in the cupboard, deciding which one to make and imagining how good a warm mug was going to feel between her hands.

Then she saw Quinian, sitting at the dining table where she'd left him earlier. He was now fully dressed and shaven, but still scowling darkly at the table top. Evidently lost in thought, he didn't so much as glance up when she entered the room. Not until she dropped as noisily as possible onto the chair across from him did he even acknowledge her presence. He raised troubled eyes to meet hers, causing unease to stir in her midsection. Whatever was bothering him had to be serious.

"Was there a problem setting things up?" she inquired.

He shook his head. "Not with that. The tracking technology works just fine."

They had tracking technology? That at least was good to know.

"But...?"

His face acquired a pained expression. "I'll have to show you."

Intrigued, she followed him into the living room, where a black rectangular box about the same size as her commpad sat in the middle of the coffee table. Beside it, a polished metal cylinder resembling a miniature glow-rod was emitting a pale, pulsing luminescence at one end. Quinian gestured to her to take a seat, and they settled side by side on the sofa.

"A friend... borrowed this unit for me. It's programmed with the software that the Directorate has been using for surveillance and tracking," he said.

She stared a question at him.

"He has assured me that no one will come looking for it," he replied carefully. "You might say it's a prototype. Only a handful of people even know that it exists."

"But the software is identical to what is on the Directorate's computers?"

"Essentially, yes."

"And it can access the Directorate's databank without being detected?"

"Yes, within limits. It has the capability of posing as one of the units currently installed in the Directorate's offices. It can get us onto the server and let us see what the surveillance system is recording, but without a valid password, we can't open any of the files that will show us how the data is being used."

Isabela frowned. "Is that something we need to know?"

"My friend doesn't think so. Not at the moment, anyway. Perhaps later."

"Then what is the problem?"

He picked up the cylinder. Pointing it at the black box, he said, "Show map of southern land mass."

A beam of white light the same width as the box seemed to unfurl from its upper surface. It halted half a metre from the ceiling, then expanded sideways in both directions, creating a rectangular screen. As Isabela watched, a full-colour image faded in, blurry at first, then resolving into a squarish piece of land with rugged coastlines on three sides and a straight one across the top. The picture animated, as though its topographical history was unfolding before her. A mountain range jutted skyward along the eastern coast, and bright blue rivers appeared to spring up in the interior and flow south and west to the sea, pausing now and then to pool into lakes.

"Show Stragori population distribution," said Quinian, still pointing the cylinder.

Like the rain that had pelted down that afternoon, a deluge of red dots appeared to strike the map, hard and fast, each dot shrinking on contact to make room for later arrivals. Concentrations of dots indicated communities. Gradually, they grew into urban districts that sprawled and coalesced, the largest one—Capital City—occupying the entire southern coast. The downpour continued for several minutes, colouring more than half of the land surface crimson.

"Show same information for northern land mass," Quinian commanded the computer.

The image faded out and back in as the screen refreshed itself. Now it displayed a map very similar to the previous one, except that the die-straight coastline was its southern shore and the rain of red dots lasted a much shorter time. When it finished, the communities were smaller and more widely scattered (although just as intensely red).

"Census update for northern land mass," Quinian said.

A pleasant, agendered voice replied, "As of ten minutes ago, total population of the northern land mass was 4,214,011."

"And how many are connected to the intellinet?"

A pause, then, "That number is zero," said the voice.

"Census update for the southern land mass," he said doggedly.

"As of eleven minutes ago, total population of the southern land mass was 58,490,410."

"And how many are connected to the intellinet?"

"That number is 51,765,209."

He turned sober eyes on Isabela's face. "Not seeing the

problem yet? Watch this." Pointing the cylinder at the box once more, he said, "Show same information for the island."

The screen repainted to display a bowl-shaped land mass that was roughly two-thirds the size of the mainland. Its northern coast was an uneven horizontal line, its curved bottom and sides boldly drawn in brown and green. A moment later, the bowl began to fill, as though with drops of blood. In short order, it was full to the brim.

The image was unsettling. Perhaps if the dots had been a different colour...

"Census update for the island," said Quinian.

"As of fourteen minutes ago, total population of the island was 5,201,092."

Wait a minute... Only five million when she knew for a fact that there were more than twenty million Terrans on the island at any given time? Tension creeping into every muscle of her body, Isabela straightened in her chair.

Now smiling grimly, Quinian asked the computer, "And how many of them are connected to the intellinet?"

"That number is 311,816," the voice replied.

Wrong again. Whatever that computer was counting up, it wasn't Terrans.

But Quinian wasn't finished yet.

"Computer, locate Reston Quinian," he commanded.

Abruptly, the bowl emptied, save for a single blood-red dot.

"Zoom in and provide coordinates," he continued.

The computer obeyed. Isabela stared in fascination as the map enlarged beyond the limits of the screen, bringing a grid of labelled streets into view. As though drawn by an invisible hand, a set of numbers appeared beside the solitary dot that now sat within the rectangle representing her building.

"So it knows where I am. Let's try another one, shall we?" he said. "Computer, locate Isabela Bakshi."

Her breath caught in her throat. Something about the glance he threw her told Isabela that this wasn't the first time Quinian had given that command today. Had the tracking device found her at the commhub that morning? Was all of this leading up to a confrontation? An accusation, perhaps, of duplicity?

After a pause that felt like an eternity, the voice informed them, "The location of that individual is unknown."

Isabela nearly sagged backward in her seat with relief.

"I'm no expert," Quinian told her, "but I've had all afternoon to think about this. Only one conclusion makes even partial sense to me. This may be programming from the time before the Corvou declaration of war, when there were only Stragori on this world. It was obviously designed to keep the census updated by tracking the whereabouts of every Stragori on the planet, with a subroutine that makes a separate count of the number of us who are optimized."

"And it thinks five million of the Terrans are Stragori."

His brow furrowed. "Yes, but that's not possible, unless... No. Computers can't do that. Not from a distance."

"Can't do what?"

He hesitated, then recomposed his features, visibly making a decision. "Can't analyze DNA, detecting Stragori genes. As to how they might have gotten into Terran bodies..."

"Relax, Quin. I know. I guessed the truth long ago, as I'm certain many Terrans have done as well."

His expression morphed into a mixture of confusion and

dread. "And what truth is that?" he demanded.

"That Adam Vargas and his party must have been Stragori, that the Great Terran Reorganization—whether intentionally or not—was modelled on the systems of this world, and that it's no coincidence that the most powerful families on Earth have the same last names as some of the powerful families on Stragon. After living here for more than five years, I would have to be blind not to have noticed the similarities."

Even as she heard herself speaking these words, realization burst in Isabela's brain and, undammed, the rest of her thoughts tumbled off her tongue as well. "The Stragori had probably established a presence on Earth, long before first contact was made on Mars. But it couldn't have been a formal colony or settlement, or we would have known about it. It was probably more like an infiltration."

Now he was looking concerned. "Isabela, I'm certain that wasn't—"

She raised a silencing hand. "No, it's all right," she reassured him. "However it began, it obviously changed over time. Stragori and Terrans were intermingling, forming relationships... and having children together. Blood inheritance is the reason for Stragori genes being part of the Terran genome.

"And before you accuse me of leaping to imaginative conclusions, you need to understand two things," she continued, putting a sharp edge on her voice. "First, Dennis Forrand and I have a much longer and more colourful history than you think; and second, being technologically inferior to the Stragori does not mean Terrans are *intellectually* inferior."

He recoiled as though physically struck. "Well! I guess

I've been told."

She leaned back in her seat, trying not to exude too self-satisfied an air. They were supposed to be partners, after all.

"So, we know *why* the program is identifying Terrans as Stragori," she said. "That still leaves us with the question of *how*."

"...as well as the question of where all the computing power is coming from that would enable a system to identify and track that many individuals. I'm pretty sure the intellinet alone wouldn't have that capacity, even when linked to the orbiting satellites. There must be a supercomputer—maybe even a whole bank of them—concealed somewhere on Stragon."

In fact, there was. Isabela swallowed hard. She knew where they could find just such a supercomputer, along with three Thryggian scientists tasked with tending it while they made their observations. The aliens' experiment gave them a reason for being interested only in the Stragori on this world—"stragori" in their language meant "control group"—and Angeli, Isabela, and Olivia had stumbled onto it earlier, and had taken a vow to keep the aliens' presence and intentions a secret.

Somehow, Isabela had to shift Quinian onto a different track, one that wouldn't lead him to the bunker under the island.

She thought furiously for a moment. "What if the computing is not being done in one central location? What if the programming has been parcelled out to a number of linked servers on the planet?"

But he was shaking his head. "That's how the intellinet works, Isabela. The system records video. It can count heads and match a thumbprint to a time and a location. It tracks movement with consent. No video or thumbprint means no trace. What we're looking at here goes way beyond that."

He was right. It required a far more advanced technology than the Stragori commanded or were capable of developing on their own—a technology such as the Thryggian consciousness-transfer process that enabled the Directorate to exist.

He gazed at her with troubled eyes. "I suspect this is a top secret program that no one outside the Directorate was supposed to find out about. If anyone learns that we have it—!"

She beamed at him. "You're forgetting something, Quin. I have no Stragori genes, meaning that the program cannot track my whereabouts. Worst case scenario, I take that device to the Wilderness Zone and bury it somewhere."

...like in the bunker with the Thryggians and their tank full of Stragori memory matrices.

SEVEN
ANGELI

Derwin was living on the bottom floor of a house six blocks away from Lyla's. Both homes were laid out the same way, except that Derwin's dining room had been converted into his bedroom, and the adjoining parlour was where he sat during the day. The upstairs rooms, Roger explained as he and Angeli walked, were overnight accommodations for the various caregivers who looked after him. They prepared and served him his meals, kept him clean, dressed and undressed him, and helped him to move around.

"It's interesting, isn't it," Roger observed, "how we enter and leave this world the same way—completely dependent on others to provide for our needs. The only difference is that a newborn can't communicate them using words."

True. And speaking of communicating one's needs...

"So, you're the new Oath Binder?" Angeli remarked conversationally.

"Appointed by the Town Speaker only a couple of days

ago. It's not an onerous position, and it gets rotated every three years. I'm sure they have something like it on the southern continent."

"They do, but... the population is much larger down there, and that makes a difference. What exactly does an oath binder do in a town the size of Westgrove?"

"I witness documents and sworn statements, as well as verbal agreements. Any promise given in my presence becomes part of the official record, and that means I have to be present whenever there's a tribunal, to make the truth-telling oath legally binding."

Tribunal. The word sent a shiver through her. Fortunately, Roger was looking straight ahead as they walked. If he noticed her reaction, he gave no sign.

They stopped to watch the children playing in the yard of Charlie's school. There had to be forty or fifty of them out there, aged four to eleven. The youngest shouted with laughter as they played a sport that involved chasing a large, colourful sphere across a broad, grassy lawn. Beyond its margins, Angeli saw kids batting a flutterball around a pole and swarming over an assemblage of geometrically shaped cubicles and platforms linked by rope ladders and climbing nets. Meanwhile, a group of older students had formed two lines facing each other and were having a game of double catch, with one line throwing balls and the other simultaneously tossing bean bags.

It was a scene straight out of Angeli's childhood on Earth. For a moment, she wished she were back there and eight years old again, with two loving parents and not a care in the world, and completely unaware that people like Dennis Forrand even existed.

"Listen, we should keep moving," Roger said, his hand on

her elbow urging her into a stroll. "Derwin will already have had his breakfast, and we want to catch him before he gets distracted by lunch."

"Is his memory reliable? And were any of his experiences unpleasant? I want to know what happened, but Mariah warned us not to excite him, so if answering my questions will get him angry or upset..."

Roger chuckled. "He's about to celebrate his two hundred and sixtieth birthday, but his mind is quite sharp," he assured her. "It's his body that's failing him. And as for the excitement part, let's just say that my grandfather is far from ready to give up worldly pleasures. You'll see for yourself when we get there."

From the moment they stepped through the front door of Derwin's house, Angeli understood what Roger meant. Back on the mainland, the dying were placed in a clinical environment, where everything was kept sanitary and the air smelled freshly cleaned. Here, it was redolent with a fragrance that brought back memories of Terran apples cooked with cinnamon and vanilla.

"Is someone baking?" she asked.

"Tasselberry cookies," came the cheerful reply from the kitchen. "They're Derwin's favourite, especially when he has company."

The owner of the voice came out to the front hall then, wiping her hands on a red and white flowered apron. She was a plump woman with short grey hair, laughter in her bright green eyes, and dimples in both cheeks.

"Mariah stopped by last night and told us to expect you," she went on. "I'm Idita, by the way. Go on into the parlour. Gretchen will bring him in to join you in a few minutes, and then I'll serve the tea. He's feeling frisky today, so we're running a little late."

Angeli's eyes widened. Two hundred and sixty years old and feeling frisky? She tried to imagine what that might look like, and couldn't. At his age, what did it even mean?

She didn't have to wait long to find out. As soon as she and Roger had taken their seats in the cozy front room, a connecting door swung open and Derwin appeared, leaning on the arm of a woman who looked about Angeli's age. She was wearing a loose-fitting purple and green top over a pair of baggy grey trousers.

Derwin was nearly bald. What little hair he had lay in wisps across his brown-spotted scalp. His skin looked like leather on his face and like parchment on his hands, where blood vessels sketched road maps just beneath the dermis. The rest of him was clad in a burnt orange pullover and a pair of black trousers whose legs disappeared down the tops of his fleece-lined slippers.

With Gretchen supporting him, he shuffled forward and finally eased himself down onto a broad, tan-coloured armchair. He gazed fondly down at her as she bent to position his legs on a darker tan footstool and cover them with a lap blanket. Not until Gretchen stood up and adjusted the neckline of her blouse did Angeli realize what exactly the old man had been looking at.

Meanwhile, Roger was struggling to keep a straight face. *Frisky. Right.*

Derwin gave Gretchen a grateful smile and said, "Thank you, my dear." The gratitude was probably genuine, but there was a glint in his eyes that belied the sickly-sounding tremor in his voice.

Idita came in with a tea tray and set it down on the low tiled table in the middle of the room. She thrust a preemptive cookie into Derwin's grasping hand, then poured out three cups of a fragrant amber brew and set one of them down on the small round lampstand beside his chair.

"You be good now," she cautioned him on her way out of the room.

He cackled and took a large bite of his cookie, with a glance at her departing back that suggested he'd rather be sinking his teeth into something else.

"Hello, Grandfather," said Roger, waving his hand as though to remind Derwin that he was not alone.

The old man held up a finger to pause the conversation until his mouth was empty again.

"Grandson," he acknowledged with a grin—and, Angeli couldn't help noticing, speaking in a much stronger and steadier voice. "And who have you brought me today? Could it be the mysterious Eva Moss, with questions that only an old reprobate like me can answer?"

"As a matter of fact, it is. She's just returned from the southern continent and she wants to know the truth about the great emigration."

"Filled your head with nonsense about that, did they?" Derwin said, the years seeming to fall away from him as he locked eyes with Angeli. "Well, I'm not surprised. Those numquats have been marinating in misinformation and wouldn't recognize a fact if it reared up and punched them in the nose. All right, then, go ahead and ask. I'll answer you straight."

"Roger says that you were in your teens when your parents took you down to the island. Is that right?"

"Almost. I was fourteen when the applications arrived and my father signed us up to emigrate as a family. I was eighteen when we received our departure date and were assigned our space aboard the ship. I was twenty-two when it came our turn to travel south to be processed for the off-world journey."

Derwin stuffed the rest of his cookie into his mouth, then picked up his cup in both hands and took a swallow of tea before continuing, "There were so many of us, you see, and only three vessels large enough to carry us and our mass allotment of possessions in a single trip, so they divided the list into waves. The first to be transported were unpaired adults without children. When there were no more of those to send, they began filling the manifests with families. We were part of the twelfth wave, I remember. More than a hundred families, all from Borea. There must have been five hundred of us. It took months to prepare us all for boarding, so we stayed in one of the little towns they'd built on the land mass they called 'the island'...

"...which is a silly name to give a continent, if you ask me, but that's what they called it, and the label stuck. Anyway, we'd been living there for a couple of weeks when my father suddenly changed his mind about leaving Stragon. He wouldn't tell us why, just ordered us to pack up our things and get ready to go back north."

"But he did explain eventually, right?" Roger prompted him, sounding like a child who was hearing a favourite bedtime story for the twentieth time and already knew how it ended.

Derwin bobbed his head in confirmation and replied, "He told my mother, and she waited until we were halfway home to tell me. She said he'd overheard a couple of officials talking about the southerners' plans to take over 'the northern continent', once most of us had been relocated."

"'Us' meaning the objectors?" said Angeli.

"That's what they're calling us now? It was something much less flattering back then," he said, pausing for another mouthful of tea. "After hearing what the southerners had in mind for Borea after we were gone, my father had immediately shared the information with the other families at the processing centre, and it changed *their* minds about emigrating as well. We had plenty of company for the journey back north. All one hundred families up and left at the same time, to discourage the southerners from trying to stop us.

"We heard there were other shiploads of emigrants after that, but they were from the southern continent. As soon as we got back, my father called an all-town meeting so he could warn everyone about what he'd learned. Then we reopened trade negotiations with the southerners' commercial representatives."

Derwin leaned forward to snag another cookie, but Idita had put the plate beyond his reach. Roger pushed it closer to him, and Derwin thanked him and took two, one for each hand.

"I was told there was sickness on the island," Angeli said. "That the objectors were quarantined there and millions of them died before a vaccine could be developed."

Derwin froze with his right-hand cookie halfway to his mouth and shot her an incredulous stare.

"Millions!" he hooted. "Now, that would be a trick, since only a couple hundred thousand of us in total signed up to emigrate, many of those changed their minds, and not all the ones who did leave went to the island at the same time to be processed. Someone's been japing you around, young lady." Still holding his cookie, he waggled a reproving forefinger at her.

"What about the sickness part?" she persisted.

"That part is true, but it didn't happen until long after the emigrations stopped. It was most likely caused by all the toxic waste the southerners dumped on the island, after the deal we struck with them prevented them from dumping it up here. Hah!"

What began as a laugh turned into a coughing fit that brought Idita racing into the room. She thumped him on the back with the flat of her hand a couple of times. Then she noticed what he was holding, and she drew herself up and regarded him sternly for a moment, shaking her head.

"When he eats or talks too fast, things can go down the wrong pipe," she said, addressing Roger and Angeli. "I keep reminding him he has to take things slowly at his age, but he thinks he's still only a hundred and fifty years old."

Clearing his throat with a final *harrumph*, he leered at her. "I've got another thirty good ones in me and you know it."

She blurted an exasperated syllable and headed for the door.

"Now, where was I?" Derwin said. "Ah! The negotiation. There was already a comprehensive trade deal in place, but the southerners had developed a new technology—surprise, surprise—and they were short of particular metals that weren't covered in the earlier agreement. Borea was rich with the right kind of ore, which gave us the leverage we needed to get what we really wanted: a defined southern border, created by dredging out a channel between the continents, and the right to decide who could cross it northbound."

"So, basically, you gained sovereignty over your land," Angeli mused. "And the Directorate went along with this?"

As she and Roger drank their tea, waiting for Derwin's response, he gobbled the last of his right-hand cookie, chewed and swallowed it, then replied casually, "Actually, I don't recall anyone consulting them about it. The southerners signed the agreement as an amendment to the existing trade treaty. All the other negotiated terms still applied, including our insistence on mining the ore ourselves, in ways that wouldn't harm the environment."

"Tell her who refined the ore, Grandfather," Roger prodded him.

"The southerners did, of course. We shipped it to them raw, figuring that if they were that desperate for the metal, they could damn well deal with its by-products themselves. But I thought you wanted to know about the emigrations," he added.

Peering at Angeli over the rim of his cup, he sipped another mouthful.

"I do," she assured him. "Were the emigrants told in advance where they were being sent?"

Now he was scowling at her. "Of course!" he snapped. "No one with a working brain would have stepped aboard a ship without knowing what to expect at the other end of the journey."

"So, the space colonization program was already in place...?"

"Stragon never had a colonization program. The southerners may have planned for one, after the emigrations were halted, but the Directorate must have stepped in and stopped them, because it was never implemented. Good thing, too. Imagine the technopoison those geniuses would have spewed out into the galaxy!" Derwin shuddered visibly at the thought.

"But they were colonizing another world. Even if it was just the one—"

He made an impatient sound. "We weren't colonizing, we were emigrating," he corrected her tartly. "What happened was, the Directorate had sent out exploration vessels shortly after that document was dug up on the southern continent—"

Alarms began shrilling at the back of Angeli's brain. "A document?" she echoed softly.

He gave her a strange look. "You really don't know? Those southerners must have tampered with your memory when you weren't looking. An excavation crew working on an extension to the tunnel system came across an abandoned bunker—some sort of observation post, they gathered—and a few artifacts and a single piece of paper were found inside it. That discovery was a world-shaking event. The writing was in an alien language. A team of experts worked on it for months. Once their translation was complete, the Directorate shared it with the population."

"Was it about an alien experiment?" she asked. A chill settled into her core as she recalled what the Thryggian observers had told her, Isabela, and Olivia not that long ago: the Stragori were the control group, protected from outside interference for as long as the Thryggians could keep their experiment on Earth running. Ultimately, Stragon was Humanity's best hope to survive the genocidal efforts of the Great Galactic Council.

Derwin frowned. "Not that I recall. It was about how we had been brought to Stragon from another world, thousands of years earlier. It said that our home planet was out there, still habitable and populated by beings just like ourselves. If that was true, it meant the ancient myths and legends that had been passed down for millennia, from one generation to the next, were actually the recorded memories of our distant ancestors.

"Many Stragori believed the document had been planted as part of some elaborate hoax. So, to either disprove or authenticate it, explorers were sent out to find this world—and with it, the rest of our race—and one of them was successful. That's what the Directorate told us, at any rate, and why so many of us signed up to emigrate. We would be returning to our beginning for a great and noble cause: to reunite the two halves of Humanity."

As a shock wave of realization swept through her, Angeli drew an audible breath. "They found Earth," she whispered hoarsely.

Locking eyes with her, he replied, "In our ancient tales, it's called Terra. We were promised that we would be making history. Nothing less than that could have induced us to leave our homes on Stragon. Now, with the Directorate's blessing, the emigration is reversed, and a nation of Terrans have settled on *this* world... but not to make history, I'm afraid..."

Angeli swallowed hard. "Do you believe they're terrorists?"

"Terrorists? No. 'Unwelcome' would be a better word, I think. But what do I know?" he added, once more speaking in his thin, quavery voice. "I'm just a very old man with lingering appetites."

*　　*　　*

Forget about spinning—Angeli's thoughts were careering wildly now, ricocheting off the inside of her skull.

The emigration had been to Earth, timed to arrive in the chaotic aftermath of the pandemic of 2172. Thousands of newcomers with Human DNA. Record-keeping in a shambles, leading up to the emergence of Adam Vargas and his party and the Great Reorganization that was completed in 2190. It would have been so easy on a world of billions for a few thousand a year to spread out and insinuate themselves into the population. Being Human, they would have passed every test... and what better way for the Directorate to dispose of objectors than to convince them it was their sacred duty to return to the home world and mend the division in Humanity?

Except... a control group was supposed to remain separate from the one being experimented on. That was the whole point of *having* a control group.

...which probably explained why the Directorate had decided not to share its space colonization program with the Terrans, but rather to hand it completely over to them. If both groups went out into space, the Great Council was bound to find out about it and force a cancellation of the experiment, and all the Thryggians' efforts to protect Humanity would be for nothing. But that would suggest that the Directorate was aware of the experiment... or that the Thryggians were influencing its decisions somehow...

...but if they were, how to explain the mass emigration? Was this something the Thryggians had engineered, believing that interstellar traffic could be kept secret if it were restricted to just the two worlds?

"They promised us we would be making history..."

Had Derwin just shown her a way to persuade the

Boreans to support a Reformation? Or was it a reason for her not to try, since the north had been burned once before and wouldn't fall for the same line again?

As though sensing her inner turmoil, Roger refrained from conversation as he walked her back home. For that, she was grateful. Angeli seriously doubted whether she could carry on a coherent discussion right now, with anyone.

Returning to Lyla's house, she found the door unlocked and a note on the kitchen counter. Lyla had gone to the market for dinner ingredients and would make lunch for them both when she returned. Angeli would be alone for the next hour, at least. It was a perfect time to study the map Forrand had given her.

A swath of wall between her bed and the closet door made a good place to project an image. Closing the curtains to darken the room, she inserted the data wafer into the reader and pressed P on the keypad. A moment later, she was looking at a hand-drawn sketch of three separate land masses, seemingly piled one atop another, labelled "North", "Mainland", and "Island", as well as the eastern coastline of a fourth, much larger land mass labelled "Galandra", situated on the other side of a body of water called simply "Sea".

After five years, Angeli was quite familiar with the squarish chunk of mainland and the bowl-shaped "island" beneath it. Although neither land mass showed details beyond the mountain range that bordered their eastern shores, her eyes went automatically to places of particular relevance. On the mainland, they identified the approximate location of the Directorate's former offices (no longer in use since the building housing them had recently been blown up). On the island, Angeli visualized where Isabela's apartment ought to be, in an urban district near the bottom of the bowl and walking distance from the caves that opened onto the southern beach. One of them disguised the entrance to the Thryggians' secret bunker.

It was tempting to let her thoughts tarry in the past. However, her mission was in the present, and it had brought her here, to a place she now knew most southerners never visited. Evidently, that made it (in their estimation) too distant and inconsequential to bother mapping in detail... which might explain why she was studying a hand-drawn sketch instead of something more polished.

Projected onto Angeli's bedroom wall, Borea appeared only slightly smaller than the mainland, but it was much more detailed, showing a web of waterways, several large lakes, and a continuation of the mountain chain that paralleled the eastern coasts of the other two land masses. It was also sprinkled with towns. She counted twenty-two of them, marked with varying sizes of dots, most likely to indicate each one's relative importance and population. Assuming that someone other than Forrand had created this map, at least that much of her pre-mission briefing had been accurate.

At the sight of all those black dots, however, a sense of urgency set in. Forrand had given her a year to win the hearts and minds of these people, but there were reportedly more than two million of them, and they were spread all over the continent. She knew how much distance lay between urban districts on the mainland. Travel time would need to be calculated and taken into account. And what about all the northerners who lived and worked in the various Industrial Zones?

Angeli found the appropriate keys on the reader and zoomed in on "North". The enlarged version took up the full height of the wall. Unfortunately, no scale was supplied and no roads were indicated, only geographical features; however, each of the towns now bore a name—Cedarvale, Kettleby, Whitewater, Moortop, Rivercross... That one was double-underlined, she noted, making it more important than any of the others.

Was Rivercross the capital city, perhaps? She would have to ask someone who'd travelled there how long the journey had taken. Then she could devise her own scale. Or maybe one of the houses in Westgrove had a sign out front that said *Map Maker* and she could barter some cookies or a pie or something for a more useful document.

Lyla returned, trailed by an antigrav cart loaded with groceries, and Angeli hurried downstairs to help her put them away. Some of the items were obviously baking supplies: flour, sweetening, dried fruit, and shortening. Others were just as clearly intended for meal preparation: pieces of meat, vegetables, and a variety of cheeses. There was a transparent bottle of pale yellow oil as well, and a large sealed container that held a thick, creamy liquid. On Earth she might have guessed it was salad dressing, but here...? It could be anything from soup base to soap. Northern cuisine was shaping up to be an adventure— several of the items were things Angeli had never seen before.

"The heggen stays on the counter," said Lyla. "The spargrass goes into the fridgerator." When Angeli hesitated, Lyla pointed to a bundle of thick, sharply pointed green stalks. "Don't tell me you've forgotten what spargrass looks like, Eva," she chided. "You haven't been gone *that* long."

Oops!

Angeli hastened to reply, "No! Of course not. It's just—It looks a lot different on the southern continent."

Lyla was washing root vegetables and lining them up to dry on a cutting board beside the sink. "I expect that's true of a lot of things," she commented wryly. "Well, this is what the plant is *supposed* to look like when it's grown in the right climate. Kate always liked to eat it raw, even as a child. She's probably feeding it to baby Fallon that way too."

Raw? Really?

"Everything that grows in the ground down south is so tough and fibrous, you've got to boil it for an hour or more just to make it chewable," Angeli remarked.

"Well, I'm not surprised. The southerners have polluted their environment with industrial waste and by-products. Meanwhile, we have the perfect conditions for agriculture up here. Rich soil, clean water. That's why we're so adamant about keeping this continent out of southern hands—we don't want them ruining our environment as well. So tell me, what do they do with the stuff that can't be boiled—feed it to their animals?"

Animals.

Hearing the word seemed to strike a gong in Angeli's brain. "There are no animals on the southern continent, not even as pets."

"And again, this comes as no surprise," Lyla said with a sigh. "Caring for living creatures requires empathy, something computers are notorious for lacking." She looked as though she wanted to say more, then evidently changed her mind.

When everything had been put away, including the towel-dried vegetables, Lyla set to pulling lunch ingredients out of the refrigeration cabinet. She worked with practiced speed, and soon she and Angeli were sitting at the dining table tucking into heggen-and-cheese sandwiches made with bread so light in texture that it fairly melted in one's mouth, even without the help of the pale rose-coloured tea that Lyla had brewed to wash it down.

Angeli's assignment was to find out as much about northerners as she could. Derwin had told her one sure way to motivate them, but it had already been tried and might not work again. She needed to gather more intel. That meant getting out of the house and exploring the town, preferably without blowing her cover as a northerner returning home.

"Next time you go to the market, I'd like to go with you," Angeli decided.

Lyla's face lit up. "Yes! I'd love the company. Tomorrow morning we'll both go out."

"You shop every day? But there's enough here to feed—"

"—ten or eleven people? How do you think I put credits into my account?" Flashing her a grin, Lyla went on, "I have a full table most nights of the week. At seven credits per place setting, plus a few more for each cake or pie that goes out my door, I'm able to manage quite comfortably. And in another hundred years or so, I'll have enough set aside to afford the kind of attention that Derwin is getting right now."

"So, those weren't gifts you were handing out last night."

The other woman's smile broadened. "No, they weren't... except for Ben's. Warders, firefighters, and medical emergency responders perform a valued service to the community. The town is therefore constantly in their debt, and we repay it by providing them with their basic necessities—shelter, clothing, medical treatment, and food—free of charge. Ben has a seat reserved for him at my table for whenever he chooses to make use of it. He also receives a monthly deposit of credits for his personal use, and a separate deposit into an account dedicated toward his old-age care."

This was all sounding very familiar. In fact, what Angeli had heard and seen of Borea so far was strikingly Earth-like. It strongly suggested that the purpose of the Great Reorganization had been not only to bring order out of the post-pandemic chaos, but also to reshape Terra as much as possible in the North's image.

The question gnawing at the back of her mind was: Why?

Was it to make all the relocated Stragori feel at home on a planet they were in the process of taking over? And had the Directorate decided to model this new Earth on the northern continent rather than the mainland because the objectors' level of technology was closest to the Humans' and a sudden leap forward in that area could raise suspicions? Or had Derwin been correct in pointing her to a more sinister motive, involving the annexation not of Earth but of the resource-rich land mass to the north?

The two women ate quietly for a few moments. Then, as though sensing the heaviness of Angeli's thoughts, Lyla asked with determined brightness, "Is there anything in particular that you want to get at the market?"

Unexpectedly, Angeli realized there was. "I had a tasselberry cookie at Derwin's this morning and it... reminded me of home."

"Aha!" Lyla crowed. "I had a feeling you might have grown up in the marshes, and I was right! Very well, then, my dear avatar—tasselberries you shall have."

EIGHT
DENNIS

The plains of Galandra were legendary, as were the huge beasts that roamed them. The first explorers to encounter a herd in the wild had brought back unbelievable stories of shaggy-haired, horn-headed creatures twice the height of a grown man at the shoulder... along with the dead bodies of those in their company who had unwisely broken from cover and attempted to get closer to one.

Dennis Forrand stepped down from the hovering avcraft into a brisk westerly wind, and found himself gazing upon an undulating sea of chest-high, blue-green grasses that stretched unbroken all the way to the horizon. The afternoon sun was sulking behind a screen of clouds. The resulting light had an artificial quality to it, a strange whiteness devoid of warmth or welcome.

Behind Dennis, a crew member offloaded his luggage, depositing the two bags on the ground beside his feet. Then the hatch slammed shut and the hoverer took off, the wash from its vertical jets powerful enough to bend nearby vegetation to the ground and shove its former passenger almost off his feet.

The pilot was in a hurry to be gone. He hadn't wanted to make this flight in the first place. Only the threat implied by invoking the Forrand name had overcome his resistance, and then he'd doubled his fee, demanding payment in advance so that his widow would have something if he didn't come back. There were stories about that region, he'd said, terrifying stories about avcraft being knocked out of the sky by monsters, and the people aboard them never being seen again. Pilots had to be out of their minds to fly there... or desperate for the risk bonus... or both.

Dennis had heard those same stories, and had written them off as exaggerations circulated by people who wanted to be left alone. He valued his solitude too. He often sought it out when he needed to think. But this was not one of those times, and in this vast and empty expanse of land where he now found himself, he was suddenly working to breathe, as though even the molecules of air had scaled up here and were too large to be taken into his lungs. He wasn't just alone in this place—he was insignificant. A negligible speck of life. An existence too trivial to matter.

Like a solitary germ in an operating room, he thought, a moment before the rumbling sound of an approaching vehicle caught his attention.

Dennis turned to his right and saw two things. The one directly ahead made his heart leap. A truck the colour of a dusty road was arrowing toward him along a track that had evidently been worn into the grass over time by the repeated passage of wheels. Meanwhile, the one that he noticed from the corner of his eye set his pulse racing for a different reason.

Not twenty metres away stood one of the multi-horned beasts, taller than Dennis at the shoulder, its massive, angular head lowered as though about to graze... and it was watching him intently with large yellow eyes. How something that big could have stolen up noiselessly behind him, Dennis did not know. He took a reflexive step backward, then froze in place, debating with himself which would be safer: staring back at it, or averting his gaze.

All at once, the truck skidded to a halt and a woman dressed top to toe in leather emerged from the driver's side door. She appeared to be about his age, with dark blonde hair and a natural squint to her eyes. Dennis couldn't help noticing that her jacket and matching trousers bore the same mottled markings as the skin of the beast currently in front of him.

"I gather this is your first look at a living auroch," she called cheerfully as she strode over to join him. "Don't be alarmed. He's inside an inclusion field. I doubt that he'd purposely hurt you in any case—this is one of the calves from the domesticated herd, so he's just being curious. We've bred the viciousness out of our own livestock, but— word of warning—an auroch in the wild is a nasty piece of work. It'll come after you for simply making eye contact with it. I'm Heidi Walberg, by the way. Sylvain asked me to pick you up. He's expecting you."

Dennis jerked a thumb over his shoulder. "That's a *calf*?" he said, his voice rising in disbelief.

"One of several born this year. It's been a good breeding season." A pause, then, "A far cry from the slab of meat on your plate in your favourite fancy restaurant, isn't it?" she asked, her brown eyes twinkling with humour.

Heidi reached down and hefted one of his bags. "We shouldn't keep Sylvain waiting," she told him. "The base isn't far from here, and there'll be time to answer all your questions later."

He helped her to secure his luggage in the back of the truck, then climbed in on the passenger side.

"Do you work for Sylvain?" Dennis asked as the vehicle bounced and swayed along the trail.

"Not exclusively," she replied. "I'm a geneticist by training, an animal healer by occupation. Sylvain is a member of the syndicate that owns the herd, and I'm contracted to work for the syndicate." Throwing him a sidelong glance, she continued, "I'm the one they call on to trank the juveniles when it's time to dehorn them. Puberty is tough on these kids. When their coats begin to shag up and the hormones start flowing, they get the urge to alphabetize."

"Come again?"

"They have to establish their ranking within the social hierarchy. Alpha, beta... you get the idea. There's a lot of pushing and shoving, and fights can break out. Those horns make sharp weapons. Juveniles in the wild have been known to maim and even kill one another while jostling for position in the herd."

"It sounds an awful lot like politics to me."

Heidi laughed. "Sylvain feels the same way. That's why he—I'd better let him explain it."

They were driving north in what should have been the heat of the day but felt more like the nippiness of early morning. Heidi opened the windows, allowing a steady breeze to cross the cab. Dennis heard her *Ah!* of contentment and noticed that she had unfastened the front of her jacket.

"So this is spring in Galandra," he remarked, crossing his arms for warmth.

"In this part of the continent, anyway," she replied. "The hot season will reach us in another six or seven weeks. The herd should be well on its way to cooler pastures by then, with calves strong enough to survive the journey."

"It must be a long one."

"It is. The auroch migration covers about a thousand kilopaces each way, over some pretty rough terrain."

His surprise must have shown on his face, because she laughed and told him, "Welcome to the world of migratory animal husbandry. Shaggy coats aren't practical in higher temperatures, so we had a choice: give every beast a close haircut twice a year, or let our domesticated auroch follow the dictates of their DNA while we travel along with them to keep them safe. We owe them that, after taking away their best means of self-defence from predators."

Predators. There were stories about those as well. The thought of possibly encountering animals even more dangerous than the wild auroch was raising additional gooseflesh up and down Dennis's arms. Trying his best not to sound concerned, he asked, "Are there any predators in particular that I should watch out for?"

"As long as you remain on the base, there's nothing to worry about. The force fields are quite effective at protecting us and the herd without upsetting the ecological balance. It's during the migration that we become vulnerable to attack, and you won't be with us then."

So, Sylvain had already decided how long Dennis's visit would last? He should have expected as much.

"We're almost there," said Heidi, pointing through the

windscreen.

He looked straight ahead and saw the dark outlines of several buildings that appeared to be rising from the ground as they approached. On flat terrain and from a distance, with nothing to serve as a reference, he could only guess at their actual size. However, there was no doubt in his mind that this was a compound of some kind.

"Hang on," she said, pulling a device from her jacket pocket. "I have to make an entrance in the force field. It's going to feel a little strange when we go through it..."

Strange? That was putting it mildly. For a good ten seconds, Dennis could swear that every molecule in his body had shed its bonds and was jumping for joy. A couple of minutes later, the truck lurched to a halt in front of a long, single-storey structure that formed the bottom of a broad, U-shaped yard. He slid down to stand on the ground, still feeling a little buzzy, and took a look around.

All the components of the base had been made the same way: rectangular buildings with brick and stucco facings, steep peaked roofs, sturdy painted wooden doors. Dennis identified a couple that were clearly for storage, and one with a red cross over the door that had to be the med centre. The rest, he guessed, were residences for the syndicate's employees, none of whom were in evidence at the moment.

"Is there anything breakable in your luggage?" said Heidi.

Startled, he wheeled and found her looking down at him from the truck bed, holding one of his bags over the side. Dennis hurried to relieve her of it, and of the second one as well. Then she jumped down, told him, "Sylvain is waiting for you inside," got back into the cab, and drove away.

He picked up his bags and carried them to the door. After the way Sylvain had been forced to leave Earth all those years ago, Dennis knew better than to expect a warm welcome; however, considering how far he'd travelled to get here, it would have been a civil gesture to at least acknowledge his arrival by coming outside to greet him.

Dennis knocked on the door and heard a surly voice reply from the other side, "It's unlocked. Get in here and give me the bad news!"

So, that was the way it would be? Fine, then.

Squaring his shoulders, Dennis shoved the door open and carried his bags over the threshold. Then he dropped them on the floor, took a moment to gather himself again, and went in search of his inhospitable host.

The building was organized as a series of single-use rooms, strung out along a corridor that ran in both directions from a central vestibule. Becoming more annoyed by the second at having to play hide and seek, Dennis found two laboratories, a kitchen, and a dining hall before finally locating Sylvain. He was sitting behind the desk in what appeared to be an office, co-opted to store a cot (apparently slept in) and some fitness equipment.

Dennis paused in the doorway, willing the other man to look up at him.

Eventually, he did.

"Hello, Uncle."

Sylvain scowled. "Oh, you've decided we're related now? Or did you just get yourself kicked out of the family as well?" He touched a series of buttons on the control pad set into the arm of his chair. Dennis watched as it seemed to glide around the desk and out into the middle of the room. That was when he realized that the chair was rolling on wheels and had a built-in footrest.

It explained a lot.

"What happened to *you*?" Dennis asked.

Sylvain shrugged. "I got careless. Got distracted, let my guard down around the juveniles and didn't move out of the way fast enough when they decided to hold a head-butting contest. Serves me right, I guess. Long story short," he said dryly, spreading both his arms in an encompassing gesture, "welcome to the rest of my life."

Linda and Gilles would probably say it was a well-deserved life. Very few in the Forrand clan had ever had much sympathy for Sylvain, the only family member ever to be deported from Earth to Stragon "for the good of Humanity". He'd reportedly continued making trouble for the Directorate on the Stragori mainland, eventually escaping to Galandra with a group of like-minded agitators scant hours ahead of the serving of an arrest warrant on him for sedition. Back on Earth, Sylvain's name had been spoken like a curse whenever the subject of Stragori politics had arisen at the Forrand dinner table.

Privately, however, young Dennis had always felt a sneaking admiration for his outcast uncle. Judging by the stories Dennis had heard about him, Gilles's younger brother was a rebel to his very marrow, a "loose cannon" with rigid beliefs and uncompromising courage. There was something inspiring and romantic about a man who stuck to his principles with that much passion. Sylvain might even have been the reason Dennis became involved in Terran politics.

Shaking off the memory, he asked, "What do the healers say about your condition? Because I know a few good ones on the mainland who would—"

"—love to conduct experimental surgery on my ruptured spinal cord? Or try out a bunch of new neural therapies? No, thanks," Sylvain replied with distaste. "I've had more than enough of that with the healers on Galandra."

Something in his tone made Dennis ask, "How long ago did you say this happened?"

"I didn't, but it's been nearly ten years, and thanks for finally asking. And what about you, Nephew? Are you stepping into my shoes as the black sheep of the family? Is that why you're here, to pick up some pointers?"

"Actually, I'm here with questions that I think you can answer."

Wariness crept first into Sylvain's gaze, and then into his voice. "Oh?"

"Someone with an agenda is impersonating Gervais Forrand and usurping the powers of the Directorate."

Sylvain's complexion darkened. "And you think *I* know who it is? Or have you come all this way just to accuse *me* of—?"

Dennis strode into the room, stopping just short of looming over the man in the wheeled chair. "I'm not accusing you personally of anything, Uncle," he declared loudly, cutting the other man off. "I'm suggesting that a member of the radical group you founded may be the impostor, and I'm giving you a chance to help me identify them and undo the damage they've caused."

"How dare you!" Spoken in low, menacing tones, these words conveyed a much deeper rage than any amount of shouting could have done. "Just because you were once someone important on Earth, that does not give you the right—"

"You're right, it doesn't," Dennis returned. "But I'll tell

you what does. While you've been out here herding your animals, I've been on the mainland, investigating all the known radical organizations, past and present. I saved Stragon First for last, because I knew it was yours, and I also remembered how you've always operated. Subterfuge was never your style, Uncle. You've always attacked an issue head on, regardless of the consequences.

"What's happening on the mainland, on the other hand, is covert subversion, and it's been going on since before I arrived on-world, twenty years ago. Whoever is behind it has been spreading lies and disinformation to convince people that the Directorate has always been cruel, corrupt, and oppressive. That it cares more about the Terrans of Earth than about the people on our own home world of Stragon."

"That it *cares*—!" Sylvain's hands curled into fists on the armrests of his chair. "If you've been investigating, then you also know how little we Galandrians care about current events on the mainland, and how little everyone on the tripartite continent cares about what happens to *us*. No one cares about the whole planet anymore, Nephew. No one. Stragon First used to care. We spoke up on behalf of all Stragori, and our reward was slander and exile. So tell me, why should we give a damn now?"

"Because someone is sowing the seeds of revolution, and if it's allowed to happen, what follows will be political chaos. And then, just as Adam Vargas and his team did on Earth, the Gervais impostor and their allies will be able to step in and impose their own version of order on Stragori society—all of it, not just the mainland. They will redraw boundaries, redistribute wealth and resources... and put themselves permanently in positions of power. Then we'll find out what cruelty and oppression really feel like.

"I'm not asking you to care, Uncle. I'm asking you to help. The worsening street violence and the bombing attempts on buildings and gatherings all over the mainland—those are just a foretaste of the bloodshed to come. Meanwhile, the Directorate has been in the paralyzing grip of an extremist who continues to push the planet toward revolution by fuelling public unrest."

Visibly deflating but still wearing a skeptical expression, Sylvain said, "So, you believe this extremist—the alleged Gervais impostor—is part of a radical group. And you're certain you've cleared every group except mine?"

"Every group that I'm aware of and every splinter that's fallen off them in the last twenty years. That's how long I've been working on this. Using my network of contacts, I've managed to do a deep background check on each member of each organization. Most of those people were influenced to join by all the misinformation they'd swallowed, and while some of the genuine radicals are capable of hacking into the intellinet, none of them have the necessary intel and expertise to pull off the impersonation of a Director. I'm not out to shut down the protest groups. People have the right to dissent. It's the impostor I'm hunting, along with anyone who has knowingly aided and abetted them."

"And that hunt has led you to me." Sylvain stared into his lap for a moment. "All right, let's imagine for a moment that you're right, and by some remarkable quirk of fate it turns out that one of my former fellow Firsters is the individual you're looking for. What then, Nephew? Arrest? Imprisonment? Summary execution?"

Dennis smiled inwardly. Sylvain's departure from Earth

had predated his nephew's rise in the Terran political ranks. He knew nothing of the Earth Intelligence Service, nor of the many other covert projects Dennis had undertaken during his career. More to the point, he had no idea what this particular Forrand was capable of. If he ever found out that Dennis had routinely ordered the deaths of adversaries who knew too much about his operations, Sylvain would be shocked. He might even become one of those adversaries. Best, then, to keep him in semi-darkness, at least.

"None of the above. I don't work for the government, Uncle. I'm a free agent, not answerable to anyone but myself. Once the impostor is identified, I intend to turn them. Give them a chance to clean up their mess. No one but us has to know it was them who made it... and I'm sure we can think of ways for them to demonstrate their gratitude for being spared the embarrassment of exposure."

Sylvain scowled. He appeared about to say something, but Heidi chose that moment to step into the room and announce, "It's nearly dinnertime, boys. Can you two find the dining hall on your own, or do you need an escort?"

The men shared a significant look.

"To be continued?" said Sylvain with a hard edge on his voice.

"To be continued," Dennis confirmed.

He let Sylvain lead the way. Dennis followed the rolling chair along the beige plaincoated corridor, past the vestibule and into a large, wood-panelled room where about a dozen men and women sat on backless metal benches to either side of a long, white-enamelled trestle table. Instead of a centrepiece, he saw a double stack of dinner plates and what looked like a vase with eating utensils growing out of it, positioned in the middle of the table. Sylvain took his place at its head, manoeuvring his protruding footrest beneath it with practiced ease. Meanwhile, Dennis paused just inside the door, feeling suddenly and annoyingly awkward.

The table was fully occupied. Oh, there was an empty chair at its foot, but he recognized Heidi's jacket slung across its back and realized that the seat had already been claimed. Sylvain was right: being important on Earth did not translate to being respected on Galandra. Dennis was an outsider here. Like a student who'd been added to the rolls halfway through the school year, he would have to be introduced and acknowledged before being fitted in.

"Move it or lose it!" Heidi's voice sang out as she passed him from behind, carrying a large jug of gravy. She deposited the jug carefully beside the dinnerware. Then she turned to face him and said, in a tone of voice reminiscent of his mother's whenever his manners fell short of her high standards, "We sit down to eat here, Mr. Forrand."

He replied automatically, "Yes, ma'am."

That broke the tension. Laughing, the people on the farther bench slid left and right to make room for him among them. Heidi remained long enough to oversee the distribution of the plates and cutlery. Then she pivoted and left the room again, returning moments later at the head of a parade of kitchen staff bearing oval metal serving platters loaded with generous portions of meat, thick slices of bread, and three different kinds of steaming hot vegetables. Once the platters were lowered onto the enamelled surface, their bearers quickly departed, leaving the diners to serve themselves.

Salivating as he inhaled a symphony of delectable aromas but uncertain what the protocol was, Dennis held back, taking his cues from the behaviour of the others. Surprisingly, no one was saying a word or making a move toward the food, not even Sylvain. It was as though someone had hit pause on the dinner scene in a video. Then Heidi settled herself onto the chair at the foot of the table—clearly her usual spot—and Dennis understood: whether or not Sylvain could be considered the father figure of this little community, Heidi Walberg was definitely its mother.

"We have a guest," she announced. "This is Dennis, a member of Sylvain's family. He'll be visiting with us for the next while, so be kind, and behave yourselves. Now, let's eat!"

At last, a flurry of happy chatter broke out. Hands reached forward to grasp serving utensils, plates were passed around to receive portions of each food item, and Dennis was treated to one of the best steak dinners of his life.

"That's how auroch is *supposed* to be cooked," Sylvain declared when he and Dennis were once more alone in his office. "Those fancy mainland chefs with their gourmet spices... they think meat has no flavour if they don't add it themselves. Well, they're right about the stuff that's grown in a lab, but real meat doesn't *need* help to taste good."

Dennis cleared his throat. Yes, the meal had been delicious, but a culinary dissertation was not where he wanted this after-dinner conversation to go. "Can we get back to what we were discussing earlier?"

"What we were—? Ah, yes. Politics." He made a face. "Since you're here, you obviously feel that you've exhausted all other avenues of investigation. But you have advantages that I don't—a network of spies and a set of working legs spring immediately to mind—so I have to ask: what exactly do you think I can do for you?"

"I want you to introduce me to the rest of Stragon First."

Sylvain leaned his head back and burst out laughing.

"What's so funny?" Dennis demanded.

The other man had to calm down before he could speak. "You are, Nephew. You're priceless! You want to meet my radical movement? You've already been introduced. You broke bread with them not half an hour ago."

Dennis was momentarily at a loss for words as well, but for a different reason. "You're serious? That was Stragon First? All of it? Every member from when it first came together?"

"Mm-hmm," said Sylvain, grinning broadly. "All of us. Me and my fellow exiles from the mainland. We owned and worked at a genetics lab, which we shut down and moved to Galandra when some serious charges were filed against us. Then we encountered the auroch, which native Galandrians had been hunting and eating for centuries. We saw a business opportunity, turned our skills to making it happen, and haven't looked back since. We closed up the lab, formed the syndicate, and buried Stragon First.

"You're hunting in the wrong place, Nephew. We were never revolutionaries. We were scientists who foresaw the consequences of the Directorate's plans for Earth and decided to speak out against them. We targeted particular policies to protest. It was never our aim to overthrow and replace the entire government, not then and certainly not now."

"With a radical-sounding name like Stragon First?" said Dennis, raising a skeptical eyebrow.

"It was relevant when we came up with it. Growing up on Earth, I had no idea how the Directorate's priorities were affecting the living conditions on this world. Then I came back here and—never mind. It's all moot. The movement's been dormant for the past fifty years."

"And yet, my contacts on-world tell me that Stragon First is still active, with chapters on Galandra and the mainland, and possibly one on Earth."

At hearing this, Sylvain's eyes widened briefly, then narrowed. "Someone else must be using our name, and I think I know who it may be. You and your contacts need to look into a fellow called Nestor Quan."

"I've heard of him..." *...in reports from EIS and Daisy Hub, before the war. Attempted murder, attempted theft, espionage... Quan was a busy man, until Earth Intelligence got hold of him...* "He insinuated himself into the scientific community on Earth, partnered up for a while with one of the pre-eminent Terran geneticists, cheated him out of all his patents, may have been responsible for killing him, then got himself hired as a Stragori government operative. About ten years ago, he was disavowed by the Directorate, fled back to Earth, and disappeared. There's a death notice filed in the Official Records Office on the mainland, but no remains were ever returned to Stragon."

"I'm not surprised," Sylvain said. "He always struck me as a slippery character, so I wouldn't trust that death notice if I were you. When we were just starting up our lab on the mainland, Quan came looking for a research position. His credentials were impeccable, and he knew all the right things to say—a smooth talker, that one—but something about him put me off, and I turned down his application. A few years later the business was up and running. We'd started Stragon First and were making ourselves heard in some important circles, and Quan came back, this time with an extremely radical agenda and an ultimatum: if we didn't help him bring an end to the Directorate, we would regret it."

Dennis drew a long, slow breath. He knew what *he* would have done at that point, but this was Sylvain's story, not his. "Can I assume that you called his bluff?"

"I sent him packing. It was the right thing to do. I told him to go back home to Galandra and swore that if he activated his agenda, I would personally see to it that *he* regretted it."

"Quan wasn't bluffing," came Heidi's voice from the doorway, startling both men.

Sylvain spat an exasperated syllable. "We don't know for sure that he was responsible," he reminded her sharply.

Scowling, she strode into the middle of the room. "He was the only one with a motive," she informed him hotly. "Maybe he didn't do it himself. Maybe he stayed on Galandra, pulled some strings, and got someone on the mainland to lay those false charges against us. It doesn't matter. He got what he wanted. And did I overhear correctly? Did that evil little man set himself up as Stragon First when we were gone? And activate his wretched plan?"

"That's what my intel suggests," Dennis told her. "I have reason to believe that someone in the current version of Stragon First is responsible for impersonating the leadership of the Directorate and destabilizing the mainland. And they've managed to do it with anonymity so far."

"Well, I wish you good luck with your hunt, Nephew," said Sylvain.

Heidi drew herself up, crossed her arms over her chest, and levelled a cool stare at his face. "So, Quan wasn't bluffing, but you were? You promised to make him regret it. Was that an empty threat? Are you just going to stand back and let him get away with this?"

For several heartbeats, they locked eyes.

Sylvain blinked first. "I don't want to, but what can I do from this damn chair?" he demanded.

"A lot more today than you could yesterday," she snapped. "An opportunity has just dropped onto your lap, Sylvain. With Dennis as your legs, we can finally make Nestor Quan pay for what he's done to us. Will you at least think about it?"

Glaring at a spot on the wall, he inhaled and exhaled deeply through his nose.

"All right," he conceded, pronouncing each word with razorlike sharpness. "I'll think about it."

Dennis's sleeping quarters were in the building that formed the right-hand side of the U. His luggage had already been moved to his room, and Heidi offered to walk him there.

"Has he really been in that chair for the past ten years?" said Dennis as they strolled across the yard.

"I'm afraid so," she replied. "He spent the first five years hoping, making me take him from healer to healer in search of a cure for his paralysis. Not all of these 'specialists' were medically trained, but Sylvain didn't care.

He insisted on checking out every possibility. Every new 'miracle product' or experimental procedure had to be investigated, and every time, the result was the same. It was heartbreaking having to watch him endure so much disappointment. When he'd finally run out of rainbows to chase, reality set in. That was when the grieving began."

"And is he still grieving?"

"He's mired somewhere between depression and acceptance, with anger simmering quietly on a back burner, so yes. The staff is like our family. They've all been extremely patient and understanding, and they're loyal to a fault. Even so, his current prolonged moodiness has been wearing on everyone's nerves. So, I want to thank you for bringing him this challenge. It could be just what he needs to boot him back into action."

"You're assuming he'll agree to take it on," Dennis pointed out. "He said he'd think about it. He might refuse."

"Not likely. I've made my position clear, and deep down he knows I'm right. He also knows from long experience how unpleasant his life can become when he goes against my wishes."

All the previous clues came together with a *snap*, and Dennis could contain his curiosity no longer. "Forgive me if I'm overstepping, but... are you two in more than a business relationship?"

She hesitated, long enough to make him think she was brushing off his question. It didn't matter, though. The dimples in her cheeks and the sparkle in her eyes had already given him his answer, and her words confirmed it. "We're life-joined, Dennis. I don't know the Terran name for it, but that's what it's called on Galandra."

NINE
ISABELA

Isabela did not sleep well that night, or the next. Her mind was full of questions, all jostling and elbowing one another to be at the forefront of her thoughts.

The software on the computer Quinian's friend had "borrowed" on his behalf was almost certainly Thryggian. How had it come into the possession of a Stragori, and how had the Directorate been using the data?

How did it work? What was there in the Stragori genome that made it detectable by alien technology from a distance?

If twenty percent of the Terrans on the island possessed Stragori genes, did that mean one-fifth of the more than three billion Humans on Earth were part Stragori as well? How would that even be possible? The Stragori infiltrators would have had to rut like rabbits for a millennium at least in order to have that many descendants. Or did they reproduce differently? Did they have special qualities or abilities that set them apart from "ordinary" Humans like herself?

Resistance to disease, for example? Was that why the percentage of Human-Stragori hybrids on the island was so high—because so many more of the "ordinary" Humans had been killed by the third and fourth pandemics that had wracked Earth and decimated their numbers there over the past couple of centuries?

If the Stragori were the control group, that meant the Humans on Earth were the experimental test subjects. But what was the purpose of the experiment? Were the pandemics part of it? If so, what were they in aid of? What were they meant to prove?

Into this mental maelstrom marched a final question, one that overshadowed all the rest and made it impossible for her to remain in bed a moment longer. Isabela got up and went into the living room, where the computer and its controller still sat on the coffee table, with the signal jammer beside them.

Shortly after the three of them had moved in, Carlos had detected the listening devices in the apartment. Disabling the mics or ripping them out of the wall would have blown their EIS covers. So, he had created something that could be turned on whenever privacy was needed.

The jammer was designed to throw up a hemispherical barrier that would block electronic transmissions. Devices located within the field were still operational. They could even communicate with one another. They just couldn't connect with anything—or anyone—on the other side of the barrier.

Isabela knew from experience that Carlos's invention was effective against Stragori-developed technology. Would the jammer still block the signals to and from a Thryggian device?

Isabela had to find out.

She checked to make sure the green light was flashing. Then she picked up the shiny cylinder and pointed its glowing end at the small black box.

"Show map of the island," she commanded it, praying that nothing would happen.

But something did. As before, the screen unfurled before her eyes and acquired the same empty-bowl image as it had displayed earlier for Quinian.

Isabela's heart sank. Then it occurred to her that the picture might not have come from a server outside the barrier. Perhaps the computer had pulled it from some sort of memory buffer instead.

She had to give it something different to find.

"Show location of Anna Sturtevant."

The screen refreshed. Now it displayed a map of the northern land mass, with a single red dot pulsing in the middle of its upper left quadrant.

But that still could have come from internal memory, she reasoned, if Quinian had requested it while testing the system earlier.

"Show location of Anna Sturtevant one month ago," she added.

The computer replied in its soft, agendered voice, "That information has been moved to password-protected archives. For access, state your password."

Madre! This was worse than she'd imagined. If the Directorate was not only tracking but recording the movements of every Stragori on the planet...!

"Show location of Dennis Forrand."

The map scrolled to the right, bringing the eastern part of Galandra onto the screen. A red dot appeared in the middle of the image, just as Isabela's heart landed, hard, in the pit of her stomach.

"What are you doing?" came Quinian's voice from the doorway, followed by the unmistakable sound of a yawn.

"Getting some answers," she replied, "and not liking any of them." Glancing up, she saw him, clad in sea-green pajama bottoms and a tee-shirt, rubbing the sleep out of his right eye. His hair was tousled. Except for the beard bristle on his face, it would have been easy to imagine him clutching a teddy bear.

Adorable when sleeping, infuriating when awake. Just like all men...

Filing away that thought, she told him, "We have to warn them somehow."

"And by 'them' you mean...?"

"Dennis and Angeli. They may think they're untrackable, but they're not. This census program just showed me where to find both of them, while the signal jammer was turned on. And there's a record of their movements in a secure part of the archives, going back at least a month."

Frowning, Quinian sat down beside her on the sofa. "Of their movements. So it can know where we've been, but not what we did there. That's where the surveillance and monitoring gear comes in, I guess—all of which *can* be jammed by your device."

"And the optimization," she reminded him.

"Including the optimization," he agreed with a sigh. "You're right. All that information makes it difficult for anyone with Stragori blood to move secretly against the Directorate. It also explains why Dennis gave us the mission he did. Pure-blooded Terrans can't be tracked, and mics and securecams can be foiled."

"What about this friend of yours, the one who obtained the computer for you? Do you think they knew what they were handing over?"

He hesitated before answering. "I lied to you earlier, Isabela, on Dennis's orders. There was no friend. Not a friend of mine, anyway, but maybe one of Dennis's. Dennis gave the computer to me. And I'm pretty sure he knows what it's capable of. He told me it would help us accomplish our goal."

"Quin," she began, struck by a sudden thought, "when Dennis gave you our assignment, what exactly did he say?"

"Just what I told you. We're supposed to turn the Terrans against the Directorate—"

"Did he use those actual words, though? Did he say to turn them, or did he say to *find a way* to turn them? There's a difference."

He thought for a couple of beats. "I believe he said we were to find a way to do it, which is just another way of telling someone—"

"No, it's not," she insisted.

He uttered a groan. "Isabela, the middle of the night is not a good time to be splitting hairs like this with me."

She batted his complaint aside. "Did Dennis tell you where he got the computer?"

"No. And even if I'd been curious about it at the time, it wasn't my place to ask." The hard edge on his voice signalled that his patience was waning.

Nonetheless, she persisted, "But you are certain he knew this device could pinpoint his location and Angeli's at any moment in time."

"Yes! Maybe! Can I go back to bed now?"

"Then he must have wanted us to keep track of them,"

she said with growing conviction, "in addition to figuring out what might motivate the Terran population to rise up in protest."

"Oy!" Quinian ran his hand through his hair. "Isabela, don't you have to get up and go to work later this morning?"

"We need to find out where this computer actually came from." *...and please, Dio, let it not be from the Thryggian bunker!*

"All right. Fine. Shut it down right now, and I promise you I'll look into that first thing today."

She arched her eyebrows. "Are you actually promising, or just using a figure of speech?"

"Never mind!" he snapped. "Stay awake all night if you like. I'm going back to sleep."

With that, he stood up and left the room.

The red dot was still pulsing on the light screen. It would yield her no answers, she knew, no matter how long and hard she stared at it. However, there was a place where she might find some, provided she could sneak away unnoticed. Planning that excursion could be her project for the day.

"Computer, power off," she said at last. Then she deactivated the jamming device and followed Quinian out of the living room.

"Mrs. Bakshi, are you all right?"

Isabela emerged from the swirl of thoughts inside her head and looked into the worried face of her young teaching assistant... and for just a moment, froze.

The truthful answer was no, she wasn't all right. However, what was currently on her mind was not something she wished to share, especially not with one who'd been optimized.

It wasn't Joanne's fault if she was being used as a spy, her senses co-opted by a Directorate intent on gathering data by any means and at whatever cost necessary. The girl had no idea it was even happening.

Isabela knew, though, and the awareness had made her self-conscious—"mindful", as Quinian had put it earlier. But it was more than that. She felt as though she was negotiating a minefield and had to plan every step, keeping her eyes on the ground and being very careful where she placed her feet.

And how she chose her words.

"I think I know why you've been so preoccupied all day today," Joanne said.

"Oh?"

"You were like this last year too, on the anniversary of your brother's passing. You told me then that the memory was making you sad."

Yes, among other strong emotions, Isabela thought, relieved that the child couldn't actually read her mind, then or now. She managed a faint smile and a nod of confirmation.

Isabela and Carlos had been close. They'd successfully run Veggieville together, they'd joined Earth Intelligence together, and they'd come to Stragon together, along with Isabela's husband Vikram, to support the EIS mission on that world. Just one year later, Carlos Calvera was dead after being bitten by a poisonous insect in the Wilderness Zone. But the venom hadn't been what killed him—it had been something in the antivenin administered afterward. A rare allergy to one of the ingredients, the doctor had told her.

She hadn't believed that for one second.

"Why don't you go relax in your office?" Joanne suggested. "I can handle things out here for the rest of the afternoon."

It was tempting. The girl was certainly capable. And yet...

Isabela gazed around the classroom, where twenty-four youngsters from six to ten years old sat quietly at their computers. Each student was engrossed in whatever age-appropriate lesson or activity they'd chosen from the assignment menu she'd posted for them that morning.

"No, I think I'd rather keep busy," she replied. "I've gotten behind in my assessments, and that's usually when Dr. Quinian decides to drop by. Besides, it's late enough in the day that some of the children will want to get up and move around, and they'll need you to supervise them in the exercise room. I'll be fine."

Joanne looked unconvinced but didn't argue. Instead, she resumed circulating among the irregularly-placed desks, pausing to observe each student at work, then glancing up to check on Isabela before moving on.

Surveilling her? Or just concerned? Either way, the girl's behaviour felt wrong.

Isabela hadn't lied about the assessments. She'd just wasted the entire morning running mental circles around the problem of sneaking away to the Thryggian bunker. Her ponderings would no doubt have been more productive after a good night's sleep, but she hadn't had one. So, it was probably time she packed that train of thought away in its wheelhouse and resumed being a teacher for now.

Picking a student at random, she opened their

Completed Work file. It contained a short essay titled, "What Family Means to Me". To Isabela's astonishment, the words struck her like a series of physical blows, all but knocking the breath from her body.

Had she really assigned this topic? She who no longer *had* a family and was still grieving the loss of her soulmate?

With shaking hands, she pulled up the menu and found the activity. She had to blink away tears as she read its description: *Compose a three-paragraph essay about the most important thing in your life.*

She must have been thinking about justice and revenge when she set this assignment. She must have thought the loss was behind her, the pain and sorrow locked away behind a wall of anger. How was she supposed to assess this piece when just a glance at the title was enough to bring it all crashing down on her again?

Perhaps Joanne was right. Perhaps it was best if she put some distance between herself and her teaching duties at this time and shift her focus to something that would take her mind off the tragic past.

Like the ugly present and the possibly violent future? Of course. That would work.

It would have to be at night. That much Isabela knew as she entered the apartment at the end of the school day. The timing was still problematic, though, if she was to leave and return without Quinian finding out. For someone whose snoring could drown out an avcraft engine, he was a remarkably light sleeper. Bare feet crossing a carpet could bring him out of his room to investigate.

"I've got a name for you, and you're not going to like it."

Startled, she spun around and saw him sitting on the sofa with his arms crossed, staring resentfully up at her. He was wearing his business suit.

"You've been to the mainland," she observed brightly.

"I kept my promise and looked into the source of the census software," he growled.

Mentally crossing her fingers, Isabela walked into the living room and settled onto the easy chair adjacent to the sofa. "You found the developer?" she said.

"No." A pause, then, "I found the thief."

"It was stolen from the—" She caught herself just in time. "—from the one who wrote the code?"

"In a manner of speaking. It was created by an alien, appropriated by a Stragori, then later reverse-engineered and sold to the Directorate as a confidential surveillance tool."

"And this thief was...?"

"Gratien Forrand. He's dead now, but he was Dennis's great-great-grandfather. And the one who eventually found a way to capitalize on it was Marcel Forrand, Dennis's uncle."

More Forrands. And more skullduggery. *Madre!* How many strands of this mission would lead back to members of that powerful family? How deep down did their criminal roots penetrate the soil of this world? More to the point, how much dirt was it safe to dig up about Dennis's relatives before he turned on her and Quinian... as, eventually, he would when he found out how much they'd discovered about his family's shady dealings. As Angeli had taught her over the course of their decades-long friendship, it was the Forrand way.

Setting her jaw, Isabela shook off the image that had

risen in her mind, of a dung heap crawling with beetles. "I can see that *you* do not like that name," she said, enunciating deliberately. "What makes you so sure that *I* will not?"

"Because Dennis 'borrowed' the prototype from him without permission, and now, thanks to my inquiry, Marcel is aware of it."

Isabela was momentarily speechless. So Dennis was a thief as well? This just kept getting better and better.

"Does Marcel suspect that we are the ones who now have it?" she finally managed to ask.

"No. It's Dennis he wants to tear a strip off, once he finds him. But Dennis will be angry as hell when he learns who alerted Marcel about the theft, and then he'll be coming after me."

"You're the one who—?" She turned narrowed eyes on Quinian's face and said, "And how are you acquainted with this Marcel Forrand, exactly...?"

"Does it matter?"

"It matters to *me*. As your partner in this adventure, I believe I have a right to know."

Quinian paused to fill his lungs, his features forming an expression generally worn by someone who had suddenly found an insect in their mouth. "He's my grandfather."

If she hadn't been sitting down, Isabela would have fallen over. "You're a Forrand too?"

"Unfortunately," he replied. "On the margins of the family and unacknowledged, but... yes."

Just like Angeli. Now things were beginning to make sense. Whether acknowledged or not, whether closely or distantly related, Forrands stuck together. And they were everywhere on this world, insinuated into every walk of life and ultimately expected to serve the interests of the family, whether they wanted to or not. So, Quinian wasn't only Dennis's cousin, he was also a Forrand spy...

...which made it doubly important that he never find out about the Thryggian bunker on the island.

"Did Marcel say where the original alien device had been found?"

"Not specifically. He just mumbled something about an underground room."

"A room," she echoed, with effort keeping her voice steady. "Did he happen to mention where it was?"

He gave her a curious look. "No. Why? Is it important?"

"I... was just wondering whether it might have been on Earth," she replied, trying to sound only mildly interested.

"It could have been on Earth, I suppose," he allowed. "Marcel was rather vague on the details."

She bobbed her head, feigning satisfaction. Meanwhile, her mind was awash in questions, and the dread simmering in her stomach was about to reach a steady, rolling boil.

If Dennis had felt it necessary to steal this technology from his uncle, then the fact that Isabela could not be tracked had to be an important part of his plan. That was why he'd given her a Forrand for a partner: Dennis needed Isabela, but he trusted Quinian.

One thing was certain in her mind now. She was going to pay a visit to the Wilderness Zone, if not tonight then tomorrow night at the latest. The Thryggians needed to be warned.

TEN
ANGELI

The market was about a twenty-minute walk from Lyla's house. It turned out to be a block-long, open-air structure, a peaked roof on supports sheltering a double row of inward-facing shops with a string of kiosks running down the middle. This marketplace was surrounded on all sides by residential streets. In fact, Angeli noticed as she and Lyla stepped into the shade beneath its covering of corrugated metal, many of the shops had evidently been repurposed from residential housing. They bravely bore their large painted signs and window displays, but were betrayed by their shutters and railing-lined front porches.

"There are at least a couple dozen markets like this all over Westgrove, and probably more by now," Lyla explained as they hurried past the not-yet-open kiosks on their way to the food section.

They'd set out from the house extra early today, because the vendors whose merchandise had to travel the farthest tended to sell out quickly, and the marshes were a fair distance away. If Angeli wanted tasselberries, it had to be the first item on Lyla's shopping list, and they would have to be among the first customers of the day.

Angeli was in charge of the shopping cart, which was tethered to her wrist by a leather strap. Surprisingly, the cart hardly hampered her movements at all.

"We're a growing community," Lyla continued, "and it's important that people be able to walk to where they buy their staple goods. I imagine it's quite different on the southern continent, though."

Indeed, it was, Angeli reflected. Each urban district on the mainland held millions of people and a single sprawling commercial zone containing hundreds of businesses. To get around the district, mainlanders didn't walk if they could afford to ride, and when they rode, they preferred to move as quickly as possible. They had created a complex underground network of rapid transit tunnels and a fleet of bullet-shaped cars for that very purpose, all controlled by an AI...

...which had been housed inside the main server under the Directorate's offices before a bomb took out the computer room and triggered a tunnel collapse.

Thank goodness for fail-safes and backup systems, or the death toll inside those transit tubes would have been so much higher...

"Aha!" Lyla crowed, startling her back to the moment. "They've got some!" All at once, she was making a beeline for one of the kiosks, where a sign hand-printed in large red letters had just appeared.

Angeli followed her and found a young man and a boy setting out containers of produce on a rough-hewn wooden table. Spargrass, heggen, dannoli... Lyla was fidgeting impatiently, but the vendors took no notice. A basket of things resembling a cross between a strawberry and a plum came out. Angeli's hopes spiked. But no, this wasn't them either.

Then a tray landed in front of Lyla that made her eyes light up. "Tasselberry! I'll take all of these," she declared.

Sometimes it was better not to know what food looked like before it was prepared. Remembering that she'd let Lyla believe she was from the marshes where this fruit was grown, Angeli forced her lips into a smile.

Tasselberry had to be the ugliest thing she had ever seen. For one thing, it was long and cylindrical, about the size of a cucumber. Hairier than a coconut, pricklier than a cactus pear, and the colour of something no one should ever touch barehanded, it instantly set off alarms in her brain. Its only saving grace was that it didn't smell the way it looked. And it helped that she'd already tasted it at Derwin's house... which raised a disturbing question in her mind: how *had* its taste been discovered? How hungry or desperate did a person have to be to put something like that into their mouth in the first place?

Ten tasselberries went into the cart, enough, Lyla assured her, for a batch of cookies, several pies, and a generous amount of jam. Soon, the fruit was joined by an assortment of root vegetables, a large cut of meat (from a live animal, not lab-grown), and two huge bags of greens for that evening's dinner.

"Ben will be joining us tonight," Lyla remarked with a peculiar lilt in her voice as they strolled back to the house, pulling their purchases behind them.

The sidelong glance that accompanied her comment was as good as a wink. It gave Angeli pause. While she was trying to imagine what Krall might have told Lyla to give her the impression that romance was about to blossom between him and Eva Moss, Lyla added, "You might want to dress up a little. I understand he wants to take you somewhere private after dinner." She was practically hugging herself and bouncing up and down with excitement.

All right, Angeli understood this now. The hint of romance was clearly a ruse to ensure they would arouse no suspicions when they stole away to be alone together. What he no doubt wanted was a secret meeting about her mission. Perhaps Dennis had contacted him with new intel, or further instructions.

That had to be it. After all, she was in her fifties, and he was... She had no idea how old he was. Stragori lived twice as long as Humans. He could be thirty-five or a hundred and forty and still look young enough to be her son. There was no question that he was attractive. If they were back on Earth and she knew nothing about Stragori, they might already be dating... but they weren't, and she didn't, and she had to be truthful to herself, if not to Lyla Claire.

"Somewhere private? Well, *that* sounds mysterious," Angeli said, counterfeiting some excitement of her own. "I wonder what he has in mind."

"I guess you'll have to wait to find out," Lyla replied coyly, and went on walking.

Eva Moss had promised the twin bards an exclusive interview for their broadcast. That afternoon, they turned up at Lyla's door with armfuls of recording gear and a list of questions handwritten on a sheet of paper. The brothers were dressed *almost* the same today, Angeli noticed—the pairs of stripes on their black and grey pullover sweaters ran in different directions.

"Really, now," Lyla scolded them, blocking their entrance, "what's the rush? You've hardly given her a chance to gather her thoughts."

"You've had her all to yourself for two days, Lady Claire," Adam pointed out. (Or was it Michael? Angeli was able to spot the small differences between them, but still didn't know who was who.) "It's time to share her with the rest of us. Besides, all we've got to report today is bad news. We need something to lighten the tone of our broadcast."

His brother spotted Angeli standing in the entrance hall and thrust the paper toward her, over Lyla's shoulder. Curious now, Angeli moved closer and scanned its contents.

"It's all right, Lyla," she said. "There's nothing on that list I can't answer."

Grudgingly, the other woman moved aside, gesturing them into the parlour.

"So, what's the bad news you'll be reporting, Michael?" Angeli asked as they busied themselves setting up their equipment.

"There's been a rash of accidental deaths in the northeastern part of the continent," he replied (*stripes going vertically—got it*). "At least, they *appear* to be accidental. The warders from the affected towns are co-operating in a joint investigation to determine what's what."

"It's not that we don't have accidents up here," Adam explained. "What's got the warders' noses twitching is the fact that these fatalities happened so close to each other and in such a short span of time, and in Borea that's simply unheard of."

Grinning wickedly, Michael pretended to twirl the end of a long moustache. "Ve-e-ery suspicious!"

"All right, enough," Adam cut him off, not unkindly. "If you're ready, Lady Moss, this will be presented as a pre-recorded interview, so let's get right to the questions, shall we?"

Angeli pinned a vidcam-ready expression on her face, determined to give an engaging and enlightening interview. The questions she had previewed were about the diet and eating habits, daily routines, and entertainment preferences of the average southern "technoslave". As she responded to each one in order, a part of her mind was wondering how the Borean audience would react to her answers.

Would it surprise them to learn how many mainlanders relaxed primarily by watching other people do challenging or interesting things? That more than half of all the southerners who were gainfully employed worked at some sort of government job? That living below ground in just one or two rooms was considered to be a luxury reserved for the very rich and powerful?

Then the twins went off script.

"So, Lady Moss, what has the Directorate been up to lately?" asked Adam.

Angeli froze. Meanwhile, her thoughts were racing. Forrand had told her she might have to make and carry out quick decisions. Clearly, this was one of them. How much was it right or safe for her to say about the political situation on the mainland when everything about it was so volatile and unpredictable?

In the space of three heartbeats, she made her choice.

"Not much, actually," she replied. "There have been no new policy announcements in a while."

Now it was Michael's turn. "When government falls silent, the governed will often speculate. What juicy rumours did you overhear during your long stay south of the channel?"

Angeli leaned forward and tightened her voice. "Forget about rumours. Your viewers need to hear the truth. So, let me tell you what I've personally witnessed and experienced and know for a fact. There is a lot of tension and uncertainty in the general population down there, largely because of the spread of misinformation, and it is building to a crisis. I'm sure your audience is already aware of the two factions that have arisen in opposition to the Directorate. Their restlessness appears to be increasing, along with their reach and their boldness. Shortly before I left the mainland, there was a bombing attack on a government building. As far as I know, no one has yet claimed responsibility for the resulting damage and the loss of life. The only thing I can say at this point is that the future is unclear, but it's also not engraved in stone.

"I know you wanted me to say something that would leaven your broadcast, but I cannot in good conscience put a happy face on what's happening right now. To turn it into entertainment would be a disservice to everyone who watches your program."

At this, Michael subsided into silence, and Adam took the lead once again.

"Let's change the topic," he said. "We understand that you worked in the Directorate's offices for a while. What was that like?"

Ten minutes later, the interview was over. As Lyla was

ushering the brothers out the door, Adam gave Angeli's arm a squeeze and murmured into her ear, "Well said, Eva Moss."

Angeli took her time picking an ensemble to wear to dinner. She wanted something that would distract Krall when she told him about the interview she'd given that day. The brothers would probably edit out her political comments before airing the piece, but in case they didn't, he needed to hear about it in advance, from her own glossy, carefully rouged lips.

Judging from the wardrobe in the closet, Kate had been the practical sort well before the baby was born. There wasn't an alluring neckline or a slit-up-to-there skirt to be found. It was a shame. Angeli would have killed for something with sequins at that moment.

As if on cue, her mind spun back to the day she and Juno had set out on their year-long excursion to the Industrial Wilderness in Americas. Angeli had gone through the younger girl's luggage, tossing out anything that screamed *Eligible brat slumming...* which didn't leave Juno with a lot of clothes to wear. And now here Angeli was, ironically wishing she could blink and make one of those sparkly tops appear on the bed.

She finally settled on a tan, knee-length skirt of sueded leather over a pair of matching tights, and a cream-coloured blouse with buttons that she could leave undone at the neck, forming a V.

She hadn't meant to make an entrance. However, by the time she'd finished applying her makeup and gone downstairs, everyone else was already seated at the table.

"Lovely," said Lyla, her cheeks dimpling with approval as Angeli stepped into the dining room.

The others present all seemed to feel the same way. All except Bennin Krall, who clearly had something weighing on his mind and barely glanced an acknowledgement in her direction.

Oh, well...

As usual, the meal was excellent—succulent slices of perfectly cooked roast, with spiced vegetables on the side, and tasselberry pie for dessert. Lyla, Ben, and Angeli were the only repeat diners this evening, and the takeaways were iced mini-cakes, some light in colour and some dark. When the meal was over and the other company had left, Krall suggested quietly to Angeli that they go for a drive somewhere and talk.

She fetched her jacket. As Lyla watched, her eyes twinkling, he helped Angeli put it on.

Then they stepped out the front door.

"It would be dangerous and foolhardy for you to travel anywhere right now," said Krall.

They were sitting in his vehicle, on the side of a road that ran through a local greenbelt. It was a romantic spot. Around them, the silhouettes of trees stood out against the moonlit sky as though painted onto a swath of midnight blue velvet. Stars glittered like tiny gems overhead, and the air wafting through the car's open windows smelled crisp and clean and full of promise. On this beautiful spring night, it definitely felt like a place where lovers might spend time alone together. And yet...

He sat behind the wheel, his eyes trained straight ahead,

his voice hard and flat as an old metal coin.

"I know something about your mission," he said. "How you were supposed to carry it out. And I'm afraid I can't let you do it."

Angeli's hackles were rising. "Really! Why not?"

"Because as soon as you leave Westgrove, you'll be arrested and sent back to the southern continent. Not for questioning—for tribunal. Apparently, Mainland Security has a solid case against you for terrorism."

"Against me? Or against Anna Sturtevant, who looks like me? Anna Sturtevant died in a tunnel collapse shortly after the bombing. I'm Eva Moss."

"Unfortunately, Mainland Security doesn't care what you call yourself. When Continental Security tried to serve that warrant a few days ago, forensic analysis on the mainland had already determined that the woman seen leaving the scene of the explosion was not the one pulled from the rubble later on. Your ruse, in other words, was a failure."

He exhaled audibly through his nose, then went on, "As soon as those Continental officers returned to their station, they filed a report with Mainland Security about the dispute we had on the dock. Mainland then immediately transferred jurisdiction higher up the chain. Every warders' station on Borea has now been alerted, including mine. Planetary Security has taken over the case. They've issued orders that you're to be arrested on sight, using whatever degree of force is necessary."

He was still refusing to look at her.

Angeli went cold all over. She swallowed hard, then said in as calm a voice as she could manage, "And is that what you're doing now? Arresting me?"

"No. I've contacted the warders-in-charge in the other

towns and informed them that this is an instance of mistaken identity and that you are already serving a sentence in Westgrove. They can't disobey an order from Planetary Security. However, they've agreed to follow it to the letter. As long as they don't see you, they won't try to arrest you. Bottom line is, whatever Forrand wants you to do, you'll have to find a way to do it without leaving town."

"Meanwhile, *you're* disobeying the order from Planetary Security. And what about the other warders in Westgrove? Will they go along with this?"

He shrugged. "As their Warder-in-Charge, I'm the one they answer to, not some nebulous authority on the southern continent. You'll be safe here. And I've taken heat from Planetary before. I can handle it."

"I see." She straightened in her seat and gazed through the windscreen as well. "So, I'm a wanted fugitive from the mainland now, charged with blowing up the Directorate's offices and killing all those people." It sounded worse when she said the words aloud.

There was a rustling sound to her left.

"Did you do it?"

She could practically feel his eyes boring into the side of her head as he asked this question. She understood the reason for it, but it stung nonetheless.

Whipping around in her seat, she glared into his face and stated firmly, "No, I did not. It was sheer dumb luck that I wasn't a casualty of the blast myself." A bitter note seeped into her voice as she added, "Well, the radical posing as Gervais Forrand did say that he wanted a Terran scapegoat for the bombing. With the other operatives gone, I guess I'm it."

...thus proving definitively that this "Director" was not

the real Gervais Forrand, she realized, or he would have been protecting Angeli, not singling her out for blame. Forrands didn't backstab one another, no matter how poorly they might get along. Except for Dennis, perhaps. He was the exception to a lot of rules.

The striking irony here, of course, was that before she could claim the privileges of a Forrand, she would first have to prove she *was* one, and in her current situation that was impossible.

Krall cleared his throat and turned back around. "Then this really is a case of mistaken identity, since Eva Moss is Stragori, northern-born. There's documentation in our capital city that proves it, and townsfolk in Westgrove who'll attest to it. Perhaps we can all work together to expose the impostor and clear Eva's name."

That wasn't her assignment. Dennis had been very specific during her briefing. She was supposed to find a way to motivate the northerners to take action against the radical groups in general, not "Gervais Forrand" in particular. And yet... he'd also promised that she would be "a hero of the revolution". And wasn't organizing resistance groups part and parcel of that?

As she became aware of a not-unpleasant musky scent in the air, a strange fluttering started up in her core. Whatever the reason for it, Angeli was suddenly certain that she wanted to trust this man, and not just because Dennis had told her she could.

"Thank you, Warder-in-Charge Krall. I would appreciate that very much."

She sensed rather than saw his smile. "Call me Ben. It's shorter."

*   *   *

When Krall delivered Eva back home, they found Lyla sitting on the loveseat in the parlour, with the screen set up on the coffee table in front of her and a steaming cup of something in her hand.

"Come in!" she called, throwing them an inviting wave as they walked through the door. "It's just about to start. There's a pot of tea in the kitchen, but you'll have to help yourselves. I don't want to miss a second of this broadcast."

Angeli's heart dropped. The interview! Ben's bad news had knocked it right out of her head. As he was shrugging off his jacket, she laid a pausing hand on his arm.

"There's something I need to tell you. The twins interviewed me today. For their news report this evening. But I didn't say anything that would compromise the mission. In fact—"

"Is there video?" he demanded urgently. "Does your face appear on camera?"

Oh, shit!

The sudden widening of her eyes evidently gave him his answer.

"Well, let's see what I can do about that," he muttered, and pulled a small device out of his trousers pocket. As Angeli watched, he punched a series of buttons on its upper surface, then held the thing to his ear. Seconds passed. His expression hardened. "Too late," he spat. "They've gone to air. You'd better hope no one in Security is paying attention to this broadcast."

"Hello, out there! It's The Skinner Report, where we bring you all the news, good and bad, from across the continent," Adam's voice announced heartily from an unseen speaker in the next room.

"Are you two going to come sit down and watch the

show?" Lyla demanded.

With dread welling up inside her, Angeli hung her jacket on one of the hooks beside the front door and followed Ben into the parlour.

The scene onscreen reminded her of some of the gang headquarters she'd had to visit while raising support for the Reformation back on Earth. The twins—wearing identically made but different-coloured shirts, one blue, one green—occupied a couple of mismatched easy chairs behind a beaten-up wooden coffee table. The tabletop was empty except for a small light screen facing the hosts, and a keypad device—most likely some sort of controller—situated halfway between them.

"Good evening, viewers," said Michael, "and welcome to those of you who may be tuning in for the first time. We have a special treat for you tonight, an exclusive interview with Westgrove's very own world traveller, Eva Moss, who will give us an insider's view of life on the southern continent. But first, the news, and you'd better brace yourselves for a shock, because I'm afraid it's not good."

"Where are they?" Angeli wondered aloud.

"Damned if I know," Krall murmured. "They move around a lot."

"Shh!" Lyla hissed. "I want to hear this."

Adam had taken over the report. "—and the warders of the five towns are jointly investigating to determine whether any or all of these deaths might be connected. In Salty Springs, Harlan Scott, eighty-five years old, was killed when he apparently lost control of his vehicle and crashed it into a tree six days ago. One day later in Ryderville, the home of Geraldo Mendez, aged ninety, caught fire. When the blaze was extinguished, firefighters found Mendez's body in a downstairs bedroom, where he had apparently been sleeping. The cause of the fire has not been released to the media. However, according to a reliable source, arson has not been ruled out. That same day, two women died in two different towns, both apparently after falling downstairs. They were Darcy Gates, aged one hundred and seventeen, in Overton, and Irina DeSalle, ninety-eight years old, in Grassy Meadows. Finally, three days later, the body of Bjorn Gustavsen, aged one hundred and thirty-one, was recovered from the foot of a bluff just outside of Whitewater. Gustavsen was reportedly an avid and experienced hiker who often took to the trails alone. However, his fall occurring in the same time frame as the other 'accidents' is causing his death to be treated as suspicious. We'll be following this story and providing you with updates as further information comes in."

Krall had gone rigid in his seat.

"Did you know any of these people?" Angeli asked him.

"Not personally," he growled. "It's just—"

"And now for that special treat we promised you," Adam began.

Michael started as though stung and stared at the controller on the table. His eyes widened briefly. Then he pressed his lips together and bobbed his head.

"I'm sorry, Adam, but I have to interrupt with additional breaking news. The investigation has expanded in the last twenty-five hours to include the warders of two more towns, where deaths originally classified as being of natural causes have now been declared to be suspicious. Herman Kronen, aged seventy-five, of Cedarvale, and Leesa Punjabi, aged one hundred and forty-six, of Brightlake, both died of cardiac arrest within the same time frame as the incidents reported to have occurred in the other five towns..."

"All right, then," Krall declared, pulling out his communication device again. "If that line is open for news flashes, I've got one for them that will singe their eyebrows."

Angeli saw a flurry of button-pushing and a final emphatic finger-poke.

"...and anyone with information about any of the deaths we've mentioned this evening is asked to contact their local warder station without delay," Michael was concluding.

Meanwhile, Adam leaned forward, his attention caught by something that had evidently appeared on the controller's screen. She could practically hear him gulp as he finished reading it. Then he turned to gaze into the camera, a sickly grin spreading across his face, and said, "Due to unforeseen technical difficulties, I'm afraid that will have to be our show for tonight. Tune in tomorrow, when, hopefully, we'll have resolved the problem and will have more information and some better news to bring you. Have a good evening, everyone."

Michael had just enough time to throw him a stunned look before the screen went dark.

Lyla turned narrowed eyes on Bennin Krall. "What did you tell them?" she demanded.

"That if they aired the interview, they would be signing Eva Moss's death warrant, and I would personally see to it that they never broadcast anything again."

"What?! You wouldn't!" she exclaimed, then added a moment later, "Would you?"

"Probably not," he confessed with a sigh. "But the danger to Eva is real, Lyla, and it comes from the southern continent. It's important that her whereabouts remain a secret. I couldn't afford to mince words just now, so I said what I had to, to keep her safe."

Thoughtful silence.

"I see," Lyla said at last. "Well, I'm going to freshen my tea and pour each of you a cup, and then you're going to fill me in about this danger, Bennin Krall, so that I can keep her safe too."

They stayed up half the night talking—and drinking progressively cooler cups of tea—as Krall "read in" Lyla Claire. The more she heard, the sterner her expression became, until the normally pleasant, motherly face was positively glowering with wrath.

"No one in this town is going to give her up without a fight," Lyla declared, pounding the edge of her fist on the arm of the loveseat for emphasis. "And anyone who disagrees with that will not be welcome at *my* table."

Evidently, this was the strongest form of rejection the other woman could muster.

When everything had been said that *could* be said without scuppering her mission and betraying Dennis's confidence, Krall left for home and Angeli went upstairs to her bedroom, her brain buzzing. She was too wired to sleep now. She took out the card reader and scanned her instructions again. Perhaps there was a way for her to contact Dennis's agents in the other towns without leaving Westgrove.

She keyed in her birth name, pressed her thumb to the square in the bottom right corner of the screen, and pulled up the list of their names...

...and forgot to breathe.

Harlan Scott in Salty Springs.

Geraldo Mendez in Ryderville.

Bjorn Gustavsen in Whitewater.

Darcy Gates in Overton.

Irina DeSalle in Grassy Meadows.

Herman Kronen in Cedarvale.

Leesa Punjabi in Brightlake.

Someone had targeted Dennis Forrand's network of contacts. This was a connection the joint investigation could not be allowed to uncover. But what if it was the only one to be found?

Krall had noticed it right away. That must have been what he was about to tell her when Adam interrupted him by introducing her interview.

The remaining fourteen operatives needed to be warned. Angeli had no idea how to do that. Krall might know... but she didn't have his contact codes. Would Lyla know how to reach him? She was already sound asleep. Was it worth waking her up to find out?

No, Angeli decided. She could wait. Daybreak was only a few hours away.

ELEVEN
DENNIS

On the ranch—an old Terran term, it nonetheless seemed the most appropriate one—breakfast was quite a different affair from the sit-down meal of the evening before.

Dennis went alone to the dining hall and found it a hub of activity. There were a lot of new faces this morning, some coming off shift and some going on. It wasn't hard to tell which were which.

Always circumspect in a strange situation, Dennis chose an unobtrusive place to stand while he took the measure of the room.

A servery had apparently been opened up, attached to the dining room and accessed through a different door than had been used the previous evening. As he watched, a stream of people entered it empty-handed and re-emerged carrying trays of food. Diners came and went at the trestle tables as well. Whether coming or going, weary or rested, they all had somewhere to hurry off to, so no one was lingering over their meal.

"Waiting for another invitation?" This amused voice that floated over his left shoulder belonged to the person who'd sat across the table from Dennis at dinner—a man with bright brown eyes, a shadow of beard, and a friendly expression framed by an explosion of wavy dark hair. His name was Eldred, but everyone called him Eddie.

Falling into step beside him, Dennis replied, "Not really, but I was hoping for some enlightening conversation."

A stack of compartmented metal trays perched on a small table just inside the servery door. Eddie took two and passed one to him, saying, "Heidi figured as much. That's why you're coming on shift with me, so I can show you what we do here."

Caught off guard (and unaccustomed to being moved around like a parcel), Dennis was momentarily speechless. Eddie gave no sign of noticing.

The servery turned out to be automated. Diners took turns placing their trays into precisely shaped indentations on a moving belt, then walked alongside it, pressing buttons to select items from the menu posted at each of four stations. At the end of the line sat a row of small bins containing eating utensils, and beside them a beverage and condiment dispenser. The entire process was a model of efficiency.

As Dennis and Eddie carried their fully loaded trays to one of the tables, three other people got up and left.

"Have an easy shift, Aaron," Eddie greeted one of them in passing.

"An easy shift to you as well," came the reply.

Without another word, Eddie stepped over the bench, dropped onto his seat, and tucked into his meal. Following his lead, Dennis did the same. His mind was swarming with questions, but this was clearly not the time to be asking them. Someone was out there, tired and hungry and waiting to be relieved.

"See those two lines?"

The yard outside was even busier and noisier than the dining hall. It was also more dangerous, as people on motos crisscrossed the area, some leaving, others arriving. A wide gap between two storage sheds seemed to be the designated vehicle depot. That was where Eddie was headed now.

Following close behind him, Dennis peered over Eddie's shoulder at the screen of the device the other man had pulled out of his jacket pocket. It displayed what appeared to be a satellite image of the compound. Glowing yellow lines curved around the cluster of buildings top and bottom, then paralleled each other and ran off the screen to either side.

"They're the limits of the force fields," Eddie explained as they walked. "The outer one is an exclusion field, to keep predators and other undesirables away. The inner one is an enclosure. It prevents the herd from wandering off into danger or entering the compound. We live and work in the corridor between the fields, except at dehorning time. The barrier walls are invisible, so this thing," he added, flourishing the handheld device, "shows us where it's safe to go."

He selected and straddled a moto with a rear seat. As Dennis sat down behind him, Eddie clipped the device into a cradle attached to the handlebar. Then he thumbed a button on the keypad underneath it, and two bright red overlapping dots popped up on the screen.

"That's us," said Eddie. "Hang on tight."

With that, he started the engine, and they were off.

Within minutes, the compound had disappeared behind them and there was nothing but grassland to be seen in every direction. Well, that wasn't entirely accurate. He caught occasional glimpses of things that glinted in the sun to both sides of their path. Antennae, perhaps, or sensors. And the moto was following a trail of sorts that had been pressed into the grass by the regular passage of wheels, just as the truck had done the day before.

So, they couldn't get lost. Good to know. And yet, hard to believe.

Dennis shivered, only partly because of the morning chill in the air, and grappled his gaze onto the screen in front of them.

"Where are the auroch?" he shouted over the sound of the moto.

Not that he actually wanted to see another one up close, of course, but their absence gave his mind something to focus on besides his odds of survival if the protective technology should happen to fail.

"They're around," Eddie called back over his shoulder. "They're big beasts. Need a lot of roaming space."

"And you've enclosed it all with *two* separate force fields? What's your energy source?"

The sound of laughter drifted back to him, then was snatched away by the wind.

For a while, Dennis subsided into his thoughts. Evidently, Heidi had wanted him out of the way. Why? So she could work on Sylvain? All she had to do was ask, and he would have steered clear. She didn't have to send him all the way out—

"There!" Eddie exclaimed, pointing.

Improbably, a small building lay directly ahead.

"What's that?" Dennis shouted.

"My post," he shouted back. "And we're right on time."

However, the heavyset, brown-skinned woman who flung open the door to the shed as the moto pulled up in front of it didn't agree with that statement. Lips pursed, she gave Eddie a withering look and declared loudly, "You're late. My shift ended twenty minutes ago."

For a moment he appeared not to have heard her, busy as he was with disconnecting his way-finder and slipping it back into his pocket. Then he replied dismissively, "Yeah, that sounds about right," and dismounted from the moto.

Her chin rose as the two men approached.

Eddie paused just beyond her arm's reach. Dennis followed suit.

"Julie, this is Dennis Forrand. He's Sylvain's nephew, from the mainland."

Although clearly unimpressed by the Forrand name, she bobbed her head in acknowledgement of the introduction and even gave Dennis a brief smile, turning it off as though with a switch as she swung her attention back to Eddie.

"There's been a development," she told him.

He spread his arms invitingly and replied, "Bring me the bad news."

"It's started. They're singling out the decoy. I caught part of it on video. I think it's the male that fell and injured his leg during the last migration."

Instantly sober, Eddie nodded thoughtfully. "This means we've got—how long? Three weeks?"

"At most. I've already let Heidi know."

Dennis stood by with knitted brows, listening. He had

no idea what they were talking about, but it felt wrong to interrupt them.

"What's the status of the field generators?" Eddie asked her. "Are they up to the trip?"

"All operating at full strength. The inclusion field generators are going to need servicing soon, but we can take care of that when we arrive at the northern base. Details are in my diagnostic report on the computer. And now you are briefed," she declared. "Have an easy shift."

"And you are relieved," he responded. "Enjoy your free time."

Dennis watched as Julie swung herself onto the moto, replaced Eddie's way-finder with her own, and headed back along the route the two men had just taken.

"Three weeks until what?" Dennis inquired, following Eddie inside.

"The next migration. I'm afraid your visit may have to be cut short. We've all got a lot of work to do now: sending a team ahead to prepare the northern base, packing up all the portables and perishables, seeing to the weapons, arranging for the disposition of the carcass..."

Dennis's brain lurched. "Whoa! What carcass?"

"The one the auroch have chosen to leave behind to delay any predators that might want to attack them while they're on the move."

"The auroch do this themselves?"

"Yes. We observed the behaviour while studying the animals in the wild. It was what gave us the idea to start this business in the first place."

This post was obviously a monitoring station, equipped with a lumpy-looking cot, a battered table, and a daunting array of screens perched atop an even more daunting configuration of control panels. As Eddie settled in to perform a preliminary check of its numerous dials, gauges, and indicators, Dennis searched for a guest chair, in vain.

It didn't feel right to sit on the cot or the table, and the lidless toilet in the adjoining hygiene room was simply not an option. So, he moved casually to the tiny rear window and pretended to take an interest in the scenery, all the while keeping an eye on his host.

At last, Eddie pressed his thumb to the screen at the far right of the console and half-turned toward him. "If you want to sit down, there's a folding chair under the cot," he said, pointing. He waited until Dennis had lowered himself onto the hard wooden seat, then asked, "Where were we?"

"Auroch behaviour in the wild."

"Ah, yes—the decoy. They always pick an adult, one that has little to no chance of completing the migration. It's old... it's weak... it's injured... whatever. The wild auroch form a circle around this animal and gore it with their horns. While it's bleeding to death, drawing every predator within sniffing distance, the rest of the herd departs. The average adult auroch yields between seven and eight tons of meat. That gives the herd three or four weeks' head start. When you're travelling with calves, that makes a big difference."

"Your domesticated animals are all dehorned," Dennis pointed out, "so how do they—"

"A couple of swift kicks to the head by another auroch is generally enough to bring the chosen one down. Then one of the other adults stomps on its neck to finish the job. We've never had to slaughter one ourselves. We wouldn't be in this business if that were the case. The risk to life and limb would simply be too great. But there are two migrations per year, one in each direction, and we weren't about to pass up an annual fifteen tons of fresh, marketable meat in exchange for giving them the protection of a couple of force fields."

Dennis leaned forward. "About those force fields... you laughed earlier, but the question remains."

"You're assuming they're constantly up, draining our energy source, and they're not. We use motion and proximity detectors to trigger the appropriate generators as needed. That keeps our power usage well within manageable limits, as you can see here." He gestured behind him to one of the rows of gauges, where every needle was in the green. "We take energy reservoirs with us on the migration and set up detectors and field generators around the herd each time they stop for the night. The reservoirs are recharged when we reach base."

"And while the herd is moving?"

"We move everything in parallel with them, while keeping our eyes open for predators. Like I said, all we really do is protect the auroch. They do the rest."

Something was squirming at the back of Dennis's mind.

"They know you're protecting them from predators, and yet they still feel the need to leave a decoy?" he said slowly.

Eddie shrugged. "It's a survival strategy, still being done in the wild, and it works. Once a habit like that becomes ingrained, it's pretty near impossible to change."

The squirming grew more intense.

"They've changed other habits, though," Dennis pointed out. "They allow you to dehorn their young, for one thing. That has to go against all their instincts."

Now Eddie was beginning to look uncomfortable. "They probably realize that it's for the calves' own good. And we've shown them that they can trust us to protect them from harm."

...they realize... and they trust... and what else, I wonder?

"Listen, I know where you're going with this, and you may believe you're breaking new ground, but you're not," Eddie told him, disrupting Dennis's train of thought. "We've already considered the possibility that they might be an intelligent species. We're scientists. We tested them."

"And?"

"Heidi has the full report on her computer, but here's the short version, as best I remember it: compared to other animals that are native to this planet, the auroch has a disproportionately large brain capacity. However, auroch have no discernible language skills, and they operate on instincts that are so deeply entrenched as to make them untrainable."

Being untrainable did not necessarily equate to lack of intelligence. Angeli was living proof of that. For that matter, so was Sylvain. If these beasts were capable of seeing an advantage in trading their own defensive weapons for the protection offered by beings much smaller and weaker than themselves, then perhaps their demonstrated resistance to being trained had nothing to do with racially inherited instincts, and everything to do with simple unwillingness to cooperate.

Dennis considered for a moment, debating whether this was an argument he wanted to start while all alone with Eddie at the beginning of an hours-long shift. He decided it wasn't, and changed the topic.

"What do you do with all that meat?"

Evidently relieved that the conversation had moved to firmer ground, Eddie dropped his shoulders and relaxed back into his chair. "Some of it we keep, obviously, to feed our own staff, and some goes to the butchers who come out from the towns, north and south, to process the carcass for us, in partial payment for their services. The rest is frozen and shipped to a broker we trust on Galandra, who uses it to fill orders from businesses and eating establishments all over the planet. The broker takes a commission on sales, and deposits the balance into our credit account."

So, the syndicate didn't have to make the kill, cut up the corpse, or handle the money. Everything happened at arm's length, and their hands remained clean. It was a prime example of the way Forrands liked to do business.

"Tell me what's happening on the mainland," Eddie said quietly, breaking into Dennis's glooming thoughts. "That is why you're here, right?"

When Dennis hesitated, he continued, "I've known Sylvain for a long time, long enough to know that Forrands don't reach out to one another unless there's a problem that affects the whole clan. In any case, I very much doubt that any mainlander would consider Galandra a tourist destination."

"You're right. The political situation on the mainland is becoming increasingly volatile. Public opinion is shifting against the Directorate, we've got factions with competing ideologies resorting to violence to make their points, and unless someone does something soon to head it off, there will probably be a revolution. Or maybe a civil war. Either way, the Directorate falls."

"A civil war." Eddie drew the words out as though they had a flavour and he was still deciding whether he liked it. "Or a revolution to overturn the Directorate. Could Galandra be dragged into it?"

"I'm certain you will be. That's why I'm here, looking for help to stop it. I know Heidi and Sylvain were geneticists back on the mainland. Tell me, what was *your* area of scientific expertise?"

"I hope you're not thinking that science can halt a war," Eddie mused.

"No, but technology might."

The other man's lips pursed briefly. "Point taken. I was a biometricist. On the mainland, I assisted with the development of various types of security programming. Here, I'm the reason we can identify and track individual members of the herd."

"Do the Directorate's servers use your security programming?"

"The last time I checked, they did, but that was fifty years ago. I'd have to inspect the code before making a determination. Why? Are you thinking of hacking in?"

Actually, someone's already done that... and for all I know, it might have been you.

"Right now, I'm just trying to get an idea of what's available," said Dennis, draining all emotion from his features as well as his voice.

He was spared having to say more by the sound of a moto stopping outside the door. A moment later, Heidi walked into the building, carrying a cloth sack.

"You forgot your mid-shift meal," she said cheerfully, depositing the sack on the table. "And I'm sorry to cut your visiting time short, but I need to bring Dennis back to the compound. Sylvain wants to talk with him."

Brief though the discussion might have been, it had evidently stirred Eddie's pot. As Dennis followed Heidi outside, he saw thoughtfulness bloom in the other man's eyes.

*   *   *

Sylvain slouched in his chair, discontentment etched onto his face.

Dennis and Heidi sat across the desk from him, with the remains of their midday meal in front of them—a hearty bowl of stew served with steaming hot rolls and tasselberry tea. If he closed his eyes, Dennis could imagine that he was back on Earth, enjoying a mug of warm apple cider.

"This reminds me of home," he remarked after taking a sip.

Heidi's eyebrows arched in surprise. "You're from the marshes? I thought you were born on Earth."

"He was," Sylvain grumped. "So was I, but I didn't get to choose when to leave it." In a muttering voice, he added, "For the good of Humanity... what a load of auroch dung... I was doing them a *favour*, for fuck's sake!"

Heidi leaned forward, her expression stern. "You can feel sorry for yourself another time," she advised him. "Tell Dennis what he needs to know."

"Fine. Not all the members of the syndicate are here on Galandra. There's one on the mainland."

That caught Dennis's attention. "Oh?"

"When we started up the lab, we needed operating capital. A friend recommended that we approach this individual, told us that he had deep pockets and wouldn't demand more than a reasonable share of our business... and she was right. For twenty percent of the lab, he became our silent partner. When the false accusations started flying and we had to close up shop and run, he helped us get away. He also offered to finance our next business venture, in exchange for a piece of the revenue. We took him up on that, made him a member of the syndicate. It was a good deal for him. While we were here doing all the work, he was across the sea, watching his credit balance grow."

"The point is," Heidi added, "he knew all about Stragon First. He may as well have been part of it."

...and they'd been funnelling credits to this individual for the past fifty years...?

His mental alarms shrilling, Dennis asked, "Did he also know about Nestor Quan? About the ultimatum?"

Heidi and Sylvain traded questioning glances.

"Hard to say," Sylvain finally replied. "He's been a silent partner in every sense of the word, for decades. But I suppose anything's possible."

"We know nothing about his political leanings, if that's what you're getting at," said Heidi. "But I don't think they matter. He's all about profit, and he plays the long game. If he's backing a business run by a radical, it's only because he sees it as an investment opportunity, with a payoff somewhere down the line."

Dennis cleared his throat. "In that case, there's something *you* need to know. My investigation of Stragon First led me here, convinced that you were still at the head of it, for a reason. I'd been back-tracing the flow of credits, from Stragon First's account on the mainland—"

"That's not right," Sylvain blurted. "We closed that account decades ago, from Galandra."

"Well, there's no record of such an instruction having been issued, so someone on the mainland must have blocked it," said Dennis. "It's been open this whole time, and receiving deposits from a shared account, also on the mainland, which in turn has been receiving credit payments from your current account here. The shared account was opened nearly seventy years ago, in the names of two business entities—Primus Enterprises and Steadfast. Did you know about this?"

"Yes. It was originally set up as a way to privately fund the lab," Heidi explained. "Our silent partner preferred to keep his business dealings confidential, so he arranged for one of his companies to make occasional credit transfers to the account, and we could withdraw what we needed when we needed it, without ever having to contact him directly."

Dennis frowned. "In other words, he wanted a piece of you but he didn't want to be associated with you. And you weren't suspicious at all?"

Sylvain heaved a rueful sigh. "We couldn't afford to be. It seemed my reputation had preceded me back to Stragon. He was the only investor willing to take a chance on us. On the lab. And I knew that if the rest of the family found out—"

"The system worked, though," Heidi interjected, cutting him off, "so when we moved to Galandra, it made sense to keep the shared account open. It gave us a way to pay him his portion of the syndicate's revenue without anyone discovering that he had a personal connection to a gang of wanted criminals. Except... now you're saying that he took those credits and passed them along to a violent radical group?"

"It was probably his purpose all along," Dennis told her, "made possible by the fact that Sylvain had a deserved reputation for stirring up trouble. When you created Stragon First, you handed him a gift. He could be sure that whatever future misdeeds were committed under that banner, the blame would be directed at you, not him. My presence here is proof of that."

"That slippery son of a—!" Sylvain's face flushed red, and for an unsettling moment it appeared as though he was about to launch himself from his chair. "He's been supporting an extremist group all this time and making it look like *we're* the ones doing it?"

"Now we know where those charges came from," Heidi said, her voice drawn tight with anger. "And why he was so helpful when we decided to leave the mainland. So eager to get us out of the way while continuing the flow of revenue from across the sea. Well, Sylvain, what now? And please, don't give me that tired excuse about the chair keeping you out of the action!"

He drew and expelled a long, shuddering breath. "What do you need, Nephew?"

"Give me his real name, and help me to arrange my transportation back to the mainland. Then just run your business the way you normally would. I've got good people. They'll do the rest."

Sylvain hesitated. "Keeping our connection a secret worked for me as well, because our two families have been enemies on both worlds, for centuries."

"He's a Harris?" That explained a lot.

"Yes. I would prefer that Gilles and Marcel and the others not be made aware of any of this."

"All right. I can't promise, but I'll do my best."

"His name is Lloyd Franklin Harris. But if you decide to question him directly, be advised," Sylvain warned. "As a high-ranking member of one of the founding families, he won't be easy to get to. And he wields some heavy clout of his own."

"Then we'll be evenly matched," Dennis told him grimly. "So do I."

TWELVE
ON DAISY HUB

Olivia was looking much better today. Not what Drew would call relaxed, not yet, but she no longer appeared on the verge of tears, and—the most promising sign yet—she wanted to be put to work.

"Marion says I need something to keep me busy," she said stiffly.

"Marion?" he echoed. "You're on a first name basis with the Doc?"

It had taken Ruby years to get that familiar with the Hub's formidable Supervisor of Medical Services. Doc Ktumba was not an easy person to approach, let alone to befriend.

Olivia shrugged. "And Lydia is on a first name basis with *you*. What's your point?"

Drew was spared from having to reply by the sound of Ruby's voice on the intercomm.

"You've got mail, Chief," she carolled. "It's a message from Stragon, addressed to someone on Earth named Henry Eisner, but in care of you. What do you want done with it?"

Townsend threw a quizzical glance at the commspeaker. "Henry Eisner," he repeated thoughtfully. "I don't know anyone by that name, on Earth or anywhere else."

Olivia gasped and came to attention in her chair. "It's EIS code, Drew. Barry Novak used to sign that name when sending encrypted messages from Ops Control to off-world handlers and mission coordinators. I know because Angeli was the on-site coordinator on Stragon, and she showed me—" Her eyes filling with pain, Olivia added in a lowered and unnaturally calm voice, "It's your call, of course, but I believe you should decrypt it. Someone on-world could need your help."

All by itself, his head began to shake. "We have no one on Stragon. This could be a trick by whoever tried to infiltrate our computer system earlier."

"No one who's still active, you mean. What about Isabela? What if she's in trouble and needs to be extracted? You know it's possible—you've heard what it's like down there." A pause, then, the pitch of her voice rising in desperation, "Aren't you the least bit curious to know what's in that message?"

Truth be told, he was intensely curious about it. However, he couldn't simply decrypt it. In case his suspicions were correct, strict precautions would need to be taken in order to avoid corrupting the Hub's databases, not to mention the VICTOR master files that Olivia had entrusted to him when she had stepped down as the Chief Intelligence Officer of EIS.

Drew pressed the intercomm button on his desk.

"Ruby, would you get O'Malley up here, please, and move that message for Henry Eisner onto a fresh data wafer for him?"

"On it, Chief!" she replied breezily.

Olivia leaned forward in her chair. "If there's anything in that transmission that you think I should know—"

"I'll inform you straightaway," he assured her.

Several minutes later, Olivia was on her way down to Med Services for a counselling session with the Doc, and Robert O'Malley was standing in the doorway to Townsend's office.

"Something I can do for you, Boss?"

"Yes. I received a transmission from Stragon just now, and it's suspicious as hell. Ruby's made a copy for you. You can pick it up from her on your way off the deck."

O'Malley's eyes widened briefly. "So, what's the plan?" he asked, dropping onto the chair Olivia had just vacated. "You want me to sanitize this message before you open it? Make sure there are no pesky AIs embedded in the code?"

"At the very least. Use the segregated server that was set up to scan the Directorate's backup files. And since the contents may be for my eyes only, I don't want Trager to know that I've received this, not until after I've read it and decided how to proceed."

"That won't be a problem, but what about Walt and Lydia? The server is in their work space. As soon as I boot it up, they're going to have questions. And if I move it to somewhere private, they're bound to notice it's missing. Then they'll *definitely* want to know what's going on."

"If they ask, answer them truthfully, but keep as much information as possible to yourself."

"I think I can manage that. All right, then!" The ratkeeper bounced to his feet. "I'll get on it immediately and report back to you with either good news or bad news."

*   *   *

Two hours later, O'Malley was standing on the threshold of Townsend's office again.

"We ran every test we could think of, Boss."

Townsend glanced up from his screen. "We?" he said curiously.

O'Malley shrugged. "Walt Garfield asked the right questions."

"All right. And...?"

"It's a carrier transmission concealing an encrypted message, and as far as we can determine, it's clean." He stepped inside and handed the data wafer back to Townsend.

Drew stared at him across the desk. "As far as you can determine?" he echoed quietly.

The other man shrugged. "We didn't parse the underlying code, in case it's eyes only."

"Since when has something like a security level ever stopped you from hacking into a file, O'Malley?"

"Since Walt Garfield became involved in the exercise. He apparently draws the line at opening other people's personal mail."

"Even when the addressee has given permission for you to do it?"

"Problem is, you're not the addressee—Henry Eisner is. Or rather, Barry Novak is. This message is clearly intended for him, by way of Daisy Hub."

"That's only because the sender doesn't realize there's been a change of management at Earth Intelligence."

That in itself was suspicious, Drew realized. According to Olivia, the only two people still on Stragon who'd even been aware that the EIS existed were Isabela Bakshi and Dennis Forrand, neither one of whom should currently have a reason to reach out to Ops Control on Earth.

"...and I have to say," O'Malley was remarking, "considering Walt's own history of hacking and espionage, for the EIS among others, the man is burdened with a truly paradoxical streak of morality."

Raising a hand to pause the discussion, Drew opened his desk drawer and pressed the button to activate the privacy field around his office.

Then he continued, leaning back into his chair, "Nonetheless, would I be correct in assuming that you can probably give me a fairly accurate summary of what this encrypted underlying message contains?"

O'Malley flashed him a mischievous smile and dropped onto one of the guest chairs. "You know me so well, Boss."

"Uh-huh. Talk to me, kid."

"The sender of the transmission is Isabela Bakshi—or at least, that's how they're representing themselves. They're saying that our old friend Dennis Forrand is mounting at least two ops on Stragon. The one he's assigned to Bakshi, along with a partner of Forrand's choosing, is to turn the Terran refugees against the Directorate. The reason she feels Novak should know about this is that it's an impossible mission and she suspects it's meant to be a decoy, distracting everyone from what Forrand actually has in mind."

"Which is...?"

"She claims to have no idea. For all we know, this message could be a lure to get you to send those EIS agents back to Stragon. But if it's legit and he's decided to muck around with Stragori politics, it could destabilize the situation even further, putting millions of Terrans in danger."

Damn!

"Does the sender provide any details about the second op?" Drew asked.

"No. He's keeping her out of the loop. At least, that's what she's claiming. What do you want me to do with this, Boss? Should we pass it along to 'Uncle Henry' so Novak can deal with it?"

"If it *is* for real, there's nothing he can do for her anymore. Daisy Hub is the new EIS headquarters, and I have nine trained agents at my disposal. That makes *me* 'Uncle Henry' now."

"In that case," said O'Malley, "perhaps it would be a good idea to send Isabela Bakshi a carefully worded reply, just to let her know she's not alone down there."

"...and see what comes back to us before making any decisions?"

The ratkeeper was looking positively impish by now. "Great minds, Boss."

Dear Uncle Henry,

From the tone of your last letter, you probably aren't expecting to hear from me again, but I miss you and Cousin Selma and feel that we really need to mend our fences, so to speak. And since I was the one who decided to distance myself, I'm taking this first step at repairing our relationship.

I think about the family a great deal. I hope Cousin Grace is happy in her new home, and that Grandma is having fun taking snaps of it, and that you and Aunt Matilda are both healthy and doing well.

I am managing here. Teaching is time-consuming, but I've found a rewarding hobby. I'm trying to knit a blanket for an old friend.

Unfortunately, I've lost the tenth and final skein of yarn required and am having no success at matching the colour. My friend has urged me to unravel my work so far and try a different pattern. The one he says he prefers looks extremely complicated. I doubt that I will be able to complete it. Still, for V's sake I will make an effort.

Please give my best regards to everyone back on Earth and let me know that you've received this in the spirit in which I now send it.

Your loving niece,
Isabela

Olivia's eyes widened as she read the text on Drew's screen.

Glancing up to meet his steady gaze, she said, "This is the covering message? It's full of code."

"That's why I wanted you to see it," he told her. "There's another encrypted message underneath it. The VICTOR code is telling me the encryption was done using one of our personalized devices. However, there are ways to foil a DNA key, and the source of this transmission makes me suspicious."

She frowned. "So, you need me to verify that the sender is actually Isabela, and that there was no duress involved."

"You two go back a long way, and I was not present when you were extracted, so yes, before taking any action I want to be doubly certain it's not the bait in a con or a trap."

"All right, then," she said with a sigh, and returned her attention to the screen. "These names—Cousin Grace and Grandma—are veiled references to a previous encrypted message that I know Angeli received from Novak. She showed it to me while I was on Stragon, but only because she believed that I was still the Chief Intelligence Officer and therefore entitled to see it."

"Was Isabela entitled to see it?"

Olivia pursed and unpursed her lips. "Technically, no. However, Isabela and Angeli's history together goes back even further than mine does with either of them. Isabela and her brother and husband were all trained by Earth Intelligence, then sent to Stragon to support the mission that Angeli was coordinating on site. After Vikram died, Isabela and Angeli became apartment-mates. Would Angeli share eyes-only communications with Isabela? I think she might, under certain conditions. She always did what her gut said was the right thing, whether or not it conformed with her orders from above. And she trusted Isabela completely, as do I, to keep sensitive information a secret."

"And Novak knows all this?"

"As mission coordinator, Angeli would have sent him regular updates. Besides that, though, they'd butted heads more than once back on Earth over her problem with following the rules."

"So, if Isabela thought she was communicating with Novak, the fact that she was referring to messages he'd sent Angeli in confidence would not necessarily raise any red flags for him?"

"No, I believe he would see it as corroboration of her identity."

"All right. If the first paragraph is a request to reopen a line of communication and the second is confirmation of the sender's ID, what's this about a 'rewarding hobby' in the third paragraph?"

"The reason Isabela stayed behind was to get justice for

Carlos and Vikram. That's the only reward that truly matters to her. She's saying here that she's found a way to prove that their deaths were wrongful, and it has to do with 'an old friend'... but she has no old friends on Stragon, so..." Olivia inhaled sharply. "That's not true. There is one. Dennis Forrand. She must have made a deal with him in exchange for his help. Ten skeins... there were nine agents at the extraction point... Angeli would have been the tenth but she was... lost..." Olivia's chin was wobbling.

"...and Forrand wanting her to unravel her knitting and change patterns," Drew said, picking up the thread, "that's got to be code for dissociating herself from the EIS and throwing in with him and whatever scheme he's cooked up... which she has doubts about, evidently, but 'for V's sake' she'll give it her best shot...?"

"For Vikram's sake," Olivia said, her eyes shining with tears. "She's only doing this so her husband can rest in peace. Isabela was hoping that I would see this, Drew. She wanted me to understand, so she wrote the third paragraph for me."

And she'd sent the underlying encrypted message to whoever was wearing Uncle Henry's shoes, so that *he* would understand and—hopefully—lend a hand.

Clearly, it was time to take a closer look at that part of the transmission. And then, perhaps, to come up with a scheme of his own.

O'Malley hadn't left out much. Sitting alone in his office, Drew read the decrypted message from Isabela Bakshi as it scrolled upwards on his screen. He'd never had any personal contact with Dennis Forrand—in retrospect, it was probably a blessing—but after hearing about his machinations from Olivia, Drew wasn't surprised to learn that their deceased grandfather had sprung back to life on Stragon and was apparently up to all his old tricks.

...or as many as he *could* get up to when he no longer had the weight of the Earth High Council behind him. One thing hadn't changed, though: his politician's habit of appearing to have one foot on each side of an issue, making him difficult to read and damn near impossible to predict.

"You wanted to see me?" came Olivia's voice from Drew's doorway.

Glancing up, he gestured to her to enter. Then he leaned back in his chair and said, "You were Forrand's protégée. As such, you knew him better than anyone. I need your opinion on something. Please, sit," he added with a wave at the two guest chairs on the other side of his desk.

She hesitated briefly, then perched on the edge of the one nearest the door.

"Can you think of any reason for Dennis Forrand to want the Terrans on Stragon to turn against the Directorate? Or to seem to turn against it?"

"No! It was Gervais who—" Her face lost two shades of colour. "He said—" She swallowed hard. "He said that destroying the Directorate would avert a civil war by removing the barrier between the two factions, but in order for there to be healing, neither faction could be held responsible for it."

Neither faction? That left only one group to blame—the Terran refugees on Stragon. This plan had a disturbingly familiar ring to it. There was an AI claiming to be the backed-up consciousness of Gervais Forrand sitting on a memory bloc safely locked away on the Hub, along with copies of a series of unverified documents designed to provoke an angry Terran response.

Drew snapped to attention in his chair. "Gervais Forrand told you this?"

"No, it was someone posing as Gervais Forrand. Gilles said—"

"Gilles?"

"Gilles Forrand. Dennis's father. Our great-grandparents picked me up at the spaceport when I arrived on Stragon. Gilles told me Gervais wanted to meet me. He pointed out what an honour it was to have a face-to-face audience with one of the Directors. I had no idea at the time that they weren't flesh-and-blood people. I thought it would be an in-person meeting. Instead, a young-looking face appeared on a screen."

It was Con Game 101. Alarms should have been blaring at the back of her mind from the second the image resolved.

Doing his best to sound only casually interested, Drew remarked, "That must have made you suspicious."

"It did, but I decided to hear him out. He said the Directorate was a sham, that being digital had driven most of the Directors into suicidal depression or straight-out insanity and the ones who didn't want to die had already backed themselves up somewhere. He wanted me to organize a mission to destroy or fatally corrupt the server housing the Directorate. He told me he'd already begun laying the groundwork for unrest among the Terran population that would make a terrorist attack believable, and he promised that Dennis would help us fake our deaths and escape once the job was done. The impostor wanted my answer right away, but I insisted on checking with Dennis before I committed to anything."

"A smart move. And what did our duplicitous bastard of a grandfather have to say?"

She threw him a reproving look. "Enough to convince me that he believed this Gervais manifestation was on the level, and that what it was planning for the Terrans on Stragon would be disastrous for all the Humans on both worlds. He was confident that I would agree with him about that, and when I told him I did, he offered to help me execute an alternate operation."

"So you're telling me Dennis was *against* fomenting unrest among the Terrans," Drew said.

"Dead set against it," she confirmed. "And his mother offered to help me as well, if I decided to turn Gervais down. Dennis was actively working against Gervais's plan. I can't imagine why he would—"

"—turn it to his own purposes? Maybe it's a decoy, to divert attention from something else he's doing," Drew offered. "Or perhaps he's working a con and needs to establish his credibility."

"And Isabela is all alone in the middle of it," Olivia murmured brokenly. "I shouldn't have left her there."

All right, enough of this, he decided.

"First of all, you didn't leave her—she chose to stay. The woman is far from helpless, Olivia, as witnessed by the fact that she managed to get word to me. Second, your responsibility for any EIS agents on Stragon, including Isabela Bakshi, ended the day you handed the VICTOR codes over to me. Once you'd requested the extraction, whatever happened or didn't happen while it was in progress fell on my shoulders, not yours. And third, Isabela is not alone. According to her message, she's working with a partner, someone Forrand provided for her and evidently trusts, and both she and the partner are concerned that the mission may be impossible."

After a moment of uncomfortable silence, Olivia said stiffly, "That's not a lot of intel. Has there been any further communication from her?"

"I expect she's waiting for a response from Uncle Henry."

"And... will she receive one?"

"Do I intend to reactivate her, you mean, and have a mole inside Forrand's organization? Because—make no mistake—that is what a reply from me would mean. Do you believe that's what she wants?"

Olivia paused, considering his question. "I have no idea what she wants," she said at last. "However, the EIS's mission is to learn and preserve the truth, and when appropriate, disseminate it. That's hard to do from the sidelines."

"Agreed. However, I withdrew all EIS presence from Stragon at your and Angeli's request because there was evidence that our agents there had been compromised. Until there's a drastic change in that situation, it would be foolish to send them back to that world. Isabela is in place, presumably with an unbroken cover, and the last thing I want to do is jeopardize it. I'll have to think some more about the best way to contact her."

Getting to her feet, Olivia warned, "Don't wait too long. People who get drawn into Dennis Forrand's schemes... they can get lost. If it hadn't been for Novak and Bruni Patel, I might never have found myself again."

That said, she walked out the door, leaving Townsend alone at his desk.

THIRTEEN
ISABELA

The only way Isabela was going to be able to sneak away to the bunker was by going there directly from school. That had now become clear to her. Fortunately, Quinian (and the Directorate) would be unable to track her using the Thryggian technology Dennis Forrand had stolen. Joanne was wearing the only monitoring gear Isabela needed to worry about during the day, and the surveillance technology distributed across the island was easy enough for her to avoid in the dark. So, if she told Quin she would be working late to prepare for his next audit of her assessments, he would have to believe her. At least, she hoped he would.

The following morning, she packed some additional clothing and a couple of glow-rods into her tote bag before opening the door to her bedroom. Quinian sat in his usual place at the dining table, contemplating a plate of leftovers from yesterday's dinner.

Evidently, they were out of cereal. In fact, they were

nearly out of a lot things, including the rest of yesterday's casserole, which she'd planned to serve that evening. Isabela had forgotten how much a man could eat at one sitting. She would have to find her breakfast elsewhere today. Fortunately, there were plenty of snacks in the refrigeration cabinet at school.

"It seems one of us is going to have to do some grocery shopping," she said briskly, "and since you're still on leave and I have a full day of work ahead of me..."

He shrugged a *why not?* "Sure. I'll try to take care of it sometime this morning. And I have a couple of meetings lined up on the mainland for later in the day, so I hope you don't mind eating dinner alone tonight."

Isabela no longer gave any thought to Quinian's meetings. Like the activities of the operatives whose special orders she had filled for the past five years, they could not be her concern. Not as long as she had students to plan for and care about. The children always came first.

So, did she mind that he would be late returning to the apartment? As long as he'd first restocked the kitchen, not a bit.

At school, Isabela spent hours at her computer, feverishly completing the assessments that she'd promised would be done before she came home that evening. The time passed quickly. The end of the school day was upon her almost before she realized it.

"Did you manage to finish everything?" Joanne asked as they were helping the children get ready to leave.

Isabela didn't answer right away. Dismissal was a two-teacher job, demanding their full attention.

Hats, jackets, and outdoor shoes had to be put on and fastened. The homework and personal belongings (including unfinished snacks) of each student needed to be sorted and packed into their own schoolbag. Anything that wasn't going out the classroom door had to be stored in a designated locker. (A place for everything, and everything in its place, as the Earth saying went.)

"Not quite done yet. I'll be staying here a while longer," Isabela lied.

In fact, as soon as she knew they were all on their way, she would have to set out for the Wilderness Zone. Normally she would wait for dusk, when it was easier to conceal her identity from the monitoring securecams. However, she didn't know when Quinian would be getting back to the apartment, and being there to greet him when he arrived would spare her from having to field a lot of prying questions.

Isabela observed from the doorway as Joanne shepherded the double line of children from the schoolyard to the sidewalk, their brightly coloured backpacks and head coverings bouncing in time with their footsteps. The little parade turned left and crossed the road, headed toward the recreational complex where their grownups would come to fetch them home in time for dinner. Delivering these students into the charge of a second shift of teachers for what was basically another entire day's worth of educational activities was Joanne's final task of the afternoon. After that, she was free to pursue her own personal interests. Lucky her.

Isabela stifled a sigh. Learning was supposed to be an adventure, especially for the young. That was what she'd been trying to provide for these little ones for the past five years, with field trips, guest experts, fun fairs, theme days, plays and concerts... and Quinian had opposed her at every turn. Why did education have to be such a pressurized, non-stop *chore* on Stragon?

"Lady Bakshi?" said a man's voice somewhere behind her.

It had come from inside the school. Isabela froze in place for a moment, forcing her lungs to accept air.

"Lady Bakshi, are you there?" This was said with urgent undertones.

Isabela knew the families of all of her students, and Joanne's parents as well. Since none of them ever addressed her as "Lady Bakshi", she could be certain that the voice she was now hearing did not belong to any of them, or even to a Terran.

Cautiously, she leaned out into the empty schoolyard and glanced around. Then she swung the door shut, locked it, drew as deep a breath as she was able, and took several firm steps into the middle of the classroom. "I am here," she called out. "Where are *you*?"

"That's not important right now. Please listen, because we don't have much time. I'm contacting you at Dr. Quinian's insistence. Before he passed out, he said you would know."

He passed out?

All at once the floor was tilting beneath her feet.

Reaching out to a student's chair for support, she said faintly, "What would I know?"

"I wish I could tell you. He fell unconscious in mid-sentence. I've called the med techs. They're on their way right now."

"And you have no idea why he passed out?"

"No. He was just sitting there having some pie and kaffy, and then suddenly he was gasping and clutching his chest, and a second later he slid off his chair onto the floor."

Isabela's thoughts were racing. His chest. His heart. He must have thought he was dying. And *she* was the person that he demanded be notified? What did he think she could possibly do—?

No, she realized with a start. If he thought he'd been poisoned, it wasn't what she could do. It was what she knew. Or, to be more accurate, it was what he'd somehow found out that she knew.

If Quinian's guess was correct, time really was of the essence.

With a sinking feeling in her own chest, Isabela hurried to her office and activated the comm screen on her desk. It was blank—this connection was audio only.

"Are you calling me from where it happened?" she demanded.

"Yes. Why?"

"Because I think I know why he wanted me involved. I need to see what he was eating and drinking."

"Keep this comm channel open," the caller said. "The med techs just arrived. As soon as they've left, I'll show you a visual."

Minutes passed, in total silence. He'd muted the sound. The terrible feeling in her chest hit the pit of her stomach and bounced back up to her throat as she sat tensely staring at the featureless screen.

At last, an image appeared. Isabela was looking at the top of a table for two in what appeared to be a high-end eating establishment. Where Quinian had supposedly been sitting, she saw a mug of dark brown liquid and a small plate holding most of a fruit-filled pastry. Either one could have been tampered with before it was served.

Or afterward. The white linen tablecloth was pristine and

the setting was orderly. Even the serviette sat neatly folded beside his unused eating utensils.

"Is Security present?" she asked tersely. Chasing justice for Vikram had taught Isabela a lot about investigative procedures. Poisoning was a crime, and protecting a crime scene from contamination was a prime concern.

A pause, then, "You're speaking with them."

"Good. Now I need you to show me the kitchen."

"I'm on my way there."

The video image tilted upward, then swayed back and forth as he moved. This was definitely an upscale restaurant, she noted. The ceiling was parchment-coloured, decorated with a pattern of calligraphic swoops and whorls that led the eye from one sculpted chandelier to the next.

"Just out of curiosity, Lady Bakshi, are *you* with Security? Or Forensics? Because your manner is very professional."

Professional. That was man-code for bossy. Involuntarily, she smiled. "Neither one. I'm just a biochemist specializing in botanical poisons."

He grunted a surprised syllable.

"All right, I'm in the kitchen," he told her. "What should I be looking for?"

"Just show me what is there. If I spot anything suspicious, I'll let you know."

Commercial kitchens were apparently the same no matter which world they were on—stainless steel canyons lined with cutting blocks, cooking surfaces, and upper and lower oven doors. Pots and pans hung from neat rows of hooks overhead, while cooking utensils sprouted like bizarre floral arrangements from cylindrical containers set here and there.

The caller strolled the length of the work area, panning

the video eye to left and right. For several minutes, Isabela saw nothing that set off her mental alarms. Then her attention was snagged by a flash of orange.

"Stop!" she exclaimed. "What is that in the far right corner of the room?"

"You mean the flowers?"

He turned and walked toward them until they filled the screen. A plain round vase sat atop a small utility table. Peering over the rim of the vase were four bright orange blossoms with frilly petals.

Oh, no...!

"That looks like damselflower," she said, frowning.

"I gather it doesn't belong in a kitchen?"

"It should not even be on the mainland. Damselflower grows wild in the toxic soil of the island."

"Are you saying it's poisonous?"

"The stem and blossoms are safe to handle, but not to ingest. If any of this was in Quinian's kaffy—!" She paused for a moment, then went on in a rush of words, "It interferes with the electrical impulses of the heart, causing arrhythmia. The effect is temporary, but if the dose is high enough it can stop the heart completely, or make it beat so fast that it explodes. The Medical Services centre where Dr. Quinian is being taken needs to be alerted."

"I'll make sure they're informed. He can't have swallowed that much, though. He took just two sips of his kaffy, and he'd barely tasted his pie."

"How quickly does this poison take effect?" a third, female voice chimed in.

"Almost immediately," Isabela replied.

"Then it had to have been administered *after* he entered the restaurant," commented her caller, evidently addressing the female he was with. "Get a forensics team on site."

"Right away, sir," came her response.

"Is Security treating this as an attempted murder?" Isabela asked, fighting to get each word out in a normal tone of voice.

"It's an attempted something, that's for sure," he replied. "And in case we need your special expertise again, tell me, which laboratory are you associated with, Lady Bakshi?"

"Oh, I'm not currently working as a biochemist. That was my Terran profession. On Stragon I'm a schoolteacher. Quinian—I mean *Dr.* Quinian—is my district supervisor."

She noticed a sudden change in the tenor of the call as most of the background noise cut out.

"Now then, Lady Bakshi—how would a schoolteacher happen to know so much about the effects of this poison?"

Instantly, her guard went up, along with her hackles. "I may not be a practising chemist on your world, but I am still a scientist," she informed him stiffly. "I began studying the native flora as soon as we arrived here five years ago."

"That explains how you could recognize the flower, not how you knew what it would do to Dr. Quinian. Have you been dabbling in a little illicit experimentation, by any chance?"

He was veering dangerously close to the truth. Isabela let her anger out to play.

"Oh! You think Stragon is the only place in the galaxy with poisonous plants?" she demanded haughtily. "Earth has so many that some of them even have the word 'poison' in their names—poison oak, poison ivy, poison sumac. I've catalogued all of them, along with their DNA profiles and their effects on the Human body. Some have proven useful for medical treatments, and one of those, *digitalis purpurea,* commonly called foxglove, has a profile almost identical to your Stragori damselflower. So, I studied it as any scientist would, meaning that I also reviewed the medical files of people who had been treated for exposure to the toxin. And unless Dr. Quinian's biology is alien to both Earth and Stragon, which I sincerely doubt—"

"—the poison should affect him in predictable ways. Of course," he cut in. "My apologies, Lady Bakshi. But I'm sure you can understand—"

"Is this a formal interrogation?" she said, snapping each word at him like a whip. "Am I now a person of interest in this case?"

"Not yet," he replied mildly.

"Then how dare you question my ethics when you haven't even the courtesy to show me your face or tell me your name?"

After a pause, he continued, "This discussion is now off the record. It's obvious that Quin trusts you with his life. I appreciate that, because he and I are best friends, and I care very much about his safety. But make no mistake, if our forensic analysis gives me reason to believe that you had anything to do with what just happened to him, then you *will* be a person of interest, and you may well regret your wish to see my face and know my name. Am I making myself clear, Lady Bakshi?"

Isabela did not respond well to threats, veiled or otherwise. She threw her shoulders back and tilted her chin defiantly. "Quite clear," she spat, glaring at the frozen image of damselflowers on her screen.

"Thank you for your help. We'll be in touch."

Silence. He'd ended the call. The screen went dark, and Isabela went into mental freefall.

They would be in touch? What was that supposed to mean?

With a numbness inside her that slowed her movements, Isabela turned off the lights, put on her jacket, and went back to the apartment. She reheated what was left of the casserole, chewing and swallowing her dinner without even registering the taste of it. Then she made herself a cup of tea and took it into the living room, where she sat, and sipped, and stared at the alien tracking device for at least an hour.

This had not been her plan for the evening. She'd been hoping to get some answers. Instead, a whole flock of questions had hatched and were flying around inside her head.

How had Quinian known about her familiarity with botanical poisons? She'd never shared information with him about her past, nor about her work for the EIS. Had Dennis found out about it somehow and revealed the information to him at one of their "meetings"? To what end?

For that matter, how would Quinian even have realized that he'd been poisoned? Or had he? Perhaps she was on the wrong track entirely and his reason for wanting her notified had had nothing to do with poisoning and everything to do with the stolen technology sitting on her coffee table right now. Was the presence of damselflower in that kitchen a coincidental health violation and nothing more? Had Quinian just had a garden-variety heart attack, and had Isabela blown her cover by assuming incorrectly that it was something else? She had, after all, been talking to a stranger who claimed to be a Security officer—a fairly high-ranking one if other officers were calling him 'sir'.

...except that all Security officers were supposed to identify themselves by name and rank when speaking with members of the public. This one knew how many sips of kaffy Quinian had taken, so he must have been either watching him carefully from very close by, or actually sitting across the table from him. Who was this man who'd apparently been at the restaurant with "Quin" and refused to so much as show her his face on the screen?

He'd promised to contact her again. Had that been a threat? Was she being set up to take the blame for what had happened? Or was Quinian's friend in fact a radical who planned to blackmail her into filling "special orders" for one of the fringe groups? Was that why Quinian had been poisoned in the first place? She tried to think of any other reason there might be to target a mid-level bureaucrat in the Directorate's Office of Education, but came up empty.

Isabela now had something other than Quinian's fate to occupy the rest of her evening—the drafting of a second message to "Uncle Henry". She hated the thought of abandoning Stragon before she'd exposed the truth about Vikram's death, but under the circumstances, she might have no other choice.

"Uncle Henry" hadn't yet had time to respond to her first transmission.

Wherever he was, whether on Earth or on Daisy Hub, she certainly hoped he was listening.

FOURTEEN
ANGELI

Harlan Scott in Salty Springs. Car crash.
Geraldo Mendez in Ryderville. House fire.
Bjorn Gustavsen in Whitewater. Fall from a height.
Darcy Gates in Overton. Fall on the stairs.
Irina DeSalle in Grassy Meadows. Fall on the stairs.
Herman Kronen in Cedarvale. Cardiac arrest.
Leesa Punjabi in Brightlake. Cardiac arrest.

Angeli sat up all night, fully dressed, waiting impatiently for the sun to rise and feeling utterly helpless.

She knew why those seven people had been targeted. So did Krall, she was certain of it. But she also had a hunch regarding their cause of death. Co-tenanting with Isabela Bakshi had taught Angeli a thing or two about botanical toxins, and those two cardiac arrests had set red flags to waving inside her brain.

If her suspicion was correct, all seven of them had been poisoned by something the local warders were unlikely to stumble onto on their own. Helping them to see it without blowing her cover and maybe the entire mission, however—that was going to be a trick, as Derwin would say. Fortunately, Angeli had a hunch about that as well. But she would have to get Krall on board with it, as soon as possible.

At last, she could hear Lyla moving around. Angeli darted out into the hallway to intercept her.

"You're up early," the other woman observed placidly, on her way to the stairs. "Good. You can help me make breakfast."

"I need to speak to Ben. It's urgent." Angeli hastened to catch up to her, nearly losing her footing on the top step.

Lyla paused long enough to steady her, then resumed her own descent. "I have his personal commcode, but I promised not to use it except in an emergency," she said over her shoulder. "So, if this can wait until later—"

"It can't wait," Angeli blurted. "People are being murdered, Lyla, and I think I know how to stop it."

Bead-bright eyes gazed up at her from the bottom of the stairs. "You mean those seven suspicious deaths? You have proof that it's murder?"

"Not yet. There's someone I need to contact on the island. An expert. And I need Ben's help to do it."

"All right, but first things first. I'll make the call right after we've had breakfast."

"Can we invite Ben over here for breakfast instead? It will save time."

Lyla paused, her lips pursed. "I don't like to wake him up... but if it's really important..."

"It is! Trust me, it is, and we can't afford to lose even a minute. Please!"

Apparently, Ben hadn't slept much either. He arrived at

Lyla's house, looking grumpy and rumpled, just as the water in the tea kettle was coming to a boil.

Breakfast on Borea was something a Terran would have recognized—a flatbread loaded with slices of sausage and pieces of vegetable, all smothered under a blanket of melted cheese and washed down with cups of strong, dark tea. While Lyla set about serving it out, Angeli told Krall what she needed him to do.

For a while, they ate in uncomfortable silence. Then he sat back, evidently coming to a decision. Judging from the stern expression on his face, it was *No*.

"You're asking me to bring in a Terran consultant on an investigation that I'm not even part of. Have you any idea how many toes I would be stepping on?" he demanded. "I'd be lucky if all I got was demoted. Besides that, Continental Security has been watching the proceedings, itching for any excuse to elbow the District Warders aside and take over. Why should I risk doing something that would give them one?"

"Because she can prove that those seven people were poisoned without giving away the—" Angeli caught herself just in time. "—the other thing they have in common."

Krall paused with his fork halfway to his mouth. His eyes widened briefly with surprise, then narrowed. "You're sure about that?"

She heard the warning in his voice but went barrelling ahead anyway.

"Absolutely," she declared. "She's a botanical chemist specializing in plants with medicinal properties, including the ability to affect the heart rate."

Scowling, he came to sitting attention on his chair. "And this Terran scientist of yours is an expert on *Stragori* vegetation? The kind growing on all three land masses?"

"She's been studying it for years, so yes."

Not daring to say more for fear of blowing her cover, Angeli met his gaze, then cast a meaningful glance at Lyla, who stood with her back to them, pouring herself a second cup of tea. When she looked back at him, Angeli saw a *click* of comprehension in Krall's eyes.

"Well, we've got some plant experts of our own in Westgrove," he said. "Let's go visit one and see what *they've* got to say."

"You sound awfully sure of yourself, Eva Moss," he reproved her once they were in his vehicle and on the road, "and you nearly gave the game away back there. What makes you so certain that poison is the cause of death in all seven cases?"

"It's the only thing that makes sense. Every one of those people was working for Dennis Forrand. He's always had a knack for making enemies that are just as devious and powerful as he is. Clearly, one of them found out he had an intel network in Borea and set out to cripple it by eliminating a whole group of his contacts, using a weapon that they were sure would baffle a bunch of throwbacks like the objectors up north."

"Something organic that they figured no one would think to test for because its source is not native to Borea," he said thoughtfully. "You're right—it does make sense."

"You knew they were Dennis's contacts, even before the Skinners broadcast their names, didn't you? And something must have tipped off the District warders as well that the deaths were all related, or they wouldn't have joined forces to investigate them. What was it? Has Dennis's operation been exposed?"

"No, it hasn't. Your mission is safe." A pause, then, "The investigation is being kept confidential, so I probably shouldn't be telling you this, but it was the forensic medical specialists in each town who made the connections. They all noted something strange during their respective post-mortem exams and shared their findings with one another."

"And...?"

"And the District Warder-in-Chief put together a task force to look into the matter and issued a statement to the media that would satisfy public curiosity without compromising the ongoing inquiry."

"It was a false statement?"

"It was incomplete. Accurate on its face, but..."

"...a little behind on the facts," she supplied. "Which were...?"

"You're not going to let this go, are you? All right," he continued reluctantly, "but only because you seem to know it already. Five of the reported causes of death are wrong. No one died from a car crash or a fall. They were dead of cardiac failure before it happened.

"A healthy heart doesn't simply stop. Or explode. Not without some outside help. That's the puzzle piece that's been missing... and that your botanical expert may be able to provide."

All at once Angeli became aware that they were surrounded by trees.

"Where are you taking me?" she asked.

"To the nearest comm nexus, so we can transmit a message to the island. That is what you said you wanted to do, right?"

"I'm confused. Back at Lyla's you said you wouldn't call her in because it would be interfering in the investigation."

"And I'm not going to call her in. You are."

"Really! On whose authority?"

"Be patient, Eva Moss," he replied. "You'll see soon enough."

Angeli hadn't been expecting this. Automatically, her hand went to the side of her trousers, where she kept Dennis's two data wafers pinned inside a hidden pocket. It felt flat. Then she remembered that she'd put her EIS encrypter, along with the data card reader, in a back corner of Kate's former closet. *Damn!*

"This isn't going to work. The message will need to be encrypted."

"That won't be a problem," he told her. "I've got a plan."

A plan. Right. With luck, it wouldn't involve blowing Isabela's cover, or her own. Angeli gazed ahead and saw nothing but trees, their long leafy branches overhanging the trail like a sheltering canopy. It appeared the vehicle was remaining inside the forested barrier, not crossing through it but rather following its curving path around the town.

"The comm nexus is located inside the Wilderness Zone?" she said wonderingly.

"Well-protected from the prying eyes of the surveillance satellites, yes," he confirmed.

Krall stopped the vehicle on the edge of a small clearing containing a shed built of rough-hewn planks, with a metal pipe chimney sticking up from the roof and a neatly stacked woodpile alongside one outer wall.

"We're here," he announced, an improbable note of pride

in his voice.

Schooling her facial expression, Angeli got out of the land car and followed him inside. This dumpy little place was camouflage, she told herself. It *had* to be.

The interior of the shed was a single room only slightly better furnished than the cell in which she'd spent her first night on Borea. In addition to the cot with a pillow and neatly folded brown and blue blanket, it also had a wooden table and chair, and a pot-bellied iron stove with a well-used tea kettle sitting on it. And... there was a door in the far wall that instantly aroused her curiosity.

"Open it," said Krall, a smile tugging at the corners of his mouth.

She strode past him and twisted the knob, and the door swung silently on its hinges, revealing a tiny landing at the top of a flight of wooden stairs that were just as rough-hewn as the rest of this little cabin. With a glance over her shoulder, she followed them down into a high-ceilinged basement two or three times the size of the room above it. This space immediately filled with light, showing her a comm display of impressive, even intimidating complexity.

Krall was close behind her.

"This is our nexus," he said. "Each district has one. The hardware was purchased for us by a benefactor about twenty years ago and smuggled up here in pieces from the southern continent."

Twenty years ago? Then the benefactor had probably been Dennis Forrand. He'd used the same strategy to set up Veggieville, back on Earth.

"So, what are you thinking of telling your Terran botanist friend?" Krall asked.

"It depends on who's liable to read this before she does.

They'll know where the transmission originated, and I can't risk giving away my location, so—"

"You won't be. Giving away your location, I mean. Not unless you want to."

She stared a question at him.

With a sly grin, he replied, "We're far from backwards up here, technologically speaking. You don't need to know the details, only that a message sent using this system can appear to originate from anywhere on the planet that the sender desires, and it can't be traced back to them."

"Really!" Angeli thought for a moment. "That's fine for the message, but what about the response? Can't that be back-traced? I don't want to compromise Isabela either."

"Then give her someone else to respond to," he suggested. "After all, isn't the whole point of this to get information into the hands of the people who are investigating the suspicious deaths?"

Of course. Angeli wanted to kick herself for not realizing it herself.

"Who is the top forensics officer on Borea?" she asked.

"Sharma Dorel. She oversees medical matters for the Continental Council. If she believes the original contact was made by one of the district forensic specialists, she'll pass the information along to all of them."

That certainly simplified things. Angeli sat down at the keyboard Krall indicated and began drafting the text.

By the time Krall returned her to Lyla's house, Angeli had conceived of a way she could fulfill her mission without leaving Westgrove. The timing would be important, though. If Dennis had given her a year, it probably meant he had extensive preparations of his own to make. In the meanwhile, she would just have to bide her time, doing all the other things he'd specified in his instructions to her on the data wafer. Such as:

Getting to know the locals. Acclimatizing herself to the northern way of life. Fitting in.

Most important, though, was becoming someone they felt they could trust, so that when it was time to take action, they would follow Eva Moss's lead.

FIFTEEN
DENNIS

The next supply run to the nearest urban district wasn't for another six days, and Dennis needed to return to the mainland as quickly as possible. For double the usual fee, a copter pilot agreed to brave the airspace over the grasslands and fetch him back to the avport at the town of Lavista the following day. There, he could see about chartering an avcraft with sufficient range to cross the sea.

Eddie had been putting it mildly when he said Galandra was not a popular tourist destination. One day in the far future, that might change, after the wild rumours and horrific tales had had a chance to crumble away, leaving a solid core of apocryphal legend. Domesticating the auroch was just the beginning of the process. Eventually, the mountains would acquire a living past, portrayed as slow-moving giants turned to stone by the light of the sun; and the real giants, the huge animals that now wandered the plains or lurked in the wetlands, would die out or be killed off, leaving only romanticized memories behind.

At least, that was what had happened on Earth. Every Earthborn child became fascinated with dinosaurs at some point. Some Humans even remained fascinated with them—studying their fossilized bones, drawing them as they might have appeared, turning them into toys and entertainments.

At dinner the night before Dennis's departure, all the conversation turned on the coming auroch migration. Preoccupied with his own plans, Dennis listened with half an ear as the Firsters talked about the timing of the move, the preparations that still needed to be made for it, and a variety of possible outcomes of it. After dinner, he sat with Heidi and Sylvain once more in Sylvain's office, discussing a much more personal topic.

"Once I've determined who's leading the radical group Harris is supporting, I'll be able to shut them down," Dennis said. "In the meanwhile, I've got two teams at work, one in the northern continent and one on the island, recruiting support for my counteroffensive against the extremists. And now I have a question for you, Uncle. I've been wondering about this for decades."

Sylvain said nothing, just gazed expectantly at him.

"I know what you did back on Earth," Dennis continued, "but no one has ever explained to me why you did it. Earlier, you muttered something about doing 'them' a favour. Who were you referring to?"

"Your father knew why. He never told you?"

Dennis shook his head no.

"That's typical of Gilles. Praise in private, criticize in public," Sylvain grumbled. "All right, then, here is the straight truth. I was helping the Directorate. Its plan for reuniting Humanity was for us to interbreed with the Terrans, thus combining the two genomes into a single race once more. That struck me as being slow and inefficient, so I found a better way."

Dennis had to close his jaw so he could respond. "You mutated an alien virus and unleashed a pandemic on Earth, killing a quarter of a billion people. How is that in any way better?" he demanded.

Sylvain shrugged. "They would all have survived if your father hadn't insisted on putting the retroviral vaccine I'd developed through an additional clinical trial. That's where the Stragori genes were—spliced into the RNA in the vaccine. Any Terran who received it, whether or not they were infected with the virus, also received a genome 'upgrade' from one of the multitude of Stragori donor samples I'd collected. And just like that, more than a billion Humans were hybridized in a matter of months. Doing it the Directorate's way would have taken literally hundreds of generations and who knows how many thousands of years.

"Unfortunately, the family didn't see it that way. They shipped me back to Stragon, in disgrace."

For the good of the Human race. Of course. And then Nestor Quan had sought him out, believing him to be a kindred spirit. And when Sylvain had refused to hire him, he'd gone to Earth and found Nayo Naguchi... whose genetic experimentation with Quan's input had resulted in at least two laboratory rats with extreme longevity... which Naguchi had taken with him to Daisy Hub to keep that particular experiment out of Quan's hands after Quan had cheated him out of all his other patents...

At last, the pieces were falling into place. Quan's attempt

to take possession of Naguchi's white rat, Yoko, on Daisy Hub would have been quite effective, had it succeeded. He could have presented the rat to the Stragori public as proof of concept for a way to make any living being virtually immortal. Never mind that only those who could pay for the experimental procedure would benefit from it—Quan's target had always been the Directorate, whose one real advantage had been its longevity. Without it, the Directors would have become redundant and then irrelevant, until hardly anyone would have noticed, let alone complained, when the radicals pulled the plug on the Directorate's supercomputer.

However, plan A had failed, forcing Quan to switch to plan B—bring down the Directorate by co-opting organizations that already had anti-government agendas, beginning with Stragon First.

"Don't expect me to apologize for any of it," Sylvain said, breaking into Dennis's thoughts. "I agreed with the Directorate's goal of reuniting the Human race, just not with its methods. And if I'd had my own laboratory, working independently of Forrand Pharmaceuticals, no Humans would have died and I would probably still be on Earth, doing good."

"But then you would never have met me," Heidi pointed out, "and you always said that I was the best thing that ever happened to you, *minian*."

His expression softened as he raised his eyes to her face. "And I was right."

Dennis Forrand had crossed the sea to Galandra on a freighter. He'd used one of his shell identities, so as not to alert the wrong people to his activities. The voyage had taken more than a week. His return to the mainland, however, had to be much faster. He'd been out of touch for too long with the operatives he'd left behind on the northern continent and the island.

The flight from Lavista to the avcraft field on the western coast of the mainland gave him ten hours to formulate a general plan of attack. He could well understand why Sylvain didn't want the Forrands to learn that he'd partnered with a Harris. In Americas, the Forrands and Harrises had competed vigorously for more than two hundred years. On Stragon, the competition had been fierce and nasty for much longer than that. Betraying Humanity was a serious offence. Betraying the family, however, was worse. It wouldn't matter that he'd been driven to it by desperation. In the eyes of the older generations, it would be considered unforgivable.

Dennis stepped off the avcraft and was crossing the pavement when he saw a sturdily-built man trotting toward him, clad in a dark blue business suit and holding a small device in his hand.

"Hoy!" the man called, waving with his free hand as he drew nearer, and Dennis relaxed a little as he recognized his cousin and long-time fellow conspirator, Arno Lindquist.

Dennis changed course to meet him halfway. Then they walked toward the transportation depot together.

"I wasn't expecting to see you here, Arno. Is there a problem?"

"There may be," the other man said. "I've heard whispers on the mainland. Your uncle has been looking for you, and he's not a happy man, so I'm your Security escort for today.

My vehicle is just over there," he added, pointing ahead as they walked toward an opening between two of the hangars.

So, Marcel had finally twigged to the disappearance of his alien prize? That was a shame. Dennis had been hoping for more time to set up his pieces on the board.

"I gather he has no way to know that we're together?"

"At the moment, he's operating blind. Without the tracking technology, he can't find anyone, Terran or Stragori... and I've seen to it that the Directorate's array is beyond his reach as well."

"Excellent!"

"Eventually, though, he's going to figure out that I'm the one responsible for locking him out of the system. When he does, how do you want me to play it?"

"However you like. Just be sure to point him anywhere except where I happen to be. In the meanwhile, I'm planning an op. I need you to give me all the information you have about Lloyd Franklin Harris."

Arno uttered a low whistle. "You really want to reopen that can of worms?"

Dennis stopped just short of the land car and turned to face him. "You honestly believe it was ever closed?"

"No, it's just..." Arno's shoulders dropped. "Fine." He opened the passenger side door and waved the other man inside. When they were both seated and a signal jammer was perched atop the control panel ahead of them, he said, "I have files on three Lloyd Franklin Harrises—Senior, Junior, and the Third. Which one are you interested in?"

"Whichever one or more of them is connected to either Primus Enterprises or Steadfast. I presume you've kept your intel current?"

Arno threw him a wounded look. "Of course. 'Know thine enemies' has become the Forrand family motto. It's been a job and a half because there are so damn many of them on Stragon, but we've become very good at tracking and surveillance. You won't be disappointed with my report."

Seat belts clicked into place around them. Arno pressed the starter button and began steering the vehicle toward the main road. "Can I presume that you would prefer a hand-to-hand transfer of hard copy rather than an electronic data transmission?"

"Of course."

"All right. We can have a late dinner together at my office this evening. And while we're at it, you can tell me what has prompted your sudden interest in this particular member of the Harris family."

"I can tell you right now. I have reason to believe that he's affiliated with a radical extremist organization called Stragon First."

Arno's eyebrows jetted upward in surprise. "You're joking. A Harris, involved with Sylvain's group?"

"It's not Sylvain's any more. Now it's Nestor Quan's group. In fact, it could even be Lloyd Franklin Harris's group now that Quan is supposedly dead and buried on Earth."

"And you're absolutely certain that there's a connection?"

"I am."

"In that case, I guess I'll have to dig a little deeper for you," Arno said grimly. "Give me a couple of days to pull everything together. I'll let you know when I'm ready to meet."

Traffic around the avport was generally heavy, regardless

of the time of day. As they sat behind a long line of land vehicles waiting to make the final turn onto the AI-controlled thoroughfare, Dennis asked, "Have you heard any news from our mutual friend on the northern continent?"

"I have, and you're not going to like it." Arno paused, staring straight ahead, then said, "There have been complications."

Dennis's shoulders sagged. Complications? Of course there were. It was Angeli's assignment. No matter how many precautions were taken, glitches seemed to gravitate toward her, like iron filings to a magnet, or moths to a flame.

"What kind of complications?"

"An arrest warrant issued by Planetary Security shortly after your agent arrived in Westgrove. She's among allies and safe for the moment, but her options for moving forward are severely limited."

Not that that would stop a loose cannon like her from going ahead with the mission anyway... and probably getting herself caught... or worse. *Damn!*

"This has to do with the bombing of the Directorate's building, doesn't it?" said Dennis.

"I'm afraid so, and it's not going away any time soon. Not even a Sub-Chief of Mainland Security like me can get a terrorism charge dropped. However, the incident took place in my jurisdiction, so I was able to review the investigation that led to the warrant."

"And...?"

A large truck had finally made the turn, and the vehicles behind it were able to creep up and fill the space it had occupied. When they were stopped again, Arno replied,

"Apparently, you're not the only one with influence in Security circles, Dennis. On the face of it, everything was done by the book. Evidence was gathered and forensically analyzed, and it all pointed to one individual, who had changed her name and stowed away on a northbound ship, thus making herself look guilty as hell. Mainland and Planetary are viewing this as an open and shut case, and if either of them get their hands on her, that's what it will be."

Scowling, Dennis pointed out, "She's a Forrand, Arno. That has to get her some consideration."

"No, it just makes it worse. There are plenty of people who feel that the founding families have enjoyed a free ride for far too long. A Forrand up on charges would be like throwing fresh meat to a pack of predators."

"And there's nothing either of us can do for her?"

"Not at the moment, I'm afraid. Thing is, everything about this case felt accelerated to me. Considering what a mess the crime scene was, evidence was remarkably easy to come by, and every piece of it was damning. Not a false lead or a bit of inconclusive trace in the lot. It should have taken us weeks to sort through the rubble. Instead, it took days. It was as though someone had laid the groundwork ahead of time in order to expedite matters to a foregone conclusion."

Red flags waving at the back of his mind, Dennis jerked himself erect and half-turned in his seat. "You're saying she was targeted before the explosion even happened."

"That's exactly what I'm saying. Someone with access to the Directorate's array must have been tracking her movements for a while. We both know she was not responsible for the blast. Unfortunately, knowing and proving are two different things, and the frame around her has been masterfully constructed. The question is, by whom? As I said before, the Forrands have a lot of enemies."

"It may not be about the Forrands, Arno. Before the attack, Angeli wasn't working for me. She was heading up a covert mission for Earth Intelligence. Then the mission was aborted, and the other agents were extracted off-world. She stayed behind at my request."

"Interesting. Do you know why the abort order was given?"

"No. But perhaps that would be a good starting point for your next confidential investigation. After you've completed your research on Lloyd Franklin Harris, of course."

They were two vehicles away from the turn now. As Arno's land car lurched to a halt only centimetres from the rear bumper of the car ahead, he threw a startled glance at his passenger.

"You want *me* to conduct this inquiry? You know much more about Earth Intelligence than I do."

"That's true, but..." Dennis sent him back a crooked smile. "Are you familiar with the Terran metaphor of burning one's bridges?"

"You honestly believe that whoever is running things on Earth will be more forthcoming with a stranger than with you?"

"More receptive to one, yes. However, you won't be contacting Earth, Arno. The extraction was organized by the station manager of Daisy Hub. He's my grandson."

"Does he know it?"

"Unfortunately, yes, and what I said about Earth applies

to him as well. If he believes I sent you, trust me, it will be a wasted trip."

"A trip?" Arno's face was the portrait of incredulity. "You want me to go to Daisy Hub? Just like that?"

"He won't speak to you otherwise. I have contacts who can sneak you off-world. As for explaining your absence… Do you have any personal leave time banked?"

Arno uttered a syllable of laughter. "You're not married, I can tell. Talya and I haven't had a vacation together in decades. If she found out I'd taken leave to go off by myself on one of your errands, she would probably burn my possessions and reprogram the locks while I was away."

"Then you'll have to think of some official reason to go there. Maybe relating to the investigation of an accused terrorist? Oh, and one more thing: be careful not to mention Angeli's name. No one is to know that she's alive. Use her shell identity instead—Eva Moss."

As the land car finally completed the turn and the traffic AI took over its controls, Arno leaned back into his seat and said with a sigh, "Tell me, Dennis, do you ask this much of *all* your relatives?"

"No. Just the ones I trust with my life."

Silence.

Glancing over at his cousin, Dennis noticed that Arno's lips were pursed, as though to stem a flow of words.

"More bad news?"

Arno exhaled noisily. "Maybe. I believe you know Reston Quinian. He's working for you, isn't he?"

Dennis frowned. "Not exactly. We're acquainted, and he's doing me a favour in his spare time. Is he all right?"

"No. He had to be rushed to a Med Services centre late yesterday afternoon. At first, they thought he was having a heart attack. But now they're testing for toxins, specifically the ones produced by plants that grow wild on the island."

The frown deepened. "They're saying he might have been poisoned?"

"*We* are," Arno corrected him. "And by 'we' I mean Mainland Security. Are you also... *acquainted* with a Terran woman named Isabela Bakshi?"

"Why? Is she a suspect?"

"Should she be?" Arno countered.

"No. She would have no reason to—Wait a minute. Is Quin *dead*?"

"Not yet. Fortunately, whatever he ingested was not a lethal dose. He's being kept for a couple of days for observation, but they expect him to make a full recovery." A pause, then, "Do you have any idea why he might have been targeted?"

Arno's voice had dropped in pitch, making this a loaded question. Dennis hesitated for a moment before replying, "Do you believe he was?"

"What matters is that *he* apparently believes it, which leads *me* to believe that he has to be involved in some... extracurricular activity, shall we say? And since he's a Forrand, and you've been seen together on more than one occasion..."

"...you're naturally assuming that I have something to do with this."

Arno bobbed his head in confirmation. "You were a high-powered politician on Earth, I understand, quite a colourful figure, and he is an insignificant civil servant on Stragon, barely noticed even by the members of his own family. That would have made him easy pickings for you, Cousin. Save your protestations," he added, thrusting out a warning hand. "I know about your schemes, how you love to play the system. I did some of that myself when I was your age. You just told me you trust me with your life. So why don't you stop pretending and trust me with the truth? What's going on here?"

"It would have to be kept in confidence."

"That goes without saying. But I'll give you my word anyway."

Dennis thought furiously for a moment, then came to a decision. He'd been doling out pieces of his master plan to the various pawns on the board. What if something were to happen to him? Someone would need to pick up the threads and carry on. And who better to take on that task than a Forrand who was a Sub-Chief of Mainland Security?

"All right. I'll read you in. But not here, and not now. There's someone I need to speak to first." He paused, then added, "In private."

Centuries earlier, the Directorate had conceived of an ambitious plan: an underground transportation network linking up all the urban districts on the southern continent. However, enthusiasm for the project had waned as the cost of bringing it to fruition mounted higher and higher, and the plan was eventually scaled back to serve the southern half of the continent only. Work that had begun on the northbound spurs was summarily halted. In short order, they were stripped of anything that might prove useful before being walled off from the rest of the system.

Nonetheless, one spur, which was privately owned, remained untouched. It had been purchased during the pre-construction phase by Gratien Forrand, the then-eldest member of the family, and had subsequently been handed down from generation to generation as a "curiosity"—like owning one brick of a castle, or the naming rights to a far-distant moon. The deed had accompanied Gervais Forrand to Earth and had eventually been passed to Dennis's uncle, Marcel, who had brought it back with him to Stragon. Marcel had then made himself a lair by placing a barrier across the mouth of the truncated spur and setting up housekeeping on its sole completed landing platform.

This retreat had also provided a perfect hiding place for "found and rescued objects", as Marcel was wont to call them. By the time he'd settled in, only a handful of Forrands even remembered that the property existed, and he made it clear that he expected them to keep the knowledge to themselves. Dennis hadn't betrayed Marcel's trust—he'd merely visited on a day when his uncle was busy elsewhere and had quietly "borrowed" a couple of items from Marcel's collection. It was a semantic distinction the older Forrand had evidently taken exception to.

The Wilderness Zone north of Capital City, the main urban district, had once been a broad, unbroken strip of forest, thick with old growth and underbrush. Now it was sliced into roughly rectangular segments by a series of two-lane paved roads that routed land traffic through the industrial and agricultural areas to the smaller urban districts along the northern coast of the mainland.

On Dennis's instructions, Arno took manual control of the car, made a right turn onto Shiremede Road, and kept his eyes open for a metal canister lying on its side atop a post on the left-hand side of the pavement.

"There!" said Dennis, pointing ahead.

Arno pulled up alongside the object and stopped the car.

"All right, we've found it, whatever it is," he said. "Now what?"

"What it is, is a reproduction of an old Terran artifact called a snail-mail box. On Earth, it was used to leave written messages and small parcels for the owner of a piece of property. In this case, it marks the beginning of the path to the owner's residence," Dennis explained, straight-faced, "which on Earth would be called a driveway."

"Uh-*huh*."

Arno negotiated the turn onto a barely discernible trail and followed it deeper into the forest.

"A snail-mail box," he mused. "It does sound like something Marcel would own. He was practically foaming at the mouth when I spoke with him earlier. Are you sure you want to go into this meeting alone?"

"That depends. Were you talking about me at the time?"

"No, I was informing him about Quin's situation."

"In that case, I'm confident I'll be all right," said Dennis. "There's a clearing not far ahead. Park in the middle of it. I'll go the rest of the way myself."

"If you insist," Arno said. "And if you're not back here in less than an hour..."

"You'll come and save me?"

"I was going to say that I'll leave you to find your own way home, but since you asked nicely—for you, anyway—I suppose I can swoop in and rescue you."

Dennis chuckled. "I'll be fine, really."

The spur had been well concealed from the main system underground, but for one who knew what to look for, there was access from above. Originally, it had been an emergency exit in case of a power failure or other catastrophic incident. Now it was a private entrance marked by a hinged slab of metal on the edge of the clearing, half-hidden by brush and fallen seed pods.

Dennis paused for a moment to savour the forest ambience. The spring breeze was crisp and refreshing, and rich with the scent of new growth. As he recalled from his previous visits, the air below was recycled from the main tunnel system and—though filtered and safe—would not be half this pleasant to breathe. In a word, it smelled claustrophobic down there. However, if he wanted to talk to Marcel, Dennis had no choice but to join him below ground.

Pulling open the hatch, Dennis found the top of the ladder and stepped onto it. As he descended the metal-lined shaft, he saw Arno get out of the car and stand watchfully beside it.

The ladder had steps, not rungs. That made the climb down easier, along with the fact that a tide of light seemed to rise from below Dennis's feet, illuminating his path to the tiled floor of the platform. Overhead, the hatch was closing by itself. He heard the low-pitched hum of the lock cycling. Evidently, Marcel had been expecting him.

"You took your sweet time getting here," his uncle's voice rasped behind him as Dennis let go of the ladder and turned to face him. "Come to return my gadget, have you?"

All the Forrands were robust, but Marcel took things to a whole new level. A full head taller than either of his brothers, he packed a great deal of muscle onto an already heavy frame, topping it off with a face that seemed purposely designed to inspire fear. His expression grew even more threatening when he was smiling. In his former line of work, that had pretty much been a requirement.

Arno belonged to a branch of the family that had never lived on Earth, so there was a lot about Dennis's uncle that Arno didn't know, and that the Forrands who'd repatriated to Stragon preferred not to discuss.

Marcel had built and run a criminal empire on Earth, for the sole purpose of frustrating the Harrises' own ambitions to do so. Whatever they got into, they found that he'd dived in as well, only deeper and smarter and ultimately with more success. Extortion, theft, tech fraud, even flesh-peddling—Marcel had matched their every move. For fifty Earth years, he'd managed to keep the Forrands and Harrises locked in a stalemate.

Finally, the Harrises had had enough. Together with the criminal elements of several other founding families, they financed the construction of a space station where they could continue their pursuit of immoral profit free from interference—Ginza Hub. They then pulled all their illegal enterprises off-world and onto the station, leaving Marcel's organization all alone in Planetary Security's crosshairs. At that point, Dennis's uncle had had no choice but to shut down his own businesses, fake his death, and move back to Stragon.

Now it was seven decades later, and Marcel was in the prime of his life, still as strong and physically imposing as ever. Since Dennis was about to go toe to toe with the Harrises, having someone at his back who could probably snap any one of them like a twig—and would immensely enjoy doing it—seemed to him to be a fine idea.

"Your gadget? I'm afraid I don't have it with me, Uncle. I've literally just returned from Galandra. I was visiting Uncle Sylvain. He had things to tell me that I was sure you'd want to know, and I couldn't wait to share them with you."

"With me, before anyone else," Marcel rumbled, his deliberate pronunciation giving each syllable a menacing undertone. "We've spoken three times in the last twenty years. The last time you came here, it was to steal something of mine. And now, all of a sudden, you're itching to share? This has a bad smell to it, Nephew."

"Well, maybe I can give it a sweeter aroma: I'm mounting an op against the Harrises, and Sylvain has just signed on."

"Really! He's supporting this endeavour all the way from Galandra? With what?"

"With whatever I need. He recently learned that a Harris was responsible for driving him off the mainland and defaming his character. Now he wants revenge, and I've promised to give it to him. And I've come to ask you to help me do it."

"*Have* you? And why should I fall in with your latest scheme?"

"Because there's a very good chance that what happened to Quin was also the work of the Harrises."

Bushy eyebrows rose and fell as Marcel's eyes first widened in surprise, then narrowed. "What do you know about that?"

"Enough to realize that it makes sense. Quin as Quin doesn't have enemies—how could he? He's content to be a mid-level functionary in a government department that offers no path to political power. With no ambition, he's no threat. To anyone. Quin as a Forrand, however—that's a different story. Forrands do have enemies, and our worst and most persistent enemies have always been the Harrises."

Marcel shifted his stance. His expression shifted as well,

as he visibly digested this food for thought. Finally, grudgingly, he said, "Much as I hate to agree with you, I'm afraid you may be right about one thing: the kid is a nobody. In my experience, there's only one reason to target a nobody, and that's to get to somebody else to whom that nobody matters. No one outside the family is even aware that Quin and I are related, so I doubt that it was done to get *me* to back off. Since you're the only other Forrand who's ever paid him any attention, the message must be for you, Nephew. So tell me, what is my grandson to you?"

"He's a minor player in my current op," Dennis said with a shrug. "His co-tenant on the island is the primary operative. She's a full-blooded Terran and can't be tracked using your software. His job is to occupy her spare bedroom, pay attention to what she's doing, and report back to me on her progress. That's it."

"Hmph. That may be the way you see it, but don't be surprised if the Harrises take a different view. Or if Quin does. He's been stuck in that dead-end job of his for going on thirty years, and now you've dropped an adventure in his lap. Fancying himself a spy could well have led to whatever's put him in the Med Services centre."

"If you're right," Dennis said disgustedly, "then his cover may already be blown, and soon hers will be as well. Damn!"

"You couldn't have known, Nephew. But look on the bright side," said Marcel, flashing an evil grin.

"There's a bright side?"

"Absolutely. Now you've got me. And I'm a lot harder to take down than you or Sylvain will ever be. Have a seat and let's talk business. My kind of business."

This was what Dennis had been hoping for. Finally able

to relax, he let his gaze roam around Marcel's hideaway.

Nothing about it had changed since the last time Dennis had visited. The spartanly furnished apartment was contained completely within the confines of the landing platform. In the centre, a smart-upholstered sofa and armchair sat facing the bullet car track, from behind a low oval-shaped table fashioned out of something resembling plastiplex. To one side was a minimalist kitchen with a cooking surface and a set of storage and refrigeration cabinets. To the other side, an array of comm gear backed up against the half-tiled wall, next to an unadorned metal door.

Behind that door lay the alien bunker. The underground room had been discovered during the excavation of the Forrand family's privately owned tunnel. Most likely a hastily abandoned observation post, it had held some documents—which had been surrendered to the Archives for translation—and a couple of artifacts that were removed from the site by Gratien before anyone else could claim them. The artifacts (identified only as "alien-made objects" in his inventory of belongings) later became part of his estate and were included in the string of bequests that ended with Marcel's inheriting the tunnel spur, along with the bunker, which he was now using as a storage room for his various "finds and rescues".

"Do you think Gratien knew the bunker existed when he purchased this tunnel?" Dennis said.

"Dunno. It's a safe bet the Harrises knew about it, though. They were about to make an offer when Gratien slipped his bid in ahead of theirs and bought the spur out from under their noses. They were outraged. As consolation, the Transportation Department proposed selling them a different one, but they declined. It was this spur or nothing. Meanwhile, the deal was done. The records had been filed, the credits had been transferred, and the mutual hatred between our families became even more deeply entrenched. And speaking of hatred, what exactly is your plan for avenging the disgrace of my youngest brother?"

Dennis dropped onto the pale orange armchair. Its upholstery immediately darkened by several shades, to complement the blue of his jacket. "Nice," he remarked, then replied, "I'm still gathering intel about the Harris that Sylvain identified. Once I know all about him, I can figure out the best way to come at him."

Marcel gave him a dubious look. "You're going to come at him? Not face to face, I hope. We already have targets on our backs, just for being Forrands. The last thing you want to do is add a bullseye to your forehead."

"Then what does your experience tell you I should do?"

Marcel leaned back against the sofa cushions and crossed his arms over his massive chest. "Did you ever hear how I framed Willy Harris for burning down his father's brothel...?"

"You're lucky I'm a patient man," Arno growled as Dennis got into the land car beside him and buckled up. "Where to now?"

"Is that offer of dinner still open? We have a lot to discuss."

SIXTEEN
ISABELA

Isabela spent half the night drafting her second message to Drew Townsend and preparing it for transmission to Daisy Hub. Then, exhausted, she fell into bed and spent the remaining hours until dawn in a fitful slumber. Shortly after sunrise, a loud, harsh noise yanked her out of a dream and propelled her, trembling, onto her feet on the floor. It took her several seconds to get her bearings and identify the source of the commotion.

"All right! Enough!"

Isabela threw on her dressing gown and hurried to open the apartment door. Vikram had made her a spyhole for times like this, but she didn't care. She was too busy preparing the piece of her mind that she was going to give to whoever was rude enough to be leaning on that buzzer at such an ungodly hour of the morning. She thumbed the latch release and waited impatiently for the door to slide aside.

Standing in the hallway was a message carrier. Or rather, he was wearing the uniform of one—the two-tone blue jacket with embossed shoulder patches and the blue and white billed cap bearing the embroidered logo of the island's delivery service.

"I'm sorry to disturb you so early, ma'am," he said, giving her an ingratiating smile, "but this transmission is from the government and they put a rush on it. Are you Isabela Bakshi?"

Her anger instantly dissipated. "Yes, I—From the government? Are you certain?"

"Yes, ma'am, it's from the Continental Council," he replied brightly, and held out his proof-of-delivery pad for her to thumbprint.

"The Continental Council?" she echoed, frowning. "Not the Directorate?"

"No, ma'am. It's from up north."

Her heartbeat quickened. The northern continent. Angeli was on the northern continent.

Moments later, Isabela had accepted delivery of the data wafer and sent the earnest and apologetic young man on his way. With growing excitement, she hurried back to the bedroom to fetch her decrypter and commpad from their hiding place. She inserted the decrypter and wafer into their respective ports on the commpad. Then she sat down on the sofa to read the text that came up on the screen.

It was in Stragori, but the EIS device wasn't finding anything to decrypt. That was strange.

Please respond to: Lady Sharma Dorel, Medical Oversight Officer for the Northern Continent of Borea

Pursuant to inquiries arising from a number of ongoing investigations of suspicious fatalities in my jurisdiction among others, I am requesting your assistance...

"...in your capacity as an expert on the properties of flora originating from the island on Stragon...?"

What was going on here? First Quinian had known about her special skills, and now some government official on the northern continent had apparently found out about them. Was her cover unravelling? Would she have to go into hiding in the Wilderness Zone, as Moe had done?

Then the meaning of the words in the message sank in, and she had to reread them to be sure she hadn't misunderstood.

Quinian's poisoning wasn't an isolated occurrence. Someone with the same expertise as hers was apparently using it to commit murders—plural—on another continent. What a horrifying thought! And yet, how comforting to know that she wasn't being considered a suspect in these northern investigations. No one would be asking her to consult on them if she were.

As well, this Lady Sharma Dorel person wasn't asking for Isabela's physical presence at the crime scenes—all she wanted was information. Send her a data file by return transmission? That much Isabela could certainly do. It would take her some time to pull everything together, of course, since the idea of writing a toxic substances cookbook had never once crossed her mind, not even jokingly, in all the time that she had lived on Stragon.

Isabela was wide awake now. Clearly, her day had begun. Might as well wash up and get dressed for work. Quinian hadn't done the grocery shopping before he was poisoned, so breakfast and lunch would have to come out of the snack drawer at school again. Perhaps she would stop somewhere on her way to the commhub with Uncle Henry's message and pick up a few items for dinner. She would need something in which to carry them, of course...

Spotting her tote bag on the floor beside the sofa, she snatched up the bag, felt its unaccustomed weight, and recalled with a start that she hadn't unpacked the extra clothing and glow-rods she'd put into it the previous day.

Then a thought occurred to her that made her skin crawl.

She was attracting attention lately for something other than her teaching prowess, from the kind of people whose notice she'd been specifically warned to avoid—Security... government types... and a whole array of "authorities". Isabela's cover wasn't entirely blown—"they" knew what she was capable of, but not what she had done, or for whom she'd been doing it. Not yet, anyway. However, "they" wouldn't think twice about invading whatever privacy she had left in order to uncover her remaining secrets. What if one of them were to break into her apartment? What would they find?

Her jaw clenched as the answer came to her. Nothing. They wouldn't find a damn thing.

Quickly, she scooped up the alien technology from the living room and dropped it into the tote bag, along with the signal jammer and, after a heartbeat's consideration, her EIS gear from the bedroom. Technically, that was alien technology too.

Weeks earlier, Dennis had instructed her and Angeli to destroy these items. Now, at last, she understood why.

Well, *that* had been unpleasant!

Isabela returned to school from the commhub shortly before lunchtime with heat in her cheeks and a knot of anger in her chest.

The helpful young woman who had assisted her with the

transmission of the earlier message to Uncle Henry had been nowhere in sight today. Instead, Isabela had been confronted—actually, "accosted" would have been a more accurate way to put it—by a brusque, malodorous man with a filled-form fetish. It had taken her nearly an hour to answer all the questions on the screen to his satisfaction. Then he'd quoted her an exorbitant price for the delivery to Daisy Hub, and had grimaced with distaste and snapped at her when she'd reminded him tartly that messages to members of the founding families travelled gratis.

Offended by his manner, she had demanded to speak with his supervisor.

He'd snarled at her that he *was* the supervisor.

After that, there had been nowhere for things to go except downhill.

Eventually, at the cost of all of her patience and most of her self-control, the message to Daisy Hub had been accepted for transmission free of charge. She had the log entry to prove it. However, the scene at the counter had been ugly enough to make her think twice before returning there with any future mail, and that presented a problem.

It was the only commhub within practical walking distance of the school or her apartment. To get to a more distant one, she would have to rent a wheeled vehicle. Not only would the transaction be recorded, but every vehicle on the island was equipped with an anti-jamming device that turned off the engine if its location signal stopped broadcasting.

So much for remaining untrackable.

"A man came to talk to you while you were out, Mrs. Bakshi," Joanne reported while Isabela was hanging up her jacket in the cloakroom.

She stiffened as a remembered voice surfaced in her mind. *"We'll be in touch."*

Madre! As if this day hadn't been stressful enough.

"Is he going to return later?"

Silence.

Isabela spun to face her teaching assistant. The girl looked close to tears.

With a second, colder knot forming in the pit of her stomach, Isabela asked softly, "Where is he?"

"In your office. He refused to leave. It made me nervous, and I didn't want him anywhere near the children."

"You did the right thing. I will take care of this."

Isabela checked that the technology in her tote bag was still concealed by the fabric of her extra clothing. Then she marched into her office, bag over her arm and anger at the ready.

The man occupying the guest chair in her office looked innocuous enough. (At least he'd had the decency not to take the seat behind her desk.) Rangy of build, bland of features, and of indeterminate age, he got to his feet and straightened his suit jacket as she came through the door. It was a quaint, polite gesture. Despite being tall, he wasn't particularly imposing. So what about him had made Joanne nervous?

Wordlessly, Isabela crossed the room and settled onto her own chair, placing the tote bag on the floor beside her. She expected him to sit back down as well. Instead, he walked to the door and quietly closed it. When he turned to face her, his expression had acquired a hardness that instantly set off her mental alarms. This had to be the face he'd shown her teaching assistant earlier.

"You're Isabela Bakshi?" he said, his tone making it more

a command than a question.

She recognized his voice. Reminding herself that this man was in *her* office, not the other way around, she drew a steadying breath. Then she leaned forward on her elbows on the desktop, elevated her chin, and stared directly and fearlessly into his eyes.

"Yes. I am. And you are the Security officer who contacted me yesterday. Are you finally ready to tell me your name?"

Still stone-faced, he reached into his jacket pocket, pulled out a familiar-looking object, and placed it on the desk in front of her. The green light was blinking.

"Do you know what that is?"

She bobbed her head once, then returned warily, "Do *you?*"

He dropped back onto his chair. "It's Quin's. He can't have it with him at the Med Services centre, and I can't be caught carrying it around. I thought since you two were—" He scowled briefly. "Once he's back home, if you could give it to him...?"

"Of course. Does this mean that you no longer believe me to be a person of interest?"

"No. It's still an official interview. We've just concluded the unofficial preamble."

"I see." Isabela turned off the signal jammer and dropped it into her tote bag. Then she came to attention in her chair and said in her most businesslike voice, "I hope the official part begins with you properly identifying yourself."

In response, he pulled up the sleeve of his jacket and showed her his badge—a metallic insignia embedded into his right forearm. Of course. Members of law enforcement, like the military, were routinely optimized, and this conversation was now being transmitted to a server somewhere.

"I'm Sub-Inspector Norton Harris, Capital City Security," he informed her. "I have some follow-up questions for you regarding your relationship with Doctor Reston Quinian. You can answer them here and now, or you can accompany me back to the station. It's your choice."

"As I told you yesterday, I am a schoolteacher and Dr. Quinian is my supervisor. Our relationship is purely professional."

"Is it? Isn't it true that for the past two weeks you and he have been sharing an apartment?"

Comprehension suddenly dawning, Isabela leaned back against her chair.

Harris knew what the signal jammer was for, and Quinian must have shown him how to use it. He'd had it with him at the restaurant, from which Harris had contacted her after Quinian had passed out. The jammer must have been off to allow him to make that call—but had it been on earlier, perhaps?

Had Quinian been having a secret kaffy date with someone? And was Harris there to monitor it? Or was he the person Quinian had been meeting with? The image Harris had sent her of the tabletop had shown only a single place setting, but he'd certainly had time to remove a second set of dishes and tidy things up before taking the snap.

Was the relationship between Harris and Quinian more than either of them was letting on?

"Answer the question, Lady Bakshi. Are you co-tenanting with Dr. Quinian?" Harris repeated impatiently.

"Technically, he is co-tenanting with me, since I've been living in the apartment for the past five years and he only recently moved in, but yes, it is true. That does not make our relationship any less professional, however."

"Would you characterize it as a friendly co-habitation?"

Isabela's posture stiffened again. This question was part of an official Security interview. Whatever she replied would be on the record and usable against her should she find herself embroiled in a tribunal.

For several heartbeats, she thought furiously.

A friendly co-habitation? The honest answer would have been no. Neither one of them had chosen to be in this situation. Up until Angeli's departure, they'd barely tolerated each other. And besides devouring her food stores at an alarming rate, the man snored like a badly-tuned moto engine, robbing her of sleep. But telling all that to Security would have painted her as having a motive for wanting him out of the way. Harris already knew that she had the means. No opportunity, but she could have bribed or tricked someone into poisoning Quinian for her. She would have to pick her words carefully.

"It is too soon to tell," she replied at last. "We are still settling in and getting used to each other."

"I've looked into the housing records, and you seem to have had a lot of bad luck with the people who have shared that apartment with you. Dr. Quinian is your fourth co-tenant in the past five years."

Isabela bristled. "That is *almost* correct. I was not the one with bad luck—they were. My brother was bitten by an insect in the Wilderness Zone. My husband was killed while trying to break up a street fight. And my best friend had the misfortune to be in the transit tunnel adjacent to the Directorate's offices when a terrorist bomb went off inside the building. And what is your question, exactly?"

"How do you do it?" This was spoken in a warm and

soothing voice. As he no doubt intended, the abrupt shift in tone momentarily shook her off balance.

"I—What are you talking about now?"

"Losing a brother, a husband, and a best friend, all in such a short time, and you're so composed. Most people I know would have gone to pieces and then into mental health therapy. But you...!"

Isabela's training kicked in. She could see where he was trying to lead her, and decided not to follow. "Clearly, I am not one of the people you know, Sub-Inspector," she pointed out, putting a razor-sharp edge on each word. "And not everything about me or anyone else can be found by scanning a computer file. Grief is a personal experience, and teaching has been my therapy. Are we close to the end of this interview? I have students to attend to."

"We're almost done," he told her. Just like that, the warmth was gone and the tough-as-nails Security officer was back. "Are you acquainted with a man named Dennis Forrand?"

Frowning, she replied, "I knew a man by that name, back on Earth. A prominent politician. He died there in a vehicle accident, about twenty years ago. Why are you asking about him?"

"What was the nature of your connection to him?"

"It was a business relationship. He hired me and my brother to manage a model town he'd set up in one of the agricultural zones. And I repeat, how is this relevant to your investigation into the poisoning of Dr. Quinian?"

Ignoring her question, he thrust another at her. "You are aware that Dennis Forrand is not actually dead? That he is alive and well and living on Stragon?"

Evidently, Isabela was not the only person of interest in

this case.

"That may be true," she said stiffly. "I would not know. I can honestly tell you that I have had no personal contact with him since Earth year 2387."

He nodded with apparent satisfaction. "And now we are done." He shifted his weight and began rising from his chair.

No, she thought stubbornly, *we are not.*

"Not so fast, Sub-Inspector Harris," she said. "Now I have a couple of questions for *you.*"

He paused halfway to his feet, tilted his head curiously, and slowly settled back down again.

"First, what is Dr. Quinian's condition?" she asked.

"He's stable and resting comfortably. They should be sending him home in a couple of days. And second?"

"Was I right? Was it the damselflower?"

"Until the lab results come back, it's too early to say. All I can tell you is that you correctly identified the flowers in the kitchen. Unfortunately, none of the staff would admit to having brought them in, and nobody knew how or when they'd first appeared." He paused for a couple of beats, then said, with exaggerated patience, "*Now* are we done?"

"Yes," she replied distractedly. "You may go."

His lips worked soundlessly for a moment. Then he got up and left.

Her eyes followed him out the door, but her mind was elsewhere—on the northern continent, on Daisy Hub... and wherever Dennis Forrand happened to be right now. She hoped he was safe. She would need his help to prove that Vikram had been murdered.

"Are you all right, Mrs. Bakshi?"

Joanne was hovering on the threshold of the office, her young features contracted into a portrait of concern.

Isabela pinned a reassuring expression on her own face. "I am fine," she replied, getting to her feet and rounding the side of her desk.

The Forrand family circus could wait. So could the Thryggians. Isabela had students to attend to, and a report to prepare for a medical officer on the northern continent. It would take her the rest of this day and part of the next to pull everything together. With luck, the transmission fee would be something she could afford.

The sun was setting, and once again, Isabela was sitting alone in her living room with a cup of hot *jekhailla* tea in her hands, staring darkly at something in the middle of her coffee table. This time it was her signal jammer. Beside her on the sofa lay her tote bag, containing enough alien technology to blow up her cover like a radical group's bomb if the Stragori authorities ever caught onto what she was doing.

It was at times like this that she was grateful to be living on the island. On the mainland, urban districts had become dangerous places to be. Radical extremists making trouble had put local Security on constant high alert. Search raids had become commonplace in response to increasingly more frequent incidents of violence. Terrans who'd taken up residence there were being advised not to be found outdoors after dark, for their own protection.

On the island, that reality seemed distant and surreal. People went about their business, having pushed the constant presence of surveillance devices firmly to the back of their minds. There was Security, of course—an all-Terran plainclothes organization that kept watch and kept the peace—but terrorism was a Stragori problem, confined to the seething mass of beings north of the strait.

Isabela had spent the previous evening and most of her morning assembling and drafting her report to Lady Sharma Dorel. Because today wasn't a school day, she hadn't had to wait before taking the transmissible file to a commhub—the same one as she'd used twice before.

This decision had not been made lightly. The unpleasant memory of her most recent visit there was still fresh in her mind. However, Isabela's inner teacher had weighed in, reminding her that it was wrong to give up on people, no matter how rude and disrespectful they might have been. So, early that afternoon she had marched up to the counter with data card and filled-out form both in hand... and had found yet a different clerk waiting to serve her, this one an older version of the helpful young lady she'd met before.

As it turned out, replies to government requests were accepted and sent without question, and travelled free of charge. Isabela had left the commhub with a third entry in her transmission log and a smile on her face.

Unfortunately, the smile had not lasted. Once back home, she had spent the rest of the day with her thoughts, and her thoughts had not been very good company.

Quinian would be returning to the apartment sometime tomorrow—he'd contacted her from the Med Services centre to let her know. Isabela was not looking forward to the conversation they would be having when he arrived.

In the meanwhile, she'd become discomfortingly aware that she was now in possession of stolen property. It was twice-stolen, actually, once from the Thryggians by Gratien Forrand, and a second time from Marcel Forrand by his nephew, Dennis. They might argue that finding a lost or abandoned object did not constitute a theft, but deep down, Isabela knew better. The Thryggians could not possibly have intended the Stragori to have the use of such a precise and comprehensive tracking tool.

According to Quinian, the damage was already done. Marcel had sold the Directorate copies of the software to put on its various systems, and that meant there was a good chance the Thryggians were already aware of the transgression. Returning the stolen technology to its original owners would be no more than a gesture of good will. Nevertheless, it was the right thing to do. At the very least, it would remove the bad taste that rose to her mouth each time she thought about the device lurking at the bottom of her tote bag.

Tonight might be her only chance to accomplish that without Quinian finding out. So why wasn't she already on her way to the Thryggian bunker? What was stopping her?

The answer was depressingly simple: once she'd disappeared the tracking device, she would have to disappear herself as well, and Isabela had no exit strategy in place. No extraction timeline, no firm commitment of assistance from Daisy Hub... in fact, not even a reply yet to her first message to Uncle Henry. Only a fool would openly betray one of the most powerful families on Stragon without anticipating their revenge and making prior arrangements to flee beyond their reach.

Isabela was no fool. A pawn in Dennis Forrand's latest scheme, undoubtedly, and trapped in a bargain she was pretty sure he would find a way to logic himself out of... but not a fool.

If Townsend could not or would not help her, the only other avenue of escape she could imagine was to hide out in the bunker with the Thryggians, quite possibly for the rest of her life. Self-imprisonment? That was not a practical option, even if they agreed to take her in (which was by no means a certainty).

No, she was forced to concede, there was no right choice in this matter. She was alone, surrounded by Forrands. She would have to continue following the path Dennis had laid out for her and hope it took her somewhere she could live with later.

A loud buzzing noise yanked her mind back from the abyss of her ruminations, so suddenly that she nearly spilled her tea down the front of her clothes. Someone was at her door. Not Quinian, surely! Security?

With trembling hands, she put her cup down on the coffee table. Then she went to the spyhole and peered out into the corridor.

It was a message carrier. In fact, it was the same apologetic young man who had brought her the early-morning transmission from the northern continent. With a sigh of relief, she unlatched and opened the door.

"Are you Isabela Bakshi?" he asked.

"You know I am," she replied.

"Yeah, I do," he said, blushing a little as he extended his proof-of-delivery pad to be thumbprinted. "But we're supposed to verify the identity of the recipient each time. It's the rules."

Moments later, he had departed. Her hands shaking now for a different reason, Isabela dropped the data card onto the coffee table and rifled inside her tote bag for the commpad and encrypter.

Oh, please, let this transmission be from Uncle Henry...

*   *   *

Dear Niece,

Aunt Matilda and I were pleased to hear from you and would like to stay in touch from now on. While time and distance make visiting impossible for us at the moment, you may continue to communicate with us through the Townsends on Daisy Hub.

How is your blanket coming along? We understand how frustrating it can be to be pulled up short before a project is completed, especially when it is intended as a gift for a friend, but we are confident that you will find a way to get it done. Meanwhile, if your friend's pattern proves to be too difficult, just let us know. Aunt Matilda has some favourite patterns of her own that she can send you.

Cousin Grace and Grandma send their love and best wishes, added to mine.

Uncle Henry

So, deactivated did not mean disowned. Weak-kneed with relief, Isabela collapsed onto the sofa to read the decrypted version of this message:

Keep us apprised of developments but do nothing that will alert Forrand or your partner to EIS's awareness of your situation. We are gathering intel from a variety of sources and will share any information we feel may benefit you. Best of luck.

Keep doing what she was doing, in other words. At least Novak wasn't asking her to do anything that would undermine Dennis's plan... although it wasn't entirely clear what those "patterns" referred to. Was there another operation in the works?

Madre! She hoped not.

SEVENTEEN
ON DAISY HUB

Four Days Later

"There's a ship coming through the Gate, Drew." Lydia Garfield's voice on the intercomm sounded flustered. "ETA is about sixteen hours. The pilot claims to be transporting some kind of Stragori official. He says his passenger is requesting a private meeting with you, in person."

Sitting at his desk on AdComm, Townsend swivelled his chair and gazed through the transparent wall of his office at the video display suspended over the tactical work station. It was showing a vessel configuration similar to the profile of the diplomatic shuttle Vinson Trager had piloted from Stragon to Daisy Hub not that long ago. Trager had been taking up his position as the Directorate's appointed envoy and liaison officer on the Hub. So, why was this meeting request not coming through channels, Drew wondered.

Had his response to Isabela Bakshi been intercepted, prompting a reaction by the Directorate? More to the point, was there a safe and covert way to find out?

"Huh!" Townsend got to his feet and crossed the deck to join Lydia at her communications console.

Trager's shuttle had broadcast its diplomatic status, along with a warning not to scan it. Nothing like that was crawling across the bottom of the tactical screen this time. Perhaps this "official" wasn't all that official.

"How many are aboard?" he asked.

She pressed a button, bringing a screen to life on her console.

"Accessing tactical data now. Medium range scan shows two living beings. I'm guessing one of them is the pilot. What do you want me to do?"

"Respond to the hail. Then put me on the comm with them. Put it on speakers."

Expertly flipping switches on the Hub's new—and to someone like Townsend, dauntingly complex—communications array, she declared loudly, "Approaching Stragori vessel, this is Daisy Hub Control. Please stand by for the station manager." She turned her head and gazed up at him. "They're blocking the video, Drew. It's audio only," she said softly. Then she moved her chair out of his way.

The mic was built into the top of the console. He stepped closer and announced himself: "This is Drew Townsend, station manager of Daisy Hub. I understand your passenger is requesting a private meeting with me. Can you tell me what this is regarding?"

"Wish I could, sir. He won't even let me say his name or identify my ship over the comms."

This did not bode well.

Drew and Lydia traded speculative looks.

Then a different, deeper male voice piped up, speaking in heavily accented but grammatically correct Standard. "Mr. Townsend, I appreciate that by insisting on utmost secrecy, I'm putting you in a difficult position. However, trust me, it's nothing compared to the risk I'm taking simply by travelling here. If you'll permit us to dock, I'll explain the purpose of my errand. It's a confidential matter that could make a huge difference to the fate of Stragon, and it mustn't be discussed remotely."

Townsend was far from reassured by this. The Repository was still in its infancy, not yet ready to make a huge difference to anything at this point. Nonetheless, he was intrigued.

"You gonna take that bait, Boss?" said O'Malley's voice behind him.

Lydia shot out a hand and slammed it onto the mute button as though killing an insect. Then she turned her head and levelled a reproachful stare at the interloper.

He responded with a shrug.

Meanwhile, the speakers had gone silent. Breaths were likely being held at the other end of the call as the two beings on the ship awaited the station manager's decision. Finally, Drew made it. He gestured to Lydia to unmute the mic.

"You have my permission to dock, but not to enter the station until I know what this is about. Contact Hub Control when you're two hours away. You'll be assigned a portal at that time."

"Thank you, sir." The pilot sounded relieved. "Will do. This is—um—Out."

"Are you certain about this, Drew?" Lydia asked once the channel was closed again. "We've had problems with mysterious visitors before. What if Dennis Forrand is trying to plant monitoring devices on the Hub again? What if this alleged official is optimized and recording everything so we can be blackmailed later?"

"All of which, if true, would present a clear and present danger to our operations here," he allowed. "But he's given us fifteen standard hours' advance notice of his arrival. That should be enough time to prepare an appropriate welcome for him, wouldn't you say?"

"You know," O'Malley mused, "there were recorded conversations on the memory blocs that Trager brought us from Stragon. I could make some voice comparisons, see if anything leaps out."

Townsend shot him a look. "I ordered that data to be wiped from our systems."

"And you believe I can't recover it?" O'Malley's expression crumpled. "Boss, I'm hurt!" he declared dramatically.

"Go!" said Townsend, shooing him in the direction of the tube car doors. "See if you can identify him."

"What about Trager, Drew?" Lydia cut in. "It's not like he's the enemy—not any more, anyway. And he's spent the past few years on Stragon, observing events from a vantage point inside the government. I'll bet *he* can give us some useful intel."

Perhaps he could. But would it be *reliable* intel?

Townsend thought for a moment, recalling: Trager had originally been planted on Daisy Hub by the Stragori Directorate to prevent Yoko, the Überrat, from falling into the hands of the radical faction. Once exposed, he'd been relatively easy to turn into an ally, especially against the Corvou. However, after the war, he'd returned to Stragon, where he would have been debriefed before being transformed into a diplomatic liaison and reassigned to the Hub.

So, although Trager might not be the enemy, and the Doc had confirmed that he carried no implants, Townsend was not entirely convinced that this particular Stragori could be considered a friend. He was, after all, the one who had brought memory blocs aboard the station, seeded with misinformation and containing an AI infiltrator. True, Trager had been as shocked as everyone else to discover how he had been used. Nonetheless...

"You may be right, Lydia," Drew replied, "but I want to know a lot more about this 'confidential matter' before deciding whether to bring the Directorate's representative into the discussion. Besides, he's not the only one aboard with recent experience of living on Stragon. While O'Malley is searching the database, I want to find out what more the extracted EIS operatives can tell us. And what Moe has to say. After all, he's spent his whole life on-world."

"Okay. One at a time, or all at once?"

Townsend glanced toward the conference table in his office. He wanted the agents all together, comparing stories and jogging one another's memories, but nine adults would overflow that limited space.

"All at once, in the caf," he decided. "Call the meeting to start in one standard hour. Include Olivia. And Ruby. As second in command, she'll need to be informed as well."

"And Captain Rodrigues?" She paused expectantly, eyebrows raised.

Of course. He'd almost forgotten. This new Hub's comm system was permalinked to the Rangers' command centre on K Deck, and all ship-to-Hub and Hub-to-ship transmissions were monitored for security purposes. That meant Rodrigues and his people were already in the loop. Excluding him now would be pointless.

Townsend inhaled deeply and surrendered to the inevitable. "And Rodrigues," he said, "but let me be the one to issue the invitation."

Daisy Hub had been rebuilt and upgraded following the Corvou war. Ranger Detachment Zulu now occupied what would have been Decks K, L, and M of the old station, and that was how Townsend's crew continued to refer to them. M Deck hangared the detachment's three space shuttles; L Deck held an armoury, storage facilities, and living quarters for eighteen beings; and K Deck was the Rangers' version of AdComm. The two command decks were identically configured, and Townsend's and Rodrigues's offices were identically equipped, right down to the security keypad concealed in the upper right-hand drawers of their respective desks.

As Townsend stepped off the tube car on K Deck, the Ranger commander looked up from his screen, leaned back in his chair, and silently beckoned his visitor to come in and sit down.

"Well," he remarked once Drew was seated, "this is certainly shaping up to be an interesting day. Are you here to include me in it? Or to ask me to mind my own business? Because you know what my answer has to be to a request like that."

Townsend knew. When Daisy Hub had formally allied with House Trokerk, he had co-opted Zulu Detachment to be his Second Shield—the Nandrian equivalent of a palace guard. Ranger Captain Paul Rodrigues and his people were therefore not only responsible for patrolling part of Sector Three of Earth space, but also honour-bound to preserve the safety of House Daisy Hub and its crew.

Rodrigues had made it clear at the time that he did not consider Chief Officer of the Second Shield to be an honorary post. He took *all* his Security responsibilities quite seriously. Now that there was a potentially dangerous Stragori ship headed for the station, that was probably a good thing.

"I'm meeting in the caf in about an hour with the Terrans we evacuated from Stragon," Townsend told him, "and I think you should be present, to gather intel and perform a threat assessment."

"And depending on my report, are you prepared to rescind your decision to let this unidentified vessel dock with the Hub? Don't forget, the last time you refused an unknown alien craft access to the station, it triggered an interstellar war."

Townsend winced inwardly. The Corvou war had been devastating, not only to Humanity but also to the forty-two alien fleets that had joined the fight on Earth's side. None of those fleets were back to full strength yet, and one of them had been Stragori. Now a Stragori was demanding an audience on what he claimed was a top-secret matter of planetary importance. Might denying his request be the flashpoint for another major conflict? Just contemplating this possibility was enough to roil his already complaining stomach.

Drew's antacid tablets were in his desk drawer, on AdComm. He needed to get back there.

"Why don't we hear what the nine agents have to say, and then make the decision together?" he suggested, hurriedly getting to his feet.

Rodrigues took the hint. "In the caf? Fine, I'll be there."

Townsend was the last person to arrive for the meeting in the caf. He'd made the mistake of going to Med Services for something stronger than antacid tablets, and Doc Ktumba had insisted that he lie down until the ulcer medication kicked in.

The Doc was a formidable woman, tall and solidly built, with dark brown skin and a will so inflexible that her disapproving glare was enough to silence even the strongest opposition. Townsend could be obstinate too, but not when he was in constant pain. So, he had just spent an hour on his back on one of her biopod beds.

The caf's circular tables normally seated four each. Today, the nine former EIS agents had divided themselves up evenly among three of the tables, Ruby and Olivia were sharing a fourth, and Rodrigues had chosen to sit by himself at the one directly behind them. All eyes turned to Drew as he entered the room.

Every medicine had side effects. The one he was on right now kept trying to fog up his brain. Willing his thoughts to stay focused, he paused on the threshold to activate the privacy shield, then walked to the serving counter and turned to face these newest members of his crew. He'd had an hour to consider how he could frame the purpose of the meeting without revealing too much information. They were just field agents, after all, with no need to know what was about to land in his lap.

"Due to recent developments on Stragon, and based on your debriefings, I've requested that Captain Rodrigues perform a threat assessment," he began.

There was much shifting of position and swivelling of heads. Drew paused, expecting the Ranger to recognize the cue and stand to take charge of the meeting.

Nope. Rodrigues remained firmly seated.

Swallowing hard, Townsend went on, "Questions have arisen, and we're hoping that you, as a group, can provide some answers. For starters, we need names. Names of people you've interacted with on-world, even if it was only once or casually. Names of places you've visited."

"And names of organizations associated with those people or places," Rodrigues chimed in. "Any small detail could turn out to be important."

Since the Ranger still seemed content to stay where he was, Townsend took over again. "Every one of you told me earlier that you felt you were being actively blocked from acquiring useful intel," he reminded them. "Now we want to be more specific. Intel from where? From whom? And when? At what point do you suspect your cover was compromised?"

A burly man with a full red beard stood up to reply. Drew pulled his name out of memory: Philip Nussbaum.

"I can't prove it, but if I had to guess, I'd say I was made shortly after we stepped off the ship on Stragon. I started running into dead ends right away."

Drew glanced around and saw heads bobbing in agreement.

"Dead ends?" Rodrigues echoed. "What kind of dead

ends?"

At this, the room fairly exploded with frustrated voices.

"Every time I identified a source, they became unavailable somehow..."

"...shunned me. And I was undercover, revealing nothing..."

"...played my role to perfection! But the way people kept looking at me, it was as if they knew..."

"...may as well have been wearing a sign saying 'Secret Agent! Say nothing!'"

"...so we had to resort to kidnapping and drugging them, and even then, nothing useful came of it..."

"If only we'd had more time!" declared a dark-haired woman at the table farthest from the Ranger. Her name was Marie Ouellette, Drew recalled, and she'd been a public speaker back on Earth. She certainly had the voice for it. Her words rolled over the room, commanding everyone's full attention.

"More time on-world, you mean?" Rodrigues asked her.

"No," she replied. "More time during the day. I applied for five jobs on the mainland that I was perfectly qualified for. Any one of them would have positioned me to make contact with potential sources at the workplace. Didn't get a nibble. Each time I followed up, I was told the job had been filled. But there was an opening in maintenance if I was interested. Or serving food. Or watching over children. Five times this happened. I ended up managing a vehicle rental depot on the island and advancing the mission in my spare time."

"Hey, at least those were urban postings," Nussbaum pointed out, his complexion darkening. "They kept wanting to send me to an Agricultural Zone. The closest I was able to get to intel during business hours was by taking a job delivering messages and packages in the commercial district."

"It's because we had to reject being optimized," came a tenor voice from the third table. Drew swung his gaze in that direction and saw a fellow with large, watery eyes and negligible hair—Elliot Darling. "People with implants get the best jobs on Stragon. So, we were relegated to menial or entry-level positions that prevented us from naturally cultivating the kind of relationships that would have yielded the best intel."

None of this was news to Townsend, but Rodrigues was hearing it for the first time.

"Relationships with...?" he said.

"People with connections. People who know things about politicians and power brokers and captains of industry." Olivia's voice startled the others into silence. She'd been so quiet that they'd forgotten she was there. "Also, labour leaders and activists... and, in a pinch, the criminal element. Any or all of those would have had their finger on the figurative pulse of the Stragori people."

"What about the military? Or Security?" the Ranger persisted.

She frowned. "A smart agent would avoid them, because—"

"—on Stragon they're all optimized, and constantly reporting to the Directorate," Drew said, finishing her thought.

"Which means we have to avoid them as well, regardless of their stated intentions," Rodrigues concluded with a significant look at Townsend.

Damn! If he sent that Stragori shuttle away and later

found out that the risk to its passenger had been real...!

"Angeli was made early on as well," Olivia said. "I don't know whether they knew she was coordinating the operation, but someone was toying with her. She was placed where she could download files from the Directorate's server, but everything she came up with was either trivial or misleading. She told me that before she—" She gulped a breath, her eyes shining with tears.

Drew had to unclench his jaw in order to speak.

"So, the mission was compromised from the outset. Was there a leak?"

"It was that damned Nestor Quan," Olivia muttered bitterly. "He had someone on the outside, I'd bet my life on it."

Rodrigues looked puzzled. "Don't you mean on the inside?"

"Quan *was* on the inside. He was a radical spy, held prisoner for years at Ops Control. He kept himself useful by feeding the Chief of Ops intel about the Directorate's plans, one morsel at a time. If Quan's captivity on Earth and the EIS mission to Stragon were both part of a greater plan by the radical faction, then it's no wonder our operation failed. We played right into their hands."

Her own hands curled into fists on her lap.

"Thank you all for your input," Drew announced to the gathering. "It's been most helpful. However, we still need you to search your memories and draw up lists of names. You can transmit the lists to Ruby when you're done. Any last questions?"

"I've got one," said Nussbaum, rising to his feet again. "Was this a simple precautionary exercise, or is there an actual threat to the station that you're not telling us about?"

Rodrigues fairly bounced off his chair to reply, "There is no clear and present danger yet. However, we're practically on Stragon's doorstep and the situation on-world is combustible, so there could very likely be one soon. It's best to be prepared."

The other man grunted a syllable of acceptance, and Drew declared the meeting over.

As the attendees were filing out, Rodrigues came over to Townsend and said softly, "I'll be needing a copy of those debriefings as soon as you can send them to me. I want to get up to speed and have a strategy in place before your secretive visitor arrives."

"Sure." Drew would have said more, but his wristcomm buzzed, derailing his train of thought. "What is it, Lydia?"

Rodrigues snorted impatiently and walked away.

"Another message just arrived from Stragon, addressed to Uncle Henry. I thought you'd want to know immediately."

"Yeah, thanks." Townsend glanced helplessly around the room. He still had to talk with Moe. And decrypt this latest message from Isabela Bakshi.

It never rained but it poured...

"Do you want the good news first or the bad news?"

O'Malley's voice was close by. Townsend opened his eyes and found the ratkeeper standing on the other side of his desk.

The kid cocked his head. "You okay, Boss? You look a little—"

"I'm fine," he snapped, dropping the fresh bottle of antacid tablets into his desk drawer and slamming it shut.

The debriefing of the Human-Nandrian hybrid called Moe (short for *homo saurius*) had been singularly unproductive. He might as well have been living all alone on an asteroid for all the useful intel he was able to provide.

Drew felt owed some signs of progress right now, no matter how slight. So, he added in a calmer voice, "What's the good news? Have you identified our mysterious would-be visitor?"

"I found a voice print on our system that matches the voice of the passenger on that shuttle. His given name is Arno. No last name is mentioned."

"It's not much to go on," Drew remarked wearily. "And that's the good news? What's the bad news?"

"The audio clip containing his voice is part of a conversation with Dennis Forrand, and I don't think either of them knew it was being recorded."

"What were they discussing?" Townsend asked.

"Nothing of import. They were making a lunch date... and cracking wise about the Directorate and how useless it was becoming."

So, *if* the clip was genuine and undoctored, both of these men were anti-Directorate... and apparently they were being monitored... and one of them was now on his way to the Hub, supposedly at great risk to himself.

Peachy, Drew thought sourly.

"Is there a time and date attached to this voice clip?"

"Yes, but it's too corrupted to be readable. The meeting could have taken place last interval or twenty years ago. It's impossible to tell."

Of course it was. This intel had a distinctly fishy aroma about it. Just like everything else they'd gotten from the

Directorate's memory blocs, it was best taken with a huge grain of salt, and then not actually swallowed.

"All right, then. Thanks, O'Malley. That's good work."

The kid shrugged. "Not that it did much good, but you're welcome anyway."

As O'Malley headed toward the tube car, Townsend consulted his chronometer. Eight hours to go. Rodrigues should have finished perusing the debriefing records by now and come to the same conclusion as Drew had done: Stragon was an unholy and irretrievable mess and they would be well advised to steer clear of it, if not for the millions of Terrans stranded smack in the middle of it. Under the circumstances, could they really justify sitting on their hands on the sidelines?

His intercomm buzzed.

Speak of the devil.

The second he opened the channel, the Ranger's voice barked at him, "Townsend, we need to talk, right now."

It had been one of the most difficult negotiations of Drew's life, but he and Rodrigues had finally hammered out a plan.

When the Stragori shuttle was on final approach, Ruby buzzed Townsend from Communications to announce, "That ship we're expecting just requested docking instructions, Chief, and the Rangers' advanced scan shows no explosives or ordnance of any kind on board. Are we a go?"

"We're a go," he confirmed. "Notify Rodrigues. Tell him I'll meet him there."

In the end, and with the right technology in place, the solution to their problem had been simple. The most secure location for a clandestine meeting was aboard the shuttle itself, and the safest location for the shuttle—and for everyone aboard it—was on Daisy Hub's hangar deck. It had taken some work to reassure their visitor of that, but Ruby could be charmingly persuasive when she set her mind to it.

One of the features of the new and improved landing deck was that it was now equipped with an airlock and an antigrav platform, both specially designed to wrangle small craft in a gridded space. No longer was it necessary to empty the deck of living personnel each time a ship was cleared to enter the station. Once the air had cycled back in and the inner doors opened onto the hangar deck, the platform would rise and deliver the vessel to its designated tie-down position.

That was where Townsend and Rodrigues stood waiting for the shuttle to arrive. The Ranger was holding two face shields—curved pieces of dark blue plastiplex with adjustable straps attached to them.

When the platform had withdrawn and the docking clamps were applied, the pilot's tentative voice came over the comm: "All right, we're here. Now what?"

Rodrigues stepped around to the front of the craft, holding the face shields in the air. "Put me on your forward screen," he instructed. "Do you recognize these?"

"We can see you," said the passenger's voice after a moment. "Are those masks?"

"They're two-way face masks. It's an old Earth technology, adapted for use in space helmets. Wearing these will conceal your identity without blocking your vision. If you'll pop your hatch, I'll place them just inside the entrance so you can test them for yourselves. Then, once you're both wearing them, your pilot is going to disembark and remain with me on the deck while Mr. Townsend climbs aboard to speak with you. You can close the hatch to prevent us from overhearing anything. Doing that will also block our surveillance systems from recording your meeting, thus equalizing the risk to you and him both. Is that acceptable?"

"Yes, quite acceptable," he replied.

Five minutes later, Drew was standing in the centre aisle of what appeared to be a standard model four-passenger shuttle. This one lacked the homey touches and embellishments that had marked the parlour-like interior of Trager's diplomatic vessel. However, the seats were honey-coloured and looked comfortable enough to sleep in. A jacket had been draped across one of them. At the other man's inviting gesture, Drew sat down on one of the remaining three chairs. His visitor took the seat opposite, then turned to face him.

"Mr. Townsend," he began, "I want to thank you for finding a way to make this meeting possible. I realize it involved a significant leap of faith on your part, one that I intend to make worth your while."

These last words set off alarms at the back of Drew's brain.

Really? He put us through all this so he could make us a deal?

"First tell me, are you optimized?" Townsend demanded.

"I used to be, but when you rise high enough in the food chain, being an open book becomes a liability. Besides, I'm a Forrand, like you and Olivia, and that still carries some weight on-world. It gives us choices others don't have... although that might not be the case for long."

Used to be? Like Trager, who was ex-military and had

been taught how to remove his implants if he were captured, without permanently damaging his nervous systems? From the neck down, this visitor had the physique of a wrestler. Drew could easily imagine him wearing a uniform.

"There's a revolution brewing on Stragon, Mr. Townsend. From here, it may seem like nothing more than a distant rumble of discontentment, but on the mainland, blood has already been spilled. Bombs are exploding, people are being attacked in the streets, and it's just a matter of time before the hatred boils over and begins claiming lives on the other continents as well. That's partly why I'm here—to brief you fully on the seriousness of the situation and ask for your help—but I also have a question that only you can answer."

Frowning, Townsend asked, "And what is the source of your intelligence, if I may ask? Because we've already been burned by supposedly reliable sources on Stragon."

"In my case, it's personal experience. Listen, Forrands have been known to lie to the world, it's true, but we don't lie to one another."

"Well, *my* personal experience tells me you're lying to me right now, about one Forrand in particular, anyway."

The visitor nodded sagely. "Dennis does have a habit of stopping just short of a lie to get what he wants from other family members. He's a politician. I'm not. So, think of it this way: would you rather remain ignorant about your grandfather's master plan, and be surprised and angry later on, when you find out how he's manipulated you into furthering it? Or would you prefer to be read into it up front, so you can decide whether and how you wish to participate?"

This was a novel approach. Townsend decided to play along.

"You would give me the choice? And respect it once it's made?"

"I would. All the while hoping, of course, that it would be to work together with us to head off the coming storm and, with luck, save the lives of millions of Terrans *and* Stragori. However, I understand that you have limited resources and many heavy responsibilities, so there would be no hard feelings on my part if you decided not to become involved."

Uh-huh. Drew stared at the featureless mask, considering. Evidently, Dennis wasn't the only manipulator in the Forrand family. Guile was probably written right into their genes. And his own, for that matter—Drew was a Forrand too. But this Arno was right—it was better to be informed.

"All right, then. Read me in. What's the old scoundrel up to now?"

"Gladly. But first, I would like an answer to one question, if you please. What made Earth Intelligence abort the operation on Stragon and order the extraction of all your agents?"

For a long moment, it was all Drew could do just to breathe. When he could once more form words, he blurted, "How do you know about that? The orders came from Earth."

"So did your grandfather. And so did your sister, who made contact with him shortly after her arrival on Stragon. Did you really think the distance between our two worlds would stop Dennis from taking an interest in your activities?"

Drew swallowed a sigh. Maybe not... but he had thought it reasonable to expect that cutting off all communication with Forrand would at least have sent the message that his interest was unwelcome and he should mind his own damn business. And now, thanks to Olivia—!

No, he decided firmly, he would not go down that path again. Blaming her had caused them both too much pain already.

Instead, he snapped, "Ops Control learned that the mission had been sabotaged years earlier by the radical faction. Covers were blown and agents were being fed disinformation. When Olivia realized that they'd been targeted to die in—and be blamed for—a major act of terrorism, she decided to hasten the extraction process by having me organize it from here. Does that answer your question... Arno?"

The other man froze momentarily, then bobbed his head. Without seeing his face, Townsend could only guess at the meaning of that gesture. In the end, however, he decided it didn't matter, as long as his own questions got answered.

"You promised to read me into Dennis's 'master plan', as you put it...?" he prompted.

"Of course, but I need to fill you in on some background first. Do you know who the founding families are?"

"No. What exactly did they found?"

"The Reorganization of Earth. Adam Vargas and twelve others, all from different Stragori clans, including a couple that had been at war with each other for hundreds of years—the Forrands and the Harrises. On Stragon, they fought for dominance on the mainland. On Earth, they fought for wealth and power in Americas. On both worlds, the conflict continues to this day, growing fiercer and more destructive with each passing decade. Forrands have been the victims of assault, vandalism, character assassination, and most recently, an attempted murder."

Struck by a sudden thought, Drew ventured, "Is that what you believe is fuelling the current political unrest on Stragon?"

"There's reason to suspect that the Harrises are behind it, yes. If they can destabilize the mainland by turning people against the government, then they can seize power. We know they're supporting at least one extreme radical group and using it to encourage violence. We also know that they plan to solve what they term 'the Terran problem' by blaming everything that's been happening on the Humans from Earth. However, the *real* Terran problem is—"

"—there's no practical way to get twenty-seven million people off the planet before the hatred the Harrises are stirring up embroils the entire population in open revolt," Townsend supplied grimly.

"The fact that most of the Terrans are living on an island twenty kilopaces south of the mainland has provided some protection for them up until now. A slow ferryboat ride over deep water gives hotheads a chance to cool off. But there have been some hate-driven incidents in Capital City, things that we've downplayed or covered over. Terrans have been harassed... beaten..."

"Killed and then blamed for their own death?"

Once again it was impossible to read an expression behind the dark mask, but the slump of the other man's shoulders was eloquent.

"You know about that from Olivia. I should have realized."

"Is his widow ever going to get justice for him?"

"It's doubtful, but Dennis has promised her he'll try."

Right. Drew and Olivia both knew how self-serving Dennis's promises were.

"I'm not sure what we can do from here to help you change the situation on Stragon," Townsend said. "All of my agents have been exposed, so returning them to the planet is not an option."

"Very true. However, there is a service you are uniquely positioned to provide. When Dennis established the Earth Intelligence Service, its mission was to learn and safeguard the truth, and then reveal it at the most effective time. Is that still the case?"

"It is. But we're calling ourselves The Repository now."

"Because you've become a repository of information. How appropriate. Well, I've brought you some to add to your collection," Arno said. "Dennis has been researching the various anti-Directorate groups, and I've maintained a comprehensive database on the Harrises. Given the hostility between our two clans, I expect the Harrises have been tracking the Forrands just as closely. Anyway..."

He reached under the jacket on the chair behind his and brought out a bluish-grey cloth sack with a drawstring fastening. "This contains a memory bloc. It's not a trick, Mr. Townsend, and it isn't disinformation. Dennis's dodgery notwithstanding, I meant what I said before: Forrands do not lie to one another. I brought it aboard without the pilot's knowledge, and you are the only person on the station who knows that it exists. Treat it as eyes only until you have studied everything that's on it, then use your own good judgment regarding who else should see it."

Holding the bag by the strings, he passed it carefully across the aisle and into Townsend's care.

"Does Dennis know you're giving this to me?"

"Of course. It was his idea."

Drew was confused. "Then why all the secrecy? Who are you afraid will find out you left Stragon to come here?"

A pause, then, "I'm afraid I can't tell you that. Read the files on the memory bloc. Then perhaps you'll understand. In the meanwhile, let me give you the broad strokes of what your grandfather has in mind..."

Half an hour later, Townsend stepped out of the shuttle. Reversing the order in which things had been done before, the pilot went back aboard, Rodrigues retrieved the two masks, and Drew cleared the vessel to depart. Then he and the Ranger captain watched as the anti-grav platform glided silently over, lifted the Stragori craft, and carried it through the open hatch into the airlock.

"So? Was it worth the risk?" Rodrigues asked him as they headed toward the tube cars.

Drew was suddenly aware of a gathering heat in his core. The risk? Certainly. The unrelenting stress of what he now knew, however, was another matter. He would need something stronger than antacid to douse the embers that Dennis's master plan was threatening to kindle to flame in his stomach.

Assuming a neutral expression, Drew replied with a sigh, "Well, I know more than I did before, but how useful the intel will be remains to be seen."

"But you will keep me in the loop regardless, right?"

"Of course!"

Rodrigues hit the call button for a tube car. While they waited, Drew sensed rather than saw the Ranger's gaze settle on the cloth bag he was holding.

"What's that?" Rodrigues asked quietly.

Drew had already decided on his response. Wordlessly, he loosened the drawstring and let the other man look inside.

"Another Stragori memory bloc?" Rodrigues said, shifting his incredulous stare to Townsend's face.

The door chose that moment to slide open. Drew waited until they were in the car and moving upwards before he replied, "This one is on the level, I think."

"You *think*?!"

"Hey, I'm not letting my guard down yet," he retorted irritably. "The last attempt to infiltrate our systems failed because we took precautions, and we'll take them again. The contents of the bloc will remain eyes only until I know what's on it and am certain that it's safe to share. At that point I will happily read you in, Paul, but not a second before."

Rodrigues lapsed into a silence that thickened the air, filling it with unspoken words. When the car stopped and Drew stepped off it onto AdComm, the Ranger put out a hand to prevent the door from closing again.

"You've changed, Townsend," he declared, "and not for the better, I think."

"Yeah. Blame it on the weight of all the hats I wear." *...and the secrets inside the head that they're on.*

Making a beeline for his office, Drew dropped the cloth bag onto the desktop and flung open the drawer containing the heavy-duty antacid tablets the Doc had recently given him. He popped a couple of them and sank onto his chair, inhaling deeply to mitigate the pain from his ulcer until the medication took effect.

"I've got those lists of names for you, Chief. Sending them to your unit now."

He punched the intercomm button. "Thanks, Ruby." Then he settled back and let his thoughts wander to the conversation he'd just had with Arno Forrand. Or maybe he wasn't called Forrand. After all, Olivia Townsend and Gael Dedrick were Forrands, and there were probably many other cousins with different surnames as well. How many Harrises might there be with names other than Harris, he wondered. They might not even realize they belonged to one of the founding families until someone they trusted pointed it out to them. And because of who the founding families were, these unsuspecting relatives might even have been born and raised on Earth—

Sudden realization burst over him. *They might be aboard the Hub.*

Now the urgent need for secrecy was making sense.

Drew hit the intercomm button again. "Ruby, I need Walt Garfield up here right away."

That streak of morality of his was about to come in handy.

The Mezzanine was the unofficial name of Deck C-1. Located immediately below AdComm, this was where all the servers and databases were kept. As well as being O'Malley's and Walt Garfield's primary workspace, it was the communications technology centre of the station.

Today, it was a private area where Townsend could sit, alone and unmonitored, and peruse the information on the Stragori memory bloc. Walt was the only other person on the Hub besides Rodrigues that Drew trusted with ironclad certainty to keep secret the fact that the bloc existed, at least until Townsend was ready to share its contents himself.

Walt had uploaded the bloc to a piece of rogue technology, a dedicated server unconnected to any of the intranets or systems on the Hub. There, he had put the coding through a series of diagnostic tests to ensure that the data was free of worms, parasites, or any other kind of unwanted passenger. Once he'd confirmed that it was clean, it was cleared to be read.

Drew watched the data scroll upward on his screen, relieved that it appeared to be exactly what Arno had promised: intel about the members of radical groups. There were a lot of them, some marked as being more involved or more dangerous than others. Once this data had been correlated with the lists of names provided by his agents, they could begin to determine how the EIS mission had been undermined, and by whom. Unfortunately, with no operatives actively assigned on-world, that was about all they could do with the information besides store it in The Repository's databank.

Then he got to the file containing the Harris family tree. The Terran branch was impressively broad and contained some names he recognized from the news feeds. The parent tree on Stragon, however, was enormous. There had to be thousands of twigs on hundreds of branches, and at least a hundred different surnames. Never having visited Stragon, Drew found all this interesting but not relevant... until his gaze was captured by one name in particular. All at once, pieces fell into place in his mind, tumbling and scattering his words until the only ones that reached his mouth were, "*Son* of a *bitch!*"

*   *   *

Townsend stormed off the tube car and onto AdComm, still cursing loudly. His first order of business was to swallow two more antacid tablets. By then, Lydia was standing at the entrance to his office, her features etched with concern.

"What can I do to help?" she asked.

He slipped the bottle into a pocket of his trousers and told her grimly, "You can warn Captain Rodrigues that I'm on my way to see him. And tell Ruby to meet me there."

"What about that message that arrived for Henry Eisner?"

"It can wait. Right now we have a rodent problem to take care of, and I'm not talking about Yoko or Akiko."

EIGHTEEN
ON STRAGON

Quinian was escorted home from the Medical Services centre by two Security officers with badges embedded in their forearms and humourless expressions on their faces. Warned ahead of time by his comm message, Isabela had stuffed all the traitorous EIS technology back into her tote bag, then concealed the bag at the back of her wardrobe. Finally, she had prepared a pot of *jekhailla* tea, hoping it would calm her nerves while she waited for company to arrive.

The sight of Quinian hobbling through the door with the aid of a cane sent Isabela's heart spiralling into her stomach. He looked so fragile!

As he made for the living room and eased himself onto the sofa with an exhalation of relief, disquieting questions arose in her mind. How long did these officers intend to remain in the apartment? As a possible person of interest in his poisoning, was she now expected to move out so that he could be in some sort of protective custody? And if that was the case, how were they supposed to work together to carry out Dennis Forrand's plan?

"Are you certain you'll be all right, Dr. Quinian?" one of the officers inquired.

"Absolutely!" he declared testily. "Don't you two have a crime to solve or something?"

The second officer turned to Isabela and informed her, "A med tech will be stopping by each day to assess his recovery. It was a condition of his early release from the Medical Services centre."

"Early release?" Whipping her gaze back to Quinian's face, she saw him put a silencing finger to his lips.

At last, the officers departed. Isabela waited until they were outside the building. Then she fetched her tote bag back to the living room and set up one of the signal jammers on the coffee table. Apparently, Quinian had been holding his breath. It gusted out of him as soon as the green light began blinking.

She went to the kitchen for another cup and poured him some tea.

Sitting down beside him, she demanded, "You left against medical advice? Talk to me, Quin. What's going on?"

"I couldn't stay there. Too many Harrises in the building. I was vulnerable."

"Too many—!" She leaned in, frowning intently. "You know who poisoned you, don't you? And you were afraid they would find you and finish the job."

Wearing the face of a man struggling to make a life-altering decision, he took a deliberate sip before replacing his cup on the coffee table. "Norry was. He told me to go somewhere safe. Right now that's here."

"Who is Norry?"

"An old friend. You'll be meeting him today. He promised to stop by."

Moments later, the door buzzer sounded. Isabela peered through the spyhole, saw a familiar face out in the hall, and went cold all over.

"Quin!" she whispered hoarsely. "It's the sub-inspector who interrogated me!"

He nodded. "Norton Harris?"

"Yes, Nort—" As comprehension dawned, Isabela felt as though she'd just been smacked in the head. The clandestine kaffy date. The need to keep up appearances. *Norry. Of course.*

Donning her sternest expression, she let him into the apartment.

"Lady Bakshi," he said pleasantly.

"Sub-Inspector Harris. Are you here to question me further?"

"I'm here to see *him*, actually."

Quinian picked up the jamming device and turned it to show him the green light. In that moment, the tough Security officer lost all his hard edges, seeming to morph into an entirely different person before Isabela's eyes.

"I'm so glad you're all right!" Harris exclaimed. He rushed over to sit beside Quinian and gave him a hug.

"Would one of you be good enough to tell me what is going on?" she demanded in her most teacherly voice. "First you tell me you couldn't stay where you were because of the Harrises. Now we are welcoming a Harris into our home?"

Quinian gave her a sheepish grin. "Not just any Harris. Norry and I have known each other for going on seventy-five years."

"Our families don't get along," Harris supplied. "The feud began literally thousands of years ago, and it's become entrenched, with the hatred being passed down from generation to generation. Fraternization is considered by both families to be a betrayal, one that my family in particular deals with quite harshly."

"So, you believe they found out that you and Quin are friends—"

"More than friends, actually," said Quinian with a fond glance to his right.

"More like brothers?" she said.

"It goes even deeper than that. Some of those meetings that I told you about were—"

"—trysts? Using a signal jammer to foil the local surveillance devices?" she supplied.

Madre! These two were the Stragori version of Romeo and Juliet!

To Harris, she went on, "Do you believe that is why he was poisoned? Because your family found out and decided to remove him from your life?"

"Nothing else makes sense," he replied grimly. "I'm afraid I owe you an apology, Lady Bakshi. I was in a difficult situation. I'd already lied to my superiors about my reason for being first on the scene, so I had to continue the investigation."

"And you cast suspicion on me in order to protect your family?"

"My family? No. It was my relationship with Quin. We'd managed to keep it a secret for a very long time by avoiding being seen together in public places like restaurants. Then he acquired that jamming device, and we dared to meet for kaffy, and... you know what happened next. You were never really a person of interest. I used that as an excuse to visit you at your workplace and drop off his jammer. In fact, you wouldn't have been dragged into the case at all if Quin hadn't insisted that I contact you."

...which once more raised the question in her mind. Isabela turned to Quinian and demanded, "How *did* you know that you had been poisoned?"

"By a fluke," he replied wearily. "Whenever Norry and I met somewhere, we never arrived together. This time, I entered the restaurant through the kitchen and noticed the flowers. I'd seen the same ones in your apartment when I first arrived, so I knew they were native to the island, and I'd already learned that anything grown in that soil was dangerous. I was two sips into my kaffy and a couple of mouthfuls into my pastry when it suddenly felt as though my chest was in a vise. Immediately, I was certain that my order must have been tampered with by whoever had brought those flowers."

"And you knew I had expertise in this area because...?"

His complexion darkened. Dropping his gaze to his lap, he said in a voice that was barely more than a murmur, "Dennis showed me your file."

She shouldn't have been surprised, she knew. Dennis had spies everywhere. He'd probably opened a dossier on every EIS agent who'd come to Stragon.

Their mission had focused on the mainland, where most of the population lived and worked... and that gave Isabela an idea.

"You know," she began, sinking onto the armchair, "there is another crime scenario that might make sense."

She told them about the data request she'd received from

the northern continent.

"Wait a minute. You're suggesting that a serial killer could be out there, using damselflower toxin as their weapon of choice?" Harris ventured. "That Quin was simply in the wrong place at the wrong time and my family had nothing to do with it?"

"I do not have sufficient information to propose a theory," she corrected him. "All I know is that there have been enough suspicious deaths up north to get the continental government's top forensic specialist involved. And it makes me wonder whether Mainland Security ought to be taking a second look at recent cases of death declared to be by natural causes."

Harris paused to consider this. "The recommendation would have to come from someone higher up than me, but I believe it could be managed. If all the victims turn out to be connected somehow, it could even spark a joint investigation between the two continental Security forces."

"But Norry, what if that investigation leads directly to your family?" Quinian's features were pinched with anxiety.

"In that case, they'll either have to face justice or they'll do whatever it takes to avoid it. Either way, I won't be part of it. I'll quit the force, change my name, get rid of these damned implants, and move to the northern continent to grow dannoli. Everyone loves dannoli. And it would probably be a better-paid occupation than what I'm doing right now."

As he said this, there wasn't so much as a twitch of a smile on his lips.

"But there's a high risk of death if the implants are removed," Isabela pointed out. "Doesn't that worry you?"

He gave her a strange look. "Where did you hear that?"

"From my teaching assistant. She had a brochure, given to her when she had the optimization procedure. It said that the implants are grafted directly onto the subject's neural systems and removal is fatal eighty to ninety percent of the time."

"Where did she go to have this done?"

"It was some large medical research company on the mainland. I don't recall the name."

"And they knew she was Terran?"

"The preparation for surgery included a DNA test, so I assume they would have found out. Why do you ask?"

"Because there are different grades of implants," Harris explained. "The highest level of technology is organic. Take it offline and it atrophies and is eventually absorbed by the body. That makes disconnecting from the intellinet a quick and simple operation, perfectly safe when it's performed by a trained medical specialist. When this technology was perfected, fifty or so years ago, the Department of Medical Science issued a directive that organic implantation would be the standard for all optimizations going forward. Unfortunately, a lot of the older, inorganic technology was still sitting around in storage, and no one followed up to ensure that it was properly disposed of."

"And that's the kind Joanne received?"

"It sounds that way. In which case, the fatality rate of eighty to ninety percent is correct. I'm sorry."

An idea was glimmering on the edges of Isabela's mind. "Do you think it might have been chosen for her because she is Terran?"

"Hard to say. There are dozens of companies performing this procedure. But they are required by law to make each patient aware beforehand of the risks of implantation."

So, every Terran optimized using the old technology should have received the same brochure. That ought to make the search more manageable. And if ever there was an injustice capable of rousing an entire population to anger while Security was busy chasing down serial killers...

Dennis was in for a surprise. All at once, the make-work assignment he'd given her was looking much more feasible.

Angeli had never considered herself to be an expert cook, but she wouldn't have called herself a novice, until now. To pass the time while waiting for the expected pronouncement from the District Chief of Forensic Medicine, she had asked Lyla to teach her how to make some northern dishes. The lessons had been eye-opening, to say the least. Some of the results had also been tear-producing.

Spices grown north of the channel, she'd learned, were used sparingly for a reason. They were all strongly-flavoured, and some imparted a variety of tastes depending not only on which foods they seasoned but also how the foods were prepared. The same was true of herbs, although they tended to be milder. Mistakes with herbs were easier to cover up, and for the most part still edible.

She'd had no idea cooking a meal could be so complicated. It was like learning to speak a new language with the wrong kind of speech organs.

Today, she watched with trepidation as Lyla dipped a spoon into the pot of heggen sauce Angeli had prepared to be the basis for that evening's dinner casserole. The recipe was Lyla's. However, on impulse, Angeli had thrown some additional spices into the mix—some crumbled dok leaves and about a tablespoonful of shavings from a root that smelled like ginger when dry but tasted peppery when wet.

Lyla had stood over the bubbling pot, waving the steam toward her nose. The more she'd sniffed, the more quizzical her expression had become. Finally, she had reached for the spoon to conduct the all-important taste test.

Angeli watched, every muscle taut, as Lyla blew gently over the sample, then took it into her mouth. She closed her eyes, initially nodding with satisfaction. Then, she frowned. Her head tilted. Her lips compressed with concentration.

The suspense was killing.

At last, Lyla opened her eyes and said, "Remarkable! I don't know what you've added, but it has created something new and delicious. I'm going to call this 'Eva's Heggen Sauce', and it will be my pleasure to serve it to my guests tonight. Be sure to write the recipe down so you can reproduce the taste and texture."

Two hours later, guests began arriving. There were ten diners in total, including Krall and the Skinner brothers. Krall was out of uniform and apparently off-duty. Adam and Michael were once more identically dressed except for the colour of their shirts, and they had brought their technical gear, stowing it in the parlour before they sat down at the table.

They'd received important news to report in their next broadcast, Angeli could tell. The twins looked ready to burst with it. She hoped it was something to do with the investigation, but knew better than to ask about it at dinner.

The casserole was a huge success, as was the dessert: a

triple-layer cake with tasselberry jam filling. Lyla had made sweetmeat tarts that afternoon. She sent five of her guests out the door with a bundle of six tarts each and put the remaining pastries on a plate to serve with evening tea later to Krall, the Skinners, and Angeli.

"There's been a break in the case!" Adam declared when they were finally alone together in the parlour. "We have the text of an advisory issued today by the Office of Medical Oversight to every district on Borea. Forensic medical specialists are being directed to re-examine all the fatalities they've handled during the past year and retest to eliminate the possibility that botanical toxins might have been involved."

"Botanical toxins!" Lyla exclaimed, shooting a significant look at Angeli. "Really!"

"Sharma Dorel sent a statement to all the news gatherers, asking them to warn the public about invasive species from the two southern land masses," Michael said. "She attached a file of information about some plants in particular that everyone's to watch for. People are to report any that they find to the warders."

"Did she provide any illustrations of these toxic plants?" Angeli asked.

"Yes, and we're going to be putting them onscreen as part of every newscast from tonight on," Adam replied.

"That's good," she said. "In fact, that's *very* good. Anything you can pass along to help people identify them could actually save lives. Some of the deadliest blossoms are also the most beautiful, so Boreans might be cultivating them without realizing how dangerous they are."

Michael frowned. "But where would they have gotten the—? Oh!" His eyes widened. In a hushed voice he added,

"They could have been smuggled across the channel."

"And who knows?" she stage-whispered back to him. "The person who brought them north could even be the one responsible for those suspicious deaths."

As his eyes narrowed thoughtfully, Angeli repressed a grin. She'd just planted a seed. It would be interesting to see what it sprouted into.

Dennis had taken up residence in the unregistered apartment above a small-goods store in one of the poorer areas of Capital City.

On Earth, the neighbourhood would have been designated as a Zone by the District Council, dropped to the bottom of the funding priority list, and allowed to fall slowly into ruin as residents departed to find better housing elsewhere, leaving empty structures behind. On Stragon, the ground floors of all urban buildings were kept habitable at Council expense to ensure full occupancy. For an annual fee, additional storeys could be registered to receive regular attention by Council-approved tradesfolk. That made them legally rentable quarters. It also meant monthly inspections, and periodic visits to make repairs— which tended to happen more frequently in the older areas.

That was not what Dennis wanted. What he wanted more than anything was to live and work in total privacy. So, upon his return from Earth, he had looked for and found a reasonably maintained building owned by someone who was handy with tools and saw no advantage to paying what she termed "protection credit" to the District Council.

The little flat above her store was perfect. Nothing was

new or pretty, but everything was in good working order. Dennis had no visitors of any kind and always used the back door. He'd also arranged for his rent to be paid with randomly spaced credit transfers from an alias account set up for that very purpose. The building owner appreciated his discretion and repaid it with her own. No one even knew she had a tenant.

This was where he'd set to work earlier, extending the leaves of the battered wooden dining table and spreading out the pages of hard copy Arno had given him. Now the past and present of the Harris family on Stragon lay before him like an open book. He'd read every word, greedily absorbing information and pausing only to rest his eyes, eat whatever came to hand, and use the hygiene cabinet.

Finally, with the data processed and Arno hopefully on his way back home from Daisy Hub, a plan was coming together in Dennis's mind.

As it turned out, Lloyd Franklin Harris Jr. was Dennis's target. Arno's further research had revealed that approaching him directly was going to be out of the question. The CEO of Primus Enterprises conducted all of his business from his home—a large, heavily fortified compound that he shared with his immediate family members, surrounded for kilopaces in all directions by flat, cultivated land. It was old school security, and it worked. The kind of technology required to sneak up on Harris's position undetected had not yet been invented—on Stragon, anyway—and even after going without sleep for two days, Dennis was not furry-brained enough to think that marching up to the front door and announcing himself would be a good idea.

Drew Townsend might be able to facilitate a stealth

approach. He had, after all, managed to spirit Olivia and those nine operatives off-world without tripping any Planetary Security alarms. It shouldn't be a stretch for him to put Dennis, Marcel, and a small strike force inside the walls of the compound. The question was, what kind of incentive would make him willing to participate in such a mission?

Dennis couldn't think of a single one offhand, not without sacrificing the board pieces he'd already put into play. All right, then. Time to come up with a plan B. Outside of those walls, Harris would be vulnerable. What could make him leave the safety of his lair?

Perhaps, if he felt another family member was in danger...? No, that wouldn't work. Everyone he truly cared about—his wife, his children, their spouses, and his grandchildren—was inside the compound with him. Lloyd Franklin Jr. clearly knew how much danger his crimes had put them in and had decided not to take any chances with their safety. Or his own. The rest of the Harris clan didn't matter to him.

Ah, but what if the target believed his master plan was about to fall apart?

To be credible, the news would have to come from another Harris, one with more seniority in the family than Lloyd Franklin Jr. possessed. He would move quickly from that point, so it was best not to set things in motion until the rest of the board was ready and waiting.

In the meanwhile, it might be prudent for Dennis to hedge his bets by requesting assistance from Daisy Hub. The message couldn't come from Dennis himself, and there were limits to what he could safely ask Arno to do for him, especially knowing that a Harris occupied a position of trust aboard the station. The Sub-Chief of Mainland Security had already taken an unconscionable risk on his cousin's behalf.

Angeli? Angeli was fearless and had probably defied Dennis and held onto the requisite EIS technology, but she was also supposed to be dead. In any case, her shell identity was trapped up north by a bogus arrest warrant.

That left just one person the Townsends might listen to. She'd already agreed to help him carry out his plan and knew how high the stakes were. He couldn't imagine her refusing to do him this small favour.

Dennis went to the coat rack and found his spring jacket. The sun was low in the sky, making this a perfect time to pay a visit to the island. Perhaps he would stop on the way and pick up a treat to sweeten the conversation he was about to have with Quin and his beautiful and spirited— dare he say thoroughbred?—apartment-mate.

Anyone tuning in to The Skinner Report that evening would have seen the twins broadcasting from an empty science classroom. The school setting had been chosen deliberately to serve as a backdrop to the botany lesson that took up the first hour or so of their show. The brothers made a good team, Angeli thought. Adam delivered the text, and Michael handled the visual aids.

The gist of their presentation was quite educational. After living with Isabela for more than a quarter of a year, Angeli had considered herself well-informed about the dangers of the Wilderness Zone on the island. However, even she was astonished to learn just how many ways there were for the plants that grew there to kill or cripple an unwary visitor.

That Vikram and Isabela had ever seen the Zone as a great place to picnic now struck her as being either incredibly brave or incredibly foolish. And Moe had *lived* there, even picking and eating fruit off the trees, for goodness' sake! No wonder the little monster had been suffering with constant belly pain.

Then came the punch line:

"Now we have a message for the person or persons responsible for bringing these dangerous plants onto Borean soil," said Adam, showing his sternest face to the vidcam. "Our Security forces are the best on the planet. They are putting the pieces together as I speak, and they are going to find out what you've done. And then they will find you and make you pay for your crimes, whatever they may turn out to be.

"This is not a threat. It's a promise. Justice may be an empty word south of the channel, but it's a sacred principle in Borea, as you will learn at first hand soon enough."

"That's our newscast for tonight," said Michael. "Stay safe, everyone, and tune in tomorrow for more information about these unfolding stories."

"Was this what you had in mind, Eva Moss?" Krall whispered into her ear when Lyla went into the kitchen to brew a fresh pot of tea.

She responded with a smile, "It's a beginning."

NINETEEN
ON DAISY HUB

So, Dennis Forrand was determined to take down the flesh-and-blood Harris who was impersonating the current most prominent member of the Directorate, and Townsend was being given the *choice* of whether or not to bring Daisy Hub into the fray? If true, that would be a first. Drew seriously doubted whether his grandfather was capable of passing up an opportunity to meddle in his and Olivia's lives. Being dragged into Forrand's various schemes had already changed them both, and not for the better. Townsend was damned if he'd let it happen again.

That said, three-and-a-half days' travel from Stragon was apparently not far enough away to shield them from the fallout of on-world events, and Arno's research had revealed a potential threat that needed to be dealt with immediately: Vinson Trager was a Harris.

Trager had been career military when the Directorate had chosen him to infiltrate Daisy Hub before the Corvou war. He'd not only been trained to be a formidable fighter, he'd also been physically modified to be very hard to kill. Supposedly, he was now a diplomat, but there was a lot of truth to that old Earth adage about leopards not changing their spots.

Rodrigues had agreed with Townsend that when push came to shove, as it was eventually bound to do, the Stragori liaison would become a threat to Daisy Hub and everything it stood for, unless steps were taken to secure his loyalty.

Turn him or terminate him. It was every agent's obligation to protect the organization, with lethal force if necessary, and Trager knew too much to be cut loose. If he refused to swear allegiance...

Rodrigues had also agreed that the safest location in which to conduct this confrontation was his fishbowl of an office on the Ranger detachment's control deck, in sight of at least five Space Installation Security officers at all times. So it was that Drew found himself sitting at the head of the Ranger captain's plastiplex-topped conference table, popping extra-strength antacid tablets in anticipation of the stressful interview ahead, while Rodrigues and Ruby McNeil took their places facing each other to either side of him.

The First and Second Shields of House Daisy Hub were now present. There remained just one chair to fill, at the foot of the table.

As one, then two standard minutes ticked past, Townsend's annoyance simmered slowly in his stomach.

At last, Trager made his appearance. Escorted to the interview room by two of Rodrigues's largest and strongest constables, he paused on the threshold and swept the area with his gaze.

"Well, here we go again," Trager declared heartily. He walked over to the vacant chair and sat down. The men who'd accompanied him waited for their captain's gesture of dismissal, then stepped outside and shut the door.

Meanwhile, Townsend was doing his best to maintain a neutral expression while willing the antacid to kick in. Rodrigues, he knew, had a forbidding face that he could turn on and off like a spigot. And a glance to his right showed him Ruby, leaning forward on one elbow and staring intently at Trager as though daring him to make a wrong move.

"This is becoming a regular thing, Townsend," Trager remarked casually. "Am I supposed to feel intimidated because I'm outnumbered?"

This man was far too relaxed for Drew's liking.

"That's *Hak'kor* to you, Mr. Trager. And they're here as witnesses, so you can't deny anything later on."

"I see. And what terrible crime are you accusing me of this time?" Trager said.

"The same one, actually, but based on different evidence," Townsend replied. "It has recently come to our attention that the Harris and Forrand families are waging an undeclared war on each other, and that you and I are on opposite sides of it."

"Does it matter? The conflict is on Earth and Stragon, not Daisy Hub."

"It matters to me," Townsend said, deliberately enunciating each syllable. "How long have you known about this situation?"

Trager exhaled audibly before replying. "I knew before I came here as Max Karlov that Daisy Hub had been funded and staffed by a Forrand. It was only logical to assume that the station manager and some of the crew would be Forrands as well. But to me, that was irrelevant."

"Oh?"

He leaned forward. "This may be difficult for you to believe, *Hak'kor*, but not every Harris hates every Forrand. There's a branch of the family that continues to nurse some long-ago grievance—it's a powerful and prominent branch, unfortunately—but they're the only Harrises who still care to remember it. Quite honestly, the rest of us are just doing our best not to be caught up in a senseless generational feud, and I'm sure the same can be said of the members of your clan as well."

"Well, this may be difficult for *you* to believe, but it appears that you're tangled up in that feud whether you want to be or not, and now that you've brought it aboard the Hub, so am I."

Townsend's words seemed to push Trager backward in his chair.

"What do you mean?" the Stragori demanded, frowning.

"You work for the Directorate."

"Yes. I was placed on detached duty from Planetary Security. I told you this when I arrived on the Hub years ago."

"Who assigned you to your current post as liaison between the Houses? Was it one of the Directors?"

"The posting was approved by a Director, but it was created and I was chosen for it by your counterpart, the *Hak'kor* of House Stragon, Louis Forrand."

"Did you speak with him personally?"

"No. I'm not important enough to rate an audience with the *Hak'kor*. His wishes were conveyed to me by his second, the *Kalufah*."

"By tradition, the First Shield contains the members of a single ruling family," said Townsend. "So, which Forrand holds the title of *Kalufah* in House Stragon?"

"Gervais. I know what you're thinking, Townsend, and you're wrong. The AI on that memory bloc that called itself Gervais Forrand and claimed to be the *Hak'kor* was a piece of software programmed to lie to you. The real Gervais Forrand is back on Stragon. He's the one who gave me my orders."

"I wouldn't be too certain of that. According to my great-grandmother on Stragon, Louis Forrand went quiet shortly after the alliance was concluded with House Trokerk, and the next-eldest Forrand, Gervais, took over as head of the family. He has also become the face of the Directorate. And since the House and the Directorate are pretty much interchangeable labels for the same thing on your world, as they are on Daisy Hub, I think it's safe to assume that he's usurped the *Hak'kor*'s power and position as well."

"There's nothing intrinsically wrong with that. If the *Hak'kor* is ill or incapacitated, the *Kalufah* is supposed to take over as leader."

Frustration sharpening his voice, Townsend said, "You're talking as though they're both flesh-and-blood beings. Your *Hak'kor* and *Kalufah* are disembodied minds, Trager. They're code inside a computer. How could Louis have become ill or incapacitated, except through outside interference with his programming?"

"What are you implying, Townsend? That someone purposely tampered with the Directorate's server? That's impossible. It has impregnable security, and for damn good reason."

"I'm not implying, Trager—I'm stating it outright. The First Shield isn't who people think it is. The real Gervais Forrand can't possibly be communicating with Louis, and he can't be the *Kalufah* who gave you your orders. Olivia met Gervais when she was on-world, and she says he's barely lucid. He's in no shape to be running *anything*."

The furrows in the Stragori's brow deepened. "How did she—?"

"However it's happened, or been made to happen," Townsend continued, batting away the question, "there's an impostor claiming to be Gervais Forrand, who is conveniently no longer a flesh-and-blood person but has been issuing orders through a server to the rest of the Forrand family. It's a perfect cover from which to *ruin* the Forrand family. And who do you suppose would be most interested in doing that?"

Trager said nothing, just shook his head in disgust. Meanwhile, Townsend was hitting his stride.

"You don't need to answer—we already know it's one of the Harrises," he said. "But here's my problem: that same impostor has also been issuing orders to you. They put you aboard Daisy Hub twice. The first time it was supposedly to protect Yoko, but I'm willing to bet there was more to your assignment than you were at liberty to discuss. The second time it was to deliver those memory blocs for safekeeping, and it turned out they were a ploy to plant an AI in our infonet systems, along with a tonne of disinformation. Fortunately, the impostor underestimated us. I sincerely hope you won't make the same mistake," he concluded, slowing his words as he lowered his voice almost to a whisper.

In response, the Stragori stiffened to attention in his chair, his military training practically clicking into place.

Leaning as far forward as he could without getting to his feet, Drew went on in the same menacing voice, "Understand this, Mr. Trager: the only reason you're still here is the way you reacted when you found out your

Kalufah had played both of us. That's why I welcomed you to The Repository instead of ordering the Second Shield to terminate you."

"You would have had me killed? I'm officially a diplomat. It would have been an act of war."

Only if they found your body, Townsend thought grimly before continuing, "You're a diplomat with a handler on Stragon, and whether or not he's a Harris, whoever's been pulling your strings is a crook. He's a liar and a fraud, and one way or another, he is going down. He's already in multiple crosshairs. It's just a matter of time. This is not someone worthy of your loyalty, Trager. To him you're nothing but a pawn in some power game that he's playing, and he'll sacrifice you without a second thought whenever it suits him. He used you like a tool to get to me. I saw how shocked and angry it made you feel when you found that out." Drew paused to let this reminder sink in, then added, "You don't have to play his game, you know."

The alien barked a syllable of laughter. "I can play yours instead? You've already given me my choices, *Hak'kor*: throw in with you or die. Frankly, I don't much care for either one."

"I don't blame you. So let's start with something a little easier to digest. Swear to me, before these witnesses, that you will keep secret what you know about The Repository and its activities, not revealing it to anyone, including your superiors on Stragon and the other members of the Harris family."

Improbably, Trager chuckled and sank backwards in his chair. "Beyond what I've already reported, you mean?"

For a moment Townsend was at a loss for words.

Ruby's razor-edged voice sliced through the silence.

"What exactly have you told your contacts?"

"Your cover story, as established in the last meeting we all attended: that Daisy Hub aspires to become for Humans what the Central Archives is for all the other races—a repository of information and resources."

She narrowed her gaze. "That's it?"

"That's it. You made it quite clear that the rest was privileged information, so I kept it to myself. Whatever you may think of me, I am not—and never was—a spy. A soldier, yes. A bodyguard, yes. A messenger, yes. A conduit for official communications between two Houses, yes. But nothing more than that."

"I want to believe you, Trager," said Townsend. "So, I repeat: do you swear, before the First and Second Shields of House Daisy Hub, that you will never reveal its secrets—not those of The Repository, nor of its activities—to anyone, including House Stragon, the Directorate, and the members of your own extended family?"

"I can swear to that."

Weasel words. As Drew was opening his mouth to call the alien out, Rodrigues leaped to his feet and beat him to it.

"That's not an answer, Trager!" he growled, leaning on his knuckles on the tabletop. "Yes or no, do you swear to keep secret what you know?"

"Yes, I do," came the defiant response.

"And do you also swear before us present that you will do everything in your power to prevent Daisy Hub from falling under the control of any enemy identified as such by the First or Second Shield?"

Trager inhaled deeply through his nose. Then he raised his chin and replied, "I'll help you defend Daisy Hub from an aggressor, Captain, but I will not become one on your behalf. It's not why I was sent here."

"Aggression can take many forms, Mr. Trager," Rodrigues pointed out. "For example, what if it's a fellow Security officer who's been seconded by the Directorate and sent to spy on us? Would you let us know about it? Would you help us to turn them in order to eliminate the threat? Would you—"

"Would I be loyal to you instead of to the planet I swore an oath to serve all those years ago and still consider to be my home?"

Leaning forward, Trager locked eyes with his interrogator.

"I think you've got it backwards, Captain. If the reason for the covert assignment was that the Directorate had been lied to or was not in possession of all the facts, then I would owe it to my government to enlighten them, thus eliminating the need for the assignment. However, since I've just sworn to protect your secrets, I would only reveal information that does not jeopardize the security of House Daisy Hub.

"On the other hand, we're trained not to follow orders blindly, so if an operative arrived on the station who'd been... misinformed, shall we say?... then I would owe it to my fellow officer to correct whatever false data they'd been given—again, sharing only as much as you would consider safe to tell them—and I would then trust them to make the right decisions going forward, as I would hope you're prepared to do for me.

"If what you expect is that I'll toss aside all previously taken oaths and be your man instead of Stragon's, the answer is no. But I wouldn't advise trying to terminate me—at least, not until after the petition for *ssalssit essendi* arrives from House Stragon."

The First and Second Shields all snapped to attention at once.

"Wait a minute," Ruby interjected. "You're saying they want to formalize an alliance with us?"

Trager nodded confirmation. "They wanted it to be a surprise, but..." His lips twitched briefly. Then his features settled into an expression more befitting an official envoy.

"And when can we expect the process to begin?" Ruby asked.

"The request from the *Hak'kor* should be coming through diplomatic channels any day now."

"Relayed by the person who's pretending to be the *Kalufah*, of course," Drew remarked, not bothering to conceal his distaste.

"Maybe he is, but it doesn't make the petition itself any less legitimate or worthy of consideration," Trager informed him. "And if you have no further questions for me...?"

Three pairs of eyes were now staring expectantly at Townsend. He could almost feel them boring into his head. They hadn't exactly neutralized the threat to the Hub, but it seemed to be on hold for the time being. Realistically, that might be the best they could hope for.

"Mr. Trager, despite being a Harris and answering to a superior who is beneath contempt, you appear to be a man of honour," said Townsend. "So, I will trust you until you give me a reason not to, at which point I may very well order you thrown out an airlock in your underwear. Do we have an understanding?"

Trager stood up and bowed from his shoulders. "We do, *Hak'kor*."

Once the Stragori was dismissed and on his way back to wherever he'd been earlier, Drew, Ruby, and Rodrigues continued the discussion.

"So, now the impostor plans to draw us into *ssalssit essendi*," Townsend mused. "It's an interesting change of tactic."

The other two at the table traded speculative looks.

"Could it be a ploy to try to acquire Yoko's clone in lieu of an egg exchange?" Ruby ventured. "That's what we gave the Nandrians, after all, and we know that the radicals have been trying to get their hands on her for years."

"I suspect it's a lot bigger—and a lot worse—than that," said Rodrigues, "although claiming Yoko could be part of it, if the impostor is a flesh-and-blood person. After all, she's living proof that a genome can be tweaked in order to create immortality without having to upload one's consciousness into a computer. Whoever is impersonating Gervais Forrand is clearly out to grab as much power as possible. Having the ability to hang onto it for a very, *very* long time...? That would be a bonus."

"The Doc would never let it happen, though." Ruby shifted uncomfortably on her chair. "Not by way of an alliance ritual, anyway. Yoko isn't just living proof of concept—she's the whole experiment. Naguchi encrypted all his notes and recorded them inside her DNA. That's why the Doc fought so hard against cloning her earlier. She only consented to do it because the Nandrians have a strict code of honour, and she knew Trokerk could be trusted not to misuse the information if they stumbled across it. She won't give in a second time, especially with what's going on right now in House Stragon."

"If Yoko is the gravy, then there has to be another

reason, a purely strategic reason, for wanting us as allies," Townsend mused, "and somehow I doubt whether it's as altruistic as Trokerk's was when its *Hak'kor* demanded to join with us."

"If I may?" Rodrigues piped up. "I have a theory, and you are definitely not going to like it. I agree with Ruby that this alliance is a ploy. There's no doubt in my mind about that. Impersonating Gervais Forrand has given someone control over the interface between the Directorate and the Stragori people, as well as power over all the Forrands on Stragon. Speaking hypothetically, what if that's not enough? What if the impostor is a Harris so invested in the feud that they want to control—or ruin, or eliminate— every Forrand everywhere, and the power grab is simply a means to that end?"

As the implications of Rodrigues's question sank in, Townsend went cold all over. Every Forrand everywhere? There had to be hundreds if not thousands of them on Earth, most of them hybrids as unaware of their Forrand connection as he and Olivia had once been. And what about the Terrans who had carried the Forrand genes out into space, to the colonies and the hubs?

"If that's true, you're talking about an enormous undertaking," Ruby pointed out, and for a disconcerting moment Townsend thought she'd been reading his mind.

"Not if it begins by controlling House Daisy Hub," said Rodrigues. "Trager as much as said that this station is a Forrand stronghold."

Ruby gave him a puzzled look. "But why an alliance? Wouldn't that make the *Hak'kor*s equals?"

"Yes," Townsend cut in, suddenly realizing where the Ranger captain was going with this, "but it would also obligate the Houses to each other."

"Exactly," Rodrigues confirmed. "If the objective is control and you can't take it directly, then you find a different route, one that lets you pull strings from a distance. The impostor must know that a physical attack on the First and Second Shields of another House, especially one not engaged in *tekl'hananni*, would bring the wrath of the Nandrian government down on Stragon's head, so that tactic is out of the question; and covert ops haven't worked out well for them either. All that's left is plan C: if you can't beat them, join them. Or rather, join them to *you*. Make an alliance that morally obligates them to come to your defence."

"Cement the alliance, then pick a fight?" Ruby said uncertainly. "That only makes sense if your ally actually has the resources to help you."

"If I'm right about this, then the impostor must feel that we do," Rodrigues replied. "Or maybe he's hoping we'll die trying. Or..." he added with a helpless shrug, "I might just be wrong about the whole thing."

Townsend swung forward onto his elbows on the tabletop. "You're not wrong, Paul. It's a power grab with an ulterior motive," he declared. "Stragon is on the brink of a revolution. A formal alliance between our Houses would drag us into that conflict on the side of the Directorate, which equates to the side of whoever is impersonating Gervais Forrand."

"Okay, it's remote control, I get that," Ruby said impatiently. "But with Earth's Fleet off the table, all we have is one shuttle and a Second Shield consisting of a Ranger detachment that's not actually under our command. We don't dare call on the Terran government to help us meet our obligation to an alien House—they'll brand us as traitors to Earth for making deals with other races behind the High Council's back. So I repeat, what kind of support could we realistically bring to a shooting war?"

"The clandestine kind. Black ops. Sabotage," said Drew. "We were able to extract ten Terrans on short notice and get them off-world without triggering any Security alarms, so the impostor knows that we have the resources to mount stealth operations. He's no doubt known for some time as well that a Forrand is in charge of the station. Once the uprising began, we'd be the ones the Directorate called on to defend it from its enemies on-world. And as the leader of the Directorate, Gervais Forrand would be the one to identify who those enemies are."

As comprehension dawned, Ruby's eyes went saucer-wide. "Oh. My. *Lord!* Fake Gervais could turn us like a weapon against anyone who stood in his way, just by labelling them as rebels or terrorists." Her voice was little more than a horrified whisper.

"The Terrans on Stragon would very likely be his first targets. According to Olivia, scapegoating them has been his intention all along," Townsend confirmed. "He also apparently knew who our EIS agents were and was going to frame them for a bombing in which they would conveniently have died. By extracting them when we did, we managed to set his plan back temporarily, but that's all. He's going to keep trying. Let's hope he also keeps underestimating us, because I'm afraid this threat won't be neutralized until he's been exposed and House Stragon has reinstalled its former *Hak'kor*."

Rodrigues breathed a long-suffering sigh. "I know that look. I'm going to need deniability, aren't I?"

"You've got something in mind, Chief? A Daisy Hub

specialty, perhaps?" said Ruby, now grinning impishly.

"The good news is, I've thought of a way to beat the impostor at his own game," Townsend replied. "The bad news is, in order to pull it off, I'll have to do something I promised myself I would never, ever do."

"Which is...?" said Rodrigues, frowning.

"Trust me, Paul, you don't want to know."

Alone once more in his office, Townsend pulled out the VICTOR codes and set to work drafting a message.

Dear Niece,

Aunt Matilda has found a pattern that she thinks your friend would like. Please show it to him, and give him our best regards. Also, let him know that she's not done searching her files yet, so there will most likely be more such patterns to come.

Affectionately,

Uncle Henry

While the encrypter worked on the message underlying this one, an old Earth saying rose to the surface of Townsend's mind—*The enemy of my enemy is my friend.*

...for now, at least.

He hit the intercomm button on his desktop. "Lydia, I need you to transmit a message for me, to Stragon. And would you have Walt and O'Malley come up here, please?"

"Sure thing, Drew."

"You should sit in on the meeting as well. I have an important assignment for the three of you."

TWENTY
ON STRAGON

Quinian was even quieter than usual during dinner. Sitting hunched over his plate, he used his fork to play "musical food", arranging and rearranging the bits of casserole and occasionally putting some of it into his mouth. After watching him do this for half an hour, Isabela couldn't stand the silence any longer.

"Talk to me, Quin," she said. "The signal jammer is activated, so you can speak freely. What are you thinking?"

He raised haunted eyes to her face. "Right now?" he said. "I'm wishing I'd never met Dennis Forrand. He's the reason someone just tried to kill me. If I hadn't been with Norry at the time, I'm pretty sure I would be dead right now." He paused to blow out a breath. "You told him that you'd known Dennis on Earth."

"Yes. He was different back then. My brother Carlos and I were whistleblowers. Things would have gone badly for us if he had not helped us to escape to the Agricultural Zone."

"Whistleblowers? I'm not familiar with that Terran term.

Does it have anything to do with family circuses?"

Struggling not to laugh, Isabela explained, "A whistle-blower is someone who feels compelled to report their employer to the authorities for illegal or immoral activities. Carlos and I had consciences. The pharmaceutical company we both worked for had none. We brought what they were doing to light and were immediately let go."

"I imagine it would have been difficult for you to find jobs in your field after that," Quinian remarked thoughtfully.

"It was impossible. So, when Dennis told us about Veggieville, we jumped at the opportunity."

"You were lucky he found you, then."

"We certainly thought so at the time."

He gave her a strange look. "But now you don't?"

"The company we worked for was called Harris PharmaLabs," she said, "and the scandal cost them half their business. So you tell me, Quin—was it luck? Or was it a reward for crippling Forrand Pharmaceuticals' largest competitor?"

He opened his mouth to reply, but before he could get a word out, there came a loud buzzing from the direction of the front door.

Isabela went and peered through the spyhole. When she saw who was standing out in the hall, she nearly fell over. *Speak of the devil!*

"Brace yourself, Quin," she called over her shoulder. Then she pinned a hospitable expression on her face and opened the door.

Dennis hadn't aged a day. He looked exactly as she remembered him from forty years earlier.

"Well, this is a surprise," she said, moving aside to let him enter.

"I should have contacted you ahead of time, I know, but this was spur of the moment. Have you finished dinner? I brought dessert."

He thrust a container toward her and her hands reached out automatically to accept it.

"How thoughtful," she remarked, also automatically. The item felt heavy. It had to be a pie, or one of those melon-spice cakes. "I'll serve this out. Why don't you go sit down?"

As Dennis approached, Quinian leaned back in his chair as though repelled by an unpleasant odour. If Dennis noticed, he gave no sign, just plopped himself down with a small sigh onto the chair facing his cousin's and said, "I contacted Med Services and was informed that you had discharged yourself and gone home. You had a close call the other day. How are you feeling?"

"A lot safer here, thanks."

Covertly monitoring this exchange from the kitchen, Isabela opened the container and discovered that what Dennis had brought was a bantilla loaf, loaded with chunks of sweetroot and sowerberry and thickly iced with chocca. She cut three generous slices, put each on a small plate, and carried them all on a tray to the dining table.

"I hope you like *jekhailla* tea," she said. "It's already brewed."

"Whatever's on hand will be fine," Dennis assured her. He put a forkful of the baked treat into his mouth, then gave her a closed-lipped smirk.

After glaring at his dessert for a moment, Quinian pushed it, untouched, to the middle of the table. "You didn't come all the way down here just to check up on me," he said accusingly.

Dennis raised a hand to pause the discussion while he chewed and swallowed. "As a matter of fact, you're right," he replied. "I was hoping we could have a little meeting about a project I have in mind."

Another one? *Madre!*

Isabela fetched the signal jammer from the living room and waved the flashing green light in front of his face before placing the device on the table.

"Ah, thank you," he said. He dropped his fork onto his plate. "I'm here to read you both into it, because I have a small favour to ask... of Isabela."

Quinian gave her a look that clearly said, *Your turn.*

About to pour the tea, she sat down and crossed her arms over her chest instead. "And the nature of this favour?" she demanded.

"I need you to send an encrypted message for me, to the station manager of Daisy Hub."

Isabela stiffened to attention in her chair. He couldn't possibly know about the two transmissions she'd already sent to Uncle Henry. Was this some sort of test, to see whether she still had her EIS technology?

"Is there a reason you cannot send it yourself?" she asked deliberately.

"There is. Drew Townsend is my grandson. To say that we're not on the best of terms would be a gross understatement. And it's vital that he open and read what I have to tell him, not simply delete it out of hand."

"Can I assume that it will already be encrypted when you give it to me?"

"Of course. It's eyes only, and I'm certain you will need at least the appearance of deniability."

"And I will compose the covering message myself." This

was not a question.

After a beat, he nodded assent.

Quinian had been watching the back-and-forth like a spectator at a ping-pong match. "You said you were going to read us in?" he prompted, impatience in his voice as well as stamped on his features.

"We're convinced that we've identified the individual who is posing as Gervais Forrand. He's barricaded himself within a fortified compound and we need stealth technology in order to get a team inside and take him down."

"What makes you think Townsend can help you with that?" Isabela asked.

"The ship that was used to extract a number of Terran agents was invisible to Stragori Security. It would be perfect for our purposes."

"You're talking about attacking and possibly killing someone. Do we want to know the name of that unfortunate individual?" said Quinian.

"All you need to know, Cousin, is that it's a Harris. A Harris who hates all Forrands and may even have been behind your near-death experience the other day."

"So, you feel it would be a justifiable killing," Quinian said.

"Why are you so certain that I plan to kill him?" Dennis demanded. "Do you really believe that I want this senseless feud between our families to continue?"

Quinian said nothing, just stared a challenge at him.

Finally, Dennis huffed out an exasperated syllable. "I promise you, I will not be murdering *anyone*," he declared. "The object of this operation will be to remove the impostor from his compound, get his confession on the record, and turn him over to a tribunal for punishment."

"In that case, I agree to send your message," Isabela cut in. "But the cloaked ship to which you refer is owned by aliens, who may or may not be within contact range, so do not be surprised if the answer comes back no."

"Is there a plan B?" Quinian asked him.

"There will be," said Dennis grimly as he got up from his chair. "And plans C and D if necessary. Somehow, we are going to make that bastard pay for what he's done."

The children were having their afternoon snack break. Joanne sat at her desk, staring straight ahead and occasionally poking an index finger into the air in front of her. She was no doubt prowling the intellinet for interesting data drops or entertaining vidclips to watch.

Isabela cleared her throat loudly and touched her teaching assistant on the shoulder to get her attention. "I'm sorry to interrupt, but... do you mind if I ask you a question about your implants?"

Joanne blinked hard a couple of times, then turned in her seat and replied, "Not at all, Mrs. Bakshi. Ask away."

"Do you know whether your parents were offered more than one type of implant to choose from?"

Her adolescent features contracted in thought. "No. But if there was more than one type, I'm sure they picked the best one for me."

"Do you remember where you went to be optimized?"

"I don't remember the name of the place. It was a large laboratory near one of the ferry docks. Why? Are you thinking of getting the procedure too?"

Isabela consciously widened her eyes. "I'm just gathering

information at this point. Maybe I should be asking your parents these questions. Or... do you still have that brochure you showed me earlier?"

"I'm sure it's somewhere in the house. But why not just access the intellinet? The answers you need are probably all there."

Actually, Isabela thought, whatever this company put out online was probably a pack of lies, carefully curated to keep its administrators out of a tribunal chamber. A printed brochure, on the other hand, was concrete evidence, hard to tamper with and even harder to argue with.

Those people had no idea of the trouble that was heading their way. And maybe Dennis Forrand had known exactly what he was doing after all, giving this assignment to a whistleblower like Isabela Bakshi.

After dismissal time the following day, as Joanne was shepherding the double line of students through the schoolyard and across the road, her mother arrived at the school for a pre-arranged meeting. Melora Santos had four daughters—Joanne was her youngest—and the family resemblance among all five of them was striking. With their long dark hair, intelligent green eyes, and confident, even aristocratic bearing, the Santos girls looked like recordings taken of their mother at different ages.

Isabela greeted Melora with a smile, accepted the brochure she held out, and ushered her into the office, where the signal jammer had previously been set up and activated.

"You've been a wonderful role model for Joanne, Mrs. Bakshi," she said, sitting down on one of the guest chairs.

"She's already signed up for online and somno courses to earn her teaching degree."

"She is a talented educator. I'm sure she will do well."

Isabela took in the friendly, relaxed expression on the other woman's face and felt a twinge of guilt for what she was about to do. Not to the laboratory management—they richly deserved what was about to land on them—but to the Terrans they'd persuaded into permanently accepting dangerous, outmoded technology into their bodies. She was going to open their eyes, make them aware that they were the victims of a crime. Destroy their peace of mind. And, with luck, make them angry enough to band together and take action.

"Joanne tells me you've been asking about the optimization procedure."

Isabela paused to choose her words. "Yes. I have been doing some research, and it has made me curious to know more. Do you mind answering a few questions?"

"Not at all. It's advisable to find out as much as possible when considering something like this. Best if you do it before committing to the surgery so there won't be any regrets afterward."

"How did you find out about it?"

"From a woman I met at a clothing store on the island."

"An employee?"

"No, another shopper. She'd just been promoted at work and was excited about picking out a new wardrobe to go with her new job. We started talking about business attire and ended up discussing optimization, since that was what she said had opened the door to promotion for her. There were some brochures on the counter. She suggested I pick one up on my way out the door. Hector and I want Joanne to have every opportunity for success in her life, so we decided implantation was worth considering."

"Interesting. Was this other shopper a Terran?"

"I don't know. A couple of years ago, I would have said, 'Of course! Who else would be shopping for clothes on the island?' But now, with everything that's been happening on the mainland..." Mrs. Santos pressed her lips together and slowly shook her head.

Isabela took a minute to skim through the brochure. As she'd expected, it was a sales tool, touting all the benefits of optimization and downplaying the disadvantages. Nowhere on the folded sheet of paper was there mention of choices. Or a date to indicate how old the information was. Or a list of venues offering the procedure.

"There is only one contact code given here. How did you select the lab where the procedure was to be done?" Isabela asked.

"All the appointments are made through the Health Department at the Directorate. We input the code and a clerk gave us a choice of three dates and times. The location depended on which date we picked."

"I see. And you said you researched this beforehand?"

"Yes, on the intellinet, and we also spoke to several other people we knew who'd been optimized. No one had anything bad to say about the procedure. It's delicate neurosurgery, so it can't be rushed, of course. Plan to lose an entire day out of your schedule. The implants are small, and recovery time tends to be no more than a couple of weeks for most people. There is some soreness, but the pain is controllable and it fades with time. I don't know what else I can tell you, Mrs. Bakshi."

"You can give me the name of that clothing store," she

said, adding privately, *I'm betting your newly promoted shopper makes regular visits there.*

Mentally planning her undercover shopping trip, Isabela arrived home and found the message carrier standing outside her apartment door with his index finger aimed at her buzzer button.

"Stop!" she cried, and he obligingly froze in place. "My co-tenant recently came home from a Med Services centre and is probably sleeping. Who is the recipient of the transmission?"

He consulted his proof-of-delivery device. "Isabela Bakshi."

"I am Isabela Bakshi."

"Can you prove it? I'm sorry, but it's the rules. I can't give this to you out in the hall without seeing proof of your identity."

Madre!

"But if I open the door to you, that is all right?"

"Yes."

"Fine!" Stepping past him, she pressed her thumb to the lock and waited for the door to slide aside. Then she crossed the threshold and turned to face him. "Hello. I am Isabela Bakshi. What have you brought for me today?"

Clearly, this young man's mind marched in straight lines only. His features screwed themselves into a portrait of helpless confusion.

Leaning forward, she said, gently and deliberately, "The fact that my thumbprint opened this door is proof that I live here."

Understanding finally shone behind his eyes. "Oh!

Yeah!" he said, and he offered her his device to imprint, followed by a data card.

She took it into her bedroom to read, noting in passing that Quinian's door was closed. Good. She had already made up her mind about next steps and didn't really want to get into an argument with him. Some things were just too blatantly obvious to be debatable.

Isabela inserted the card into her commpad. As the message came up on her screen, a thrill raced through her. It was a "fat" transmission—file attached. And... patterns? Had Novak decided to become involved in Forrand's schemes after all?

She reread the text. It said nothing to indicate the "patterns" were for Dennis's eyes only. Fumble-fingered with excitement and by now desperately curious, she pressed her EIS encrypter into place and opened the attachment.

It contained the details of a plan. Her hand rose to cover her mouth as the bulleted list scrolled slowly upwards. It was doable. Yes, definitely doable. And it was signed by Drew Townsend, not Barry Novak.

This was an unsettling development. How did Olivia's brother fit in? Had he intercepted her two earlier messages? Was he taking matters into his own hands? Or had Novak perhaps put him in charge of operations on Stragon because of where Daisy Hub was located? That was what *she* would have done.

Well, as some wise person had once said, there was nothing to be gained by borrowing trouble. She was much too busy for that. Isabela had a message to relay to Dennis Forrand, and an operation of her own to finish planning.

Once a whistleblower, always a whistleblower.

TWENTY-ONE
ON DAISY HUB

O'Malley and Walt Garfield stepped out of the tube car together on AdComm and went directly to Townsend's office, where three guest chairs sat waiting in front of the station manager's desk.

"You wanted to see us, Boss?" said O'Malley.

"Lydia mentioned something about a special assignment," Walt added as he lowered himself onto the seat farthest from the door.

"It's an important assignment," Drew confirmed, "and it's something that I'm confident the three of you working together have the skills to accomplish."

Lydia appeared then and slid onto the chair they'd left vacant, nearest the entrance to his office. Townsend opened his desk drawer and hit the button to activate the privacy shield.

"When we extracted those EIS agents from Stragon," he began, "we left one behind, by her own choice. I respected her wishes and deactivated her... and it appears Dennis Forrand immediately scooped her up and put her to work on an operation of his own. She's contacted me twice now to let me know what he's planning, because she doesn't think it's going to work."

"She needs an exit strategy," Lydia murmured.

"Or he needs a better plan," said O'Malley. "Is that what this is about, Boss? Us coming up with one?"

"It's already done, Mr. O'Malley," Townsend replied. "Lydia has transmitted the encrypted details to our former agent on-world, to be passed along to Forrand. Once I've received his acceptance, the op will be a go. He'll have some prep work to do on his end, just as we will on ours, and your assignment is a big part of it."

Leaning forward, Walt asked, "What's our objective?"

"Don't you mean Forrand's?" O'Malley cut in.

Sharing a knowing look with Townsend, Walt replied, "Why should we bother propping up his plan that isn't going to work if we can replace it with one that will, and will benefit our own organization at the same time?"

"Walt's right," said Drew. "We're doing this for ourselves. We know that leadership of the Directorate—and by extension, of House Stragon—has been usurped by an impostor claiming to be Gervais Forrand. We've also just learned that House Stragon will soon be requesting to join with House Daisy Hub in *ssalssit essendi*."

"Now *that's* a tangled web," Lydia remarked.

"Accept the request and you legitimize the impostor," Walt mused. "Reject it and you not only cause offence to Stragon, you force the Directorate to look to House Trokerk for help if and when the fighting begins, turning it instantly into an interstellar conflict. You're saying you know a way out of this mess?"

"I am, and I do," Townsend told him. "This is now an

official Repository operation. We're going to flush out the impostor and return the previous *Hak'kor*, Louis Forrand, to power."

"That's a tall order, Drew," said Lydia, frowning uncertainly. "Do we even know what happened to Louis when the impostor took over?"

"We don't have to know. You three are going to recreate him on a memory bloc."

For several beats, Townsend watched calculating glances pass back and forth in front of him. Then Walt broke the silence.

"You want us to build an AI like the one the Directorate tried to sneak onto our systems before?"

"One just like it, yes, only this one will believe it's Louis Forrand. I'm not looking for a permanent substitute. It just has to last long enough and be realistic enough to convince the impostor that it's game over, and that Louis is back with a vengeance. Please tell me this is doable."

O'Malley was shaking his head. "I don't know, Boss. Stragori technology is a lot further along than ours."

"But not as far along as the Stragori think it is, according to Olivia's report. Could you use the first AI as a template?"

"Maybe," said Walt. "I haven't reinitialized the server yet. As long as it hasn't been overwritten, we might be able to find enough of the original AI code to piece something meaningful together. It's going to take time, and it won't be complete. But it could be sufficient to get us started."

"We'll need information about Louis Forrand as well, to help us fill in some of the gaps," Lydia pointed out.

"Fortunately, we have a source aboard the Hub," said Townsend. "Trager had Second Shield status and was present at Stragon and Trokerk's *ssalssit essendi*. Ask him to tell you what he knows about the *Hak'kor*."

"You're certain he'll cooperate?"

"No, but you can feel free to remind him that it's in his own best interests as well as ours to ensure that an alliance takes place between our two Houses, and that it's something your *Hak'kor* will not consent to as long as there's an impostor running House Stragon."

"What's our time frame, Boss?" O'Malley asked.

Townsend had already done the math. "Ideally, about seven to ten station days."

"Then we'd better get to work," Walt declared.

Once the memory bloc had been built, they needed a way to deliver it to Stragon without being detected. That was where Gorse Pirrit's *Night Cloud* came in. Able to throw up an impenetrable cloaking field, the Eggenali-built craft had slipped unnoticed through the Stragori defensive perimeter once before, to extract the endangered EIS agents. Vin Trager had been the one who had procured it for Townsend's use. However, Drew was still debating whether to read him into the operation this time around, so it would be best if he spoke with Pirrit himself.

Townsend strolled over to the main console where Ruby McNeil sat monitoring local comm and vehicle traffic.

"When are Gorse and Ixbeth due back?" he asked.

"Should be any day now, Chief. Or maybe longer. A twenty-first birthday is a big deal. Leslie Eberhart's family wanted to do Lania's party up right, and Ixbeth was determined not to miss a moment of the celebration."

Drew felt a pinch of envy. It had been a long time since he'd been able to enjoy anything as normal as a family birthday party. Or even a family.

His surviving biological family, with the exception of his sister and one cousin, Gael Dedrick, consisted of people he preferred not to be associated with. The Warrior Kings had called themselves his family for six years, until they'd betrayed him to Security. Caught in possession of stolen goods, Drew had spent the next five years in detention. That was where Bruni Patel had taken him under his wing. Bruni had been the older brother Drew never had, for nearly twenty years. Then he'd been murdered.

Working as a field detective out of the 33rd Precinct, Townsend had had a history that made people wary of getting too close to him. So, no family there.

Finally, he'd been sent by the EIS to manage the crew of Daisy Hub, who were, according to Rodrigues, "a band of merry lunatics". At least, they'd been that way until the Corvou had come along and declared war on Humanity, effectively knocking the merriment out of everyone in Earth space.

Townsend cared deeply about the people who worked for him. Some of them he even thought of as his friends. But whoever had said that it was lonely at the top was absolutely right. None of them were family—not to him, anyway.

"Let me know the moment Pirrit enters our landing deck."

"You've got it, Chief."

"How long do you plan to go on like this?" Doc Ktumba scolded.

Townsend gazed up into her face from the biopod where

he'd been lying while the medication she'd administered took full effect. His vision was finally clearing. For the past hour, the room around him had been a blur, mostly white with streaks of chrome, and prismatic explosions near the ceiling, like tiny stars going nova. The intensity of the light had fatigued his eyes, making it difficult for him to keep them open.

So, lulled by the barely audible chorus of humming and whirring that emanated from the diagnostic technology hovering around his bed, he'd dozed. At some point he'd noted that the pain in his stomach had subsided to a dull, distant ache, and that the air he was breathing smelled and tasted faintly of citrus.

Good thing there are no Nandrians aboard the station...

Townsend murmured a relieved, "Ah!" and instantly, it seemed, the Doc's face was hanging over him, her eyes flashing.

"Are you *trying* to perforate your stomach lining?" she snapped.

Uh-oh.

"Who snitched?"

"Nurse Fermi saw you in the caf. She just told me what you were eating for lunch. Spicy goulash and three cups of Jensen's java. You've always struck me as being highly intelligent, Mr. Townsend, so why do you keep eating food that will exacerbate your ulcer?"

"Prescribe a diet for me that has some taste to it and I'll stop."

"Stick to it long enough and you'll be safely *able* to stop," she told him, scanning the readouts on the screens over his head. "I once had a patient like you. Stubborn. Refused to follow doctor's orders."

"Let me guess—he died prematurely."

"Actually, he lived to a ripe old age, after I had a talk with his wife... and his employer. You can sit up now," she added.

When he was seated on the edge of the biobed, she stood in front of him and went on sternly, "The bacterial infection that initiated your problem has completely cleared up, so the antibiotic has done its work. Now you need to do your part: the factors preventing this gastric ulcer from healing itself are dietary and stress-related.

"Since you apparently have no interest in bringing either of them under control, I'm left with no choice but to give you an ultimatum. If you won't take the measures I've prescribed, I will be forced to declare you medically unfit to run this station, The Repository, and House Daisy Hub, and will assign Ruby to replace you, in every instance. Is that understood?"

There were two mantras on Daisy Hub. The first was, *Turn them or terminate them.* The second was, *Never argue with the Doc.*

"Yes, ma'am," he said with a sigh.

The yogourt surrogate Drew now had to eat twice a day by order of Doc Ktumba was chocolate-flavoured. That was its only saving grace. Developed by the Hub's agronomist, Ajda Grey, shortly before the Corvou war, it contained no dairy product but was full of calcium and other nutrients and was great for coating the stomach lining.

The Doc's other stipulation (for the time being, at least) was that under no circumstances was he to eat at his desk. She said it was to remove him from a stress-associated environment, but Townsend knew better. She just wanted to make sure there were witnesses to every one of his meals. That way she would know whether he was cheating on his diet.

When Drew's wristcomm buzzed halfway through his dinner, it felt like a reprieve.

"Gorse and Ixbeth are on their way back to the Hub, Chief," Ruby told him. "ETA is about three days. And you've got mail. A message from Stragon, addressed to Henry Eisner."

A reply already? That was quick. *Too quick.*

"You're sure it's genuine?"

"It seems genuine. Want me to isolate it just in case?"

"Yes, and have O'Malley check it for any irregularities. I'm on my way—" Suddenly aware of eyes turning in his direction, Townsend cursed silently and switched gears. "Scratch that. I'll be returning to AdComm after I've finished eating."

"You've got it, Chief."

He could swear he heard her smile.

Dear Uncle Henry,

I hope you and Aunt Matilda are doing well. Please thank her for her offer of knitting patterns. I look forward to seeing them.

Meanwhile, my friend has decided to take up knitting. He has found a pattern he would like to try, but I'm not sure it's the right level of difficulty and am struggling to find the right words to tell him so. Perhaps you can help me find them.

As ever, give my love to Grandma and Cousin Grace.

Isabela

Curious, Townsend decrypted the underlying message. His jaw sagged when he read Forrand's request.

Sneak a Stragori strike team inside a compound housing a high-ranking member of a rival Stragori family?

It was no wonder Isabela had expressed reservations about this. It was a shortcut to open warfare. With luck, Forrand would see the wisdom of going along with Townsend's plan instead. And if not...

Best not to borrow trouble. Just the thought of it was causing Drew's stomach to churn, and he'd nearly used up his daily quota of antacid tablets.

Damn this ulcer...

TWENTY-TWO
ON STRAGON

Given the rising probability of an unaccompanied Terran female encountering violence on the mainland, Isabela decided it would be safer if she invited Dennis to return to the apartment so that she could give him the copy she'd made of Drew Townsend's encrypted message.

Once again, Forrand appeared at her door bearing a gift of rich pastries and wearing an insincere smile. Isabela dredged up a matching expression and waved him inside.

Quin was sitting on the sofa, looking discontented, with the signal jammer blinking silently on the table in front of him, and Isabela made no move toward the kitchen. Evidently realizing that there would be no offer of tea today, Dennis remained standing just inside the door.

"I've received a message from Daisy Hub, with an encrypted attachment to be passed along to you," she told him.

"It's too soon for that to be a response to my request," he remarked, his brows drawing together.

"That is because it isn't a response," she told him. "It is a request from the station manager. More of a proposal, actually."

His frown deepened. "It sounds as if you've read it, even though it was encrypted and clearly intended for me."

"The message was addressed to me, and the covering text said nothing about the attachment being for your eyes only, so yes, I decrypted and read it, and I think you should give his plan serious consideration." Isabela raised her eyebrows in a silent challenge: *And I defied you and kept my EIS comm gear. Care to make an issue of it?*

He was thinking about it, she could tell. Then Quin loudly cleared his throat, and when they both turned to look at him, he arched his eyebrows as well, no doubt in warning.

Finally, Dennis thrust out his hand and said brusquely, "Could I have my part of the message, please?"

She pulled the data wafer from her pocket and placed it on his palm.

"How are you coming with your assignment, by the way?" he asked.

"I have learned about something that will trigger anger in a significant portion of the island's population," she replied. "Now it is just a matter of harnessing and mobilizing it. As you pointed out earlier, putting together a major public event will take time, but I will manage."

He gave her a long, appraising stare. "Are you being evasive with me, Mrs. Bakshi?"

Meeting his gaze with a cool one of her own, she replied, "I learn from the best, Mr. Forrand."

*   *   *

Each of the fifty residential districts on the island was dotted with open or covered marketplaces that served as community centres, as well as providing space for a variety of commercial enterprises. Unfortunately, the clothing store where Melora Santos had first learned about the implantation procedure was not local. It was situated with about twenty other retail outlets and offices at an indoor mall several kilopaces from Isabela's apartment. She would have to rent a wheeled vehicle and spend at least half a day "shopping", and that meant the excursion had to wait for her next day off from teaching. It also meant that after broadly hinting at her plan to Dennis Forrand, she could no longer put off reading Quinian into it.

So, she brewed a pot of *jekhailla* and broke out some of the bantilla-filled pastries that Dennis had brought, and laid everything out for Quinian as they sat at the dining table that evening, enjoying dessert.

He responded pretty much as she'd expected, by nearly inhaling a mouthful of tea.

"You must be joking!" he sputtered between wracking coughs. "A march to the mainland? Isabela, the logistics alone will be—! Are you out of your Terran mind?"

Undeterred, she leaned back in her chair and explained, "On Earth, before the Corvou war, we had a Reformation. Nearly a million people came to the planetary capital and surrounded the building where the High Council was in session. The demonstrators had come to negotiate a fair deal for everyone who'd been oppressed by the Relocation Authority—our version of the Directorate. They presented their demands peacefully, and the strategy worked. The practice of classifying Humans as Eligible or Ineligible was abolished, along with many of the social ills that these labels had brought about."

By now, Quin's coughing had subsided, giving way to an occasional violent throat-clearing. Leaning forward on his elbows, he said, "Now I'm confused. Are you saying you want to abolish the separate designation for Terrans on Stragon?"

"Of course not. It's a fact, not simply a decision made and imposed by a government agency. But there is a social ill that needs to be recognized and remedied, and it was your friend Norry who pointed it out to me. Hundreds of thousands of Terrans have been optimized. I do not know how many of them are walking around with the obsolete version of the implants inside their bodies, but I would bet any amount that it's because the laboratories chose to let them believe there was no other alternative. The Directorate needs to shift its priorities and actively enforce the fifty-year-old ban on inorganic implants. That is why we have to have the march—to give the Directorate a wake-up call."

"Not to mention that it will stir up a lot of unrest on the island, just as Dennis wants us to do," he added. "But the protesters on Earth had specific demands."

"And so will we."

"Oh?"

"I would like to see the laboratories that took advantage of Terran ignorance for their own profit punished. They should be made to forfeit every credit received for illegal implantations, and that revenue should be used to fund research into finding a way to safely remove the old technology from their victims."

"It's a very noble goal," said Quinian. "However, there's a problem you may not have considered. What do you suppose the Directorate is going to do when their tracking software shows them all those hybrids and optimized Humans—those unwitting spies—gathering around them?"

Madre! He was right.

"They will call in Security to break up the rally," she said.

"No, Security will already be there. The Directorate will derail the protest in a way that discredits you *and* your marchers. They'll broadcast warnings and misinformation over the intellinet to everyone carrying implants. They'll get your peaceful demonstrators so riled up that they'll forget why they joined the march in the first place. And if fights break out and people get hurt, so much the better. It will give Security a reason to arrest you, and from that point forward, you'll be known as the person who led an angry Terran mob to the Directorate's front doors."

"We've got the signal jammers," she pointed out.

"They're short range devices at best, and their power supply is limited. You're talking about a huge crowd of people, and an event lasting several hours."

With no further arguments to offer, she could only sit staring numbly into his face.

"Fortunately, I know someone who can help us with that," he continued. "I'll set up the rendezvous, but Dennis can never find out. Agreed?"

Isabela perked up. Keeping secrets from Dennis Forrand? It seemed Dr. Reston Quinian had a rebellious streak.

"Agreed!"

Dennis returned to his little flat, pulled his commpad and encrypter out of their hiding place in the wall, and read the message from Daisy Hub. As the text scrolled upward on his screen, his lips curved slowly into a satisfied grin.

This would work. In fact, with only a few small modifications at his end, it would be damn near perfect. He'd always known putting Drew in charge of Daisy Hub had been the right move—that when push came to shove, the Forrand in him would shine through.

Better yet, if the timing was right, Dennis might even be able to incorporate Isabela's "major public event" into the overall plan.

Now he just needed to make some calls.

Two days later, the med techs conducted their final assessment and certified that Quin was fully recovered. That evening, to celebrate, he and Isabela took the ferry to the mainland, where they rented a vehicle and drove it through a series of "safe neighbourhoods" to a restaurant specializing in cuisine from the far northern part of the continent. That was how Quin had described it to her. What Isabela saw when they arrived, however, was quite different from what she had imagined.

For one thing, only someone who already knew where to look for this place could have found it. The restaurant was situated on one corner of a residential intersection, well away from the lights and bustle of the commercial sector of the district, and the faces it showed to passersby clearly belonged to a house. Only the smallish sign suspended from a post in the middle of the tiny front lawn and the soft glow emanating from every window hinted that it might be more than it outwardly appeared. *Ravi Motaro.* The restaurant's name was elegantly scripted in orange against a dark brown background. As Quin pulled up and parked at the curb in front of the building, the shiny raised lettering caught the light of the setting sun and seemed to burst into flame.

Isabela hoped that wasn't an omen.

Quin walked her to the front door and opened it... and another world reached out and enveloped her in sound and warmth and movement. The very air seemed to give off a soft, golden light. Minor notes coaxed from stringed instruments wafted a symphony of rich aromas through the vestibule, reminding her of some of the mouth-watering dishes that Vikram had liked to prepare back on Earth.

As she and Quin waited to be seated, Isabela could see the heart of *Ravi Motaro*, a large open kitchen with dining rooms growing out of it, like luminescent flower petals. The restaurant was busy this evening. Servers wearing long, russet-coloured tunics bustled back and forth with trays, popping in and out of view.

At last their welcoming host appeared with menus in hand. He led them to one of half a dozen small round tables in a room with only a few other diners, all apparently waiting for their meals to arrive. On each table, a candle burned inside a transparent cylinder, which seemed to pin a dusky rose-, teal-, or saffron-coloured cloth in place.

The menu was displayed on the backlit screen of a wafer-thin tablet. To Isabela's dismay, it was printed in a language she could read but didn't understand.

"What is *taharu*?" she whispered, leaning across the table toward her dinner companion.

"It's a spice. Very hot. First-timers should probably avoid it," came a response from behind her.

The woman who now stepped around to the side of their table was fine-featured, with golden brown skin and dark eyes. Her hair was covered by a scarf that seemed to have flowed upward from the bodice of her turquoise, floor-length garment. Its fabric was shot through with metallic threads that sparkled as she moved.

"Welcome back, Dr. Quinian," she purred. "And who is your guest this evening?"

"This is Isabela Bakshi," he told her. "She teaches the children on the island. Isabela, meet Nasneen Kasril, the owner of this exceptional establishment."

Nasneen nodded acknowledgement of the compliment. "Bakshi? That sounds like a northeastern name."

"I'm from Earth. My husband's family came from an eastern culture on that world," Isabela told her.

"Isabela would love to know more about the northeast mainland," said Quin. "Perhaps you could sit with us for a while...?"

The other woman swept her gaze around the dining room and out the door, then replied, "If you linger over your meal, I can join you for dessert when it's not quite so busy."

"Sounds great," Quin told her. "I'm thinking we should order the sampler, without *taharu*."

"A good choice. I'll relay it to the kitchen and instruct the staff to serve it one dish at a time."

Watching her glide away, Isabela found that she really did want to know more about Nasneen's culture. It had definitely originated on Earth. Hopefully, more of it had survived here than back home, where some recipes and a traditional garb worn only as a costume were all that remained of many old and distinctive ways of life.

The meal was a parade of savoury treats that begged to be enjoyed at length, whether or not one was waiting to be joined later. Thankfully, the individual portions were small and not too filling—which was good, since Quin had advised her to save room for dessert. He'd ordered something special, just for her.

At last the room was empty save for the two of them. Warm beverages were put in front of them that looked like muddy water but smelled like cinnamon and tasted like kaffy with chocca added. With them came a plate holding about a dozen confections, each no more than a mouthful in size, and each a different colour.

Nasneen arrived shortly afterward. She pulled up a chair and sat down between Quinian and Isabela. Then, leaning in, she said softly, "It sounded urgent when we spoke earlier. What is going on, and why do you need a favour, from me of all people?"

Of all people?

Isabela glanced back and forth between their suddenly sober faces and saw history practically etched into the way they looked at each other.

"Because you're the only person I know with both the expertise to help us and the motivation to keep it a secret," he replied, pulling the signal jammer from his pocket and placing it on the table in front of her. "I think you can guess what this is."

Nasneen barely had to glance at it. "I have seen items like it."

Quin went on, "We need to create a large signal-free zone that will maintain its diameter for several hours. This device is not powerful enough to do it. Can you boost its strength?"

"It depends. Who built it?"

"It's Terran technology, if that's what you are asking," Isabela said warily.

Nasneen slipped her a sideways smile. "Really! And how large a zone do you require?"

"Roughly the size of a marketplace," said Quin. "Is it doable?"

"I believe so. Now I just need to know why any member of my group should be willing to help a Forrand."

In the silence that followed her challenge, it seemed to Isabela as though the temperature around their table had dropped several degrees.

Then Quin placed his hands palm down on the tabletop and replied, "Because you won't be helping a Forrand—you'll be helping a Terran to help her own people." Addressing Isabela, he added, "You can read her in. Nothing you say will go any further."

As Isabela outlined her plan, Nasneen's expression grew surprised, then thoughtful.

"So," she said when Isabela had finished, "this is not for political gain. You're going after the laboratories only."

"For justice. Yes," Isabela replied.

"And if one of those labs turns out to be owned by the Forrand family, what then?"

Purposely not looking in Quin's direction, Isabela lowered her voice and said, "Then they had better be able to weather a public scandal, because I refuse to play favourites, especially not with something as important to my people as this."

Nasneen leaned back in her chair. "All right, then. I think we can do business. Safiq is familiar with Terran technology, but he won't work for free. What can you offer?"

Quin's features hardened. "How about information?"

She sat up straight again. "About...?"

"Gervais Forrand."

Her eyes narrowed. "You have my attention. Keep talking."

Quin glanced a warning at Isabela, then stage-whispered to Nasneen, "He's an impostor. The person posing as Gervais Forrand is not inside the Directorate's server. He's a flesh-and-blood Stragori who's found a way to use the server to silence Gervais and further his own political agenda. In fact, he's not even a Forrand."

"How do you know this?" she demanded.

"Dennis told me, in confidence. There's more, but it will have to wait until Safiq has delivered the modified device and we've tested it to be sure it works."

After a beat, Nasneen extended her hand to be shaken. "We have a deal."

"Who is Nasneen's group and why do they hate the Forrands?"

Isabela had waited to ask Quinian this question until they were in the land car and retracing their earlier route back to the ferry dock. In the dark of night, danger hung in the air like an oppressive fog, even in the so-called "safe neighbourhoods". It tautened Isabela's nerves and raised gooseflesh along her arms.

"Nasneen and her brother Safiq head up a moderate group whose members adhere to a set of principles laid out by one of their religious leaders thousands of years ago," he explained.

"Principles that are antithetical to the beliefs of the Forrand family, I gather?"

"Nearly every last one of them, I'm afraid. That's why I never mentioned my connection to the Forrands when I first approached the group. Eventually the truth came out. Truthfulness is one of their sacred virtues, and I had lied by omission—exhibiting typical Forrand behaviour, they said—and so the membership voted me gone.

"It was just as well that it happened before my family found out what I'd done, or *they* might have voted me gone as well. The Forrands are loyalists—or claim to be, at any rate—and view anyone who wants to curtail or abolish the Directorate as a threat to their orderly and well-heeled existence. And now you've been entrusted with *two* secrets that could ruin me if either one were to get out."

Isabela went quiet. She had secrets too, but hers were far more explosive, and that made them much too dangerous to confide, no matter how earnest and appealing his invitation might be.

The next three Skinner Reports fell into a pattern: a lesson about the toxic and dangerous flora grown in the Wilderness Zone of the island, followed by some minor tidbit gleaned from an official warder report, and capped off with a dire warning to The One Responsible that they would soon be apprehended. The investigation appeared to be stalled—"appeared" being the operative word—but the threats at the end of the newscast were becoming progressively more specific and vehement. Delivering the latest one, Michael looked ready to leap through the screen and throttle someone.

Angeli's original assignment had been to figure out how to "push the buttons" of the northerners so that they would take action against the radical groups on the southern continent. She wasn't sure about anyone else yet, but her whispered suggestion earlier had evidently found Michael's hot button, and he in turn was mobilizing the power of the media.

"You put them up to this, didn't you?" Lyla accused her after Adam had given his brother a startled look and signed off.

Angeli consciously widened her eyes. "Me? I didn't put anyone up to anything. I merely suggested a possibility."

"And now they're the ones suggesting the possibility, to who knows how many viewers across the continent..."

"Getting people riled up against a faceless criminal who has already murdered seven Boreans and may be planning to kill a few more? That seems like a good thing to me."

"Well, getting them panicked and pointing fingers at one another is *not* a good thing. This is going to end in violence, Eva, you mark my words."

The following day, her prediction came true. Krall arrived early for dinner at Lyla's house, with news to share, courtesy of a fellow warder-in-charge.

Several days earlier, two greenhouse workers had gotten into a fight in Green Haven, a town in one of the Agricultural Zones. While investigating the incident, warders had discovered a patch of what looked like yellow and purple delphins growing in a corner of the assault victim's back yard. This wildflower with curlicued, ribbon-like petals had been mentioned in the Medical Oversight Officer's bulletins.

Called to the scene by the District Warder-in-Charge,

Continental Security had promptly dug up and confiscated the plants for further analysis. Krall had then cashed in a favour and obtained a copy of the case file, including a video of the interview with the man who'd been growing the delphins. It would be the after-dinner entertainment, once all the paying guests had gone.

That evening's meal consisted of mixed vegetables, nuts, and wild grains, fried up and served on a bed of greens, then drenched with a sauce that was at once both sweet and tangy. It was a dish Angeli had "invented", without revealing that her mother had regularly prepared it back on Earth. For dessert, Lyla had made bantilla custard pies earlier in the day, with three dozen chocca tarts as the takeaway.

When the last diner had departed, Lyla prepared a pot of tasselberry tea and brought it out on a tray, along with three cups and a small plate of cookies, while Krall set up the viewing gear in the parlour. He paused the video until everyone was comfortably seated and holding a beverage.

"This took place three days ago," said Krall.

The image on the screen was like no Security interview Angeli had ever seen. Instead of trying to put the suspect at ease and in a mood to cooperate, someone had gone to great lengths to make him uncomfortable.

At first, she couldn't tell which of the two men glaring at each other across a bare metal table was the one being interviewed. Neither one wore a uniform. Both looked as though one wrong word would set them at each other's throats. The anger she could sense straining the confines of that tiny, windowless room was implacable... and at the same time strangely fascinating. It sent shivers down her back.

"They hate each other," she murmured, wishing she could tear her eyes away from the picture in front of her.

"Indeed," said Krall. "They have a history, those two."

He unpaused the playback.

The man on the left leaped to his feet as though stung and leaned halfway across the table, sending his chair clattering to the floor behind him. The other man jumped up as well, to meet him. They froze with their faces only centimetres apart, their noses practically touching.

Krall paused the video again.

"On the left we have Yuri Debenski, the delphin grower. On the right is Peter Zenkolov, a Continental Security officer for the past seventy years. Peter was Yuri's arresting officer twice before. Not for serious crimes, though."

"Then why such hatred?" Lyla wanted to know.

"Yuri is married to Peter's sister."

"Oh, dear!"

When the video resumed, Yuri slammed both his hands down on the tabletop. "Why are you interrogating *me?*" he roared into Peter's face. "I'm the one who was attacked first, remember?"

Peter's hands curled slowly into fists. He narrowed his eyes and hissed back at Yuri, "You were also growing a poisonous plant in your yard, not native to this continent. We know you've never travelled south of the channel, so where did you get the seeds, Yuri?"

"I didn't plant any seeds, you *proklyatyy* moron! I planted a plant, and it reproduced itself."

"Then where did you get the plant? Calling me names won't help your situation, Yuri. This is an official Security investigation, so you need to sit back down and tell me the truth."

The suspect huffed air through his nose, like a bull about to charge. Then common sense seemed to prevail. Groaning with frustration, he righted his chair before dropping onto it. A second later, Peter did the same.

"Yelena found it when she was walking in the woods. She dug it up and brought it home to plant in our yard. It was a single beautiful flower. I was going to divide the bulb so there would be more, but I forgot and went to work. When I came home from the greenhouse, she had already put it in the ground."

Good thing he didn't cut into that root bulb, Angeli thought grimly. She'd seen the precautions Isabela had taken when handling this particular plant. And Yelena had transplanted one whole, unaware of the danger she was in and suffering no ill after-effects? It was nothing short of miraculous.

Yuri was continuing: "The following season, five stems came up. The season after that there were two dozen. They multiplied so fast that I had to pot some and give them away or they would have overrun my yard."

"You gave them away? To whom?"

A shrug. "To everyone who admired them. My friends. My co-workers..."

"Oh, shit!" Angeli blurted. "There are patches of delphin all over Green Haven by now."

"Your co-workers," Peter was saying. "Including Sacha Nemkov, the man who attacked you? Is that what the fight was about?"

Yuri's shoulders sagged. He dropped his gaze to the tabletop, then raised it to Peter's face. "You have to believe me," he pleaded. "We had no idea this was a dangerous plant."

"Why did Sacha attack you, Yuri?" Peter pressed him,

leaning forward as though preparing to pounce.

"Sacha's youngest daughter... she had a pet. A lepke. It liked to run around outside."

"She *had* a pet? It *liked* to run?"

"It died suddenly. No one knew why. Then Sacha watched a broadcast one day, The Skinner Report."

"And he realized why the animal was dead, and he was angry and confronted you about it?"

Yuri's spirit returned. Angeli could see it in the set of his mouth. "You must know all this from speaking with him," he said, scowling. "Why are you now asking me the same questions?"

The screen blanked abruptly as the vidclip ended.

"The forensic botanist who examined the delphin taken from Yuri's yard has identified it as a nonpoisonous relative of the one growing on the island. The northern variety is called 'ribbonel'. The blossoms are similar in appearance, but the genome is different," Krall told them.

"In other words," Lyla said, throwing Angeli a significant look, "Yuri was attacked for no good reason." *I told you so.* There was no need to say the words aloud. The tone of her voice spoke them for her.

"Actually, that's not entirely true," Krall cut in. "Just because a plant is nonpoisonous to people doesn't mean it's desirable to have in a garden. Whether or not the lepke died after ingesting ribbonel blossoms, Yuri is being fined for failing to warn people about the danger to their pets, and he and Nemkov may never be on good terms again. And this," he added with a sigh, "is why people are being advised to report sightings of suspicious-looking flora to the warders instead of handling things themselves."

"Yelena found a single flower," Angeli pointed out. "If

they're as prolific as Yuri described—"

"Ribbonel is considered to be a weed in the southern half of Borea, where it's destroyed whenever and wherever it's found to be growing. However, its seeds can travel on the wind. Evidently, one of them made it all the way to the forest where Yelena happened to be walking."

"So it was a coincidence."

"Nothing more." After a thoughtful pause, Krall levelled his gaze on Angeli's face and continued, "I'm afraid you've started something that won't be easily stopped, Eva. Thanks to The Skinner Report, it's only a matter of time before neighbours and co-workers begin turning on one another all across the continent. So I'm wondering, do you have a plan in mind? Any idea how this is going to end?"

She stared fearlessly back at him. "It ends with seven murders being solved." *...and my mission being completed,* she added privately.

"You're still utterly convinced that they were poisoned with a botanical toxin of some kind?"

"I am, and time will prove me right," she declared, although with more confidence than she was feeling at the moment.

Shaking things up and seeing what fell out had always worked for Angeli before. She was, after all, a "loose cannon". But throwing an entire continent into chaos in service of a long range plan...? That was Dennis's style, not hers. At least, that was what she had thought.

How dismaying to discover that she was just as much a Forrand as he was!

TWENTY-THREE
STILL ON STRAGON

Isabela knew what she had to do next. Her first impulse was simply to march into the clothing store and confront the woman who was shilling for the laboratories. However, experience had taught her that first ideas were rarely good ones, so she decided to talk this one over with Quinian at breakfast. He was, after all, the one with connections.

"Exposing her this early on will also expose you—and anyone you tell about the march—to intimidation by the big labs," he pointed out between mouthfuls of cereal. "And if threats don't silence you, they won't hesitate to use physical violence. Remember what happened to your husband?"

A shiver raced through her. "Yes."

"You trained as an operative, Isabela. What would a spy do in this situation?"

"She is optimized, so I can't turn her... and I don't dare terminate her. That leaves only option C: turn her own strategy against her if possible," she recited from memory. "But she's—"

Struck by a sudden thought, Isabela went to her tote bag and pulled out the brochure Melora Santos had given her.

"She's handing these out," she said, dropping the folded flyer onto the dining table in front of him, "and that can't be the only store she's visiting, so she's probably leaving copies behind in each location. If I were to replace them without anyone seeing... The fronts would have to be identical, of course. We don't want her to become suspicious and actually read the text inside."

Quinian was fingering the paper. "I can match this stock. Provide me with your revised wording and I'll have the counterfeits made up for you. How many copies do you think you'll need?"

"At twenty per district times fifty, I would estimate a thousand." Noticing his sudden frown, she added, "You don't think that's enough?"

"I think it's plenty. It's just that—" He hesitated for a beat. "Covering the entire island seems a little overambitious for one person."

"Oh, I won't be doing this all by myself." Giving him a wide-eyed smile, she added, "I think it's time we had a parent-teacher meeting at the school. Don't you? One day late next week, perhaps? Will the brochures be ready by then?"

He nodded thoughtfully. "I would think so."

Dinner at Lyla's the following evening was a quiet affair. She had closed her table to outside guests while she, Krall, and Angeli digested the latest developments and decided what to do next.

The joint investigative team had finally issued its report regarding the cause of all seven suspicious deaths: poisoning by means of damselflower toxin. They had also found a common element that seemed to point in the direction of the poisoner. All seven victims had received invitations to attend the live recording of a video broadcast, titled "The Stories Left Behind".

Several episodes had been recorded over a three-day period in Edgerton, the first town due east of Salty Springs. Although thousands of people had shown up to watch, drawn by a public announcement made beforehand, only ten personal invitations had been issued. This alone had aroused suspicion among the warders.

"There had to be food available," Angeli said. "That's the easiest way to poison someone. Do the warders know who catered the event?"

"Continental Security is still looking into that," Krall replied. "The executives of the production company are being difficult to reach. My guess is that they're too busy marshalling their legal team to return Security's calls."

"How about the attendees?" Lyla suggested. "Companies that work large events generally post their names all over the place. Someone should have seen and remembered one of the signs."

Krall grinned ruefully. "Continental Security prefers to let the district warders do that kind of legwork..."

"...and there's no love lost between the two levels of law enforcement," Angeli said, returning the grin as she completed his thought, "so the warders are unlikely to do Continental's work for them. That leaves just us, and I have an idea."

"Oh, dear!" said Lyla. "Another one?"

"It's a safe bet that the people behind these poisonings are members of one of the radical groups from the southern continent, trying to stir up trouble."

"Do I want to know how you arrived at this conclusion?" Lyla demanded.

Krall and Angeli responded together. "No."

"It's better if you don't," Krall added. "Not yet, anyway. Maybe later."

Continuing her earlier thought, Angeli said, "What if we could destabilize the radical movement by turning the groups against their leaders?"

"Well," Lyla sniffed, "you've certainly demonstrated a talent for that sort of thing."

Ignoring the jibe, Angeli went on, "If we were to broadcast a powerful enough message across the continent, the radicals themselves might expose the guilty party. Then Security could move in and scoop them up."

"Like everyone taking a step backward except for the poisoner? It might just work," Krall allowed.

"But is it possible?" said Lyla. "I don't think any of our northern commhubs have the power to reach south of the channel."

"Not individually, no, but if we were to link up several of them in an array, and if the receiving unit on the southern continent is already set up to transmit to other units all over the world...?"

Angeli inhaled sharply. "You're talking about the intellinet! You can do that? Hack into the Directorate's server without leaving a trail? How?"

"The principle behind it is... Well, it's something Dennis came up with, actually. He gave it to us about twenty years ago, but we've never really tested its limits. A tech like Roger Walker can probably explain it much better than I can. Dennis's name for it was 'entanglement'."

"Entanglement? You mean *quantum* entanglement?" she blurted. "That's the theoretical basis for teleportation. Before the war, Terran scientists were attempting to teleport material objects, but—! Are you now saying you have the ability to make an electronic signal simply appear somewhere else?"

"Along with the programming to keep it travelling, yes. Late yesterday, I received a coded message from Dennis, instructing me to have the entanglement net ready for a special transmission, so I think the time has come to test what it can do. Compose your powerful speech, Eva. We'll record it and send it out the day after the next Skinner Report."

Hey there, all you radicals! You call yourselves that, as if blowing things up and ganging up on outsiders is some shiny new idea. Well, it's not. There's nothing radical about you except how willing you are to let yourselves be used like tools and then thrown away. You heard me right—I said 'thrown away'. Disposable. You've been taking orders from people who don't give a lepke's rear end about loyalty, and they especially don't care about you.

And why should they, when they're getting a sweet deal from whichever powerful family is pulling your strings? You don't believe me? Ask them where the credits are coming from to fund this little sideshow of theirs, because terrorism doesn't come cheap—your leaders have been paying out credits for bribes, for safe-houses, and for the silence and loyalty of gullible people like you. This is no grass-roots movement. Someone with wealth and power wanted it to happen, so they bought what they needed, including your leaders. Ask them! Ask them what their reward will be once the Directorate falls. Then ask them what you'll be getting out of it and watch them squirm. Because the answer is: you get nothing. Instead, you lose everything.

You're the ones who will get arrested by Security and charged with capital crimes, because you're the ones who will have blood on your hands. It won't matter that you were just following orders. You're the ones who planted the bombs and murdered people in dark alleys—not your leaders—and you're the ones who will take the blame. You're the ones who will be branded as terrorists. You will lose your families, your reputations, your freedom, and your lives. Meanwhile, your leaders—and the families who hold their leashes—get to toss you away like trash and walk away clean. They won't even admit they know you. Why should they?

While you're rotting in detention or counting your final minutes before being executed, they won't be giving you a second thought. They'll be too busy enjoying the good life they've earned by putting together a bunch of tools willing to swallow a pack of lies about doing something important, about changing society for the better. For the better? Better for who?

Who the flatch do you think you are to them? Use once, then throw away. That's the only use they have for you. So wake up! Open your eyes and look around! Listen to who's giving the orders! Think about who's taking the risks by getting their hands dirty! Because it's not your leaders, that's for damn sure. You think they're on your side? Think again! They're only loyal to themselves. Now think a third time. If you choose to go on doing the bidding of leaders who despise you, then you deserve everything that comes your way from now on, and believe me, it won't be pleasant.

Krall looked up from the hard copy Angeli had given him, his features frozen in an expression of surprise. "This is strong stuff, Eva. There are bound to be consequences."

"My mission is to silence the radical groups. Can you think of a better way to accomplish that than by sowing distrust among their ranks?"

"And if it backfires, and the leaders of all the radical groups get together and order their people to hunt down the source of the transmission?"

"If your entanglement machine does what it's supposed to, they'll think it's the Directorate," she returned.

"That's precisely my concern. Since bringing down the Directorate is their stated goal, you could be firing the first shot of a war."

"When Dennis was briefing me for this assignment he promised that I would become a revolutionary hero, and you can't be a revolutionary without starting a revolution. Ben, nobody ever accomplished anything without taking a chance. Let's do this."

Krall threw up his hands in surrender. "All right, then. I just hope we don't live to regret it."

After some research, Quin and Isabela had identified their putative villains: five large laboratories on the mainland whose major source of revenue consisted of grants from the Directorate for performing optimization procedures. Suspicious though it seemed, however, that by itself was not a crime. Neither was distributing brochures containing incomplete information. To justify what Isabela had in mind, she and Quin still needed solid proof that obsolete technology was being implanted in Terrans.

They needed witnesses, lots of them, all marching together on the day of the event.

The parent-teacher meeting at the school had been very well attended. This was largely thanks to Mrs. Santos. Following her and Isabela's earlier talk, Melora had joined the cause. She'd guessed the purpose of this gathering and had made a point of personally inviting every student's family to send at least one representative to it. After activating the signal jammer to ensure privacy, Isabela had turned the discussion to the topic of optimization.

The subsequent sharing of information had proven to be an eye-opener for everyone, including Isabela. She'd had no idea how many of her students' relatives either had the implants or were considering getting them. By the end of the meeting, she had a commitment from every person present to help her replace the laboratories' brochures with her own, truthful ones. Days were designated for "shopping trips" around the island, urban districts were portioned out, and each attendee left with two bundles of twenty folded flyers.

Isabela had literature to distribute as well. She'd exercised some privilege and reserved the local district for herself, keeping for last the store where Mrs. Santos had encountered the fake shopper.

This retail outlet was larger than the ones where Isabela normally browsed, although that made sense considering where it was located. Anyone who could afford to rent space in a sheltered mall could probably afford to rent a lot of it. There was no crowding of clothing on long, freestanding racks or casual piling of it on tables here. In this store, garments rode on well-separated carousels, making it unnecessary for patrons to sidle between them. The merchandise was pricey, as Quin would say, so it was important to treat it well. To let it breathe. And to give the clientele a relaxed shopping experience and let them breathe too.

Even the staff looked pricey, dressed in outfits from the store's window display. Standing just inside the door, Isabela counted four clerks—one behind the payment counter and three watching over the sales floor—and another five shoppers besides herself.

"May I help you?" asked the woman who now stepped forward to address her.

As Isabela turned to respond, she glimpsed the display of brochures on the counter to the right of the door. They were identical to the one Mrs. Santos had given her, but they wouldn't be for long.

"Actually," Isabela replied, consciously mirroring the clerk's friendly demeanour, "I was hoping to speak to your manager about a business matter."

The practiced smile never faltered. "May I tell her your name?"

"Certainly. It is Bella Calvera." That wasn't a lie. Calvera had been Isabela's unmarried name.

As the clerk disappeared into the back of the store, Isabela stepped over to the brochures and blocked the display with her body. Then, being careful not to move her upper arms, she rapidly made the switch. A moment later, the offending literature was tucked into her tote bag. Isabela turned back around and found herself suddenly face to face with one of the shoppers, a tall, slender woman with perfect makeup and long blonde hair.

When their eyes met, the woman lit up her expression and said in a gushing voice, "Forgive me, but I couldn't help noticing your interest in optimization. Are you thinking of getting the implants?"

This had to be the shill.

Thinking quickly, Isabela replied, "My niece is. Can you tell me more about them?"

"All the scientific stuff is described in here," said the woman, plucking a brochure from the rack and placing it in Isabela's hand. "But speaking as someone who recently had the procedure, I highly recommend them. Optimization is what got me my promotion at work."

That was probably not a lie, either—it would have been a reward for all the procedures she'd convinced unsuspecting Terrans to undergo.

"Congratulations," Isabela said. "And what kind of work do you do, *chica?*"

"Since my promotion, I'm in public relations. That's why I'm here, buying clothes. Image is everything, right?" She trilled a little laugh, which to Isabela's ears sounded just a bit too high-pitched to be natural.

"So, these implants are not dangerous at all?"

"Not one bit," the woman assured her. "There's some discomfort while your body adjusts to them, but once they're integrated into your nervous system, you are directly linked to the intellinet."

The sales clerk returned to tell Isabela, "Svetlana will see you in her office now."

Meanwhile, the clerk at the payment counter had picked up one of the brochures and was reading it, the frown on her face deepening gradually into a scowl. Good. With luck, the truth might even set the blonde-haired shill free as well.

The manager's office was nearly as spacious as the sales floor and clearly doubled as a conference room. Looking around her, Isabela saw nothing but metal and plastiplex, arranged in straight lines and sharp angles. Then Svetlana stepped out from behind the desk, and Isabela could guess who had chosen the décor.

The manager's ensemble was severely tailored and monochromatically grey. Her face looked drawn and sallow, as though it had begun to melt at some point and then stopped. How such a colourless soul had ended up managing a women's fashion store was beyond Isabela's comprehension. Or perhaps all the brilliant hues out front were to satisfy the tastes of commoners like herself who simply didn't understand *haute couture*. The image popped into her mind of a closet filled with various shades of grey blouses, grey skirts and pants, and grey jackets.

"What can I do for you, Ms. Calvera?" The voice was low-pitched. If she closed her eyes, Isabela might think she was being addressed by a man. "Beatrix says you've come on a business matter...?"

In fact, it had been Isabela's intention to make the switch and disappear before Beatrix found her again, but the blonde woman had delayed her departure. Now she had to fabricate a plausible reason for her visit.

Mentally crossing her fingers, Isabela met Svetlana's steady gaze (her eyes were grey, no surprise there) and replied, "Back on Earth, I was part of a very successful management team. If the owners are planning to expand by opening additional stores, I would like to be considered for... well, for your job, Svetlana."

A pained expression washed across the other woman's face. "I'm afraid that is out of the question. The owners are Stragori and the hiring policy is very clear. We always promote from within. I'm sorry that you wasted your time this afternoon, but please feel free to examine what is on offer at the front of the store."

On her way out, Isabela glanced at the brochure rack. It was empty, and the fake shopper was nowhere to be seen.

Word spread quickly. Over the next few days, Isabela received invitations to speak at parent-teacher meetings in numerous other districts on the island. Quin got busy producing flyers for her to hand out. As the date of the march approached, he would create posters as well, to put up indoors, away from prying surveillance eyes.

Isabela took attendance at each meeting and got student lists from the teachers who had invited her to speak. Then she and Quin used the alien tracking program to determine who among her audience was pure Terran and who was optimized. Together, they began building up a map of the island that showed how far demonstrators would have to travel to their assigned targets on the morning of the march. Coordination was going to be critical. Every group needed to arrive on the Directorate's doorstep at the same time.

Isabela's plan was coming together. Now only one thing was missing: the signal jammer that would ensure they had the element of surprise.

One day in late spring, a man with swarthy skin who identified himself as Safiq came to Isabela and Quin's door with a delivery of food from *Ravi Motaro*. He had rented a vehicle, which the three of them then rode to the middle of a public park roughly the size of a district marketplace. Ostensibly they were there to picnic. In fact, they were about to test the piece of technology that had been concealed at the bottom of the delivery container.

Once Isabela had spread out their blanket on the ground, Quin drove the vehicle back the way they'd come, until he was halfway to the apartment. On his signal, Isabela activated the signal jammer, and he turned around and drove slowly toward her.

Rental vehicles stopped working when the locator signal they emitted was jammed. Quin's came to a halt at the edge of the park, beside an unattended kiosk, and he got out and counted his steps the rest of the way to their picnic area. The jammed zone had a radius of nine hundred paces.

"Large enough?" said Safiq.

"If the device is located far enough away from the front door, yes," Quin replied. "Powerful enough?"

"I have modified it to pull energy from a strap-on battery, which you will find inside the food container marked 'haliji'. It is fully charged and should maintain the field for at least twenty consecutive hours."

So saying, Safiq extended his hand for payment. Quin pulled a data card out of his pocket and placed it on the other man's palm.

"Give this to Nasneen with our compliments," he said. "I believe she'll find it a satisfactory payment for your work."

Safiq turned the card over a couple of times, then tucked it away in his belt pouch. "And my transportation?"

Quin gave him a sympathetic look. "The same as ours, I'm afraid. Isabela and I will walk you to your car."

Things were working out perfectly, but Marcel was difficult to convince of that.

As he sat with Dennis on the sofa in his underground lair, pouring out twin goblets of sowerberry wine, he growled, "You're placing an inordinate amount of faith in the reports coming from operatives at opposite ends of the continents, Nephew, especially when neither of them has the full picture."

"One of them is your own grandson," Dennis pointed out.

"The dull little bureaucrat who fantasizes about being a pirate. Right," he added, simultaneously slamming the cork back into the bottle with the flat of his beefy hand.

Dennis picked up his goblet and swirled its golden contents around a couple of times. "There's more to Quin than you think. Certainly more than he's shown to this point."

"What? He's had a near-death experience and now he's a daredevil?"

Dennis grinned. "Not quite. But he's definitely colouring outside the lines now. In some respects, I would even go so far as to say that you and he have a lot in common. You really ought to give him a chance, Uncle." He took a sip of the wine, savouring its taste and the way it felt in his mouth for several seconds before he swallowed. "This is excellent. Do I want to know where it came from?"

"Nope."

"Figured as much."

"Am I ever going to get my gadget back?"

"Probably not."

"Figured as much." Marcel cleared his throat and turned to face the bullet car track. "So you're positive the timing lines up?"

"Absolutely."

"And the impostor will be forced out of his stronghold?"

"I guarantee it."

"And Arno Lindquist knows what he has to do?"

"I've made sure of it."

"And your grandson will come through for us?"

"Drew hasn't let me down yet."

There was a pause as Marcel's gaze swivelled. Dennis could practically feel it drilling into the side of his head but resisted the urge to turn and meet it.

"There's a first time for everything, you know," Marcel reminded him quietly.

"I know." Dennis took another thoughtful sip. "But we've come this far. I guess we'll be finding out."

TWENTY-FOUR
ON DAISY HUB

"**C**hief, O'Malley just called up from the Mezzanine," came Ruby's voice on the intercomm. "He says there's someone down there you'll want to meet."

Townsend leaned back reflectively in his desk chair. Someone he didn't know was on the computer deck immediately below AdComm?

Then things clicked together and he cursed himself for slow-wittedness. Of *course* there was someone there, but not on the deck. It had to be the AI on the dedicated server. They'd done it! And not a moment too soon.

"Tell him I'm on my way."

Townsend stepped off the tube car on Deck C-1 and found Lydia, Walt, and O'Malley standing around one of the computer stations, looking proud enough to burst.

"We haven't given him a voice yet," Walt cautioned, "but you can communicate with him by using the screen and keyboard."

"Most of his memories still need to be filled in, but he

definitely has a personality," Lydia added.

Drew sat down and keyed in the first line: *Hello. I am Drew Townsend, station manager of Daisy Hub. Who are you?*

I AM LOUIS FORRAND, THE SENIOR DIRECTOR OF THE STRAGORI PLANETARY GOVERNMENT AND THE HAK'KOR OF HOUSE STRAGON. WHERE AM I?

Your consciousness—

AND WHY CAN'T I FEEL MY ARMS AND LEGS?

Your consciousness has been saved—

BUT NOT MY LIMBS? WHAT THE FLATCH HAVE YOU NUMQUATS DONE TO ME?

—saved to a server on our computer deck. This was done for safety reasons, since your original server has come under attack by radical forces on-world. In fact, your existence has been digital for quite a long time.

THEN WHY CAN'T I REMEMBER BEING UPLOADED?

We are in the process of locating and restoring your memories.

NICE TRY! HOW WILL I KNOW THEY'RE GENUINE? FOR THAT MATTER, HOW DO I KNOW YOU'RE NOT MANIPULATING ME RIGHT NOW WITH A PACK OF CAREFULLY CHOSEN LIES?

"Told you," Lydia murmured.

Gritting his teeth, Townsend poked punishingly at the keyboard:

Because we're both Forrands, and Forrands do not lie to one another.

SAYS YOU.

"Prickly son of a bitch, isn't he?" Walt remarked.

I HEARD THAT. BRING ME MY PANTS AND MY SHOES. I'M LEAVING.

Drew sighed inwardly. This wasn't going to be easy.

*　　　*　　　*

In retrospect, it shouldn't have come as a surprise. From the moment that Townsend had arrived on Daisy Hub, nothing had gone right the first time. Well, he could give them a few more days. With luck, O'Malley and his team would be able to turn this belligerent coot of an AI into something that could be used to fool the impostor. But Drew wasn't about to hold his breath.

Turn him or terminate him.

If those were his only two options, it might be time to roll out plan B... whatever it turned out to be.

No sooner had that depressing thought crossed his mind than a familiar, painful sensation kindled in his midsection. He did some rapid mental calculation. Four more antacid tablets and he would exhaust the daily quota the Doc had imposed on him. She had made it clear that he would not be denied medication, but there would be a price to pay for not taking care of himself—a stern lecture would come with anything further that he requested from Med Services.

Fortunately, his deskcomm chose that moment to buzz, distracting him.

"The Pirrits are on approach to the Hub, Chief. Their ETA is roughly twenty station hours," came Ruby's cheerful voice through the speaker. "And Mr. Trager has asked to have a word with you. He's on his way up to AdComm right now."

Lovely. This was probably about the petition for alliance from House Stragon. Another ember to add to the slow-burning fire in his belly.

Moments later, the Stragori liaison was standing in the doorway of Townsend's office, his eyebrows elevated appraisingly. "Have I chosen a bad time?"

Drew rearranged his features into a neutral expression, then gestured to Trager to enter and sit down.

"I've come to offer my assistance," said Trager. "Or at least, a suggestion or two."

Intrigued, Townsend leaned forward on his elbows. "Go on."

"After telling your people everything I could remember about Louis Forrand, I couldn't help speculating about why it might be necessary. The fact that the ones requesting the information were all computer tech specialists led me to one remarkable conclusion. If it is your intention to impersonate Louis Forrand the same way that someone else is impersonating Gervais Forrand—and for the same reason—then I would urge you to reconsider."

"Oh? Why?"

"Louis Forrand went silent fifty years ago, just as Gervais was inducted into the Directorate. If an impostor skewed the uploading process in order to replace Gervais in the eyes of the public while managing somehow to lock Louis away at the same time, then he has had decades to solidify his position. To make Gervais over in his own image, both literally and figuratively. Meanwhile, fifty years is not that long for a Stragori. People still retain detailed memories of the way Louis presented himself, and the way he represented the Directorate and House Stragon. His speech mannerisms, his word choices... not to mention his pronunciations. Every being carries their origins in their voice. You have agents aboard the station who are fluent in Stragori, but not even the ones who speak it like a native are entirely accent-free."

"Accents and inflections can be counterfeited using exemplars. I'm sure we can find some samples of Louis's speech patterns on those memory blocs you brought us," Drew pointed out.

"The ones you ordered to be sealed in their containers because of the high probability that they would corrupt your systems? I would not advise that, Mr. Townsend."

"Then what would you have us do, Trager? We need a convincing Louis Forrand facsimile and the clock is ticking."

The Stragori smiled faintly. "I understand that you were a Security officer in your former life. Did you ever have occasion to solve a crime by putting yourself in the place of its victim?"

"Not often when it was a murder, but for something like a kidnapping—" Drew's eyes widened as the solution to his problem seemed to burst like fireworks in his brain. Overtaken by a sudden sense of urgency, he sprang to his feet. "Thank you, Mr. Trager, you've been most helpful."

"I do my best," came the reply. Trager stood up as well. He put out his hand and let it be clasped briefly, then added before heading out the door, "And don't look so surprised. Didn't I tell you the first time we met that I'm not your enemy?"

As soon as the Stragori had disappeared into a tube car, Townsend hurried down to the Mezzanine, where O'Malley and Walt Garfield sat conferring at one of the computer stations.

"Forget about visuals," Drew told them briskly. "Louis will be sending out a voice message only, in Stragori."

O'Malley frowned in puzzlement. "But if people are accustomed to seeing as well as hearing their Directors make announcements—"

"He won't be making an announcement. He's a kidnap

victim, trapped inside a box. He'll be calling for help and railing against his captor."

"Boss, that's brilliant... I think..."

"Do we have language programming in our systems?" Townsend demanded.

"About a hundred different lexicons in the files I copied from the Central Archives," said O'Malley. "We may still have the translation algorithms as well, from when we were uploading the Stragori documents earlier."

"Voice samples?" said Townsend.

"Quite a number of them, actually," Walt replied. "We'll need at least a couple of Louis's audio clips if we're to reproduce his timbre and cadence."

"Timeline?"

Walt and O'Malley exchanged calculating looks.

"A day," said Walt. "Maybe less."

"Good. Give our AI his speaking voice and make ready to translate mine, then prepare to record our next conversation."

Sixteen hours later, the *Night Cloud* glided from the airlock to its tie-down on the Hub's landing deck, and Townsend was there to greet it.

The Eggenali ship was a wonder to behold. The same pure black as deep space, it looked more like the void that would be left if a sleek, shuttle-sized craft with backswept wings were to be neatly excised from reality. If one stared at it intently, the curve of its hull appeared to shift back and forth between convex and concave, almost as if it were breathing.

This was the vessel that had penetrated the Stragori

defence perimeter and rescued the Terran agents a short while ago. Its owners—Gorse Pirrit and his mate, Ixbeth Minegar—had taken a tremendous risk by doing so. They had defied the harsh terms of a treaty imposed by the Great Council millennia earlier and were wanted fugitives outside of Earth space. Now Townsend was having to ask them to return to Stragon, this time to make a delivery, and although hopeful, he wasn't at all certain that they would agree.

Ixbeth was a rare, pure-blooded Kularian. Gorse was a Kularian-Praxtan hybrid from the planet Eggenar. Both were members of felid species, although Ixbeth was much more catlike, having tawny fur all over her body and a stubby tail at the base of her spine. Gorse was furless and tailless, with dark skin and a face that suggested rather than depicted feline features. Both were telempathic as well, and came from cultures that had developed psi-powered technology, including for interstellar travel.

That was why the *Night Cloud* went nowhere without both of the Pirrits aboard—it was partly psi-powered.

"You're looking very serious, Mr. Townsend," said Gorse as he leaped down from the hatchway. It was hard not to notice how lightly he landed on the deck. *Like a cat.*

"I have another favour to request, Mr. Pirrit. I wish I didn't need it, but..."

"The birthday party was very enjoyable, and thank you for asking," Ixbeth cut in, a warning flashing in her turquoise eyes.

Lowering his voice, Gorse said to Townsend, "Perhaps you and I should discuss this privately a little later on."

"Of course. And how is Lania doing?"

Practically beaming now, Ixbeth replied, "She's thriving,

surrounded by her new family. Dedrick and Eberhart made the right decision, letting Eberhart's brother and his mate adopt her."

Feeling somewhat redeemed by this exchange, Townsend nodded pleasantly... and filed the information away. Lania Dedrick was a genetically modified Human with the same psi powers as a Kularian. Yoko and Akiko were genetically modified Terran laboratory rats with lifespans so long they were virtually immortal, and with encrypted scientific data concealed within their DNA. All three could very well figure in The Repository's end game.

After some thought, Townsend decided to put off meeting with Gorse until confirmation was received from the computer deck that the AI could now speak in something closely approximating the voice of the real Louis Forrand. After all, there was little sense in discussing delivery details for a parcel that didn't yet exist, and nothing to be gained by needlessly troubling the Pirrits' domestic waters.

Walt's estimate of the time required was off, but not by much. The following afternoon, he sent a message to Drew's desk, inviting him to come and help them test their work.

"You complicated the assignment by requiring that everything be both translated and recorded," Lydia explained, "so we had to come up with a workaround. Under the circumstances, this is the best we could do."

Townsend's heart already sinking, he said, "Walk me through it."

"Do you have a script?" Walt asked him.

In fact, he did. There were specific things he needed the

Louis Forrand surrogate to respond to, so Drew had spent considerable time crafting a list of carefully-worded prompts.

As it turned out, the process was roundabout, but not all that difficult. Townsend spoke his lines into a mic, pausing for several seconds between them. As he did so, the computer recorded his voice and used it to translate the prompts into Stragori. The resulting playback sounded remarkably lifelike. Not that it mattered, since his wasn't the voice that the Stragori people would be hearing.

"Now comes the tricky part," said Walt. "The AI will respond to these in spoken Stragori, with emotion, in the closest imitation of Forrand's voice that we were able to create. But his answers will have to be translated into Standard in order for us to know what he's saying. The computers can translate simultaneously—that's not the issue. Problem is, we can't rehearse this before we record it, and we can't rerecord it to correct mistakes. We only get one take, and it has to be perfect."

Of course it did. They were running a con on the AI, and they were all going to have to think on their feet. Townsend had nearly forgotten how good the rush of adrenalin that came on the heels of that thought made him feel.

"Then I guess it's show time!" he said.

The recording went even better than Drew had hoped. The AI ranted for a good half-hour, giving O'Malley and his team plenty of material to work with. After that, there was just one more thing Townsend had to do before approaching Gorse Pirrit to ask for his help.

The package is ready for delivery. Allowing four days for transit time, please supply timing and safe landing coordinates for a cloaked shuttlecraft, and passwords to ensure the security of the hand-off.

Townsend stared for several long moments at the message he'd just drafted. The last time the *Night Cloud* had paid a visit to Stragon, it had landed on a deserted beach in the Wilderness Zone at low tide, lingering only long enough to take on passengers and then departing, all in the middle of the night. Logically, that was when and where the rendezvous should happen again. But this errand was for Dennis Forrand, not the EIS, and Dennis didn't concern himself with the safety of his pawns.

Tempted though Drew was to simply specify the same coordinates again, Olivia had impressed on him the need to keep that spot on the beach a secret. Isabela had remained behind to pull up the rope ladder that provided access to it from the top of the bluff. She was a trained EIS operative and could be trusted to keep sensitive information to herself. The same could not necessarily be said about Forrand's people, and that was who would be taking delivery of the package.

So, Townsend chose what he hoped would turn out to be the lesser of two evils. He encrypted the message on his screen, attached it to a bland, folksy covering letter to Isabela, and gave them both to Ruby to transmit to Stragon. Then he crossed his fingers and hoped that Forrand wouldn't direct the *Night Cloud* to an airfield in the middle of an urban district.

Or a war zone.

TWENTY-FIVE
ON STRAGON

One week later, in the fourteenth hour of the ninth day of the fifth month of the year, a message was transmitted to every person on Stragon. It blared out over the intellinet, apparently coming from the Directorate's server. Those who were optimized heard it through their implants as a woman's voice, harsh and trembling with barely-controlled rage. The rest found it in their voxmail, marked 'Most Urgent Listen Immediately':

Hey there, all you radicals! You call yourselves that, as if blowing things up and ganging up on outsiders is some shiny new idea. Well, it's not. There's nothing radical about you except how willing you are to let yourselves be used like tools and then thrown away. You heard me right—I said 'thrown away'. Disposable. You've been taking orders from people who don't give a lepke's rear-end about loyalty, and they especially don't care about you...

Instantly, the 'net lit up with comments and reactions, the majority of them laced with profanity and demanding to know what the hell was going on. At first, people assumed that the main server had been hacked somehow. But that was impossible. The Directorate's security was impregnable. Therefore, the message had to be real and coming from somewhere inside it.

It didn't take long for the leaders of the radical fringe groups to realize they were in trouble. This strident appeal to their followers to bring them down was a clear indication that their friend inside the Directorate was gone. Gervais Forrand had either been found out and silenced or had actively turned against them. Either way, they were on their own, surrounded by subordinates who were now looking at them suspiciously and asking questions they'd rather not answer. The radical leaders began making arrangements to flee to Galandra before their own people could take them out.

Isabela and Quinian heard Angeli's voice delivering this broadcast and shared an astonished look.

And Dennis Forrand chuckled to himself as he prepared to make some calls and send some messages. One of them was going to Drew Townsend, in reply to the latest transmission from Daisy Hub.

Angeli had completed her mission successfully.

The date of the march on the Directorate had been finalized.

At last, Dennis could tell him that the operation was a go.

The central division warders' station in Westgrove was a larger version of the one guarding the entrance to the Wilderness Zone—a box-like structure with dark brown walls, small barred windows, and a bright red door. Perched on a pole stuck into the ground in the middle of the tiny front lawn was a painted sign displaying the words WESTGROVE WARDERS STATION NUMBER 1 in large block lettering.

It wasn't often that Krall had occasion to question one sibling at the behest of another, but Ella Thurman had been insistent. Her sister, Marjorie Harris, was up to no good. After deserting the family forty-two years earlier and going south to find a wealthy life mate, she was back in town, too cheap to rent proper accommodations. Instead, she'd simply turned up on Ella's doorstep and begged her way into her sister's spare bedroom.

Something had told Krall that this was more than just a matter of wanting an unwelcome house guest to leave, so he'd dug a little deeper. Marjorie's husband, it turned out, was part-owner of both the production company and the catering firm that had recently spent several days in Edgerton. It was reason enough to send his warders out to find her and bring her in for questioning.

Less than an hour later, Marjorie Harris was located and peacefully taken into custody in the district's largest marketplace. Half an hour after that, she arrived at the warder station and was escorted into a smallish, windowless space furnished with a square wooden table and four matching upholstered chairs.

Marjorie was looking flushed and a little dishevelled, Krall noted. As he and Andy Birtles observed her on the monitoring screens in the booth next door, she prowled around the room, discovering and peering into each concealed, corner-mounted surveillance eye in turn. Then she checked the underside of the table for a hidden mic before finally settling onto one of the chairs.

"She's no stranger to interrogation," Andy murmured.

"She has an arrest record," Krall confirmed. "I checked. That's probably why she headed south. It wasn't to find a wealthy family to marry into. It was to get away from her own and make a fresh start."

"Then why did she come back?"

"Good question. Let's add it to the list and get some answers, shall we?"

The two warders had barely crossed the threshold of the interview room when their subject sprang to her feet and demanded, "Where is my sister? I have to speak to her."

"And you will," Krall replied, "but first we need to talk. Please make yourself comfortable, Lady Harris. Warder Birtles here can bring you something to drink if you'd like. This may take a while."

Shaking her head, she sank back onto her chair. "When my husband hears about this—"

"He'll be welcome to join us here," Krall said, raising his voice to cut off the rest of her threat. "Until then, we're just going to have a conversation, you and I. We're not accusing you of anything, but we believe you have information that can help us solve a case, so for your own sake I would advise you to answer truthfully. Will you do that?"

As her chin came up in a silent challenge, Krall breathed a sigh and sat down facing her. He hadn't expected her to make this easy for him, but some level of cooperation would have been nice. Well, if this was the way she wanted to play it...

"Fine." He pulled up the list of poisoning victims on the screen of the pad he'd brought in with him, then placed it on the table in front of her. "Do you recognize any of these people?"

She leaned forward warily and read the names. "No," she replied, "I don't know who they are."

"Really? That's strange, because they've been all over the news lately."

"I don't follow the northern news," she informed him coolly. "I'm more concerned about what's happening on the mainland."

"Well, let me bring you up to speed, Lady Harris. These seven Boreans from seven different towns all have two things in common. First, they were all invited to attend the recording of a video broadcast called 'The Stories Left Behind', in Edgerton, and they travelled there to be part of the audience."

"So did a couple thousand other people," she pointed out, notes of anxiety creeping into her voice.

"Quite true. But *only* these seven died of damselflower poisoning within days of leaving Edgerton. So Security looked more closely, and we discovered a third thing these people had in common. They were among a group of ten winners whose names were drawn by the production's hired catering company to receive a package of tasty treats as a parting gift, 'for the road, and the story *you* will leave behind'.

"Forensic testing has determined that those treats were poisoned. Since they were prepared on site in Edgerton and damselflower is not native to Borea, our medical specialists have ruled all seven of these deaths to be planned and deliberate murders."

Her face lost shades of colour. "And you think *I* know something about them?" she demanded. "That's ridiculous!"

Krall leaned toward her and softened his voice. "You may

not realize that you know it. The crimes were committed during the time the video crew was in Edgerton, and you were on site with them. It's possible you saw or heard something that can lead us to the murderer. We're asking for your help here. Any small thing could turn out to be important."

Her spine straightened as though pulled by a string, and a look of consternation swept across her face.

Krall and Birtles exchanged knowing glances. This woman was torn. She knew something but didn't feel safe or comfortable revealing it.

"Are you sure you wouldn't like something to drink?" Birtles said, smiling. "Some kaffy, maybe, or water? Unfortunately, we're not allowed to offer you anything stronger than that."

Her lips twitched momentarily upwards. "No, thank you, Warder."

"Lady Harris, we're aware that your husband is part-owner of both the video production company and the firm that handled the catering for the event," Krall resumed, "so that gives you an insider's perspective. Did you notice anyone on the crew or among the catering staff who was behaving strangely or didn't seem to fit in?" Krall asked.

"Any new hires who made you nervous or uncomfortable in any way?" Birtles chimed in.

Her shoulders sagged. "I shouldn't have come to Westgrove," she muttered.

"Why did you, then?" said Krall.

She leaned forward earnestly and replied, "Because everything is falling apart on the mainland. You must have heard about the bombings, and the attacks in broad daylight. I wanted to make sure my children would have somewhere safe to go. Somewhere where they could grow up happy and... normal. I thought if I reconnected with my family..." She went silent for a moment. "But even after all these years, they want nothing to do with me. I should have realized it was a daydream."

Visibly recomposing herself, she gazed directly into Krall's eyes and informed him, "There's nothing I can tell you about either of those two companies. I've found that my marriage works much better if I keep my nose out of the Harris family businesses. I'm just a fan of the show who came up here to be part of the audience for the recording sessions and to try to visit my family, and that's all. That's my statement. Give me some paper and a pen and I will record it for you."

"Paper and pen?" said Birtles, glancing in confusion from her face to the two computing devices on the table. "Why wouldn't you—"

"This is the northern continent, is it not?" she said haughtily. "The land of low tech?"

"But—"

"It doesn't matter, Andy. She's refusing to talk and she wants us to have it in her own handwriting," Krall told him. "Get her what she wants and find someone to drive her to her sister's house. She's free to go."

On her way out of the station, Marjorie Harris handed Krall a folded sheet of paper. "I'll be returning to the mainland tomorrow, to my husband and my children," she said archly, "and I didn't tell you a damn thing." Then she departed, her shoulders squared and her head held high.

Birtles came to stand beside him. "I don't get it, Ben. She was obviously withholding information. Why did you release her?"

Krall had been perusing her "statement". Smiling, he handed the page to his partner and replied, "Because she just gave us an anonymous tip. Once she's back home, this gets entered into our system as such, but not a minute before. The Harrises are vindictive and don't tolerate betrayal."

Two days later, Krall contacted the District Warder-in-Chief, who made a call to Continental Security, passing along for further action the names of two men who'd been added to the catering staff just before the Harris-owned production company set off for Edgerton.

Continental responded with a grudging thanks, then girded their loins for a jurisdictional battle with Mainland Security.

That evening, Krall also transmitted a detailed report to Dennis Forrand. Then Krall, Lyla, and Angeli sat under a cloud of frustration as they sipped tea in Lyla's parlour, bemoaning the fact that all their poisoning suspects were out of reach on the southern continent.

Mainland Security would probably use that as justification for wanting to take over the investigation, and once Mainland started digging, there was no telling what sort of dirt might be revealed.

TWENTY-SIX
ON DAISY HUB

"**A**re those the correct coordinates?" said Walt. Townsend swivelled the screen to show him the decrypted message that had just arrived from Dennis Forrand. "They're the ones he sent me. Apparently, he wants the ship landing as far away from the Directorate's server as possible."

"That makes no sense. Not if the plan is to sneak our audio file onto the intellinet via that server. The farther the package has to travel once it's delivered, the greater the chance that something will go wrong."

"He's a Forrand, Walt. To him, it makes all the sense in the world, and that's all he cares about."

The other man blew out a heavy breath. "He's changed our plan. Well, he's boots on the ground and we're way the hell out here, so it's possible he knows something we don't. I guess this boils down to a question of whether you trust him. Do you?"

Good question.

Townsend thought for a moment, recalling what Olivia

had told him earlier about people getting pulled into Dennis Forrand's schemes and losing themselves. This was Forrand's plan now. Did Drew trust him not to foil it by making changes on the fly? Certainly. Dennis was a past master of the con game. In addition to being a ruthless bastard who would do anything to win, he was calculating and meticulous in his methods. Any changes he made to Drew's scenario could only be intended to improve the odds of its success.

Unbidden, Arno's remembered voice bobbed to the surface of Drew's mind: *"Forrands have been known to lie to the world, but we don't lie to one another."*

That sealed the deal.

"I trust him as much as I need to, Walt. I'm green-lighting this."

At last, armed with the final details, Townsend could approach Gorse Pirrit for the favour he needed.

He found the Eggenali sitting alone at a table in the caf. At the same time, so did Vin Trager. Gorse looked up from his mug of Chef Jensen's famous sludge, saw them both bearing down on him, and waved invitingly to them.

When Drew pulled up beside him, Trager said, "You may as well join the party, *Hak'kor*. I figured out your plan days ago."

"Really!" Townsend levelled a dubious stare at him. "Now, that's interesting, because I didn't know myself what it was until this morning."

"Then perhaps you don't know yourself, period."

Gorse frowned. "Do you two need some space? Because I can go elsewhere."

"No, stay where you are. We need to talk," said Trager. "You too, *Hak'kor*." The title didn't sound at all respectful when he used it. However, he was right about the need for a discussion.

Yielding to the inevitable, Townsend sank onto one of the empty chairs. Also inevitably, Chef Jensen bustled over and put a spoon and a bowl of yogourt surrogate in front of him. It was peach-coloured, but Drew had learned the hard way not to get his hopes up.

"The ulcer's misbehaving, is it?" said Trager with sympathy in his eyes but not his voice.

"Preventative measure. Doctor's orders," Drew replied. Then, to change the subject, he turned to Gorse and asked, "Where is Ixbeth? You two are usually together."

"She's in Med Services, being checked over."

"Is she all right?" Trager asked.

"Normally, the flight back from New Elysium wouldn't have bothered her at all," said Gorse. "She's mentally linked to her twin brother, and together they're a powerhouse of psi energy. In her current condition, however, she doesn't have access to him—or to me—so it's no wonder she's feeling exhausted."

In her current condition?

Townsend stared a question at him.

"Pregnant Kularian females bond completely with the kits developing inside them," Gorse explained. "That mental connection supersedes and excludes every other."

"So, you're going to be a father," said Trager, grinning broadly. "Congratulations! When is she due?"

"In about seven intervals. For obvious reasons, it's only a guess, but so far everything seems to be following the textbook." Addressing Townsend, he added, "Are you here to ask for that favour now?"

"I'm afraid so. I need your ship for another stealth mission to Stragon—just to drop something off and come back. But if Ixbeth isn't up for this—"

"I know someone who might be," Trager cut in, "someone the *Hak'kor* has already shown he trusts, and who has been a student of the mental disciplines for some time."

It took a moment for Drew's brain to click in. "You're talking about Yorell Enne. But she's a Reyot, and unless I'm mistaken, the Reyota are telepaths, not empaths like Gorse and Ixbeth."

"You're not mistaken, Mr. Townsend," said Gorse. "However, the Reyot and Kularian races diverged from a single species. Just as every Kularian is a latent telepath, every Reyot is a latent empath. I have a technology that can access and amplify Yorell's latent talent, giving her the ability to at least maintain life support aboard the *Night Cloud*. So, as long as she is willing to risk entering alien space, she would be a good choice for this mission."

As long as she was willing. This was by no means a certainty. Madame Enne was not only The Repository's Head Librarian, she was also the Reyot High Councillor who had set out to foil the Great Council's plans to annihilate Humanity, thereby becoming an outlaw. She was as much a wanted fugitive as the Pirrits were.

Townsend swallowed the further objections that had dropped onto his tongue. Gorse was right. Madame Enne was their only hope. Now all he had to do was make her care about a single parcel delivery to a world that was in the process of tearing itself apart.

*   *   *

"I hate to think what this place would be like if you didn't have me to put it in order, Mr. Townsend," Yorell scolded, barely glancing up at him as her long fingers flew over the keyboard of her computer.

The plastiplex-walled cubicle next to Drew's on AdComm was now the office of The Repository's Head Librarian. Like The Repository itself, it was a work in progress. However, now that it was finally equipped with a chair designed to accommodate her tail and her oddly-fashioned legs, she had settled in and begun "putting things in order" with a vengeance.

Townsend remained in her doorway, glad that Reyota could only read the thoughts of other telepaths. He wasn't sure he wanted Yorell to know what was on his mind right now.

Even in her current reduced circumstances, the disgraced former Prime Docent of the Central Archives was a force of nature. Bipedal and a head taller when standing than the tallest Human on the station, she was a powerful figure with grey facial fur that darkened as it neared her hairline, and a striking, pure white mane.

Eventually, she swivelled her chair and met his gaze. "Is there something I can do for you, Mr. Townsend?"

"I have a favour to ask. It isn't onerous, but it might be a little dangerous."

She smiled. "I know. Gorse Pirrit needs a co-pilot. Mr. Trager came to see me earlier."

Of *course* he did.

"So, you've had a chance to think about this."

"Indeed."

"And what is your answer, Madame Enne?"

"I would like to propose an exchange. A favour for a

favour."

"I see. And what favour would you require from me?"

Her smile brightened exponentially. "I don't know yet. But you can owe it to me. I promise that it will not be onerous... but it might be a little dangerous."

In spite of himself, Townsend had to chuckle. "All right, Madame Enne, we have a deal."

Later, he went in search of Trager and found him on B Deck (vessel maintenance and repair) finishing up a conversation with Lucas Soaring Hawk, the Hub's propulsion systems engineer.

"You knew about Ixbeth before we met in the caf, then pretended you were hearing it for the first time," Drew said accusingly as he walked Trager back to the tube car. "Why?"

"Yes, I knew, because I was interested enough to ask Gorse about their flight back to the Hub. And when I went to tell Yorell about the coming blessed event, the conversation turned to the problem it was probably going to cause for you," came the unruffled response. "You should spend less time worrying about your problems and more time talking to your crew about them, *Hak'kor*. You'd be amazed at how much help they can be. As for the reason for my pretense..." He shrugged. "As the liaison between two *Hak'kors*, I try to do things the Nandrian way. It would have been dishonouring to you—not to mention disrespectful of me—if I were to suggest the solution before you were even aware the problem existed, and since I was going to be the source of the solution, that meant you needed to learn about the problem from someone other than me."

"I had to state my need, then let you find a way to fulfill

it, so that honour would accrue to both of us." The importance of honour as currency had been one of the first things Gavin Holchuk had taught Townsend about interacting with Nandrians.

Trager nodded sagely. "Indeed."

TWENTY-SEVEN
ON STRAGON

In the middle of the night following the second day of the sixth month of the Stragori year, Warder-in-Charge Bennin Krall put on his darkest clothing and drove to the coordinates Dennis Forrand had transmitted to him earlier. They denoted the middle of a broad clearing in the forest, just inside the easternmost edge of the Wilderness Zone, approximately one and a half kilopaces from the Westgrove commhub. Krall pulled to a stop in the covering shadow of the nearby trees, angling the vehicle so that he could observe the clearing through the windscreen. Then he doused the headlights, turned off the engine, and waited.

He'd been told that a parcel was going to be handed off to him at this location, that it would be something Dennis wanted broadcast over the intellinet by way of the Directorate's server, and that exact instructions would come with it.

Spring was a season of wet weather on Borea. Within

moments of Krall's parking the land car, fat drops were splatting down onto the windscreen from the foliage overhead. Minutes later, the rain was coming down hard, obscuring his forward view entirely and forcing him to turn on the wipers.

So much for being undetectable.

All at once he noticed something strange about the rain falling into the clearing. The drops appeared to be changing direction in mid-air, as though they were bouncing off something he couldn't see. Intrigued, he got out of his vehicle and moved in for a closer look, heedless of the downpour that immediately began soaking into the fabric of his jacket and trousers.

The *snick* of a latch froze him in place. Then a light appeared in front of him. It hovered at his eye level for a moment, growing larger and taking a rectangular shape, and he realized that he was watching an invisible door slide aside.

Krall was instantly wary. "Who's there?" he called out.

"The nights are brisk up here," came a male voice from the direction of the opening, speaking in heavily accented Stragori.

It was the password from Dennis's earlier notification about this meeting.

With an inward sigh of relief, Krall gave the coded response: "Be glad it isn't cold enough to snow."

At this, two beings appeared in what was clearly the hatchway of a cloaked ship. Krall saw a face even darker than his own, with vaguely feline features, and another, even more alien-looking, with a paler complexion and a thick mane of white hair.

"We understand you're expecting a special delivery," said

the second being, whose command of Stragori was considerably better than their partner's.

"You understand correctly," Krall replied. He stepped forward to receive a cloth-wrapped bundle from the second being's hand. "Do you have further instructions for me?"

"No. We are just the messengers. Perhaps with the parcel?"

"I'll check. Thank you." His final words were spoken to a rapidly closing door. Tucking the bundle into the inside pocket of his jacket, Krall hurried back to his vehicle.

On the third day of the sixth month of the Stragori year, the captain of the ferry boat taking on passengers for the first island-to-mainland crossing of the morning noted with some surprise an unusually large number of commuters boarding his vessel. Most of them carried hand-lettered signs. He squinted and was able to make some of them out:

My body, my choice.

Full consent means full disclosure.

Terrans are not disposal units.

Ferries on early runs generally carried a fraction of their total capacity. Today, he was filling up fast and would probably have to leave some travellers behind to catch the next boat.

It appeared a protest was brewing on the mainland. Should he notify Security?

Then he took a closer look and noticed that many of these passengers were school-aged children. He'd heard that the island might be harbouring terrorists, but he seriously doubted whether any of them were *that* young.

Besides, they were all chattering happily and moving peacefully along the ramp. Maybe it was harmless. A class trip, perhaps? That would be out of the ordinary, certainly, but as long as everyone behaved themselves during the crossing, surely it was nothing to raise an alarm about.

Sub-Chief of Mainland Security District One Arno Lindquist had called an emergency meeting of all his division commanders.

"I've received a tip that a situation is about to develop, and I'm putting all of you on high alert. Recall everyone on your rosters. No one gets the day off today."

"What kind of situation, Sub-Chief?"

"According to my source, there's going to be a mass protest by the Terrans against some of the medical laboratories in the heart of our district."

"You're expecting terrorism, sir?"

"Not from the Terrans. But I'm concerned that once the protest begins, some of the more radical fringe groups may decide to use it as a distraction while they run around doing damage. As well, many large businesses, including the medical labs, have hired their own private security. The sight of a large crowd at their doorstep could panic them into unleashing their goon squads, and I don't want any violence breaking out, especially since I'm told there will be children present. You're not to let a single protester get hurt today if you can avoid it. Am I clear?"

"Yes, sir!" came the many-voiced reply.

"So what's the plan, sir? Do we know which labs are being targeted?"

"As a matter of fact, we do," Lindquist told him, "and

that's going to make our jobs a lot easier. BioFuture in division one. ExcelMed in division four. Harris Research Labs in division seven. MediCorp in division eight. Spence BioTech in division fourteen. I want each of these protests protected in two ways. As well as having uniformed Security present and visible—"

"And armed?" one of the commanders piped up.

"—and ready to handle any sort of threat expeditiously," Lindquist continued grimly, "we also need to have officers in plainclothes mingling with the crowd, prepared to identify and apprehend any known radicals who have infiltrated the demonstration for the purpose of causing trouble. Division commanders with responsibility for the affected locations are hereby authorized to draw reinforcements as needed from neighbouring divisions in order to accomplish these assignments.

"The rest of you will double your coverage of likely targets in other areas of the district. Be the presence that deters anyone who's even *thinking* about criminal activity from turning thought into action.

"Let me just reiterate, people, that your first priority today is to keep the peace, and by so doing to protect all those who are peacefully protesting at those five locations. Division commanders, you now have your assignments and are dismissed."

"With respect, sir," said another of the commanders, "do you not want us pre-emptively picking up the leaders of those radical groups?"

"Actually, someone else is taking care of that."

The freighter made port in Galandra at mid-morning and

was met by a battalion of Security officers with lists of names and snaps of faces to go with them. In rapid succession, all fourteen passengers were rounded up and put into vehicles bound for the nearest detachment headquarters. After ten days on a working freighter, they were a sorry-looking lot, rumpled and out of sorts and not about to go quietly.

A portly gentleman with florid features shrugged off the hand of the officer who was urging him toward one of the land cars. "This is outrageous!" the man declared loudly. "What are we being accused of?"

"By us? Not a thing, sir," the officer replied pleasantly. "We have some questions for you, and then we have orders to hold you until your return transportation can be arranged. It shouldn't take more than a couple of weeks."

"Return transportation?" a woman with an unruly mass of short brown hair exclaimed from the back seat of another car. "You're sending us back there?"

"You've been flagged as potential threats to peace and order and are being denied permission to enter," said a second officer, "so yes, we'll be sending you back to the mainland."

"On whose authority?" bellowed a third voice, deep and indignant, from somewhere in the rear of the procession.

The officer escorting the portly detainee turned and announced in a stern voice, "On the authority of someone much higher up the food chain than any of us, including yourselves. Now. Please be seated in your indicated land cars. All your questions will be answered once we reach the station. Until then, you have the right to be silent. Exercise it."

*　　　*　　　*

Isabela had made a point of boarding the ferry for the first crossing of the day. So had Quin and Melora, at the other two docks on the island. Once disembarked on the mainland, they'd remained to welcome each additional boatload of demonstrators with shouted encouragements and reminders.

Isabela had done the math. One hour before the beginning of business hours, the island docks would fill rapidly with actual commuters waiting to board, so the protesters had to get off to a much earlier start if they were to arrive in the necessary numbers. If everyone showed up to the ferry on time, the protest would launch with roughly two thousand hybrid Terrans with signs, divided into five groups and besieging the entrances of five different laboratories.

There would be additional warm bodies joining in as the day progressed. Stragglers, parents of very young children... hopefully, some Stragori as well who were sympathetic to the cause... and of course, the several hundred pure-blooded Terrans who would lead the final march on the Directorate. However, this last group would not be giving away their intentions by carrying placards.

Standing on the front steps of the building nearest the ferry dock—BioFuture, the laboratory where Joanne had received her obsolete implants—Isabela gazed out over the crowd. It had grown since her arrival, swelling with newcomers until a virtual carpet of Humanity lay over every bit of lawn and pavement, right down to the roadway.

Making themselves quietly visible around the margins of this gathering, she noted, were a number of uniformed Security officers. Isabela hoped they were there to protect the protesters, not to try to intimidate them. These people had already shown they didn't frighten easily. Now signs were rising and falling in time to a chant that grew louder and more defiant with each repetition:

NO MORE LIES! BRING THEM OUT! MAKE THEM PAY!

All right, this was enough, she decided. Whatever happened here was already going out over the intellinet, courtesy of the optimized members of the crowd. She might as well start things rolling.

Isabela went to the front door of the building and leaned on the enter buzzer. A minute later, she heard the *click* of a latch unfastening and the door slid aside just a crack, giving her the narrowest glimpse of what appeared to be an anxious female face.

"They're not here," said the owner of the face.

"Who is not here?" Isabela demanded.

"The ones you're here to see. As soon as you began showing up, the CEO had building Security escort the entire executive committee out the back way. They're gone." There were tear tracks on this woman's cheek, and a tremor in her voice. She sounded in fear for her life.

Isabela and Quin had not only planned for this, they'd hoped for it. Isabela turned and gestured to the crowd for silence. Immediately, the chanting stopped.

"We are not here to hurt anyone," she announced in her loudest teacherly voice. "We only wish to make ourselves heard." Addressing the woman behind the door once more, she added, "We have a message to deliver. Who is the highest-ranked individual on the premises right now?"

"That would be me," came a man's tenor voice through the door. "I'm Dr. Selwyn, Assistant Head of Research."

"And everyone above you has fled, leaving you to face

the consequences of their criminal actions. What does that tell you about them, Dr. Selwyn?"

As the door slid open some more, a man's round face filled the space where the woman's had been. He wore a pained expression.

"Nothing we didn't already know, I'm afraid," he said. "What's the message?"

"Under the circumstances, it's more of a request, and an invitation. If you'll just step outside for a moment...?"

He took a step backwards instead. Isabela was confused. Then she realized what he must be thinking, and she stepped aside to give him an unimpeded view of the crowd.

"Very well, then, stay inside, but come closer and have a look," she invited him, adding as his face reappeared in the opening, "As you can see, we have many children with us, as well as their parents and a number of teachers. We travelled quite a distance this morning to speak with your CEO, but since that will not be happening, perhaps there is something else we can do. Would it be possible to have an educational tour of your facilities? Some of the parents would naturally accompany each tour group as chaperones."

"I—I think that could be arranged," he stammered, obviously taken aback.

"Wonderful! Would you like them to be organized according to age level?"

"That... would be most helpful, actually."

"We'll need a few minutes to sort them out. In the meanwhile, I have an invitation for you and everyone else in the building, if you wouldn't mind conveying it to them. When we leave here, we will be continuing on to the Directorate's current location to demand that the ban on non-organic implants be enforced. Anyone on staff who feels the same way as we do is welcome to join us."

His lips curving slowly into a smile, Selwyn said, "I'll be sure to pass that along. Now, if you'll excuse me, I have some preparations of my own to take care of. I'll need about ten minutes."

As he disappeared back inside, Isabela turned to face the crowd and announced, "Ten minutes, everyone. Let's get organized!"

With that, a couple dozen Security officers exchanged bemused glances, a hundred or so signs fell to the ground, and the teachers present got busy herding their young charges into classroom-sized groups. Isabela watched the sudden flurry of activity with immense satisfaction.

She'd been trying to put together field trips like this for her students for years.

Warder-in-Charge Krall had found two data wafers inside the package he'd picked up the night before, one of them containing a file titled, "Read Me Then Erase". As he'd hoped, it told him everything he needed to know.

He was still debating with himself over whether to share the information with Eva Moss. After all, from the reports he'd been receiving, her assignment for Dennis Forrand had already been accomplished. Her blistering transmission had flushed the most radical leaders out of hiding and straight into the hands of the authorities, thus silencing most of the fringe groups.

On the other hand, her mission had been part of the set-up for the greater operation currently in progress. She had to be wondering how she fit into Dennis's long-range plans, and whether they included getting the charges against her dropped so that she could return to the life she'd left behind her, either on the island or back on Earth.

That thought saddened him. Krall hadn't wanted to admit it earlier, but he'd grown quite fond of Eva in the time that they'd been working together. He was going to miss her when she left.

As though to second the thought, his stomach growled. Krall checked his chronometer and noted that it was time for lunch. Dennis's instruction had been quite precise: the message on the data wafer was to be broadcast on the intellinet at the turning of the sixteenth hour, on the dot. Good. It meant Krall had time for a relatively leisurely meal before setting out for the commhub in the Wilderness Zone.

After their tour of BioFuture, the children and their parents spread blankets on the lawn around the building and sat down to eat the lunches they had brought with them onto the ferries earlier that day. As Isabela had hoped, the picnickers were joined by BioFuture employees, many of whom had decided to take the afternoon off and participate in the march, and by the Security officers, who had also brought their meals with them and would be escorting the marchers to the Directorate later on. There was a relaxed, almost party atmosphere surrounding the event.

Commcalls from Quin, Mrs. Santos, and one of the other two group leaders had confirmed that similar things were happening at their locations. Meanwhile, waves of pure-blooded Terran adults were boarding the ferries, on their way to the mainland to join the hybrids for the final part of the protest. The timing would be critical. Everyone had to be in place before the turning of the sixteenth hour.

Quin and Isabela's plan was brilliant—rout the decision-makers and turn their staff—but its success hinged on the cowardice of the top executives, and Dennis and Arno had known from the start that Harris Research Labs would be "a tough nut to crack", as the Terrans would say. Its CEO was not one to tolerate the presence of a large, chanting crowd on his doorstep, and he was certainly not going to let them force him out of his corporate lair.

So, extra steps had needed to be taken.

First thing that morning, Sub-Chief Lindquist had dispatched a special violence prevention team to the site, headed up by Sub-Inspector Norton Harris. Their orders were quite specific: under no circumstances were they to permit company goons to be deployed outside the building.

By all reports, the strategy had worked. A peaceful demonstration had taken place. A message had been delivered to those inside, along with a request (warily accepted) and an invitation (regretfully declined). Then there had been a picnic on the company grounds.

At the turning of the fifteenth hour, it was time for Dennis Forrand to swing into action.

He arrived at the rear entrance to Harris Research Labs with twenty minutes to spare, greeted the armed Mainland Security officer guarding the door, then went inside the building and boarded the lift. The CEO's office was on the top floor, at the end of a long and intimidating corridor lined with firmly closed metal-slab doors. His was the only one flanked by building security—at least, Dennis assumed that was who the two burly men wearing identical dark blue jackets were. They came to attention and stood scrutinizing Dennis with narrowed eyes as he approached.

Stopping just out of arm's reach, Forrand said pleasantly, "Tell him D.F. is here to talk. He'll see me."

"No need, sir," said one of the guards as the door slid aside on its own. "He's evidently expecting you."

Of course he was. Lloyd Franklin Harris Senior had surveillance eyes all over his domain. He would have known about Dennis's arrival from the moment Mainland Security opened the rear door to admit him.

With a nod to Harris's protection detail, Dennis proceeded through the outer office and into the CEO's sanctum.

It resembled a luxury hotel suite, but with a massive desk slightly angled to the right just inside the entrance. Behind the desk was a floor-to-ceiling window, and standing there gazing out at the crowd that was finally walking away from his front lawn was a tall, lanky man with thick white hair pulled back from his face and curling down over his shirt collar. He was clean-shaven except for a luxurious and well-kept handlebar moustache.

"You've got some nerve, Dennis," he growled over his shoulder, "showing up here after siccing the Terran mob on me. We had a pact! You don't attack my family, I don't attack yours. That was the deal."

"We also agreed to warn each other about attacks from other members of our respective families. It's a shame you've chosen not to honour that part of the agreement."

Harris spun to confront him. "You know how large my

family is. If some distant cousin of mine has—"

"It's your son, Lloyd," Dennis interrupted, slicing off the end of whatever excuse the other man was about to offer. "We may not be responsible for the behaviour of our offspring, but we keep track of them. We make sure we know what they're up to, and that's why you know damn well why I'm here. Lloyd Junior has not only recently attacked individual members of my family, but has also, for the past fifty years, been mounting an all-out offensive against the entire Forrand clan. This is precisely the situation we wanted to prevent, because we both realized there was only one way for it to end. Or have you changed your mind about that?"

Lloyd Senior blew out a breath and eased himself onto the chair behind his desk. "I haven't changed my mind, Dennis. You've got details?"

Forrand sank onto the guest chair, counting off on his fingers as he enumerated all the offences Lloyd Junior had committed against Sylvain, both directly and indirectly.

"That explains why I wasn't aware of it," Harris said. "He obviously decided to keep his dealings with your uncle confidential and Stragon First at arm's length, to ensure that any blame for their actions would land on Sylvain—all of which is despicable, but hardly what I would call an all-out offensive."

"Sylvain is not the only Forrand your son has framed for terrorist activity. Anna Sturtevant is my daughter. She's in hiding, with a warrant out for her arrest for the bombing that killed over fifty people. Olivia Townsend is my granddaughter. She was forced to flee off-world before a similar warrant could be served on her for that same bombing. And there are other Terrans with Forrand blood flowing in their veins. In fact, there are five million hybrids on the island, many of them distant members of your own family, and they're all being wrongfully labelled as terrorists."

"By the Directorate, Dennis."

Impaling Harris with a cold, hard stare, Forrand rose from his chair to lean over the desk. "By your son, Lloyd, posing as Gervais Forrand, who now *leads* the Directorate, and who occupies the dominant position in the Forrand family as well. Your son is an impostor and a usurper."

Harris leaned forward as well. "That's quite an accusation, Dennis. Can you prove it?"

Surreptitiously checking the time on his chronometer, Forrand retorted, "I have people working on that. In the meanwhile, more and more of us are becoming aware of the impersonation, both inside and outside of the Directorate, and it's no mystery which family would have the greatest motive for bringing the Forrands down. When the truth comes out, as it very shortly will, I guarantee you there will be retaliation, so you can consider this my warning to you of an imminent attack on your family."

"If what you've said is the truth, there will be no safe place for Lloyd Junior on Stragon."

Dennis shrugged. "Choices have consequences, Lloyd. I'm just the messenger. What happens next is not my concern."

All at once, a loud buzzing sound was emanating from the intercomm unit on Harris's desktop.

"Mr. Harris! On the intellinet!" came a woman's frantic voice. "It began a few seconds ago. A priority broadcast! It's going out everywhere!"

Throwing Forrand a suspicious glance, Lloyd Senior

opened his desk drawer, pulled out a small device, and inserted it into his right ear.

Dennis remained just long enough to watch an expression of horror wash across the other man's features. Then he got up and calmly left the office.

How dare you! I am Louis Forrand, the Senior Director of the Stragori planetary government and the Hak'kor of House Stragon! How dare you lock me away like this! And what have you done with Gervais Forrand? No, it doesn't matter how many times you say it, you are not Gervais Forrand and you never will be! That is why you've imprisoned me here—because I know the truth about you. You're not a Director. You're an evil little man with large ambitions and no morals or ethics whatsoever! Well, you can't keep me prisoner indefinitely. I'll find a way to let people know what you've done. And when I get out, I will find Gervais, and then we will make you pay! Do you hear me? The Directorate will hunt you down, and House Stragon will make you pay!

None of the protesters gathered around the building that now housed the Directorate's executive offices received this transmission. Not with Quin standing at the centre of the milling crowd, with the modified signal jamming device flashing green inside his pants pocket.

Not until the mob swelled large enough to spill beyond the jammer's range.

NO MORE LIES!

On the front steps of the building, surrounded by fellow pure-blooded Terrans, Isabela heard the chanting and saw the signs waving and felt nothing but optimism. Everything was going according to plan. Not only the Terrans were protesting this injustice—some Stragori who had seen the marchers passing by had dropped what they were doing and joined their ranks as well.

MAKE THEM PAY!

On the margins of the protest, uniformed Security officers had been patched into the intellinet. They stiffened to attention and became more watchful as eyes widened and urgent whisperings percolated the air around them. Crowd control had abruptly become much more hazardous than before.

NO MORE LIES!

The whispers spread like wildfire toward the front of the demonstration. Like flame on a fuse. Isabella turned to face the protesters and saw Security wade into the crowd, bellowing to everyone to be calm. But the chant had new meaning now, and thousands of angry voices rose up as one, drowning out their admonitions.

MAKE THEM PAY!

Within seconds, the number of officers standing behind Isabela at the front entrance of the building tripled. She switched on her mic and asked for the crowd's attention... and was ignored, once... twice... three times. Disconcerted, she felt a hand on her arm and heard a man's voice in her ear: "We'll take it from here."

NO MORE LIES!

That was when she realized what Dennis had done— what he'd had in mind for her all along—and a red-hot tide of rage swelled inside her.

"No!" she shouted, shrugging away from the officer. "You won't. I will. Give me your whistle."

"My what?"

"Your whistle!" she repeated impatiently. "I know you carry one. A device that makes a loud, shrill noise."

"You mean my screamer."

"Whatever you call it. Hand it over!"

Responding reflexively to the commanding tone of her voice, he complied.

Isabela put the screamer close to her mic and triggered a couple of short, sharp blasts.

A moment later, the only sound people were hearing was the ringing in their ears.

"Thank you, for finally giving me your attention!" she declared into her mic. "You have just experienced a practical demonstration of the downside of optimization. What you heard over the intellinet may or may not have been true. That is not the issue. What it did, however—that is the issue. Whether intentionally or not, it changed you from a peaceful group of protesters into a potentially violent mob by distracting you from our purpose in coming here today.

"So, let me remind you of what we are protesting against and what we hope to accomplish..."

As she pressed the screamer back into the officer's hand, she heard him murmur, "Lady, you are *good!*"

Urgent calls were being made.

Lloyd Franklin Harris Sr. contacted several people, including Lloyd Junior.

Lloyd Junior already had matters in hand, but he thanked his father for alerting him to the threat.

At half-past the sixteenth hour, two men wearing work attire and protective gear parked their vehicle next to a squat, grey stone building on the edge of a treed area in the middle of the mainland. Carrying tool kits, they approached the door, which was locked. Opening it required the entering of a seven-digit code. As one of the men stood glancing nervously around, the other one pulled out a communications device and made a call.

"We're here. What's today's code?"

He punched keys rapidly with his free index finger, then grunted a 'thank you' and terminated the connection. The door slid aside, permitting them access to a seldom-used room equipped with banks of computer gear and monitors, all protected by transparent, form-fitted coverings. Moving quickly and quietly, the men crossed to a door that opened onto a flight of metal stairs, which they descended somewhat more noisily into the basement.

This was where one of the Directorate's remote back-up servers was kept, behind a floor-to-ceiling barrier of woven metal slats guarded by a console. One of the men switched on the overhead lights. The other one went directly to the console, where his partner joined him a second later.

"What does he want us to do? Delete the software?" the second man said.

"Nah. Our orders are to blow up the server, same as we did before. Fingers will point to the Terran terrorists, and no one will ever realize there was an AI planted inside it."

"Is that a confession I just heard?" This voice coming from the darkness under the stairs froze both the men in place.

"It sure sounded like one to me, Sub-Inspector Bashir."

Two Security officers stepped into the light, one of them holding a weapon and blocking the bottom of the stairs. The other was holding a comm device.

"Did you hear all that at your end, Sub-Chief?" he said.

"We did, loud and clear," came the response. "Can you

see anything that looks like a bomb?"

"No, sir. The saboteurs apparently brought the ED with them, but we never gave them a chance to open their tool kits."

"All right, then. Search both suspects on site. If they're clean, bring them in for questioning, minus their toys. If they're not, detain them in place and keep this channel open. I'm dispatching the nearest disposal unit to your location."

Three hours later, a convoy of land cars arrived at the entrance to the Harris family compound. The break-and-enter crew at the server back-up site had given Mainland Security everything they needed to get an arrest warrant for Lloyd Franklin Harris Junior. Warned to expect resistance, the officers had come armed and in force to execute it. However, they were in for a surprise.

To begin with, the outer gates swung wide for them as soon as they announced themselves, and the inner yard was empty. The door to the main residence was opened by a woman dressed in a maid's uniform. Everything about her looked starched, including her facial expression and the blonde bangs that swept diagonally across her forehead.

"You're too late," she informed them. "You're welcome to come in and look around, but the family is gone."

"Gone where?" demanded the leader of the detail.

"I don't think even Mr. Harris knew. Men wearing dark blue jackets came in cars a couple of hours ago. They said Mr. Harris Senior had sent them to take the family somewhere safe. Gave them half an hour to pack their necessaries, then whisked them away."

"What about the private security guarding the compound? Where are *they*?"

"Mr. Harris dismissed them just before he left. They were out of here like a shot. It's just me and the kitchen staff now."

The officer cursed disgustedly. "And the rich and powerful get away with murder yet again. Why do we even bother?"

The metal bench at the foot of the Directorate's front steps had ornate wrought iron sides with curved armrests. As Quin and Isabela sank down onto it, she let out a contented sigh. This had been a very successful day. Thousands of people had come together in peaceful demonstration, with only the one hiccup, easily handled. They had made their voices heard by those in power, had received a promise that action would be taken to redress their grievance, and then, their purpose achieved, had peacefully disbanded.

That wasn't the end of it, of course. Isabela wasn't naïve. She knew there was still a lot of work to do—messages, reminders, visits by delegations. But they'd taken the first step. Change on a social scale was a process that needed warriors to fight for it and midwives to bring it along, and either role suited her just fine.

By sunset, the lawns and paved walkways around the Directorate's offices were nearly empty, and the surrounding streets were rapidly clearing out. Besides a noticeable increase in foot traffic in the vicinity, the only sign that there had been a mass event at this location was the overflowing condition of the District Waste Management receptacles sporadically distributed around the grounds. Isabela the teacher was pleased that the protesters had picked up after themselves. Having them bring their children with them had apparently also spurred parents to set an example of good citizenship.

Of course, the fact that the Directorate was now sharing a building with District Security Headquarters might have had something to do with it as well. With that many official eyes watching from the windows, the odds of being caught and fined for littering public property went up dramatically.

"We make a good team," Quin remarked. "I just wonder how this is going to affect our adversarial relationship going forward."

"Oh, it's not going to be adversarial. Not when it comes to my students. Don't forget, I know things about you now. You are going to see the wisdom of my teaching ways."

He chuckled and leaned his head back, turning his face to let it soak up the late afternoon sunlight.

"It appears you were right, by the way, about the Directorate broadcasting propaganda to disrupt the protest," she said. "Do you know what it was about?"

"Not a clue." He stifled a yawn. "You may recall that I was in the middle of a signal jamming field at the time. Nothing was going out or coming in. But I'm sure you'll be hearing all about it from Joanne tomorrow morning at school."

"Excuse me—are you Lady Isabela Bakshi?"

Startled, they turned and saw a female Security officer walking toward them. She halted smartly beside the bench.

"Lady Isabela Bakshi?" she repeated.

Isabela nodded warily.

"Sub-Chief Lindquist would like to have a word with

you, if you wouldn't mind."

Her heart dropped. *Uh-oh. What now?*

Throwing Quin a worried glance, she followed the woman inside and up a sweep of stairs to the second floor, where a uniformed officer waited to usher her into an office not much larger than her own at the school. Behind the unimpressive desk stood a floor-to-ceiling wooden shelving unit filled with hard-bound books—volumes and volumes of them, all with identically-lettered spines. Every title dealt with an aspect of law enforcement: its history, its psychology, its technology, its philosophy, its ethics.

In a corner of the room was a partly closed door. By leaning forward, Isabela was able to see that it was a tiny hygiene closet, currently occupied by a sturdily built man with dark hair... and he was shaving his face.

Isabela liked tidiness in a man. Vikram had been meticulous in his habits. But having a total stranger shave before a meeting with her made her uneasy. What sort of "word" did he have in mind?

Lindquist emerged from the closet, wiping his hands on a towel.

"Well?" he said cheerfully. "How do I look?"

She sifted her mind for a noncommittal reply, finally coming up with, "Very presentable."

Tossing the towel back through the door, he dropped onto his chair and leaned forward confidentially. "I have a date tonight with my wife. It's a special occasion."

Instantly, Isabela relaxed. "I think she'll be pleased."

"I won't keep you more than a minute or two, Lady Bakshi," he assured her. "First, I want to congratulate you on the way you regained control of the people you'd invited to meet you in my front yard today. That situation could easily have erupted into a riot."

"Thank you."

"Don't thank me until I finish. That said, I must warn you that the next time one of my officers tells you to step back and let Security handle something and you shake him off and pull a stunt like what you did today, placing yourself and others in possibly mortal danger...? There *will* be consequences. My people are trained for situations like that. You were just damned lucky. It's not to happen again. Am I making myself clear?"

Doing her best to look chastened, she replied, "You are."

"Now, in light of some information that recently came to my attention, I've been reviewing a number of old cases, checking to make sure there are no irregularities in the investigative process. One of them concerns the untimely and unfortunate death of your husband, Vikram Bakshi, and I regret to say that I did find reason to question the way the investigation was handled. I am therefore reopening the case. I can make no promises about this, Lady Bakshi. We will follow the evidence, thoroughly examine and analyze it, and draw an impartial conclusion backed up by science. And then I will notify you, among others, of our findings. I trust that will be satisfactory to you?"

So, even a ruthless bastard like Dennis Forrand could be a man of his word.

Relief cascading through her like a waterfall, Isabela said in a voice thick with tears, "Very. Very satisfactory, Sub-Chief. Thank you!"

TWENTY-EIGHT

Sprawled on Marcel's sofa, Dennis raised his fifth goblet of sowerberry wine in a jaunty salute. "I would call this a very successfully completed operation," he declared.

Misinterpreting the gesture, Marcel topped him up. Then he poured the rest of the sparkling orange liquid into his own glass, carefully placed the empty bottle on the low table in front of them, and leaned back against the cushions with a sigh of satisfaction.

"Indeed! When I left Earth, you were still a boy. I had no idea there was a criminal mastermind lurking inside you, or I would have recruited you for my organization."

Dennis chuckled. "So, where did you send Lloyd Junior and his family?"

"Tempting though it was to simply make them all disappear, I put Lady Harris and her offspring on a ship bound for Earth space. She actually thanked me for it."

"I can't believe you handed them over to a smuggler. Was that wise?"

"Never fear, Nephew. I know the captain well, and he knows what will happen to him if any harm comes to a relative of mine aboard his vessel. I told him she was my cousin. Now she can change all their names and make a fresh start on one of the Terran colony worlds, far from the Harris malignancy. Meanwhile, Junior still has a debt to pay to Stragori society."

He took a thoughtful swallow of his wine.

"You let him live?"

"Oh, I did worse than that."

Dennis gasped dramatically. "Don't tell me you turned him over to the authorities!"

"Don't *you* tell me I had a choice in the matter. Giving Sylvain his pound of flesh would have been fun for about six minutes, after which Security would have come looking for me... and there goes my low profile. So, we drugged Lloyd Junior unconscious, gift-wrapped him, and delivered him to Mainland Security, tied up with a bow and accompanied by a handwritten note enumerating all his prosecutable transgressions. It's quite a list. There's definitely a tribunal in that man's future, and not much future following it. Data tampering is still a capital offence on this planet. And speaking of data tampering, do I want to know how you managed to access the Directorate's server connection to the intellinet?"

Dennis gave his uncle a mischievous grin. "There was no data tampering involved. Just a highly advanced communication technology originating from somewhere off-world. And that's all I'm going to say about it."

Angeli and Lyla were having tea and biscuits in Lyla's

parlour when Krall's land car pulled up at the curb in front of the house.

"Better get out a third cup," Angeli observed as they watched him trot, scowling, up the walkway to the front door. "He looks like someone with news to share."

By the time he'd joined them inside, a steaming cup of tasselberry tea sat waiting for him on the coffee table, beside the replenished plate of biscuits.

"I've heard from our friend on the southern continent," he told Angeli. "Mainland Security has identified the persons responsible for the bombing of the Directorate's offices, and they have the ringleader in custody. You've been cleared. The charges against you are in the process of being dropped, and once Planetary Security's arrest warrant has been voided, you'll be free to travel again, wherever and whenever you want to go."

It was good news. Angeli knew she ought to be relieved to hear it. And yet...

Since the day she'd turned sixteen and Dennis had recruited her for his grand plan, nothing about her life had been what anyone would consider normal. The past few weeks had been a reminder of what she'd given up—the relaxed pace, the daily routines, and the feeling of belonging to a community. Contentment. Somewhere between the Reformation and the EIS, she'd forgotten what that was like. Now, she was torn. Her mind was rebelling at the thought of leaving it behind again. But realistically, how could she stay here?

Lyla looked from one to the other of the sober faces in front of her, then cleared her throat and said, "I think I'll give you two some space." With that, she picked up her cup and left the room.

"What if I don't want to go, Ben?" said Angeli after a pause. "I mean, there's still the matter of the damselflower poisonings to be settled, and it doesn't feel right to be leaving in the middle of things."

He shook his head. "You wouldn't be. That case is about to be closed. Mainland Security is laying charges against the part-owner and two employees of the catering company as we speak."

"How did they know who Dennis's contacts were?"

"All he would tell me is that they used a Forrand family tree. What's important is that seven murders have been solved and your mission has been accomplished. You can go home, wherever that is." A pause, then, "Unless you'd rather stay and make one for yourself here...?"

"Why, Bennin Krall," she teased him, "are you saying that you would miss me?"

"You want to hear it out loud? All right. Eva Moss, or whatever your actual name is, I'm asking you to stay in Westgrove."

Her heart constricted with longing to say yes, but she had to be honest with herself.

"Ben, I wish I could, truly, but I don't think I would fit in. What would I do here? I can't be Lyla's house guest forever, and I don't have any skills to contribute to the local economy. You told me yourself that sooner or later I would have to have something to barter with."

"I did, didn't I?" He paused, his lips pursed in thought. "Then you give me no choice but to recommend you for the next wardership that opens up."

She had to close her jaw to reply. "You want me to be a peace officer? Why?"

"Because I've seen how you operate, and how you think,

and you're the sort of person who's either going to be enforcing the law or running around breaking it. And we can't have a relationship if you've got a criminal record."

"A relationship," she echoed. "You do realize that I'm in my fifties?"

He shrugged. "And I'm in my nineties. As long as we're both adults, what does it matter? Besides, I happen to know that you're half Stragori and will probably live another century at least. Listen," he added, taking her hand in both of his, "you don't have to answer right away. Take your time and think about what you want to do. I'll accept whatever you decide. And so will Lyla. Right?" he called over his shoulder.

The landlady's grinning face appeared around the corner of the doorjamb. "Of course, I will."

In spite of herself, Angeli smiled back. Westgrove had been feeling more like home with each passing day. Maybe this would work for her. Maybe she and Bennin Krall could have a relationship after all. It was certainly worth a try.

But... the loose cannon becoming a cop? Dennis Forrand was going to either pop a blood vessel or split his side laughing.

Drew Townsend was in the caf, staring down the bowl of yogourt surrogate that Jensen had just put in front of him. The chef had been experimenting with flavours again. Some made this chalky goop actually taste like food. Unfortunately, orange-pineapple wasn't among them.

"Doesn't *that* look appetizing," Trager commented as he dropped onto the other chair.

Drew glanced up and made a sour face at him, then

shoved the bowl to the centre of the table. "So, what have you heard through your official diplomatic channels, Mr. Trager? Was our stealth mission a success?"

"Your part of it was. Thanks to the parcel you arranged to have delivered, the Harris family has received a rather painful boot squarely in its seat of power. Two high-ranking members have been arrested on various charges, along with a bunch of their minions, and fake Gervais is no more. Louis is still missing, so Émile Forrand has taken over as the leader of the family and *Hak'kor* of House Stragon. The Directorate are in the process of choosing another Senior Director to speak for them as well. Things appear to be settling down for now."

"But...?"

"To use a Terran analogy, I'm afraid you've just thrown a bucket of water at a wildfire. The Forrands have come through this whole mess relatively unscathed, which I suppose counts as a win for them against the Harrises. However, the animus against the Directorate continues to spread, meaning that the radical faction can only get stronger. Eventually, Security will no longer be able to keep a lid on the violence, and there will be either a revolution or a civil war... and you're going to have a decision to make.

"Centuries ago, Stragon came to the rescue of your world. Adam Vargas and his team brought order out of the chaos that followed the second pandemic. We stepped up again when the Corvou declared war on Humanity. Now Stragon is the world in need of rescuing. What are you going to do, *Hak'kor*? Is House Daisy Hub going to stand by while Stragon destroys itself?"

The question seemed to fan the embers in Townsend's midsection. He pulled the yogourt back toward him and shovelled a spoonful of it into his mouth. Forcing himself to swallow it gave him a moment to think, and to decide. The Stragori were the control group. The Great Council posed the greater threat to that world. However, the slide toward bloody conflict was the more immediate one.

"Relay a message through diplomatic channels to the new *Hak'kor*," Drew said at last. "Tell him that if he chooses to present a petition for *ssalssit essendi*, the *Hak'kor* of House Daisy Hub is willing to meet with him and discuss the terms of an alliance."

Trager got to his feet and bowed from the shoulders. "I'll take care of it right away," he said. Then he left Townsend alone once more with images of wildfires burning a path through his mind.

Arlene F. Marks has been writing since the age of 6, and she has no plans to stop. A veteran teacher of the craft, she has authored two popular literacy programs for the classroom. Her short stories have appeared online and in print, notably in an anthology of reimagined fairy tales, *Grimmer Tales Volume One*. She is also the author of the Sic Transit Terra space opera series (from Edge Publishing) and *Adventures in Godhood*, her first of several recent releases from Brain Lag Publishing. *Remains to Be Seen*, the sequel to *Weekends Can Be Murder*, is scheduled for release in 2025 as well. Arlene lives with her husband on the shore of beautiful Nottawasaga Bay, where she spends time exploring imaginary worlds, collecting interesting-looking owls, and dreaming of one day having a tidy, well-organized office.

www.thewritersnest.ca

If you enjoyed *The Stragori Deception*, try:

In a universe of gods and gladiators, an extra-galactic intrusion could spell the end of everything.

Rowan fights a secret war against alien pirates bent on subjugating mankind. At least, that's what she thinks.

When aliens arrive looking like God from the Bible, who can you trust?

Manhattan rose like a phoenix from the rising seas. But its troubles are just beginning.

See all 50+ titles at brain-lag.com